LORI FOSTER

The Somerset Girls

ISBN-13: 978-1-335-77349-4

The Somerset Girls

HQN
22 Adelaide St. West, 40th Floor
Toronto, Ontario M5H 4E3, Canada
www.Harlequin.com

To Ruby Dooby:

You're a very special little girl, a personality without compare, an utter delight all of the time and a force to be reckoned with. You were the model for my seven-year-old character Sadie—from the beautiful red hair to the big blue eyes to the kind heart and the fashion sense. Love you bunches!

And to Patricia Schaffer:

When I asked readers on my Facebook page for a volunteer to be the "not nice" lady in the book, you stepped up! That actually makes you really nice, so I hope you enjoy the story. Thank you for offering up your name—even though I'm quite sure you would never be a gossipmonger.

And to everyone else who volunteered, thank you, as well! After writing so many books, I often look to you, my Facebook friends, for the names of my secondary characters.

Hugs to all!

Dear Reader,

Oh my goodness, I'm *soooo* happy to share *The Somerset Girls* with you for several reasons. First, sisters Autumn and Ember run a rescue farm, and if you've read me before, you know how very much I care about animal welfare. Writing them was like channeling all my most heartfelt emotions. They love animals as much as I do, but unlike me, they're actually bringing them all home. (I donate a book each year to a no-kill animal rescue because, sadly, I can't bring all the animals home. My elderly cats would be horribly upset.)

Even better, Autumn meets a single dad with a seven-year-old daughter he loves with all his heart—and I modeled her off a very special little girl who is near and dear to me. From the vivid red hair and big blue eyes, to the independence and quick wit, to the often fun fashion sense, it's all taken from sweet Ruby. Writing that character was made easier because of my love and familiarity with her. However, please know that Ruby has never dealt with the serious issues that my book girl Sadie faces. Ruby's mama is a wonderful person and a phenomenal mother who has always kept her very safe, loved and secure.

Lastly, because I have two sisters I adore, I love that these sisters are close. Not alike—sisters seldom are—but they work around the differences and love each other unconditionally. They have disagreements but don't hold on to grudges. Better still, they're *there* when needed. To me, that's how family should be…but isn't always.

So this is a book of emotional conflicts and unending love, of hurt and healing, of loss and triumph. Of family, with all the good, bad, hilarious and embarrassing moments thrown in.

I sincerely hope you enjoy it!

Lori Foster

PS: Autumn is a reader, too—and she loves suspenseful romance from the amazingly talented Karen Rose. So to my friend Karen, thank you for the inspiration and the happy hours of reading!

Chapter One

A refreshing shower, ice cream and the book she was reading. As Autumn Somerset got the unhappy pigs into the back of her truck, she repeatedly recited the awards that awaited her at the end of her day.

A day that should have ended...oh, about three hours ago.

As a designer, she'd wrapped up appointments promptly at five o'clock. Yes, she'd been thinking about that tub of carrot-cake ice cream in her fridge even then. In fact, she'd thought about it since it had arrived a few days ago. Being a dedicated member of an ice-cream club had its perks, like new flavors every month. Her efforts at healthier eating meant she only consumed ice cream on Mondays, Wednesdays, Fridays and holidays.

True, every so often she created a holiday all her own. Like Cleaned the Kitchen Day. Or Completed a Job Day.

Or Mother Didn't Insult Me Day. That particular holiday earned her two scoops.

This being a Monday, she didn't even need a fake holiday.

"Sure do appreciate it, Autumn."

Forcing her mouth into a polite smile, Autumn turned to the man who had, over the past two years, gotten several pets that he then no longer wanted. *Ass*, she thought in her head, but what she said was, "It's no problem at all, Ralph."

"Got that first pig thinking it'd be small, ya know? Like a dog."

"Yes, I know." He'd thought he was getting a miniature pig— then he'd found out differently.

"Got the second one to keep it company, but that first one outgrew it in no time—"

"I do understand." And, damn it, she wanted her ice cream. If she had to converse, she'd rather do it with the pigs that were now squealing inside the cage of the truck. "I have to get going so I can get them settled." Trying for a speck of diplomacy, she suggested, "You should really think about gifts other than pets, don't you think? Perhaps your kids would like a nice swing set? I could design one for you."

"Can't afford that."

Smile locked in place, she volunteered her sister without pause. "Ember and I will help with that, okay? But only if you promise me, no more animals."

His face lit up.

Good. One job down. She'd tackle Ember next.

At least her sister loved animals as much as she did—which, honestly, might be the only thing they had in common other than blood.

By the time she got the pigs to the farm, it was after nine o'clock. Pavlov, their six-year-old redbone coonhound, met her in the yard, jumping around the truck in excitement. Because she lived on a farm, Pavlov didn't have to be locked in the house while she was away. The doggy door let him in when he wanted—to her side of the house, her sister's, or their parents' separate residence—but more often than not he preferred to visit with a cow or mule or even a turkey.

"Hey, buddy. Miss me?"

Too busy seeing what new friends she'd brought home, Pavlov paid her no attention. Never had a dog been so taken with other animals.

"Anxious to meet, huh?" While Pavlov bounded around, jumping into the truck and then out again, she set the pigs loose in the wide-open pen.

He barked in excitement.

Noses to the ground and already rooting through their new digs, the pigs moved forward. "I present Matilda and Olivia."

Pavlov, aptly named, went into the pen, too, only because the gate was open. With the sun splashing crimson across the sky, she waited, arms folded over the wooden post, while they got acquainted. It warmed her heart to see the pigs so happy. The smaller of the two ran circles as he explored the area. The biggest one found the shade and then rolled around, wallowing in freedom.

How often had Ralph even had them outside? She'd taken them from the basement, poor babies. Yes, they'd been fed and had straw to lie on, but it wasn't the same. Farm animals needed fresh air and sunshine.

Here, at the Fresh Start Farm, they'd get that…and more.

"You're home now, babies." Stepping into the pen, too, Autumn found a grassy spot to sit and spent another half hour lavishing love, scratches and hugs on the affectionate animals.

Finally, as the sun sank behind the trees and mosquitoes filled the air, she headed in. All it took to get Pavlov to come along was to open the gate again.

The dog walked through every open door, every single time. That, in part, accounted for his name.

Because he'd jumped into the truck bed, she took her time driving the short distance, going gently over ruts and small hills so she wouldn't jostle him too much, and then parked on the gravel lot behind the sprawling farmhouse. Porch lights had automatically flicked on.

"Race you in," she told Pavlov and then took off running. Ears flopping, he gave chase and they hit the door together, her laughing and him barking.

Unfortunately, after getting two steps into the foyer, she found Ember waiting on her.

"About time!" Ember stood from the couch, where she'd been flipping through a design magazine. "Where have you been, anyway? It's late. And ewww, Autumn, you reek."

"Nice to see you, too." Putting the shower on the back burner, she made a beeline to her kitchen sink, where she washed her hands and arms up to her elbows.

Pavlov ate the food she put into his dish like he hadn't been fed in a month, which was just his way, then drank noisily, splashing water everywhere. Finally, with slobbering chops, he greeted Ember.

Laughing, Ember said, "You are such a pig, Pavlov."

Speaking of pigs…

As Pavlov headed into the living room and his big pillow bed, Ember shook her head. "I take it he's sleeping with you tonight?"

Pavlov varied his routine, sometimes staying at her side of the house, sometimes Ember's, and sometimes even with her parents or their hired man, Mike. "Looks like."

"That dog is so fickle."

"He loves us all." Ignoring the reason for her sister's visit, Autumn took the ice cream from the freezer.

"Is that going to be your dinner?"

Unwilling to debate her eating habits, Autumn pointed a spoon at her. "I volunteered you today."

With a groan, Ember flopped into a chair at the table. She, at least, looked fresh and pretty in a sundress and cute sandals. Her dark hair, much like Autumn's but with reddish streaks supplied by a salon, didn't look frazzled and wasn't soaked in sweat.

No matter what Ember did, she never seemed to sweat. If she hadn't been her sister, Autumn might dislike her on principle alone.

"Ralph gave us two pigs, one miniature—maybe—and one definitely not. I just got them settled, thus the lovely aroma you noted."

"What a jerk! Two dogs, a cat, ducks and now pigs? What part of 'not animal-friendly' is he not getting?"

Luckily they'd found good forever homes for the dogs and cat. It was a little tougher with the farm animals, since they didn't want them turned into food. "That's why I volunteered you. I promised him we'd build a swing set for his kids, *if* he'd stop getting animals."

Skewing her gloss-covered mouth to the side in thought, Ember frowned, then gave a decisive nod. "I should have enough scrap wood to make something nice. Good thinking. You draw it up and then help me put it together, and you've got a deal." She offered her palm.

Autumn high-fived her. "It's a genius plan, thought of spur-of-the-moment, but only if it actually works." More often than not, they agreed on most everything when it came to saving animals. They were well suited to run the animal rescue together.

The rest of life? Not so much.

Using that as a perfect segue, Ember gave her a sideways look. "Speaking of genius plans—"

Autumn froze. Ember's plans were always proof positive that they led very different lives.

"—guess who's in town?"

Shrugging, Autumn shoved a big bite of ice cream into her mouth. She had a feeling she'd need it.

Looking like a magician about to perform an amazing trick, Ember announced, "Tash Ducker."

The ice cream stuck halfway down her throat. Disbelieving,

suffering a mix of dread and curiosity, Autumn choked. When she finally got her breath, she asked, "Tash is back?"

Many years ago—sixteen, to be exact—she'd had a ridiculous crush on him. Two grades above her in high school, and oh-so gorgeous, she'd gotten severely tongue-tied whenever he looked her way. Even after they'd graduated, she couldn't seem to look at him without going mute. Once he'd finished college, he'd moved away and she hadn't seen him since.

Going into self-survival mode, a necessity with her family, Autumn replied, "Huh" with as much nonchalance as she could muster. To further that lie of disinterest, she asked, "What'd you do today? I tried to call you about the pigs, but you didn't answer."

"Now that I know it was about pigs, I'm glad." Ember flashed the smile that made all the local guys stupid. "Actually, I had a date and didn't want to be interrupted. I figured whatever it was, you could handle it."

That answer, given far too often, took some of the delight from the ice cream. "So…what if it had been an emergency?"

"You didn't leave a message." One eyebrow lifted. "I assume you would if it was life or death?"

"Meaning you'll only answer my calls if someone is dying?"

"Meaning," Ember stressed, "that just because you don't date doesn't mean I shouldn't. Besides, I'd already checked in on Mom and Dad."

Well, that was something. Hopeful that Ember wouldn't start in on her lack of a social life, Autumn nodded her gratitude.

"They needed groceries, and I swung by to get their stuff on my way home."

"Thanks." A few years ago, their dad had suffered a debilitating stroke, leaving him largely dependent on the care of others. Ten years older than Tracy, their sixty-year-old mother, Flynn Somerset still had his wit, but not the use of one arm and one leg.

Together, she and Ember had built their parents a small house on the forty acres left to them by their grandparents. It made helping them easier and more convenient, plus Autumn liked that she could get to them in minutes if anything came up.

As a designer, she'd fashioned the house for her father's disability, making everything wheelchair-accessible and putting all handles and light switches lower, so he could reach them. The walk-in tub and shower made bathing so much easier. An open floor plan kept the home airy and filled with light, and made it possible to see their dad from almost every room.

Ember, who'd learned carpentry from him, had overseen the construction...and they'd only butted heads a few times in the decision-making process. When it came to design, Autumn insisted on having her way.

That wasn't something that happened very often.

Their parents loved the end result because they still had their independence, but weren't really alone.

The old farmhouse had been divided into a duplex with Autumn living one side, Ember on the other. One interior door allowed them to visit without going back outside.

Ember used the door quite often, always on the presumption that Autumn had nothing "good" going on.

True enough.

However, Autumn never dared to intrude because Ember was the opposite, meaning she always indulged in the good stuff—aka, man candy.

"That's where I saw him, by the way. At the grocery."

Avoiding eye contact, Autumn asked, "Mom and Dad are all settled now?"

"Yup." With a knowing smile, Ember said, "But hey, you're changing the subject. Want to tell me why?"

"I wasn't," she lied. Everyone knew lying to one's little sister wasn't a sin. Heck, it barely counted at all. "You mentioned them so I thought I'd—"

"Avoid talking about Tash?" Ember didn't bother to hide her amusement.

Oh, how that sisterly laugh annoyed her—enough that she gave up any pretense of disinterest.

Whispering, because seriously, this was nerve-racking, Autumn asked, "You're sure it was him?"

Just as quietly, Ember leaned in and replied, *"Yes."*

With just a tiny bit of evil hope, Autumn asked, "How's he look?" By now he could be balding. Maybe he'd picked up a beer belly. Lost his studliness altogether. She was thirty-two, so that made him thirty-four. Plenty old enough for him to have drastically changed.

Ember leaned even closer. "He's even hotter now."

Deflated, Autumn sat back in her seat. "Figures." Tucking back into her ice cream, she tried to picture him a decade older, but failed. In her mind, he looked the very same. Young, healthy, energetic...and disinterested in her. "Did he say why he's back?"

Deflecting, Ember rolled a shoulder. "He's moved here for good."

Hmm. What was her sister up to? "Settling here with his wife?" That'd maybe make sense.

"He's not married."

Okay, so she wasn't married, either. She knew her reasons. But what were his? "You know that how?"

"I talked with him. In fact, we talked about you."

Lord. The ice cream must have numbed her brain, because she couldn't think of a single thing to say. Left eye twitching, she stared at Ember instead.

"I have a plan."

After pushing back her chair in haste, Autumn put space between herself and whatever nonsense her sister contrived. With a definitive *"No,"* she headed for the sink. *Whatever it is, ten times no.* After rinsing her bowl, she stuck it in the dishwasher and tried to make a strategic retreat to the shower. "Later."

Ember jumped into her path. Wearing an expression of extreme disappointment, she shook her head. "Just look at you, Autumn."

"That's a little hard to do."

"You know what I mean. You've given up and just don't care anymore. The good news is that I can fix it."

It? They'd had this conversation too many times. Truthfully, she'd never cared that much about the things Ember obsessed over, like makeup, hairstyles and the trendiest clothes.

Crossing her arms under her boobs, Autumn said, "You mean me. You want to fix *me*."

Damn it, she was the *it*.

Rather than deny it, Ember pinched the air. "Just a tiny bit. Like…" She looked at Autumn with obvious disapproval, and lamented dramatically, "Your *hair*. I'm not sure if that started out as a ponytail or what, but now it's just a mess."

"I loaded and unloaded pigs." She pointed at Ember. "By myself, if you'll recall, since you refused to answer the phone."

"I'm very glad you saved them from Ralph. That's one thing we don't need to work on—your compassion."

Hallelujah. She had an asset.

"But those clothes? I'm the builder, you're the designer, but you dress like you work—"

"On a farm? With *pigs*?"

"That was later and you know it. This afternoon, you met with clients."

Autumn shrugged.

"You should wear pretty dresses that flatter your figure, not pants that look like they came from the back of Grandma's closet."

A slow inhale didn't help. True, she was something of a visual mess. Inside, she mostly had it together. And, damn it, she liked herself. So she dressed for her own comfort? Big deal. Everyone else could bite it. "How about you don't dissect me, and I won't dissect you?"

Ember gave a small flinch. "I don't mean to be insulting—"

God save her if she ever did mean it. Every time Ember or their mother got started, her stomach hurt. She hated that she didn't measure up, and biting back sarcasm only made it worse.

"Autumn, stop that." Ember started to draw her in for a hug, then sniffed the air and changed to giving her a small shake instead. "It's just that you're pretty and you practically hide it. It wouldn't take much to really make you stand out—and as an incentive I already..." She drew a breath as if to gird herself.

For Autumn's ire. Meaning it had to be bad.

"What?" Alarm chased circles in her gut. "Ember, what did you do?"

"You have an appointment with Tash tomorrow."

Good thing she had a wall beside her, because Autumn collapsed against it. "You didn't."

"Did." In a rush now, Ember explained, "He needs a designer, Autumn, and you know you're the best around!"

She had compassion and design skill. Hey, the compliments were piling up.

"Forget that crazy crush you had on him—"

"It was eons ago!" Heat bloomed in Autumn's face. She hated to be reminded of her most awkward years. "Of course I've forgotten it. Maybe *you've* forgotten that I was even engaged after that."

It was the wrong thing to bring up. Ember's expression softened. "I know. Neither of us will ever forget that."

Autumn threw up her hands. "No one died, so stop looking so grim."

"You haven't dated since then."

"Choice," she emphasized. "There's no one here who interests me, that's all." *Liar, liar, pants on fire.* Sure, some guys asked, but everyone here remembered her engagement and certain assumptions came with that, making everything superawkward. "Let's forget all my past failures, okay? I'm over them, I swear."

"Great." Satisfied, Ember beamed at her. "Then it's no problem to meet with Tash, right?"

It was a massive problem, but how could she explain that after swearing it wasn't? She could only think of one excuse. "The thing is, you don't set my schedule. I already had my day booked."

Dismissing that, Ember waved a hand. "I looked at our joint calendar and, um, rearranged a few things."

Of all the intrusive, pushy, over-the-top... Straightening, Autumn squared her shoulders. "Rearrange them *back*."

"Can't." Turning, Ember headed for the shared door. "Tash is expecting you at six."

"I finish work at five!"

"Yeah, see, that's how I rearranged. Added another hour for ya. If you come straight home, I'll have a tiny bit of time to work on your appearance before you have to head to his place on the other side of the lake." She gave an airy wave. "Tomorrow, if any emergencies come up, I promise to answer the phone to leave you free and clear."

"That must mean you don't have a date."

Ember shared a slow smile. "No, but you do." And with that, she closed the door.

Feeling militant and more than a little irate, Autumn walked over and flipped the lock, then yelled through the door, "I can get myself ready, by the way! I don't need help."

A loud "Ha!" came right back to her.

They needed more insulation in the walls, and thicker doors, obviously.

Frustration amplified the discomfort of her sweaty clothes and clammy skin. Honestly, she could put up with the idiocy of the Ralphs of the world every day for the rest of her life, and it'd be easier than dealing with her family.

She really, like very badly, wanted to reopen the door and somehow intrude into Ember's life. But Ember would probably just laugh and go about her business.

Few things ever got to her. In almost every scenario, she was the life of the party, the fun girl, the one in demand.

Only one time had she ever seen her sister truly leveled, and she never wanted to go through that again.

They both had their father's coloring, with dark hair and blue eyes, but Ember had also inherited their mother's fun-loving ways.

Autumn had her mother's plump build.

She knew this because for most of her life, her mother had pointed it out.

Give Ember a break. She's a free spirit, like me. But, oh, Autumn, you poor dear, you got my big bones.

Yay. Lucky her.

Maybe she could add that info to all her social media.

Favorite movie: *A Perfect Getaway.*

Favorite music: anything by Kid Rock.

Outstanding feature: big bones.

As she walked away, she thought, *Biggest flaw: lets my family boss me around.*

Right there, in the hallway leading to the bathroom, she stalled. No, she did not have to let them do that. For a while now, she'd been working on being more assertive. Largely without success, but hey, that didn't mean she should give up.

So was it a bad thing to meet an old classmate who needed design work? No. Not if she didn't make it weird.

Would she do it under Ember's terms? Absolutely not.

She would get herself ready. She'd be professional but comfortable. By God, she had nothing to prove to her sister or to Tash.

And if Ember didn't like it, too bad.

Autumn wouldn't let it bother her.

With that decision made, she got moving again. She wanted that long-awaited shower, a comfy spot in the bed, and then she'd read.

Pavlov followed her, staying in the bathroom with her while she showered, and then he lumbered into the bed beside her as she began reading the newest title from Karen Rose. She did love a scary romantic-suspense storyline, with an evil madman and smart characters. In fact, she got so engrossed in the lives of the characters, she forgot all about her sister and hunky guys from the past and her stupid big bones.

Not until midnight rolled around did she call it quits and close the book. Not an easy thing to do, but the alarm would go off early and she had a full day—a day that would now run extra late thanks to her sister.

Tash Ducker. Her heart beat a little faster. Would he remember her? Would he see all the ways she'd changed?

Would he *like* those changes?

Autumn groaned. Maybe she'd let her sister give her just a few pointers, after all.

"You're already messing up your hair."

Putting away her dishes after a fast bowl of soup, Autumn said, "That's why I usually put it in a ponytail. Any type of hairdo just falls apart."

Tucking, smoothing and rearranging, Ember said, "If you'd let me use some hair spray…"

Shouldering away her sister's busy fingers, Autumn explained, "Hair spray gets all gummy when I sweat."

"Maybe you could try not sweating?"

Incredulous, she closed the dishwasher with a little more force than necessary and spun to face Ember. "Yeah, why don't you invent a way for me to do that? We'll sell it and make enough to save all the animals."

"Don't be sarcastic."

Why not? Her sarcasm was almost as top-notch as her compassion. When Ember pulled a tube of something from her pocket, Autumn scowled. "Now what?"

"It's just lip gloss. It won't kill you."

"I don't like it. It tastes bad."

"It does not."

"Does if you lick it…and I can't seem to keep from doing that."

Rolling her eyes, Ember gave up and put away the shiny pink gloss. "Fine. Maybe you can make the 'naked mouth look' work for you."

A rap at the screen door drew their attention and Mike, their handyman, farmhand, do-everything guy-in-residence grinned. His shaggy blond hair should have been cut weeks ago, and working in the sun had left him a little too tanned…in a most appealing way.

All in all, he looked scrumptious—but better than his stellar appearance? He did great work with the animals, never complained, accepted living in the loft apartment over the barn and was always around when they needed him.

He winked at Autumn. "A naked mouth works for most men. Don't let Ember tell you otherwise. And for the record, I think that stuff tastes bad, too."

Ember's eyes flared, then narrowed dangerously.

Uh-oh. Autumn hurried to the door and opened it. "Mike. What's up?"

"I was going to ask you that."

"Oh." She gestured lamely. "I just have this appointment in a bit and Ember wanted to practice sprucing me up and—"

Hands in his pockets, he smiled and entered. "I meant with our new members, the pigs. When did they arrive? You left too early this morning for me to ask you about them."

Mentally slapping her own head, Autumn laughed. "Right. Matilda and Olivia."

He went right past their names. "You do look great, though—but then, you always do."

Resisting the urge to stick out her tongue at Ember, Autumn said smugly, "Why, thank you."

"Her scalp sweats."

Horrified, she gasped at Ember's bald statement.

"Everyone sweats." Indifferent, Mike shrugged, then took a jab. "Unless it's different for princesses?"

Eyes narrowed at her sister, Autumn said, "I certainly wouldn't know."

"Most of us wouldn't." Ignoring Ember now, Mike asked, "Anything special you want done with the pigs? I saw that you fed them this morning before leaving, and I fed them the usual in the afternoon and evening. I've already visited with them plenty, too, and let them play under the sprinkler for a while during the hottest part of the afternoon. Is there anything else?"

God love the man, he'd silenced Ember so easily, she could almost kiss him. Well, except that he might misunderstand the gesture of gratitude. She adored Mike, but there wasn't a speck of chemistry between them.

He and Ember, however... Different story.

Autumn went over the special diet she'd come up with for the pigs, and the area of the farm where she wanted them to get a little more freedom. "I have everything written down for you." She snatched up the paper on the counter. "Most important, though, is that I want them to feel loved in their new surroundings."

"Gave 'em lots of love," he assured her. "They're already settling in."

"Thank you. Seriously. You always go above and beyond."

"It's a wonderful place you've created here."

Ember folded her arms. "She didn't do it on her own, you know."

"Few people can feel really good about their jobs, but I do."

Mike glanced at Ember, his gaze warming...and then he dismissed her. "If you don't need anything else, I figured I'd head into town for a bit. Tracy and Flynn mentioned the diner's chocolate lava cake, so I promised to bring back two slices with me."

Guilt made her frown. "Mom and Dad shouldn't impose on you...but wow, that does sound good."

His smile came big and easy. "It's not a problem. Your folks keep me entertained."

She could guess what that meant. "Mom gave you another sculpture, didn't she?" Her mother unintentionally made sexually suggestive sculptures that left Ember and Autumn red-faced more often than not. What should be one thing always ended up looking like something altogether different.

"I had to build a special bookcase to hold them all." Winking, he headed for the door, and just before he stepped out, he added, "I'll bring some cake back for you, too."

Once the door closed behind him, Ember drifted toward it, looked out, then huffed. "He didn't offer me cake."

Autumn figured he wanted to offer her sister something altogether different. "Maybe if you were nicer to him...?"

"I'm nice to everyone." Turning back with a grin, she said, "Next time we shear the sheep, I'm going to offer to give him a trim, too."

"I like his hair longer." It curled against his neck, but didn't quite touch his big shoulders.

"Because you, sister dear, are into the messy look." Giving her a critical once-over, Ember nodded. "You know, Mike is right. You do look nice without a lot of makeup."

"Dad calls makeup war paint."

"Dad enjoys harassing Mom."

"And Mom enjoys the attention."

Ember hesitated, then released a long breath. "I'm sorry about mentioning your sweaty head."

Good God, Ember made her sound like the Niagara Falls of

perspiration. "I'm often outside measuring stuff, you know." A lot of her design work was specifically geared toward kids' rooms and play areas, but she also created outdoor living spaces, man caves, she sheds, converted garages and more.

"I work outside, too," Ember pointed out.

"But you would never admit to sweating."

"Very true." She smoothed a long hank of Autumn's hair, then let her hand linger on her shoulder. "Anyway, I'm sorry. It was a stupid thing to say. Mike makes me... I don't know. Mean?" Liking that word, she nodded. "He makes me mean, but I should save all my meanness for him, not you."

Of all the ridiculous things! "He's an amazing employee. Why would you be mean to him?"

"He ignores me."

Autumn snorted. "No, he doesn't."

"He treats me the same as the animals. Or—" she wrinkled her nose "—Mom and Dad. It's disturbing." Ember flagged a hand. "He jokes with you, like you two are close pals, and I'm just a shadow hanging around."

Sudden comprehension widened Autumn's eyes. "You want him to be interested."

Ember sniffed, doing her best to look unaffected. "Maybe a little, but I shouldn't have insulted you to get it."

Especially since that tactic had backfired. Still a little amazed, Autumn said, "So you—"

"At least the jeans fit you instead of being all baggy." She tugged on a belt loop, almost pulling Autumn off her feet. "And I like your shirt. That's a good color for you."

Glancing down at her own chest, Autumn admired the bright tangerine hue. Personally, she thought it added color to her cheeks. "It's nice, right?"

"Very." With a glance at the clock, Ember urged her toward the door. "If you don't leave now, you might be stuck behind the train and then you'll be late."

Since Tash was on the other side of the lake, and it didn't make sense to take the boat then walk several blocks, she'd have to drive around and that meant crossing the railroad tracks.

"Well, shoot." She snatched up her big satchel of design materials, her portfolio, so she could show her previous projects, and slung the strap of her loaded purse over her shoulder.

Ember surprised her by kissing her cheek. "Go get him."

"Get the *job*, you mean." This trip—nice shirt and all—wasn't about anything else. But she had to admit, having Ember's approval of her overall look gave her added confidence. "I'll see what he wants first."

Bobbing her eyebrows, Ember grinned.

"Stop that." Fighting a laugh at her sister's antics, Autumn shoved open the door and hurried to her truck, aware of Ember standing there smiling like a sap…and looking like she knew a secret.

Chapter Two

A n-n-nd…of course, her air-conditioning died while she was stuck waiting for the train to pass.

For several minutes she vigorously fanned herself with a sheath of papers, which sort of, maybe, stirred the thick air a little.

Kentucky in July wasn't for wimps. On top of the ninety-plus temps, humidity settled on everything, curling her papers, expanding her hair, leaving her skin dewy and gluing her clothes to her skin.

Arriving at the address Ember had given her a solid five minutes late, she hurried from the truck and started up the walk.

Sunset, Kentucky, was a small town that, like the home she shared with her sister, had a definite divide. One side of the lake boasted farms and acreage, some heavy woods and a wide creek.

On the other side, several communities—some waterfront, some not—seemed to fill up every foot of space. This was where residents did their shopping, saw doctors or dentists and enjoyed entertainment other than swimming and boating. Two movie theaters, several restaurants, a roller rink, miniature golf and one rather rinky-dink "nightclub" made this side of Sunset the happenin' place.

Overall, Autumn preferred the quiet life on the farm, but since she did most of her regular work here, she was familiar with all the streets.

The address for Tash led her to a cozy white clapboard house with a somewhat barren yard. There were only a few trees, but since his house was in a newer section of homes, maybe land-scaping was still on the agenda. Admiring the house, with its dark shutters and paned windows, she'd almost reached the porch before she realized a young girl was peeking at her through the rails.

Pausing, Autumn tipped her head. "Hello."

Vivid blue eyes watched her. "I can't talk to strangers."

"Good rule." She double-checked the address. "I was looking for Tash Ducker? Maybe I'm at the wrong place."

"That's my dad."

Disbelief glued her feet to the walkway. Her mouth opened, but nothing came out. *Dad?* Tash had fathered this beautiful little girl?

The blue eyes narrowed warily. "What do you want?"

For such a tiny person, she did a fair job at showing hostility. "I have an appointment with Mr. Ducker."

Still scrutinizing her, the girl went to the door, yanked it open and bellowed, *"Dad!"* In one hand she clutched a beat-up Barbie, and in the other a water gun.

Autumn heard hurried, heavy footsteps, and a second later, Tash stood there, filling up the doorway and sending her thoughts into a tailspin.

Oh, my.

Yup, he still looked crazy good. He still made her heart trip. He still...well, none of that mattered.

Tash was a father.

With a height over six feet and shoulders plenty wide, he seemed a Goliath next to his petite daughter.

"There's a stranger here," the girl announced.

He looked up and spotted Autumn standing there like a statue, then relaxed with a welcoming smile.

"Damn, I forgot." Stepping out, hand extended, he said, "Autumn, hey. Good to see you."

His brown eyes were the same, the color nothing extraordinary...except for the piercing intensity, the warmth and maturity that seemed to physically hold her.

He'd changed. Duh. One of the changes was sizing her up with ripe suspicion. A cute little red-haired, blue-eyed change.

Her mouth went dry, until Tash's smile quirked.

It hit her that she just been standing there, openly gawking at him.

Get it together. Surging forward, her face hot, she managed to juggle her load and free one palm. Fortunately, she sounded mostly casual when she said, "You, too."

After briefly gripping her hand, he turned to his daughter and smoothed her stunning red hair. "Honey, don't yell like that, okay? I thought pirates were kidnapping you."

She snorted with every bit as much verve as an adult. "She didn't even get close. Besides, I'm not a baby. I wouldn't let anyone take me."

His smile widened but his tone sounded grave when he said, "Of course you wouldn't. You love me too much to leave me, right?"

She rolled those heavenly blue eyes. "Yes."

Hand to his chest, he feigned relief. "Whew. Good. So the next time you see a stranger, just keep your distance, come inside and calmly call for me, okay? See this?" He pointed to his throat. "My heart is still up there."

She giggled and leaned into his leg, getting a one-armed, very affectionate hug.

Wow. He wasn't just a dad. He was an *awesome* dad and she wanted to melt. Autumn looked at the adorable girl again. A purple-unicorn shirt worn over orange shorts with pink sandals clashed with her deep red hair. *Beautiful* hair—long, thick and silky.

Her eyes, a very bright blue, were far more striking than her own, and very direct when she glanced at Autumn again.

Tash said, "Autumn, this is my daughter, Sadie. Sadie, meet Ms. Somerset."

Extending her hand again, Autumn smiled. "It's nice to meet you, Sadie."

Still brusque, she gave her tiny hand for a quick greeting, then asked, "Why are you here?"

Charmed by her blunt manner, Autumn lifted a shoulder. "Actually, I'm not sure yet since my sister set up the appointment for me, but I bet your dad will tell me." She turned back to him and caught his curious scrutiny. "Or did you need to reschedule?"

"No, I wouldn't do that." Quickly, he held open the door. "Come on, Sadie. Join us."

"I want to stay out here."

Patiently, he said, "But I want you inside, so inside you go."

Sadie stubbornly held her ground. "I'm watching birds."

"They'll be there tomorrow."

"Not the same ones."

"Sadie," he said, his voice soft but insistent.

Grumbling, the little girl gave her a dirty look, as if she had any say in it, and preceded them into the house.

"We just got here a few days ago," Tash explained as he led her past a few large shipping boxes. "We're still unpacking and setting up. Since I saw Ember, we've had a dozen things come up."

Following him to the kitchen, where something smelled really good, Autumn said again, "I really don't mind if you need me to come back another time." She could use the time to regroup, to get used to the idea that this particular man was back in town, still a hunk, but now a father.

And...oh. Did he have a wife tucked away somewhere? She glanced around, but didn't find anyone else. Surely Ember wouldn't have been so intent on matchmaking if he was married.

"Now is fine, if you don't mind the mess. Here, have a seat." He pulled out a chair at the table, his attention glued to her face.

Autumn paused.

"You haven't changed at all."

That alone proved how little he remembered her, because she'd seriously changed a lot. "Neither have you."

His gaze cut to Sadie. "Oh, I don't know about that." He watched his daughter get into her seat, then thunk the Barbie and gun down on the table. Suddenly, he sniffed the air and turned fast. "Tacos." He went to the stove to stir something in a skillet. "You like them?"

She and Sadie said, "Yes" at the same time.

Mortification rushed through Autumn. "I'm sorry. I thought you were asking me." Oh, that sounded bad. "Not that I'm inviting myself to eat! I wouldn't. But, of course, everyone likes tacos—"

"I was talking to you," he said over his shoulder, his smile twitching at her nervous chatter. "I already knew Sadie liked them."

Swinging her legs, Sadie sat back in her seat and studied them both. "How old are you?"

Laughing, because she'd just been wondering the same thing about Sadie, Autumn said, "I'm a few years younger than your dad."

"So thirty-two."

Wow, smart. "Yes. We knew each other in school. Or rather, I knew who he was. We weren't really friends or anything."

"You didn't like him?" Sadie asked.

"She didn't know me well enough to like me," Tash said as

he moved to a cutting board, where he expertly diced tomatoes. "In high school, the difference between a sophomore and a senior is a pretty big deal."

"Oh." Sadie eyed her anew. "I'm seven."

Amazing. "I would have guessed a little older. You're mature for your age."

Beaming, Sadie nodded. "That's what Dad says, too." She slid off her seat, swiped a piece of tomato and peeked into the pan. "I'm hungry."

"You're always hungry." He hugged her into his side. "Not too close to the heat, honey."

"Mom used to let me cook."

He paused for a heartbeat, then teased, "I must be more of a worrier than she was."

Was? Had Tash's wife passed away? Autumn sat very still, feeling horrible for them both.

"Why don't you ask Ms. Somerset what she wants to drink?"

Sadie sidled over to her. "You want a beer?"

"Sadie."

Shoulders scrunched, she glanced back at her dad. "That's what Mom and her friends always wanted."

"We don't have any beer here, right? Offer cola, iced tea or water."

Disgruntled with that order, Sadie mumbled, "What do you want?"

Just what was going on here? Autumn tried to affect a carefree smile. "You know what, Sadie? You're about the most adorable, precocious little girl I've ever met. I think I'm going to trust you to choose for me."

Not budging, Sadie studied her. "What's p'cosis."

"Precocious. It means intelligent and sassy and wise beyond your years."

After giving it some thought, Sadie said, "You can have a cola."

Assuming that was a treat, Autumn thanked her.

Tash caught her eye and gave a nod of gratitude. She didn't have any idea what was going on, but she sensed some heavy-duty undercurrents.

What really surprised her? Seeing him, looking right at him, didn't befuddle her at all. He mouthed, *Thanks*, and she smiled in return.

On the way to the table, Sadie dropped the cola on the floor. It rolled up to Tash's foot before it stopped.

"Oops." Autumn turned to her…and went still at the stricken expression on the girl's face. She'd gone completely still, seemed tense and wary.

Tash saw her, too, and immediately dried his hands. As if it meant nothing at all, he said, "We must have the dropsies today, huh?"

Dropsies? Did grown men say things like that? Apparently men who had young daughters did.

"Did I tell you I dropped the seasoning packet for the beef? Luckily, it was closed, like the cola." He set the can in the sink, still talking, his voice calm and moderate. "After that I dropped the cheese, but it was open so a bunch spilled everywhere. Took me a bit to get it all swept up."

Autumn's eyes went past him to the counter, where she saw a new pack of shredded cheese…unopened.

He scooped up his daughter for a hug. She was very tiny in his arms. "Accidents happen, baby."

"But…we have company."

"So? The Pope and president could both be here and it wouldn't matter, I promise."

"And I'm neither," Autumn said, feeling her way. "I'm just a friendly neighbor who does her own fair share of dropping things, so I didn't think a thing of it."

After putting a loud smooch to Sadie's forehead, Tash set her back on her feet and said, "Grab Autumn another cola, then go wash your hands. I'll have your plate ready for you when you get back."

Sadie, still seeming unsure, looked at her, then her dad, and back again.

Pretending she didn't feel the tension, Autumn launched into babble. "You want to talk about dropping things? This one time, I was carrying a bucket of feed for a bunch of hungry hens and dropped it. Feed went everywhere and the feathers were flying! The ninnies always have fresh feed available, but they carried on like they'd found gold. I ended up slipping, and even tore my pants." She threw in a laugh for good measure. "Know what happened then?"

Sadie asked, "You have chickens?"

She nodded. "While I was down, Delilah gave me a solid headbutt and I went face-first into the mud. At least, I hope it was mud. With a lot of animals around, it's sometimes hard to tell. Delilah is our goat, by the way, not my sister—though my sister probably would have laughed herself silly." Seeing Sadie's fascination, she continued. "Then Franklin, our ornery old sheep, almost jumped on me, but luckily I got out of the way in time."

Eyes huge, Sadie asked, "You have goats and sheep?"

"And horses, a mule, two pigs—as of yesterday—ducks and a dog."

Tash carried a napkin holder and sour cream to the table. "I had no idea. You run a farm?"

"Animal sanctuary."

Surprised, he said, "I thought you were a designer."

"That, too. Ember and I inherited the farm from our grandparents, and our jobs help supplement what we need to care for the animals." She said to Sadie, "Why don't you get your hands washed, and then I can tell you both all about it. That is, if your dad has enough time...?"

"Can't wait to hear it." He put his hand to Sadie's back. "Get them clean, and I promise we won't talk about animals until you get back."

Like a shot, Sadie raced down the hall.

His expression contained, Tash stood there, gazing at the doorway she'd gone through, then he turned to Autumn. "Thank you for that. I'm discovering that things with her mother weren't always great." He briefly clasped her shoulder, his touch warm and heavy, before he moved away. "You did a great job stepping into the unknown. Not many could have handled that so seamlessly."

"I'm glad I didn't make anything worse." Posing it as a question, she said, "Sadie seemed awfully upset over something so simple."

His mouth firmed. "Her moods jump around enough to keep me guessing, but we're getting there."

That didn't really tell her anything. It wasn't her business, yet she felt compelled to ask, anyway. "I don't mean to pry, but... you're divorced?"

Keeping watch on the doorway, he worked his jaw. "For years now. We shared custody, but...it was complicated." He shook off his mood. "Sorry. None of this is your problem."

"It's okay." More than okay, because her heart ached for him. "You have Sadie now?"

"I do. She's mine and somehow I'll make everything okay." He glanced down the hall again, then turned to her. "She's been through a lot, so I appreciate your patience, especially with her less-than-warm welcome."

"Like I said, she's precocious...and pretty darned adorable."

"Right?" He smiled with her, but as their gazes held, his smile slowly faded. "Deb, my ex, crashed with her in the car. Drunk. Leaving town because it was my turn for a vacation. I actually passed them on the road, turned back...and found the car wrapped around a telephone pole." Remembered fear darkened his eyes; he worked his jaw and whispered, "Swear to God, it took ten years off my life, not knowing at first what I'd find."

Autumn could only imagine, given that her heart beat double-time just hearing about it. "Sadie...?"

"She was in the back seat, luckily buckled in, shocked, bruised and crying, but thankfully okay. Unfortunately, Deb didn't survive."

Emotion squeezed her lungs. "No child should ever have to go through that."

"On that we agree." He looked stricken, then gave a self-deprecating laugh. "Jesus, I haven't seen you in forever and here I am dumping my life history on you, when I usually don't talk about it at all."

She wanted to tell him that he could talk to her anytime, but as he said, they hadn't seen each other in years, and he hadn't know her well when they did. "I don't mind."

"You did such a great job distracting her that I guess I just—"

The sound of Sadie's running footsteps shut them both down.

Tash gave her another long look, then went back to the stove and busied himself, his shoulders set in a tense line as Sadie skidded back in, anxious to hear more about the animals.

Autumn found it hard to swallow.

More than anything, she wanted to haul Sadie close and hug her silly. Instead, giving Tash a moment to himself, she shared one funny story after another.

When Tash set a plate in front of her, she balked. "Really, I don't mean to impose. If you want to tell me what I'm designing, I can take some measurements while you eat and then, when you're done, you can let me know what you have in mind."

"You have to eat with us," Sadie insisted. "I want to hear about the dog that had only three legs."

Distracted, Autumn promised, "We found a wonderful, loving home for him. Other dogs and cats, too."

"Did you name them all?" Sadie asked.

"My sister and I can't seem to resist. But sometimes they come to us with names. When they do, we don't change them."

Again giving her that funny, pleased-but-confounded look, Tash said, "If you have the time, we'd love for you to join us. It'll give Sadie a chance to tell you what kind of bedroom she wants."

"That's what I'm designing?"

He nodded. "And a play area in the spare bedroom. Maybe a swing set outside, too?"

Clearly it was news to Sadie. The little girl looked stunned.

"Oh, fun!" Already Autumn looked forward to spending more time with Sadie. She adored kids, always had. Getting close to adults was difficult for her, but kids, with their frank manners and zest for life, won her over without even trying. "Kids rooms and play areas are my favorites."

"Perfect." Gesturing at the food, Tash said, "Dig in."

So far this visit was everything she hadn't expected, and nothing that she'd worried about. "Okay, sure. So, Sadie, while we eat, why don't you tell me what kind of bedroom you want."

Sadie shrugged. "I don't know."

"So what are your favorite colors? Favorite toys or cartoons?"

"Hmmm...baby blue," she announced around a mouthful of crunchy taco. "I like rainbows and unicorns." She paused, thought, then added, "Glow-in-the-dark stars on the ceiling and glitter."

Tash went comically still. "Um..." He looked to Autumn.

She had a full mouth, too, but she quickly nodded, letting him know it was okay. For years now she'd been managing the combined expectations of kids and parents, finding a moderate compromise that pleased them both.

She reached for her portfolio with her free hand. After swallowing, she rifled through it and withdrew a big printout for another bedroom she'd done.

"What about something like this?" She turned the paper and

pointed to the very sweet girl's bed with a flexible canopy over-head. "The stars could go here, on the canopy, so that they're closer to you at night. The bedding can be unicorns instead of mermaids, and the rainbow can be accomplished with curtains. What do you think?"

Relieved, Tash let out a breath. "That looks amazing. What do you think, Sadie?"

"I like it," Sadie hedged, "but it needs more color. Lots and lots of color."

"Most definitely," Autumn agreed. "Just leave it to me."

The process of designing everything Tash wanted took several visits over the next week. On one visit, she interrupted his work on the computer, but he didn't seem to mind. She only got a glimpse before he closed the screen, but it appeared to be internet advertising. Fascinating.

On another trip, she found Tash and Sadie at a backyard tea party, sitting on a floral tablecloth, drinking from tiny cups and eating cookies at least twice the size of the miniature plates they were on. Yes, she ate a cookie.

Or two.

And she even drank some juice from the cup.

It was extremely nice that his work allowed for impromptu backyard picnics. In a very short time, she'd already realized that Tash made spending time with his daughter a big priority.

When Sadie wandered off to pick wildflowers, Autumn had quietly asked him about the restrictions of his job.

He explained that he wanted the summer to help Sadie get acclimated to her new life. While watching his daughter, he said, "Time enough to really build my new business after she starts back to school."

"Ah, so it's a new business." While she spoke, she strolled the yard, thinking about possibilities. A number of large trees provided shade to the back of the house, but also complicated things.

Where to put the play area so it could be aesthetically pleasing, blending with the trees instead of competing with them?

"I was a partner in an advertising firm before coming here."

"Oh?" She glanced at him, then away. Being with him like this, even with Sadie nearby, was a unique form of intimacy, one she'd never experienced before. The probing way his dark eyes looked at her, the shared whispers, the...trust? Yes, she sensed that he trusted her, and it filled her with purpose. "That sounds like an important position?"

He looked at his daughter again, his gaze warm but also determined. "Not as important as Sadie."

That answer made her smile from the inside out. "No, of course not."

"Now I freelance remotely with the firm, primarily with my longest-standing clients, who didn't want to switch reps, but I'm mostly focusing on internet advertising. The hours are more flexible."

"That's wonderful. You should let the local paper know. They'd probably love to do a feature on you."

"I might, thanks." Tash stayed right with her, strolling along, making her *über*aware of him. That wouldn't do. The man was a father, for crying out loud, and she was only there to create the perfect spaces for Sadie.

Tash hadn't said it, but she knew he wanted her to feel settled in and happy.

Unfortunately, when she asked Sadie about her preferences, all she got was a shrug.

When Tash started to intercede, Autumn reached back to reassure him...and inadvertently touched his stomach. She snatched her hand away.

He caught her wrist, his strong fingers completely encompassing it. Screw the big bones—his bones were obviously bigger!

Voice low, he said, "She's holding back, but I promise you, she's excited."

Did he think she'd lose her enthusiasm? Not likely. "Give me just a second with her, okay?" Without waiting for his reply, she moved to where Sadie sat on the ground. "Mind if I join you?"

Nose scrunching, Sadie squinted up at her. "Why?"

"I wanted to talk about my plans, see if they work for you."

Another shrug didn't deter Autumn. Mimicking Sadie's pose, she sat yoga-style beside her. "So I was thinking of building something around that tree." She pointed to the mature oak. "The branches are high enough that a tree fort would be really cool."

Sadie looked up, her blue eyes rounding. "Tree fort?"

Now I've got you. Suppressing her smile, Autumn asked, "Do you like to climb?"

With a caution that Autumn now recognized, Sadie said, "Yeah, but..."

"Excellent." Arranging a drawing pad on her lap, Autumn leaned closer so Sadie could see and started sketching. She drew a basic structure around the trunk of the tree with an extension to hold swings and a slide. "You'd go up this ladder to get to the platform, through a trapdoor and then to the deck. There'd be a railing around it to make it safe, of course. Your dad loves you too much to take a chance on you getting hurt." She went on quickly, glossing over the fact that Tash was apparently a lot more cautious than her mom had been. "We could decorate the deck any way you want. More unicorns or—"

"I like pirates."

"Oh, excellent!" Running with that small admission, Autumn said, "We could make it to look like the helm of a pirate ship." Adding on to the sketch, she said, "We could put a ship's wheel here, as if you're sailing, and maybe a telescope so you could look out and see the squirrels and birds." She nudged her with her shoulder. "I remember that you like looking at birds."

Sadie chewed her lip. "It sounds nice."

"It'll be more than nice, I promise."

"You'll really build it?"

And there it was, the little girl's worry. How many times had she been promised something, only to end up disappointed? "If your dad approves, I'll draw it up and my sister, Ember, will do most of the building. She's crazy-good with power tools."

Because he'd been listening, Tash immediately joined them, lowering his muscular body to sit the same way so that they formed a small circle. "Let me see." He took the sketch pad from Autumn and then whistled. "Man, I would have loved something like this when I was a kid."

"It'll be sturdy enough to support you, I promise."

"And you?" Sadie asked, her excitement growing.

"Heck, yeah. I expect an invitation to your open house."

Pleased with her drawing, Tash asked, "Could you put in some monkey bars?" He reached out to muss Sadie's here. "She *is* a little monkey, you know."

Sadie's smile brightened, before she tempered it again.

Undeterred, Tash smoothed Sadie's hair. "Which would you want her to start on first? Your bedroom, the playroom, or the swing set?"

Her big blue-eyed gaze flickered over her dad, then Autumn. And they got another shrug.

"My suggestion," Autumn said, "is the area out here. I think Ember could start next week if that works for you. In the meantime, I could be getting stuff together for the bedroom."

It almost killed her when Sadie looked so hopeful.

Tash recognized the problem, too, because he asked, "How long do you think it'll take you to get everything done?"

"I don't need a playroom," Sadie stated, stalling Autumn's answer. "I mean..." She squirmed, drew a breath. "Dad should have an office, right?"

Gently, Tash said, "I don't mind working in the living room."

"But..." Again, she glanced at each of them, then seemed to

shore up her determination. "If we're staying here, you need an office."

Oh, my, such a beautiful little spirit. Unable to resist, Autumn put an arm around Sadie and drew her in for a hug. "You are just the sweetest person I've ever met." She even put a kiss to the top of Sadie's head, then got back to business. "So an office. We could easily do that. And truthfully, Sadie is going to have an *amazing* bedroom. I have all kinds of ideas so that it'll be perfect for playing and sleeping. It's up to you, of course, but if you want—"

"I think Sadie is brilliant," Tash said, pulling the girl into his lap. "Will you help me figure out what I'll need in an office? Including your own section, so that when I'm really busy, you can still be in there with me?"

"But…you'll have to work."

"True," he said, his tone grave. "But I like seeing you play sometimes. Maybe when it's rainy and you can't get out, or if you just feel like being close—the way I sometimes do. The office would face the backyard, so when you wanted to play, I could still see you, hear you…" He gave her a squeeze. "Hear you laughing."

"Oh! What a fabulous idea!" Creative ideas came fast and furious. Flipping to a new page, Autumn sent her pencil flying in fun designs. "You'll have to tell me exactly what you need, of course, but wouldn't this be amazing? We could take out the closet door, reframe it and make it Sadie's own little office space. The wall could be done in chalkboard paint, and we could put a few low shelves on this side for art supplies, with this shelf serving as a desk surface—" She squeaked in surprise when Tash gave her the same type of hug she'd given to Sadie, embracing her with one long arm while laughing at her eagerness.

It nearly stopped her heart. Good Lord, the man was solid. Crushed close to his side, several sensations hit her at once, like

the soft hair on his forearm, the heat of his skin, his husky laugh
and his rich scent.

When was the last time a man had held her? So long ago,
she couldn't even remember! She blinked, unsure what to say,
or what to do...

He didn't linger over the gesture, and she realized his focus
was largely on his daughter—meaning Autumn had overreacted.

That assumption proved true when he said to Sadie, "I think
I should give Autumn a down payment right now, don't you?
That way she can't back out on us."

"I wouldn't," Autumn protested, still flustered and trying her
best to hide it. She knew he'd done all that for his daughter, to
reassure her, so she needed to get her raging hormones in line
and play along. "I'm looking forward to digging in and I'm hoping to have lots of input from Sadie. She can be my assistant."

Tash asked his daughter, "What do you think? Are you up
for the job?"

"Yes," Sadie sang, and before Autumn even knew what was
happening, they were all on their way indoors, where Tash insisted on writing her a check for more than half of her esti-
mated charge.

Since Sadie seemed so very pleased, Autumn accepted the
payment with a smile.

Talk about being blindsided... Tash had a hell of a time adjusting. From the moment he'd pulled Sadie from that twisted
wreck, he'd put women from his mind. He'd canceled dates,
broken ties and devoted all his thoughts, energy and purpose
into caring for his daughter. Piece of cake. Nothing mattered
but his daughter's well-being. Being one-hundred-percent Dad
left little room for the pursuits of most single men.

Now here was Autumn, and damn, the lady packed a wallop.

At first, he hadn't thought she was pretty—was, in fact, almost plain. Average face, average build.

Until she'd smiled. Once he'd talked to her for a few minutes and watched her interact with Sadie, she looked different. Right before his eyes, she'd…glowed. With happiness and understanding.

That smile teased without trying. Her eyes, a soft blue, looked at Sadie and really saw her—not just a cute kid with a bold personality, but a young girl struggling to find her place, to adjust to big changes.

And when she looked at him? There was a sexy reserve to her manner, something that suggested she wasn't exactly interested, but was definitely full of secrets.

All combined, it made her uniquely…tempting.

It didn't make any sense.

He remembered her as a shy, quiet, nondescript little thing, who'd occasionally stare at him in school and at sporting events.

She wasn't all that shy anymore, definitely wasn't quiet—not when discussing one of her passions, like design or caring for animals—and he wouldn't call her little, not at all.

The woman had curves galore. Curves he kept noticing despite his best intentions.

Yet it was more than that, too. If she'd *only* been stacked, no problem. A sexy body wouldn't draw him so completely. But in addition to that mouth-watering figure, Autumn was warm and sweet, intuitive and caring.

He wasn't made of stone, so how could he *not* notice?

Dangerous. Appealing.

Now that he'd hired her, they'd be seeing each other more. He looked forward to talking with her again, and if he didn't miss his guess, his daughter felt the same.

It was nice seeing Sadie excited for something. Now if he could just keep her smiling…

Autumn had other appointments, but she and Tash ended up conferring on the new office space instead, and later, with that area decided, the design of Sadie's bedroom changed just a bit to include plenty of room for her toys.

Sadie had dolls of every variety, so Autumn hoped to convince Tash to invest in a really special dollhouse made locally. It was big enough for Sadie to crawl inside now, and when she was older, it could be turned and used as a special shelf for her dolls. That, she decided, should be discussed in private, though.

She never made those suggestions in front of children, because it was the parents who understood and would adhere to a budget.

She'd left Tash's house well behind schedule and spent the rest of the day running late for appointments. She got home well past her usual time, so it was a good thing Ember had tended to all the animals and checked on their parents. Autumn crashed in her bed a little after ten and only managed to read two chapters before she got too sleepy to concentrate.

She nodded off thinking about Tash. The way he'd touched her, along with the evidence that he was such a great dad, proved to be a powerful combo of physical and emotional appeal.

The man was more enticing than Rocky Road ice cream, and damn it, that scared her a little...in a very exciting way.

Chapter Three

T hat next Saturday, after working all morning on the farm, taking her parents to appointments in the afternoon and rescuing a turkey that some a-hole wanted to shoot, Autumn was entirely tuckered out.

A heat wave had affected the area, making everyone—her included—more listless. Her work was often dirty and, yes, regardless of her sister's wishes, she perspired. With the temps in the midnineties and oppressive humidity, she knew she wasn't the only one.

As she walked through the house on her way to the laundry room, she peeled off her suffocating clothes. The kiss of air-conditioning on her skin helped revive her, but only a little. Once she dropped her rumpled load onto the utility-room floor with the rest of the clothes, the heap nearly reached her knees.

A day off to catch up on chores would be nice, but she wouldn't get that until next weekend.

Sighing, she eyed the growing pile with apology. "Don't complain," she told the laundry. "No one is doing me, either." She snickered at her joke. The laundry did not.

After kicking away a sock, she dragged her tired body into the shower. Pavlov, who was indeed fickle, had decided to stay with her parents for the night, so she got into a sleep shirt and crawled into bed alone.

Just her, her Karen Rose book and lots of bone-chilling tension.

She was so deep into the story, her heart racing, that when her cell phone buzzed with an incoming call, she nearly jumped out of her skin.

Pressing one hand to her chest to contain her heart, she grabbed the phone with the other. Ember. Immediately thinking the worst, she swiped the screen and answered, "What's wrong?"

"Nothing. Jeez, can't one sister call another without you thinking the world is ending?"

"No. Not in the evening." With regret, she closed the book and sat up. "So, um, what's up?"

"I'm sitting on your stoop. Put on your swimsuit and come join me. We're going to the lake."

Her jaw loosened. Okay, so a glance at the clock showed it was only nine. Tiredness pulled at her, and the book wouldn't read itself. "Sorry, sis, but I'm in for the night."

"No, you're not. Stop being a party pooper. Other people are there swimming. This awful heat inspired an impromptu party and I want to go, but I don't want to go alone."

Not buying it, Autumn said, "You could seriously call any of a dozen guys and get a date." Heck, Ember had probably already turned down a few guys. That's likely how she heard about the party.

"I don't want a *date*. I want my *sister*."

The muted distress in her tone alerted Autumn. A year ago, Ember had gone through a heart-crushing difficulty, and there were days when it all came back. Cautiously, Autumn asked, "Are you okay?"

"*Yes.* Now get your granny butt out of the bed and come join me."

Did she really think insults would win her over? Not likely. Still, the worry didn't let up. "Ember—"

"Fine. Forget I asked. I should have known better."

Yes, she should have. Ember was the free spirit, after all. Autumn liked to put her big bones to bed early. "Listen, it's just—"

Again, Ember cut her off. "No big deal. If you need me, I'll be at the lake having fun with real people instead of book characters. Later, gator."

The call ended, and damn it, now she was alert and concerned and she knew it was impossible to turn that crap off. If she didn't check on Ember, she'd fret for hours.

Never mind that her book characters were far more likable than most people she actually knew, Autumn grumbled her way out of bed, and then rummaged in a drawer to find some cut-off shorts usually worn when she fed the animals in the morning. She thought about a bra, but in the heat, that'd be miserable. The sleep shirt was oversized and loose enough that nothing vital showed.

If Ember was down, she wanted to support her, to help her through the memories. Differences aside, that's how sisters worked.

Shoving her feet into flip-flops and doing a quick finger-comb of her hair, she grabbed her phone and keys and headed through the house for the door.

She'd go to the stupid lake, find Ember to ensure she was all right, and then she would return to reading comfortably in her bed. It'd be an hour's interruption, maybe two. Totally doable.

Fueled by indignation, Autumn jerked open the door and almost plowed into Ember, who leaned patiently against the wall beneath the porch light.

Grinning at her, her sister said, "Wow, you're fast. I thought I'd be waiting at least ten minutes more." Ember latched on to her arm so Autumn couldn't backtrack. "Come on. My car is idling so we can cool off on the way over."

She'd been duped! But, hey, at least Ember wasn't crying... *yet.* It relieved Autumn to see her sis smiling at her, even though she also noted the shadows in her eyes.

It wasn't that Autumn gave in gracefully, but she did give in. Ember might act like nothing was wrong, but Autumn knew her well, so she saw all the emotions Ember tried so hard to hard.

Playing her role—because Ember hated pity—Autumn said, "An hour. That's all."

"Sure, sis. Whatever you say."

While seating herself, Autumn noticed the wine coolers and chips in the back seat. "What's all that?"

"Snacks for the party. I brought your share, too." She pulled away from the house, saying, "You owe me ten bucks."

Great. At least Ember's car was cool. She still hadn't fixed the air-conditioning in her truck. Putting her head back and closing her eyes, she tried to ignore the blooming headache.

"Autumn? Thanks for going with me. Really, it'll be fun, I promise."

Lazily turning her head toward Ember, she said softly, "Fess up."

"About what?"

That careless attitude didn't pass muster, so Autumn just waited.

It took a full minute, and then Ember swallowed heavily. "The house I worked on today? The parents had two little kids." Inhaling a tight breath, she whispered, "One was a newborn boy."

Knowing how shattering that still was for Ember, Autumn reached over and put her hand on her shoulder. "I'm sorry."

"It's been a year." Ember's voice cracked just a little. "A whole freaking year and it still…" She went silent, her breath strained.

"You loved him. From the moment you knew you were pregnant, you planned a life around him." Miscarrying two months into her pregnancy had done more than devastate Ember—it had changed her. "Reminders might always be difficult."

"Sometimes," Ember said, her tone stark with sadness, "I still feel empty."

And so she filled herself up with parties and more men who didn't matter and a lighthearted attitude meant to hide the hurt. "I know," Autumn answered softly. "I wish there was something I could do."

With a shaky laugh, Ember swiped away a lone tear that tracked down her cheek. "You're here. That's enough."

Forget an hour. She'd stay out all night with Ember if it'd help.

"You know, I sometimes wonder where you came from." Ember went over the railroad tracks without a delay. "I mean, Mom's as flighty as they come, Dad only thinks about Mom and I'm…well, I'm not responsible like you."

"Bull. You put in the same hours I do and contribute every bit as much time to the farm and the animals."

"I try." She went quiet again. "But I haven't even asked you how it's going with Tash."

They'd both been so busy the past week, they'd barely seen each other. Only the morning after her first visit with Tash had they talked, and it had been brief. At that time, Autumn had assured her all went well and Ember had teased her about Tash being her crush.

Same old, same old.

Since Ember hadn't asked again, Autumn hadn't brought it up. She hadn't realized that a newborn at the job site had caused Ember to withdraw into her own thoughts, and now Autumn felt guilty.

Because she'd been stuck in her own head, too.

"I knew Tash had a daughter," Ember said. "And she looked so shy, I had a feeling you'd be good for her."

"*Shy* isn't really the word. More like *watchful*." Autumn pictured Sadie in her mind, with her long red hair and huge blue eyes and that contagious smile. The girl was a heartbreaker without even trying. "I'm not sure what's going on there, but I know her mother passed away. That's why she's living full-time with Tash now." She took a moment to explain about the car crash, and Tash's concerns.

"Does he seem like a good dad?"

"Absolutely." Because it was more complicated than that simple answer, Autumn gave it some thought. "I'm pretty sure his main goal right now is making his little girl's life secure."

"That's even better than being gorgeous and gainfully employed." Marking a scorecard in the air, Ember said emphatically, "Good dad."

"Yes."

"You two would be great together."

"Whoa." That was so absurd, Autumn snorted. "Did you miss the part about his focus being on his daughter?"

"Nope. In case you didn't know, men can multitask same as women. Besides, you wouldn't be attracted to a guy who didn't make his kid a top priority."

"Neither would you," Autumn reminded her. That, too, was personal for Ember. She'd faced her accidental pregnancy alone since the guy hadn't been interested—and that made Ember also disinterested in him. Granted, she hadn't been that into him, anyway, but still...

Rewinding, Ember said, "That part of you being so responsible? I mean it, and tonight is a perfect example. If you called me, would I switch plans for you?"

"I like to think you would."

Tone flattened, Ember said, "Odds are we'll never know, because you don't do lame stuff like this."

No, she retreated to her room to read. Alone. Adding in a note of lofty humor, Autumn stated, "We're different but equally awesome people."

"Hell, yeah." Steering one-handed, Ember held up her palm for a high five.

Lame, but Autumn indulged her. She liked this mood so much better than the melancholy.

Up ahead, they could see a few torches lighting up the sandy shore of Sunset Lake. Music mingled with laughter while dozens of people enjoyed the night air—single men and women, families with their kids, even a few of the elders in lawn chairs.

It was the number-one thing Autumn loved about her home— the close community.

At times, it was also the thing she disliked most. A close community could be helpful and kind, but nosy and judgmental, too.

Definitely a double-edged sword.

Ember parked on the grass next to a row of cars and trucks. Seeing the crowd gave Autumn second thoughts. "I should have worn a bra."

Laughing, Ember got the stuff from the back seat. "If you've got it, flaunt it—and sis, you've got it."

Yeah... Autumn wasn't so sure about that.

"Besides," Ember continued, as they got out of the car, "nearly everyone is in a swimsuit. In comparison, you're modest."

Looking down at herself, she was grateful nothing showed. She'd just avoid getting too close to the light. "You're not wearing a swimsuit."

"Sure I am. It's under my cover-up." Hooking her arm through Autumn's, she tugged her forward. "Come on."

The shore of the lake wasn't naturally sandy, but the county periodically replenished the sand in two specific areas so everyone could swim without getting muddy. Weather-worn gazebos sat at either end of the recreational area, and midway out on the water, buoys designated the safe-swim area, where boats couldn't intrude.

Autumn loved it here, with the sound of the waves gently lapping the shoreline, the smell of the lake water and all the trees, even the feel of the sand beneath her feet. For most of her life, though, she'd avoided it, or only come to visit during quiet nights, when no one was likely to notice her.

She wasn't comfortable in a bathing suit and didn't interact easily with others.

Ember, however, had always been in her element here. She had no problem stripping down to a bikini, and seemed to be close friends with everyone.

"Oh, look, Mike is here."

Suspicion had her giving Ember closer scrutiny, but her sister was so busy waving to every other man there, Autumn couldn't quite read her expression. Why point out Mike only to ignore him?

It didn't last long because Mike jogged over to them. Barefoot, shirtless and wearing only board shorts, he looked scrumptious and she was pretty sure Ember had to notice.

Autumn greeted him with a grin. "You've been swimming."

"Yeah." He shook his head, sending water droplets to spray them. "It's good to see you get out a little."

"Ember coerced me."

"And look," Ember said. "You're smiling." She thrust the wine coolers at Mike, who almost dropped them, and then—right there, on the spot—she peeled off her cover-up and handed it to Autumn.

Because she was braless, Autumn folded it against her chest and held it within her crossed arms.

Mike made no pretense of looking at Ember in her itty-bitty white bikini. And why should he? Autumn could be biased, but she thought Ember looked better than any other woman there.

She'd always considered confidence to be supersexy in men and women alike, and her sister had the body and the personality that warranted confidence.

"Get in the lake," Mike suggested to Ember with a smile, "and you'll warm that water up a few degrees more." Then he shocked Autumn and Ember both by turning away. "Where do you want your stuff, Autumn?"

Aware of Ember's disgruntled retreat, Autumn said, "Oh, um..." Abandoned, she wasn't quite sure what to do.

"How about over here?" Seeming in a hurry to ditch her, Mike headed toward one of the torches.

That's when she spotted Tash. *Talk about scrumptious.*

Sprawled over a large towel, resting back on his elbows, he smiled. Autumn followed his line of vision and realized his attention was on his daughter.

So endearing. The love he felt showed in his gaze, gave him a warm smile, and she couldn't be immune to it.

Wearing a life preserver over her bathing suit, Sadie sat on the very edge of the shore, where the water just reached her bottom and legs. Two boys had buckets and shovels, and together they were building sandcastles.

Even though the boys looked a few years older, Sadie was clearly in charge.

Tash looked up when she and Mike stopped beside him, and his smile brightened. "Autumn." He immediately stood. "I didn't know you'd be here."

Mike looked back and forth between them, and a calculating grin formed. "Probably because her sister dragged her along." He peered out at the water, then turned back again to ask, "Mind if I drop her stuff here?"

"No problem." Tash quickly brushed sand off the towel.

"Thanks." Putting everything behind the towel where Tash had unlaced running shoes and a cooler, Mike said, "Now you kids behave...or not." He headed back to the lake while Autumn stood there trying to figure out what to do.

Towering over her, windblown and gorgeous and smelling like sunshine, Tash smiled. "There's room if you want to take a seat."

Being unloaded on him made Autumn ridiculously self-conscious. She *could* just mosey away, much as Ember had. Though she wasn't great at mingling, there were people here that she knew. Or she could walk along the shore, enjoy the air—

"Autumn." Smile widening, he bent his knees to look into her eyes. "You don't want to join me?"

Want? Yes. She wanted that. Would she? It didn't feel right. "It seems like I'm always imposing on you. Dinner, picnics and now this. I promise, it's not a problem for me to find another place to—"

"I'd rather you stay." Her heart took a leap, until he added, "You're a familiar face."

Ah, familiarity. No reason for her unruly heart to get excited. Too bad it already made her a bit breathless. Trying to sound blasé, she said, "You grew up here."

"Ages ago, but other than the Johnsons over there, I don't think I knew any of these people very well."

The Johnsons were part of the elderly group, and they'd been in the area forever. "You used to cut grass for them, didn't you?"

"For damn near everyone." He gestured for her to sit, waited until she finally did before joining her. To stay out of the sand, he sat close, his hip nearly touching hers. Drawing up his knees, he rested his arms over them. "I had one hell of a business going until college."

Seeing him this relaxed did funny things to her. "I remember." Autumn did what she could to stay covered. The big shirt helped, and now she draped Ember's cover-up over her lap to sit yoga-style, turning slightly away so her leg wouldn't overlap his. The cover-up almost entirely hid her bare legs. "My sister used to beg our folks to hire you to cut the grass, but they insisted we do it. It was one of her most hated chores." Her smile went crooked at the memory. "She got even by wearing a halter on the rider and when guys started driving by just to whistle at her, Dad gave up."

Curiosity brought his gaze to hers. "So who cut the grass?"

"He gave her a different chore and I inherited grass duty." She wrinkled her nose. "I didn't mind so much, except for when it got really hot."

"Which was most of the summer in Kentucky."

"True."

"Why didn't you just do the halter trick?"

Laughing, Autumn glanced at him...and realized he was serious. "It wouldn't have been the same."

"Why not?"

Because no one would have whistled at me. Surely he knew that, since he was one of the guys who'd never paid her any attention.

Tash continued to watch her, waiting, so she worked up a credible and casual shrug. "Mom and Dad always saw through my BS."

As if seeing through her, hearing things she hadn't said, Tash held her captive with his gaze.

She felt herself sinking. Heck, she might've even leaned toward him a little, drawn in by his intense interest.

Luckily, Sadie laughed, breaking the spell and drawing away Tash's attention. Smiling in anticipation of his daughter's happiness, Tash looked toward her. Her antics made him grin, putting a dimple into his lean, bristly cheek. In profile, she noted his long lashes, his straight nose and high cheekbones.

The wind-tousled hair, the casual clothes over a body carved with strength and the evening beard shadow all detailed his masculinity, but it was his open affection toward his daughter that really sealed the deal.

After blowing out a quick breath to ease the squeezing of her heart, Autumn turned to see Sadie layering a clump of seaweed over the castle walls with artistic flair. The boys loved it.

"She's a charmer." The seaweed really did enhance the castle. "I'm glad she's having fun."

Tash's smile lingered. "It's why we're here. I'm hoping she'll make friends, but most of the girls are swimming and she didn't want to. Instead she corralled those two boys into building the castle she wants."

"They don't seem to mind." Flickering light played over Tash's body. He also wore board shorts, but unlike Mike, he'd topped them with a snowy white T-shirt that fit close to his wide shoulders. He had long, narrow feet, and damn it, to her beleaguered brain even they looked sexy.

The way he'd pushed back his hair, she knew he'd been swimming earlier. Already a few locks dropped forward, making her fingers tingle with the need to touch them.

"The other day when you were over..." He shifted to face her, and the way he stared into her eyes made it damn difficult for her to think. "I'm sorry if I made you uncomfortable."

That didn't make any sense. "What?"

"You realized Sadie was worried." Frustration seemed to emanate off him. "She's worried far too often. Her mom used to promise stuff left and right, but most of it never happened."

How terrible. She'd suspected something along those lines, and having it confirmed helped explain some of Sadie's cynicism. "She's afraid to get too excited."

He nodded. "You saw that, and I appreciate the way you reinforced things. I know you don't normally take payment upfront, but—"

"You're apologizing for trusting me in advance?" Since getting paid wasn't always that easy, she laughed. "Believe me, not a problem. And, hey, if I helped to convince Sadie that you're here to stay, I'm glad."

Dark, serious and sincere, his gaze held hers. "It was nice seeing her happy and I was grateful, so I hugged you. But you froze up, so I figured I'd overstepped."

Ah, so that's what he meant. Feeling like a dolt, Autumn vehemently shook her head. "Nope." *Get it together, girl.* "I mean, it's fine. That is, I knew it wasn't... I knew you were..." Voice going firm, she stated, "It was about Sadie." *Oh, gawd.* She never got this tongue-tied anymore. *Dumb, dumb, dumb.* "I understand."

As if her blathering reply had amused him, his smile twitched. "You do, huh?" Bumping her with his shoulder, he said, "I'm glad one of us does."

Now what the heck did that mean?

Without giving her a chance to find out, he nodded to a couple who said hi as they passed. Next he tossed back a beach ball that got away from some kids. Then he passed on the beer offered to him by a small group.

He might not know these people, but they gravitated to him all the same. No one offered *her* a beer. Of course, they all knew she didn't drink often, but still...

Running a hand over his hair, he said, "It's finally cooling down a little. An hour ago, just sitting still could make you sweat."

His restless hand had further disrupted his hair. Autumn remembered that back in high school he'd get blond streaks from the sun. Now, though, it was a pure sandy brown.

Whatever his life used to be, there must not have been too many beach parties.

Tonight it was *mostly* couples at the party, some with kids, so while everyone was friendly, no one hit on him. If he'd joined in a real party, Autumn felt certain he'd have been mobbed.

How long would he be around before he started dating some of the women she knew? There were a few from their old school days who were newly single, and, of course, there were women he'd never met before who'd moved to the area in the time he was gone.

When his smile suddenly widened, she realized she'd been staring at him and scrambled for something to say. "So…you know Mike?"

His lazy look told her he wasn't at all fooled. "Met him tonight, actually. Nice guy. He stopped by when we first got here, then made a point of introducing the other people with kids so Sadie could jump right in and play."

"He's a very nice guy," she agreed. Now that she'd managed to stop staring at Tash, she found herself stealing looks at Mike. No one would call the man subdued, and unlike Tash, he did have the attention of the single ladies… Ember included.

Oh, her sister, the big fraud, tried to pretend to ignore him, but Autumn knew her too well. She'd bet her favorite book series that they were here now because of Mike.

"Mike said he works for you on the farm?"

"He's our number-one guy." Their only guy, really, other than the occasional seasonal help.

"No kidding?" A few beats passed before Tash said, "Huh. He said he just helps with the animals."

Why did she get the feeling Tash asked about more than employment? And the way he looked at her, like he saw her in ways no one else ever had…

Very unsettling, and she sort of liked it.

"Mike does anything and everything. He's terrific about pitching in without being asked." Sometimes at home, he was her only ally. In most things, he was her backup. "We'd probably be lost without him. I know I would."

Until tonight, he hadn't seen Autumn's legs. Crazy, now that he thought about it. Even in the sweltering heat, she'd always worn slacks. Seeing them now, he had to wonder why.

He couldn't comment on it, but she looked terrific in her shorts, and he liked her hair loose and a little messy.

Before now, he'd noticed her curves, but hadn't noticed her being so damn *cute*. He thought back to high school, her awkwardness and the way she'd sometimes stare at him.

Like she did a minute ago.

Back then it had made him uneasy. The difference in their ages had mattered, yes, but also…he hadn't thought about her that way. She was a funny girl who seemed to watch him too much. He hadn't known what to make of her.

But now? Had to admit, it felt good to have her attention. He'd either been celibate too long, or attention from Autumn now meant more than it did from other women. Whatever the reason, he liked having her here with him. They'd both grown up, and *everything* was different.

Since he'd caught her staring, she seemed to be avoiding his gaze. Ordinarily, he'd be bothered by that, but damn, the way she smiled at his daughter, how she noticed every little thing about Sadie, always in a complimentary way, made him want to hug her again.

As a man, he hadn't worried for much. He'd gone through life feeling blessed, and even the divorce from Deb hadn't kept him down long. But as Sadie's dad? Worry for her was second nature.

There were moments when she seemed to own the world, holding it in her small, gentle hands. But then something would happen and she'd retreat behind a wall of uncertainty. He'd do everything in his power to make her feel loved, wanted and secure.

Because Sadie reacted well to Autumn, he wouldn't mind having her around more.

He shouldn't ask, and it damn sure shouldn't matter, but he'd already noticed how she tracked Mike, watching his every move, and then with what she'd said… Well, he had to know, so screw it. Might as well ask. "You two have a thing?"

"What?" Surprise brought her around with widened eyes and a nervous laugh. "Ha-ha. No."

Why was it so funny? She'd laughed the same way when he'd asked her about using her sister's ploy to get out of cutting grass. She seemed to think Mike, and guys in general, wouldn't be drawn to her, but he couldn't figure out why.

With his continued attention, she shook her head in further denial. "Mike works for me, that's all."

For only a second Tash hesitated to press her, but it had never been his way to tiptoe around a subject. He saw no reason to start now. "You don't look at him like an employer looks at an employee."

"Because he's also a friend?" Maybe noting his skepticism, she leaned closer. "Repeat this and I'll be forced to do you harm, but I think Ember's hung up on him. Not sure if that's a good idea or not. Either way, it concerns me."

With her that close, he couldn't help looking at her mouth. "So your interest is for your sister?"

"Why else?"

"I don't know. He seems to have the attention of a lot of women." Hip-deep in the lake, Mike carried one shapely woman on his shoulders while laughing with another. Two others stayed nearby. "They all appear to like him."

"And why not? He has a quick grin, a friendly manner and a nicely honed body." Her gaze dipped to his own "honed" body, then darted away. "But I'm not most women."

No kidding. She was different all right...in a very nice way. "Wanna tell me how you mean that?"

As if it made perfect sense, Autumn shrugged and said, "Guys, other than friends, do not interest me. Not anymore."

Though she sounded serious, he didn't buy it. "Uh-huh."

"It's true. Ask anyone and they'll tell you."

Chapter Four

B ecause she was too young, too vital and sensual to have
given up on men, Tash laughed.

When she didn't, he felt bad for misunderstanding. What
could have happened to make her so jaded?

Rather than make her uneasy, he turned his gaze toward the
lake and searched for her sister in the crowd of bikini-clad bodies. Even in the dim light, with her hair slicked back, he spotted
Ember quickly enough.

Nice curves on a tight body, probably from her physical job.
Bold attitude—the opposite of Autumn's. Overall, pretty damn
hot. And, yeah, she was flirting with one guy but keeping an
eye on Mike.

Something about Ember—maybe the way she smiled, or how
she laughed a little too loud—kept him studying her, until he
came to a conclusion. "She's a little fragile, isn't she?"

Blinking, her gaze searching his in awe, Autumn started to
speak, but nothing came out. She, too, looked back at her sister.
"What makes you say so?"

Ah, so he'd hit the nail on the head. "I've seen it before." It dawned on him where, and he shook his head. "Never mind." That was the last topic he wanted to discuss. It was bad enough that he'd already dumped info on Autumn.

There was something about her, some natural understanding and empathy, that got him going every time she was near.

It surprised him when Autumn rested her small, warm hand on his arm. "You can tell me."

Huh. She'd gone from not looking at him, almost leaning away from him, to now scooting closer.

He hadn't known many people who'd put aside their own comfort level to be compassionate. Never mind that he didn't need her compassion—he'd eventually figure things out on his own—she still appealed to him in a big way.

Normally, he was pretty good at reading women, but he had no idea what Autumn felt. She didn't outright flirt. No, all she did was sympathize and, damn it, he shouldn't confuse that with intimate interest, regardless of what his instincts said.

She lightly squeezed his forearm, then dropped her hand. "It's okay." Her smile flickered, then was gone. "I promise I'm not thin-skinned."

"What does that mean?" He didn't want her putting herself down.

"Feel free to talk to me, or you can tell me to buzz off." She rolled a shoulder. "I promise it's fine, either way."

The hell it was. Compliments flooded his brain, but they'd be out of place so he bit them back.

Misunderstanding, she started to retreat. "Sorry."

He wasn't about to let her go, so he caught her arm and they did a little more staring at each other. Damn, he felt connected to her. "Stay."

She nodded. "If you want."

Knowing he couldn't—shouldn't—kiss her, he chose to explain. "I recognize the look because Deb wore it as she did a slow slide down the deep end."

"The deep end?"

"Depression, maybe." Though that didn't begin to cover Deb's inclination to think some other guy, some other situation, would naturally be better than what she already had.

Jesus, he hated thinking about it.

"I'm not a psychologist so I can't really say. I just know she went out of her way to pretend to be happy, because deep down she wasn't." And much as he'd tried, he couldn't change that.

Firm resolve stiffened Autumn's shoulders as she searched for her sister in the lake. "I won't let that happen with Ember."

The underlying steel in her tone made him admire her even more. How many times had she taken care of her sister? "I didn't mean to alarm you. It's entirely different, right? Ember might be dealing with something, but she looks overall happy. Deb wasn't. She was usually more miserable than not."

Autumn watched her sister a moment more before deliberately relaxing, staged smile and all.

Likely for his benefit. Everything she did made his admiration grow, and it made him more curious about her.

"You said she was drunk when she wrecked?"

He rubbed his ear, wondering how succinct he could be without insulting her. "I left her because there were other guys."

"She cheated on you?"

Autumn sounded so appalled by that notion, he almost smiled. "More than once, yeah. She didn't want the divorce, but I couldn't stay."

Again, she put her hand to his arm. This time he covered it with his own. "Because of Sadie, I left her the house and car. I didn't want to disrupt her life too much."

"You still saw her?"

"We shared custody, but I gave residential to Deb so Sadie would start school with her friends. The first year wasn't so bad, but then little by little, things got worse. At first I thought Deb was just partying—" *with other guys* "—and it pissed me off because I'd worry about Sadie, you know?"

"You're her dad and you love her."

Things for Autumn often seemed very black and white, but he knew love involved multiple shades of gray. He'd lived in those hues for far too long, trying to fix what he hadn't broken.

It was in the past, but he couldn't let it go. Even now, as Sadie built a sandcastle with two other kids, he saw that she acted older. She always had, and he feared it was because responsibilities had been dumped on her at such a young age.

He wanted her to be a carefree kid, but sometimes he thought it might be too late for that.

"Deb pretended to be happy whenever I was around, but clearly she wasn't. I should have realized." That was his biggest mistake—believing the illusion, buying in to the charade. "I didn't realize she had a drinking problem until it was too late."

Autumn worried her bottom lip with her teeth, then asked, "What was she unhappy about?"

"I never could figure that out." So many times, he'd felt helpless to understand her. "We had Sadie. She was healthy and smart and, to me, perfect. We had a small house, money in the bank, and I had a great job."

"It's so much more than many have."

"To me, Sadie's a blessing. A part of me, but better."

She smiled. "Deb had red hair?"

"My grandmother, actually." His family detested Deb for what she'd put Sadie through, so talking to them only made things worse, sharper-edged. "Deb's family...they blame me, and, by extension, Sadie."

"Losing a daughter has to be tough. Maybe that'll get better in time."

"I hope so. Sadie not only lost her mom, but most contact with her grandparents, too."

"She has you, and that's what really matters."

He didn't mean to, but with Autumn listening instead of judging, he just naturally shared. "Deb used Sadie to blackmail her family for money. Whenever they gave her cash, she'd forget about Sadie while she went out looking for something to make her happy."

She leaned into his shoulder. "Depression is a very difficult thing."

And his daughter had been forced to deal with it. "So many times now, I say or do something, and Sadie makes these broad assumptions based on her life with Deb." The reality of that put a stranglehold on him. "She offers to make breakfast, or do laundry, and I don't know what to tell her. That she's too young? She is, but is she trying to feel needed?"

Autumn was clearly more familiar when commiserating with him as friends, less so as a woman with a man. In the short time he'd been reunited with her, he'd gotten to know her better than any of the women he'd dated after his divorce. She fascinated him, in more ways than one.

"Sadie's probably trying to show you how useful she can be."

Was that something Autumn had done with her own family? The way she said it led him to think so.

A deep breath didn't ease his growing sexual tension. Hell, breathing her in only magnifed the things he felt. "I helped her make breakfast."

"Oh, genius!" Honestly pleased, she gave him a squeeze. "The two of you together."

He nodded. "Blueberry pancakes, because they seemed fun."

"You have great instincts."

Until he got her approval, he hadn't realized how unsure he'd been. It was a novel feeling. Laughing at his own weakness—namely a little redheaded weakness with big blue eyes—he added, "I let her help sort the laundry, then thanked her so much she started giving me funny looks. I feel like I'm walking on eggshells with her." With Autumn now so near, he just naturally put his arm behind her—not quite an embrace, but close. "I flounder, and then I realize I'm offering her the moon, and that's not good for a seven-year-old kid, either."

Voice soft, Autumn asked, "Like her room and the gym equipment in the backyard?"

"We still want that, okay?" He knew Sadie was looking forward to the changes, even if she remained subdued about them. "Hiring you was a great idea."

Autumn nudged him playfully. "I think you've had many great ideas."

"A few," he admitted. "I want her to be excited about something, instead of so damn skeptical all the time."

The way she looked up at him heightened his tension, but in a different, far more pleasant way. "Not that you asked for my advice—"

"I'd like it." Hell, she seemed to have a very calm, common-sense way about her. She wasn't railing against Deb, which he appreciated, and she hadn't tried to baby Sadie, which would have bothered his daughter a lot.

"All right." Her gentle tone softened the rebuke when she said, "You need to relax. Kids are more resilient than you realize. Sadie probably picks up on your worry, you know? If you're second-guessing yourself, it's going to stress her."

"Shit." Trying to relieve his knotted muscles, he rubbed the back of his neck. "You're probably right." Easier said than done, though.

"From what I've seen, you're a terrific dad. Be natural with her and if she gets upset or misunderstands, explain things. Over and over again, if you have to. She knows you love her and that's the most important part."

"The thing is, she knew Deb loved her, too. Sometimes love isn't enough." He'd found that out the hard way.

"You're right. Kids crave routines and boundaries that they

can understand. If she wants chores, give her some that are age-appropriate, and maybe an allowance to go with it. Talk to her about future plans that include her. She can be your entire focus—"

"She is."

"I know it," she said, her eyes warm with understanding. "Sadie probably knows it, too, and that's a lot of pressure, like everything hinges on her. For a kid, that would be scary. It might make her feel responsible for keeping things on track."

"Well, hell." Not once had he ever considered that, yet now that she'd said it, he knew she was right. "I need to be the adult and let her be the kid."

"She needs to know you're in charge, through the bumpy times and through the easy transitions, when she's an angel and when she misbehaves."

Why hadn't he thought of it?

Again, she nudged him. "Parents are incredibly imperfect, and you don't get to be any different."

"All parents, huh?"

"Every single one. It's called being human."

Somehow she made it all sound less awful. "I don't want her to be afraid ever again."

"She's smart, but still only a little girl. A lot of things have changed in her life lately, so, of course, she's scared."

He looked out at Sadie, busy tossing seaweed at one of the boys, who tossed it right back. When it stuck to her hair, she cracked up...and so did they.

"I'm glad she's seeing what a nice place this is for us to live."

Though people walked around them, noisy with their conversations, splashing in the lake, laughing, he was easily able to tune them out. Sometime in the near future he'd like to return to this very spot with only Autumn and Sadie. They could have a picnic. The image in his mind had him smiling.

She glanced at him curiously. "Are you happy here?"

Light from the torch danced in her eyes and over her dark brown hair. It was longer now, unkempt in a natural and somehow sexy way.

She looked tired, but he knew she wouldn't say so. How he knew that, he couldn't say—except that it felt like he'd known her forever, never mind that they hadn't been close back in school.

"Tash?"

He doubted Autumn Somerset had any idea just how attractive she looked right now. He glanced down at her mouth... and then away.

Noticing her damp lips wouldn't be a smart move. Then again...too late. The longer he knew her, the more he noticed, and the more he liked what he saw.

"I'm more comfortable here than I've been in a year." In Sunset, Kentucky, he felt like he could actually breathe. "This is home, you know?"

"Yes, I know."

When things had gotten rough, this was what he'd wanted. The familiar, and maybe the good memories, too. Autumn felt like the best part of Sunset...and he hadn't even known her that well. "My parents retired to South Carolina not long after I moved away. For the longest time, there hadn't been any reason to come back." He looked toward Sadie, now making the summer equivalent of a snow angel, but in the wet sand. God, she was precious to him. "After Deb died, I knew Sadie and I needed a fresh start."

"So you came home. Smart." She, too, looked toward his daughter. "You and I both know it's a good place to grow up."

"Yeah." Here on the beach, with the evening air encompassing them, he detected the light scent of floral shampoo, maybe lotion, and soft, warm woman. How long had it been since he'd noticed a woman? He wanted to lift Autumn's hair, brush his nose along her throat, breathe her in and taste her skin. Voice a little husky, he said, "It feels right to be here."

"Autumn!" Waving energetically, a tall blonde woman started their way.

Tash barely heard Autumn's muffled groan before she plastered on a brittle smile and whispered to him, "Prepare yourself."

Taking his cues from her, he straightened when she did. They no longer sat so close and he already missed her touch.

He didn't think Autumn was prone to exaggeration, so as the woman closed in, he assumed this was about to be an unpleasant visit.

"Patricia." Autumn started to stand, but Patricia waved her back down and plopped on the towel in front of her, bringing along a lot of sand with her bare feet.

"I couldn't believe it was you! You *never* join the parties."

Autumn's smile didn't slip. "I'm here with Ember."

That made Patricia laugh. "Ember *always* joins in, and you *never* come with her."

"Sometimes I do." Defensiveness kept her shoulders squared. "Just not very often."

With a snort, Patricia said, "It's the first I've seen, especially since you-know-when."

What the hell? She made Autumn sound antisocial. Did that impression have to do with Autumn giving up on guys? And what was that *you-know-when* gibe? By the second, Tash's interest grew. He wanted to know Autumn better, and maybe this talkative friend of hers could be a start.

"So..." Patricia tilted her head toward Tash with a lot of suggestion. "Is *this* why you're here?"

"This," Tash said, because of how she'd referred to him, "is a friend from high-school days. Autumn is doing some design work for my daughter's room." Keeping it simple seemed to be his best bet.

"Daughter?" Patricia's eyebrows shot nearly to her hairline, giving her a comical look. She took in the two of them sitting there together on the towel. In a titillated whisper, she asked, "So you're *married*?"

"Good grief, Patricia," Autumn groused.

"Well, *is* he?"

The woman had a very annoying way of overemphasizing certain words. Rather than have Autumn put on the spot, Tash started to answer…but Autumn beat him to it.

"Let's back up, okay? Patricia Schaffer, meet Tash Ducker. Tash was two grades ahead of me back in school. He moved away for a while but now he's back." She turned to him. "Patricia isn't from here, but she moved to Sunset about three years ago."

"A year before you were supposed to be married." She poked out her bottom lip as if the reminder made her sad.

She looked absurd, and then what she'd said hit him and Tash froze. Wait…*what*? Autumn was engaged?

He looked at her and saw she'd turned into a stone statue. As if chipped into place, her smile remained.

Patricia enthused, "Such a weird coincidence. I mean, you know *he's* back, too, right?"

"He?" Tash asked, because Autumn didn't look interested in contributing.

In a scandalized whisper, Patricia said, "Chuck Conning."

A recognizable name. Tash wracked his brain and pulled out what he could remember, which was mostly Chuck's whiny attitude and penchant to blame others every time he screwed up.

He gave Autumn a look, but no, he couldn't reconcile the two of them together. Autumn and Chuck? Definitely not.

Patricia leaned closer. "Two weeks before they were supposed to get married, Chuck ran off with Brenda Walker. Poof. *Gone*." She looked back at Autumn, pouting again. "It was *tragic*."

And just like that, Autumn returned in full force. "Really, Patricia. I don't know why you're whispering." She dusted sand away from her legs with a little too much force. "I'm sitting right here so it's not like I won't hear you. *And*," she stressed, stealing Patricia's habit, "there was nothing tragic about it."

Bravo, Tash wanted to say, absurdly proud of her, but Patricia wasn't done yet.

She touched Autumn's hand, mock sympathy oozing from her. "I thought you should know he's *back*."

"Why?"

Confusion loosened Patricia's jaw. "Why is he back?"

Impatient, Autumn shook her head. "Why ever would you think I needed to know?"

Tash was wondering the same damn thing.

"Oh, honey. Because he *broke your heart*."

With a credible laugh, Autumn disabused her of that notion. "Not even close. Actually, he did me an enormous favor."

Incredibly dim, Patricia blinked at her. "But...how?"

Resisting the urge to roll his eyes, Tash said, "He showed his true colors before she leg-shackled herself to him. Marriage would have complicated things even more when she kicked his ass to the curb."

Looking at him in surprise, Autumn grinned. "So astute! Yes, much better before than after."

"But you'd spent all that money on the *gown* and the *church* and *flowers*—"

Autumn flapped a hand. "Some lessons are costlier than others. Besides, I found out that I like ice cream a lot more than men."

"Ice cream?" Patricia repeated.

Yeah, Tash was a little curious about that one, too.

Ignoring Patricia, Autumn grinned at him. "Did you know there are ice-cream clubs? Because I didn't, not until the whole debacle with Chuck."

"It *was* a debacle," Patricia gushed, trying to rejoin the conversation.

"No kidding." Playing along, Tash ignored the twit, too. "Like you belong to a group?"

"With a monthly subscription! How wonderful is that? Each month I get three pints of different flavors. The club emails me a tracking number so I'll know when it's arriving."

"Special flavors?"

"Oh, my gosh, *yes*. They have watermelon, and apple strudel, and strawberry shortcake. My favorite is salted caramel." She made *mmm-mmm* sounds, as if tasting it.

Tash wanted to taste *her*.

"Anyway," Patricia said a little too loudly, "Chuck is back and I heard he and Brenda have *split*." Clearly tickled by the prospect, she leaned in. "I heard he's going to look you up!"

With a dramatic groan, Autumn pretended to collapse.

She dropped back...into Tash.

Glad that she'd included him in her antics, he caught her with a laugh, and then held on, drawing her closer. It felt nice having her feminine weight soft against his side.

"Did she faint?" Patricia asked with gleeful hope.

"She," Autumn said, opening her eyes and straightening, "is dying of ridiculousness."

Tash chuckled again. "Ridiculousness, huh?"

"I have no interest in anything Chuck is or isn't doing, and I'm sure he has no interest in seeing me. It's dumb to suggest that he might."

Patricia stiffened. "Did you call me dumb?"

"Hey." Breathing a little fast, Ember showed up, standing close but not on the towel since she dripped lake water and sand covered her feet. She pushed back her wet hair and managed a cryptic smile. "I just noticed Patricia was here to...visit."

"Ember to the rescue," Autumn mumbled as she moved away from his hold.

Of course, Tash let her go—what else could he do? He didn't want to. He wanted to pull her into his lap, hug her and tell her that her strength was sexy as hell. Not many could have handled that encounter with her humor and panache. Had Ember seen Patricia and, knowing the type of woman she was, come to assist her sister? If so, that'd be a nice gesture.

Not that Autumn had needed help.

"Aren't you going to swim?" Ember asked Patricia.

"Maybe later." Glad for more of an audience, she went right back to her gossiping. "I was just telling Autumn—"

"Here." Ember reached past them and grabbed the wine coolers. "Have one. We'll drink while you tell me about it."

"But I—"

Ember caught her arm and practically hauled her to her feet. "I count on you to keep me informed."

"You do?" Patricia huddled closer to her. "Then let me tell you…" Heads together, they walked away.

Impressed, Tash watched them go. "Well, that was smooth. And Patricia doesn't seem to suspect a thing."

"Patricia is oblivious whenever it suits her." Autumn brushed away the sand before straightening her legs. "She's nice enough, but—"

"She didn't strike me as nice." Pretty legs, he noticed. Shapely and not too thin. What would Autumn look like in a swimsuit? He wouldn't mind finding out. "I'd say she borders on spiteful."

"She's just self-absorbed and she loves to be in on everyone else's private business." Autumn huffed a short laugh. "Although, since everyone here knew what Chuck and Brenda did, it was never really private, anyway."

"I recognize Chuck's name from high school, but not Brenda's."

"She moved here after you left town." Drawing a fingertip through the sand, Autumn sighed. "Soon as Chuck met her, I should have known there'd be trouble."

"Made it obvious, huh?"

Pretending it didn't matter, she shrugged. "He denied it whenever I asked, and I stupidly believed him."

"You were in love?"

"Thought I was at the time." Nose scrunched, mouth tweaked to the side, she downplayed her feelings. "Later I realized that I just liked the idea of being in love. Marriage and family and growing old together. That all sounded nice." She looked up at the sky. "Nice enough to marry Chuck. I meant it when I said he did me a favor. I'll forever be grateful that I didn't get financially tied to him."

Yeah, at the moment he was pretty damn glad she didn't, too. "When I married Deb, all that sounded nice to me, too, so I get it. The idea of sharing everything with someone…"

"Now I realize it has to be the right someone."

Very true. "Ember knew what was going on? I mean, with Patricia."

"She probably saw her with me and, knowing her as she does, assumed, or she… I don't know. She just knew."

It surprised him when Autumn leaned back to her elbows, her gaze remaining on the gray velvet sky overhead. It was a provocative pose, though he suspected she had no idea. Even when ditzy women weren't bombarding her with mean-spirited gossip, she seemed remarkably unaware of her sex appeal.

He wondered now if Chuck, the ass, had something to do with that. Had he damaged her self-esteem?

Hating that thought, Tash went to one elbow and braced on his side next to her. He watched Autumn, felt her introspection, and badly wanted to touch her. "Ember just knew?"

"Remember, we grew up together." Her gaze slanted his way. "She can look at me and tell something is wrong—same as I can with her."

"No shit?"

A silly smile played over her very kissable mouth. "No shit.

Sometimes it's nice, other times it's intrusive. That's how it is with family."

"Mind if I ask you something."

Dread made her tighten, but she shrugged again.

"Is that why you're here? You were worried about Ember so you came along?"

For the longest time, Autumn stared at him as if trying to figure out a puzzle.

Having no idea why, he lifted an eyebrow. "Problem?"

"You're not going to grill me about Chuck, are you?"

Ah, so she was used to everyone carrying on like Patricia had? It pleased him to disappoint her on that assumption. "I wasn't impressed with him as a kid, and now, as a man, he sounds about as smart and honorable as a gnat—meaning not very important, so why bother?"

The puzzlement morphed into humor. "A gnat?"

"Should I have said complete dumb-ass?" Liking the way she smiled, how it added a dimple to her cheek and a glimmer to her eyes, he stuck with his theme. "For the record, I'm censoring for your benefit. Dumb-ass is as nice as I can get. If we continue this conversation, the insults will get more colorful." He smoothed back a silky hank of her hair, tucking it behind one ear. "Maybe not appropriate to these delicate little ears."

Her smile widened—a really beautiful smile, he noticed. "Delicate ears?"

"Cute ears. Ears that inspire me." Ears he wanted to nibble. He leaned down to breathe close, "Should I bring out my ugliest descriptions?"

Feeling her shiver, he smiled and leaned away.

Covering her reaction, Autumn cleared her throat. "My delicate ears are twitching to hear them, but you probably shouldn't." She gave an exaggerated, furtive glance around. "Too many people might overhear."

"Who cares? If they know good old Chuck, I'm sure they already think the same."

"You'd be surprised. Most think he's a great guy. They probably assume there's something wrong with me." Once the words left her mouth, she looked horrified that she'd said them and followed up with, "Not that I care what they think."

Of course she did. The urge to protect her, to shield her from the ugliness of ruthless gossip, burned through his bloodstream. "Was someone stupid enough to say that to you?"

She took in his annoyance, and another smile twitched into place. "No, but I know how this town thinks. If you stay—and I hope you do—you're going to hear all sorts of things. Chuck dumping me was the juiciest bit of gossip Sunset has had in a very long time."

"Meaning not much happens around here, so they have to make the most of what a dumb-ass does?"

"Meaning half the town was involved in that stupid wedding in one way or another." She scrunched her nose again. "Chuck wanted a big wedding with all his friends, and I chose to use only local vendors, so everyone knew every damn thing about the wedding."

"Ouch." That had to smart. He remembered how he'd felt when his marriage fell apart. They'd largely kept it private, not in the spotlight of an entire town, so his situation was only a fraction of what she must've gone through. Because she hadn't buckled, hadn't run away from it all, his respect for her increased tenfold.

And she could still deal with the likes of Patricia. Amazing.

"Mostly everyone was nice about it. Sometimes too nice, if you know what I mean."

By the minute he understood Autumn, maybe better than he'd ever understood Deb, so he could easily guess how she'd reacted. "You didn't want anyone feeling sorry for you."

Her soft sigh said a lot. "But they did, and I hated the pity most of all."

"Will it bother you if he's back around?"

"It'd bother me if he stole my ice cream." She flashed a cheeky grin, but it slipped away as she grew serious. "If he really is here, it's going to be a little embarrassing. You already saw that it'll stir up the past. But I don't have any feelings left, not for him, not for what happened. Chuck is history. I got over him long ago."

So strong. He had a feeling Autumn would face any situation with guts and pride and a good dose of kindness and understanding for those who didn't give her the same. She wasn't a vindictive person, and she allowed others a lot of leeway for human error, as he'd witnessed with Patricia.

He admired her and her poise.

Also admired her legs, and her lips, her skin and hair...

Without meaning to, Tash found himself brushing the backs of his knuckles over her cheek. *Softness, warmth...*

Cravings he hadn't felt in far too long suddenly surged to the surface. He hadn't realized how he'd missed this type of connection, but it seemed natural, even right, with Autumn. "You're sure about that?" The silkiness of her skin put his awareness on the razor's edge. "No residual feelings for Chuck?"

A mix of surprise, uncertainty and something close to yearning kept her still.

Maybe she enjoyed the contact as much as he did.

Briefly, she leaned into his hand. His palm opened to cradle her cheek while his heartbeat slowed, went heavy. Lust. He'd almost forgotten what it felt like, but he felt it now in spades.

From a simple touch and shared conversation.

"Our family was still reeling over my mess when..." Hesitation gripped her and she cut herself off. Slowly sitting up, she pushed back her hair, and seemed to wage an internal battle.

Left holding air, Tash rose to sit beside her. He didn't know the problem, but he knew he didn't like seeing her this way. "I overstepped again?" And now she'd retreated. He should apologize, but damn, he wasn't sorry. In fact, he suddenly wanted to do more than stroke her skin. A lot more.

"It's not that," she promised.

"No?"

"Talking with you has been nice." She searched his face. "Really nice, actually."

"For me, too." Even now, he wanted to put his mouth on hers, lick over her lips, taste her...yet Autumn seemed oblivious to the chemistry arcing between them.

Probably for the best.

She was a good listener, and she gave excellent advice. He felt connected to her in various ways—through the history of the town and their school years, sure; as a man to an attractive woman, most definitely.

But also on a more elemental level, one he couldn't quite identify because he didn't think he'd ever experienced it before.

The last thing he wanted to do was muck it up. She'd said she was done with men—hell, she preferred ice cream now. He had to remember that.

"Have I ruined the evening?"

"No, of course not. I've had a wonderful time."

A wonderful time? By worrying about her sister, listening to his concerns and being assaulted by a nosy friend? Yeah, a laugh a minute. Given a chance, he'd show her what a good time should be. Except, she wasn't interested, and he had a seven-year-old daughter still adjusting.

Now was definitely not the time to start something.

Autumn drew him from those thoughts when she said, "Before, when I froze up, it wasn't you." She examined a fingernail. "It's just that I started to share something private, and not mine to tell." Biting her lip, she glanced at him. "I've never done that before. Slipped up and almost told things I shouldn't, so I think it's you. You're just too easy to talk to."

Well, that was something. "You don't need to confirm or deny, but I'm going to guess it's something to do with Ember, and she's still struggling with it." To keep from touching her again, he folded his arms over his knees. "It's pretty terrific that you're here for her."

"We're sisters," she said simply.

And that explained it all? Being an only child, he couldn't say for sure what siblings did, but he knew he'd do anything for Sadie.

"Dad."

Jolted, Tash looked up to see Sadie braced between the two boys, favoring her right foot. He knew her different tones, and in that single word he'd heard both worry and pain. Standing in a rush, he realized he hadn't checked on her for…oh, ten minutes or more, and now something had happened.

Chapter Five

Meeting Sadie halfway, he quickly looked her over from head to toe.

The look in her eyes, like fear of repercussions more than injury, nearly broke his heart. Hiding his frustration, he kneeled down and gently asked, "You're hurt?"

"Just a little." Sidestepping that, she said, "Hey, Autumn. I didn't know you were here."

How like her to try to tough it out. For a seven-year-old, she never ceased to amaze him.

Of course, Autumn handled it perfectly.

"Because you were too busy having fun to notice me. Nothing wrong with that." She came up to her knees. "You hurt your foot?"

One of the boys looked at him, seemed to burst and words poured out. "We were playing, right where you told her to stay. It was just a game of catch around the castle, but she cut her foot on something and it's bleeding!"

"So I see." Tash kept his tone deliberately calm as he noticed the blood on the sand.

"I told you I'm okay," Sadie insisted, wincing only a little.

"Let's make this easier, okay?" Tash reached out for her, and the boys stepped away. He scooped her up, hugging her to his heart as he came back to his feet and carried her closer to the torch so he could better see.

His petite daughter weighed next to nothing, but the bulky life preserver made her an awkward bundle.

He heard Autumn reassuring the boys. "Thanks for helping her over, guys. Don't worry, I'm sure she'll be fine."

"I don't know how she did it," the other kid said, his tone defensive. "We were just in the sand."

"A broken shell," Sadie explained with obvious exasperation. "I stepped on the stupid thing."

"Hold still, sweetheart." Tash put her on the towel where he'd been sitting, then dumped his cell phone out of one of his shoes. He used the glow of the screen to look at her foot.

Autumn touched his shoulder. "There's a first-aid kit in Ember's car. I'm sure we have a bandage or two. Want me to get it?"

The arch of Sadie's foot continued to drip blood through an open cut about an inch long. "If you wouldn't mind."

"Be right back." She took off in a loping run that briefly drew his attention.

"I'm making a mess on the towel."

"We have other towels." If he'd been watching her more closely...what? He wanted her to play with other kids. He wanted her to run around and laugh. Logically, he knew kids sometimes got hurt. "She's fine, boys, I promise. No one's fault, just an accident."

The tense boys relaxed marginally, staring at her foot in macabre horror.

"Where's that shell now?" he asked as he helped Sadie take off the life jacket.

"Here." She opened her palm to show half a mussel shell

with a broken edge. "Wish I'd found it with my hands instead of my foot."

For her benefit, he gave a brief smile. "It's a beauty. Did you want to keep it?"

When she nodded, he put it in his pocket. "We'll find a special place for it. The shell that brought Sadie Ducker low."

His joke fell flat, only earning the tiniest smile from her.

Autumn returned, coming down beside them with a compact kit. "Here's a pretreated swab." She handed the small square to him.

As gently as he could, Tash cleaned away the blood. Sadie, hurt but stoic, didn't make a sound. The two boys, who'd crowded close to see, seemed to be in agony.

When Sadie's lip quivered, Autumn began to usher them away. "Let's give Sadie and her dad enough room to see, okay, guys? In fact, you better let your parents know where you are. If they don't see you, they might worry."

Reluctantly, they turned to go. "We'll see you soon, Sadie," one boy said.

The other chimed in, "I hope you don't need stitches." Together, they ran off.

Silence fell around them while Tash concentrated on cleaning away the sand and blood as carefully as he could.

He was just about done when Sadie mumbled, "I didn't mean to, Dad."

Her small voice brought his head up quickly. She appeared very uncertain with his concentrated attention. Smiling wide enough to blind her, he lifted her foot to kiss her toes. "I know that, goose. I'm just sorry you're hurt."

"I don't need stitches, okay?" Worry added a tremble to her tone.

"I can't tell how deep it is, but I think—" His attempt to reassure her never made it out.

"No." Courage shriveling, she tried to jerk away her foot.

"Hey, easy." Given her reaction, worry surfaced. "I don't think it's much deeper than a scratch." Another smile, and this one pained him. He smoothed back her tangled hair. "I wouldn't let anyone hurt you, okay?"

She nodded, but her voice trembled when she said again, "I don't want stitches."

With perfect timing, Autumn moved in closer until her hip touched his. "Is she up on her shots?"

"Yeah." Once they'd settled in, he'd collected her medical records and found a local pediatrician. "Tetanus, too."

"Then for tonight at least, I think it'd be safe to wash it well—maybe in a bubble bath?"

Hoping that would boost Sadie's mood, Tash said, "Sure, we could do that, couldn't we, goose? We still have half a bottle of that tutti-frutti bubble bath we bought last week."

She nodded.

"Once it's good and clean," Autumn said in a no-nonsense voice, "put on some antibiotic ointment and a bandage." She smiled at Sadie. "In the morning, if it starts to look red or feels hot, you'll need to get it checked, okay? Otherwise, I don't think it's serious. Look, the bleeding has already stopped."

Eyes a little wide, Sadie asked, "Are you a doctor, too?"

Autumn's laugh was sweet and further helped to lighten the mood. "No, but working on a farm means one of us is always banged-up somehow. I know what to look for. Stitches are only used to stop the bleeding or to make it look prettier. Your feet are cute enough that one little scratch won't matter." She sat cross-legged again and did her own quick inspection of the wound. "All in all, that doesn't look too bad, right?"

Bending herself like a pretzel, Sadie peered at her foot. "Right." She shot Tash a guarded look. "No stitches, okay?"

It made him numb with grief, seeing that level of caution. What the hell had Deb put her through? What did she think would happen?

Trying to sound as cheerful as Autumn had, he said, "At least I can wrap it pretty." He put a small wad of gauze on the wound and held it in place with tape that he tied in a bow. "Ta-da."

Sadie cracked a genuine smile.

Autumn said, "So cute!"

He kissed each of Sadie's toes, then shook out another towel. "Doesn't look like it'd be necessary, but in case it ever happens again, you need to know that stitches don't hurt."

"He's right." Conspiratorial, Autumn whispered, "I got some on my behind."

For a moment, that threw Tash. He held out the towel, but didn't do anything with it. His daughter looked equally surprised.

"I was climbing over a fence on the farm," Autumn confided, "and my backside found a loosened nail...*as* I was sliding over to the other side." She flinched as if in remembered pain. "Trust me, that hurt, but the stitches were a piece of cake."

Casual as you please, Sadie said, "Mine hurt."

Tash wrapped the towel around her. "You've never had stitches, honey."

"Did, too." She ducked her face and whispered, "It was a secret."

Like a slap to the face, her disclosure stunned him. Damn Deb for asking a child to keep secrets from her father.

Never would he let her feel his rage, so he carried on as if she hadn't just divulged an awful deception that ripped out his guts. "Well, now I know, right?" He kept a smile pinned in place. "How did you get hurt?"

"I was cutting up an apple." Eyes downcast, she whispered, "I cried a lot."

"I'm sorry, baby." Tash drew her into his lap and kissed her forehead.

She peeked up at him, swallowed and said, "One of Mom's boyfriends was a nurse, and he gave me stitches."

One of Mom's boyfriends. Toward the end, Deb had a different guy every month, or so it had seemed. He hadn't liked it, but saying so had only led to arguments, followed by him losing time with Sadie.

He only missed a single beat before he asked, "You cut your finger?"

She held up her right hand. "This one."

Of course, he and Autumn both looked...and saw the short, jagged scar on Sadie's tiny ring finger, between her first and second knuckle.

Autumn gently rubbed her little hand and asked, "So you went to a hospital?"

She shook her head.

"Ah, a doctor's office then?"

"No."

Stymied, Autumn asked, "Where did he stitch you up?"

Watching Tash, Sadie whispered, "In the kitchen." And after a swallow, she added, "But I'm not supposed to tell that, either."

Though he mostly hid it, Autumn saw Tash's devastation. He did great with Sadie, hiding his anger, but this—this was just awful.

Standing, she looked for Ember. Her sister was busy pushing Patricia into a group of other people. Damn it. She needed—

As if sensing her stare, Ember glanced up, took one look at her and immediately excused herself from the group to jog toward them.

Guys looked. Ember jogging in a bikini? Yeah, even women admired her. Autumn certainly did.

Sounding more lighthearted than she felt, Autumn said, "Look, my sister is heading this way again. She's the one who'll build your pirate ship in the backyard."

Sadie said, "We met her at the grocery."

Before Ember reached them, Autumn asked, "Would you

two like to see the farm? I'll have time tomorrow." She'd make time so she could ensure father and daughter were both okay. "I could show you around, let Sadie pet the animals and feed the chickens. What do you think?"

Secrets and her injury forgotten, Sadie gasped. "Could we, Dad? Please?"

"Sure, why not? I'm curious to see the farm."

Squealing, Sadie bounced in her dad's lap. "Could I see the pigs, Matilda and Olivia?"

"They would love that. They're always excited for company."

"And the goat, Delilah, and the sheep, Franklin?"

Delighted, Autumn laughed. "You remember them all!"

Walking into the conversation blind, Ember said, "Wow, did this squirt just name four of our critters? I'm impressed!" She offered her palm to Sadie. "Give me five."

Grinning from ear to ear, Sadie smacked her palm.

It relieved Autumn to see the tension easing from Tash's shoulders. "Ember's amazed because she sometimes forgets their names."

"That's because Autumn always gets to name them." She dropped down to sit by Sadie and said, sotto voce, "She sneaks and gives them names before I even have a chance to think about it." As if inspired, Ember turned back to her. "You know what? We should let Sadie name the turkey."

"What an excellent idea!" Loving the excitement on Sadie's face, she explained, "We just rescued a turkey. Poor baby has a broken wing, but our super-amazing vet will get him all fixed up. Once we get him to the farm, you could meet him and de-cide what he should be called."

"We could name him after Dad."

Autumn choked. Ember laughed outright.

"Tash the turkey?" Happy to play along, Tash gave Sadie a squeeze and said with haughty dignity, "I'm honored."

God love the man, just how incredible was he? He took Sadie's confession on the chin, rolled with the punches and kept on teasing—all for Sadie. Autumn had the feeling he'd do just about anything to keep the shadows out of his daughter's eyes.

More than his gorgeous bod and handsome face, more than his easy presence and friendly manner, his potent dad-mode made her heart pound in a demented beat.

When Sadie's giggling subsided, he announced, "It's time for us to head home. By the time you get that bubble bath, it'll be past even my bedtime."

"Mine, too," Autumn said with a big and not entirely feigned yawn.

Ember and Sadie called them party poopers as Tash stepped into his shoes and gathered up their stuff. Autumn automatically pitched in.

Sadie started to stand, but Tash said, "I'll carry you, okay?"

"*Dad,*" she complained, looking around to make sure no one had heard him. "I can walk."

"You've got me convinced you can do anything you put your mind to, but I don't want your foot getting dirty."

Autumn cut the debate short by saying, "I'll help Tash get this stuff in his car." She wanted a moment to talk privately with him, anyway. "Ember, you'll wait with Sadie?"

"We'll talk about the playground and everything she might want," Ember promised, shooing them away. "Take your time."

Tash seemed distracted as they headed to his car. One step behind him, Autumn took in his squared shoulders, stiff with tension…which just naturally led to her looking over the rest of him, too. Firm flesh stretched taut over long bones and masculine angles, emphasizing his innate physical strength.

After what she'd just seen, she knew he had emotional strength in spades, as well.

Biding her time until they were far enough away that no one could hear, she trailed behind him…until he suddenly stopped and looked back. "Damn, I'm sorry." He held out a hand. "Didn't mean to leave you behind."

"You have a few things on your mind." When she reached him, his hand went to the small of her back and drew her alongside him. "Are you okay?"

"Furious," he answered, his tone low. "Fucking heartbroken." As if she hadn't been there to hear it, or maybe to convince himself it was real, he said, "Her mother had her keep secrets from me. My baby had stitches and I didn't know it. Worse, she had some boyfriend do it. Jesus."

Knowing he was hurting, Autumn leaned into him. Words didn't come to her, so instead she offered touch.

"I want to ask her questions. I want—*need*—to know it all. Any other secrets. Any other injuries. But I don't want to pressure her to talk."

"She's opening up little by little, right?" As Sadie adjusted, she'd talk more. Autumn felt sure of that. "You did great with her."

"If Deb was here, I could demand answers. Obviously I should have done more of that when she was alive. I just never imagined..." He cursed low. "If she didn't go to the doctor, how did this random guy even numb her finger?"

"Don't torture yourself," she advised, rubbing his arm. "She's with you now, safe and happy."

His laugh held no humor. "Is she happy? I hope so, but sometimes it's hard to tell."

They reached his car, so she waited while he opened the back of the dark SUV.

After he loaded everything inside, he leaned against the fender. The bright moon overhead highlighted his face in heavy shadows, but Autumn could guess at his expression.

She stepped closer. "Little by little, Tash. You're giving her stability, security and love. The rest will come."

Taking her by surprise, he looped his arms around her waist

and drew her against him. With his chin to the top of her head, he whispered, "Thank you for reminding me. I *will* make it all right. Just might take longer than I'd like."

Total shutdown. Good Lord, Tash had her snuggled up against his solid body in a cozy embrace and she couldn't think. Couldn't reply.

Could barely even breathe.

She did manage a nod, which meant she bumped her head into his chin, making him pull back.

Laughing, he used the edge of a loose fist to tip up her face. "You maneuver through all this so seamlessly. I know you brought up the visit to the farm to give me a second, and I appreciate it."

Another nod felt inadequate, but seriously, she was acutely aware of every firm inch of his long, hot body...and then she remembered she hadn't worn a bra. Her mouth opened, but that's as far as she got.

What could she say? *Sorry, but I'm afraid you might be able to feel my nipples?* Yup, they were at attention, big-time.

Pretty sure her ovaries were, too.

"You are so cute." Casual as you please, Tash bent and put a soft, lingering kiss to her temple. "Cute, and a blessing."

A blessing. Right. That's what this was about. The man had just suffered awful revelations about his daughter and she'd worked as a buffer. Under the circumstances, he'd be equally grateful to Ember, or even Mike.

Probably wouldn't hug and kiss Mike, though. Pretty sure Mike's nipples wouldn't be a problem.

Her thoughts were still scrambling around when he released her, engulfed her hand in his and started back to his daughter.

Just like they were a couple or something.

Now she didn't know what to think, but whatever. She liked it, even though he freed her before Sadie and Ember came into view.

Tomorrow would be a work-heavy day at the farm, but with their visit planned, she already looked forward to it.

Closing the book he'd just finished reading, Tash looked down at Sadie. Snuggled under his right arm, she smelled sweet and clean, her hair freshly braided and her injured foot sporting a clean bandage. Brown eyelashes rested low on her sleepy eyes.

He loved times like this, when she was warm and sweet, all her defenses down, cuddled close and feeling secure. With a kiss to her forehead, he said, "Time to sleep, honey."

After a lusty yawn, she looked up at him. "You lookin' forward to seein' the farm, Dad?"

"I am." Mostly he looked forward to her happiness. "How about you?"

"I can't wait. I hope Matilda and Olivia like me."

"I think they'll adore you, just like I do."

Far too grave for a child her age, she said, "Thanks for readin' to me."

The seriousness in her big blue eyes nudged a smile onto his mouth. "You look very cross about it."

Narrow shoulders lifted. "Just thinkin'."

It was their special time, something he'd started when she was too young to understand. Whenever he had her overnight, which granted, wasn't as often as he'd have liked, he always had a new book to read to her.

"I love reading to you. In fact, I was thinking we should get a few new books soon."

After a weighty pause she said, "Mom didn't like to read."

The disclosure surprised him. Trying to keep it light, he set aside the book and smiled. "What was your bedtime routine at home?"

"I'd sometimes watch TV. I had a TV in my room." Pensive, she heaved a sigh. "Mom told me to leave it on while I slept."

Maybe to drown out other noises? It didn't matter, not anymore. As Autumn had said, he had her now and he'd make her life as secure as possible. "Did you want a TV in your room here?"

"No." She bit her lip. "I mean, I'd rather you read to me."

Tash gave her a squeeze. "I prefer that, too."

Toying with a loose thread on her stuffed monkey, she asked, "Do you like Autumn?"

"Sure. Don't you?"

"I didn't like Mom's boyfriends."

His heart tripped, though he tried to hide it. "How come?"

Another shrug, meaning she wasn't ready to go there yet. Little by little, he reminded himself. Grilling her for info wasn't the way.

"If you don't like Autumn—" he ventured, hoping that wasn't the case, since he more than liked her.

"I do," she interrupted fast. Turning to face him, her gaze pointed and serious, she stated, "I like her lots."

Fantastic. "Me, too."

"Mom wouldn't have liked her."

She blurted that out, then waited for his reaction.

Knowing this was important, Tash gave himself a second to think.

For whatever reason, Sadie had chosen tonight to open up. Perhaps because of his reaction to her injury? Maybe discovering that it was okay to tell a secret had reassured her. He hoped so.

Keeping his expression and tone impassive, he asked, "Why do you think that, honey?"

"She said you liked other women and they were all nasty." Falling quiet for a moment, Sadie screwed her mouth from one side to the other, then reluctantly added, "She said you didn't care about us."

Pain cut through him, but he swallowed hard and forced a small smile. "I love you more than anything in the whole world. I always have."

Scrunching up her face, Sadie whispered, "I think *she* didn't care about us."

"That's not true, honey. Your mother loved you, it's just that she was sometimes...unwell."

Throwing her thin arms around him, Sadie said against his shoulder, "I'm sorry I kept secrets."

Emotion put a death grip on him. Cradling her close, Tash sat up and pulled her onto his lap. For a minute or so, he just rocked her, words lodged in his throat. Finally, still hugging her, he managed to say, "I want you to listen to me real close, okay, baby?"

She nodded without raising her head.

With his heart full to bursting, and his voice a little raw, he said, "You can tell me anything. I'm your daddy and I will *always* love you, no matter what."

He heard her swallow, and she whispered, "You might get angry."

"Never, ever at you." He rethought that, because damn it, he was human, so he corrected himself. "Even if I sound angry, even if you did something you shouldn't, it won't make me stop loving you. Nothing could do that, okay?"

She wiped her eyes against his T-shirt and nodded. "I sometimes mess up."

"Me, too. But we're in this together, right? This is our home and I want you to be as happy about that as I am. Sometimes, if I've had a long day, I might be grouchy. Maybe if you didn't get enough sleep, you might be grouchy. No one is perfect, right? But I'll still love you, and you'll still love me, and we'll muddle through one way or another."

For several heart-stopping moments, Sadie seemed to think about it. To his relief she finally nodded again. "Okay."

"Okay."

"Autumn's not like Mom, is she?"

One blow after another. Unsure of how Sadie meant that, Tash said, "Autumn is unlike any other person I've known."

"I wouldn't mind if she was your girlfriend."

That precious attitude made him laugh softly. "Well, I might not mind that, either, but Autumn has something to say about it."

With complete authority, Sadie stated, "She likes you."

"You think so?"

"'Course she does. Everyone likes you."

Deb hadn't... But he kept that thought to himself. "I know for a fact Autumn likes you." He playfully tapped the tip of her nose. "She told me so."

Her beatific smile squeezed his heart. "Do you think she'd do dinner with us again?"

"I'll ask her," he promised.

She gave him another tight hug. "Love you, Dad."

"I love you more." He turned and settled her in the bed, pulling the sheet and blanket up and over her shoulders, making sure he tucked in her stuffed monkey, too. "Get to sleep, okay? We have a busy day tomorrow."

"Seein' the animals." She snuggled her monkey up close and turned to her side to burrow into the pillow. "G'night, Dad."

"'Night, baby." With a final kiss to her forehead, Tash turned out the light and slipped from the room. Per Sadie's preference, he left her door open, so it wasn't until he'd gone into his own room that he dropped back against the wall, his hands fisted, his eyes damp.

Progress. Finally Sadie had opened up to him, trusted him. He felt like he'd conquered something monumental and he had the urge to call Autumn and tell her about it. He wouldn't, of course.

He could wait until tomorrow.

His mouth curved. For entirely different reasons from Sadie's, he was every bit as excited about the visit.

★ ★ ★

Ember got up extra early on Sunday morning after promising Autumn she could sleep in a bit. Fair—after all, she'd kept her out last night, so she owed it to her.

Owing her wasn't the only motivation, though. Beneath the angst of Sadie's injury, she'd felt the undercurrents between Tash and Autumn. Her silly sister thought it was all gratitude from him, but she knew men better than Autumn did.

Sure, they might have connected over his daughter. Autumn was fantastic with kids, with everyone really, and that made her extra endearing. But Tash wasn't looking for a babysitter. Far as she knew, he wasn't looking at all, for anything, except a fresh start for him and Sadie.

Yet she'd felt the vibe whenever Tash looked at Autumn.

Whatever it meant, she wanted Autumn looking well rested when she saw him again.

It was only 5:30 a.m., but with the heat, the earlier the better. By 11:00 a.m. it would be broiling hot, so she wanted to get as much done as she could before Tash and Sadie showed up.

Dressed in a light tank top, jean shorts and her work boots, with her hair up in a loose twist, she headed out a half hour later. The sun peeked over the hills, sending out a golden glow that highlighted the barn and other outbuildings, and gave stubby fruit trees long shadows.

Lucky her—she lived in paradise. She didn't ever want to take it for granted.

Work on a farm could be never-ending, but there were times, like today, when she enjoyed the routine. It gave her a chance to lose herself in monotony, to talk to creatures that didn't talk back and to soak up the unconditional love animals always shared.

By rote, she got busy working through each chore. She fed the animals and let them roam free while she cleaned their areas, giving each plenty of attention. The free-range chickens, now that they'd eaten, followed her around, pecking at her feet and tripping her up a few times.

She hadn't bothered with makeup, and good thing, considering the number of times she swiped her wrist across her face. Even this early, she started to wilt…and so did her clothes. The waistband of her shorts now hung loose, just like the neckline of her shirt. Parts of her hair escaped her tie, only to stick to her neck.

She never should have hassled Autumn about sweating, but then who knew such a massive heat wave was on the horizon? She remembered Mike calling her "princess," and not in a complimentary way. Last night he'd flirted—with her and every other woman.

Blasted confusing man. He left her muddled—a feeling she didn't appreciate, especially when most guys were easy. She knew how to flirt, but how could she flirt with him when he kept her guessing?

She realized she was thinking about him—*again*—and did her best to put him from her mind.

The grueling weather made her want to collapse and, finally, after weighing her options, she headed to the lake.

With the chores done, she wanted a dip. That'd do a lot to cool her down and clear her head.

The chickens, clucking softly, trailed behind her as she headed down the well-worn dirt path to their own little private cove. Along the way, she lifted the hem of her shirt to let air reach her midriff.

It didn't help.

When she got close to the lake, frogs leaped in and lazy fish swam away. Two turtles, resting on a partially submerged log, ignored her. A large willow tree shaded one little section, but over the rest, sunlight reflected brightly on the placid surface.

Shading her eyes, she looked around. From here she couldn't

even see the main body of the lake, just the other side of the cove full of trees, scrubby brush and cattails.

Without hesitation, Ember sat on a rock, unlaced her boots and peeled off her socks. She wiggled her toes, then stood and dropped her shorts. After laying them over the rock, she reached for the hem of her tank—

"Much as I hate to interrupt things at this point—"

Squawking, she spun around and found Mike leaning against a tree, arms folded over his bare chest, shorts hanging low, barefoot and with wet hair.

"—I feel it's necessary to point out you have an audience." He kept his gaze on her face. "But, hey, if you want to proceed, I won't complain."

Speechless, she stared at him. "You were watching me?"

"Just walked up, actually."

"Did you *tiptoe*?"

His mouth twitched. "Nope. Wasn't even all that quiet, but you seemed pretty intent on cooling off."

Well, that was something. But damn it, she stood there in panties and a tank top feeling a little exposed and a lot provoked, and he didn't seem bothered at all.

"You already went swimming?" she asked, for lack of anything more intelligent.

He ran a hand over his head, sending more water to trickle over his broad, tanned shoulders. "A day like today, the lake just calls to you."

Man, it was difficult not to snatch up her shorts like a startled virgin, but pride helped her to resist the urge. Never would she let Mike know how he unsettled her. If he wanted to be all freaking nonchalant, she could do the same.

Hopefully.

"Yeah," she said, pleased that her tone emerged as indifferent. She even turned, hands on her hips, to stare out at the water. "It's crazy hot today."

No reply.

When she glanced back, she found his attention on her rear, but it quickly shot back to her eyes. "I'll join you if you want." His smile challenged her. "I could scare away the snakes."

"Hmm." Satisfied now that she knew he wasn't immune to her, she moved closer to the rocky shoreline. Snakes often hid among the rocks. She wasn't really afraid of them, but, yeah, she'd prefer not to get too close. Plus it gave her a great excuse to keep him close.

"It's getting hotter by the second," he pointed out.

The sun hung in a cloudless sky, but it was Mike's gaze that really made her feel the heat. "Okay, sure." She turned to face him, and stared into his eyes. "I told Autumn to sleep in, and I didn't expect to see anyone else this early on a Sunday."

"I had some things to do."

What things? she wondered. Pushing him, determined to make him react, she stated, "I'm without a bra and I don't relish swimming in my shirt. I wouldn't have anything to put on after I get out."

For the longest time he stood there. Breathing. Looking at her. Thinking...things.

She hoped things about her. She wanted him to want her.

But she'd done enough to prompt him. He had to make the next move.

Too bad she hadn't worn mascara at least. Or fixed her hair. Judging by how she felt, she wasn't sure she wanted to know how she looked.

As if he'd read her thoughts, he said, "Natural looks good on you, Ember." Moving over to a tree, he snagged a white T-shirt and shook it out. "Wanna wear my shirt?"

Yup, she definitely did. Knowing it'd smell like him made her toes curl. "Everything will show through." She liked that idea, because maybe that would help to make things happen.

"You're not modest, Ember." His voice, low and rough, set her heart to beating double-time.

She honestly didn't have a modest bone in her body. But with Mike, everything felt different—mostly because he was different and she couldn't quite figure him out.

"No reason you should be," he added. "So what's the holdup?"

"All right." The spontaneous decision brought her forward, hand extended.

Rather than give her the shirt, he snagged her hand in his and drew her closer—so close that she had to tip back her head to maintain eye contact. "If we do this," he whispered, "I'm going to kiss you."

Well, hallelujah. 'Bout damn time. Feeling daring and a lot turned on, she smiled. "Is that so?"

"Fair warning."

"Duly noted." She grabbed the shirt and took two steps away. "Turn around."

One eyebrow arched. "A little modest, after all?"

Oh, no, she wouldn't make it easy for him. Twirling a finger in the air, she silently emphasized her demand.

A cocky smile curved his mouth, and he turned.

In seconds, Ember whipped off the tank top, tossed it toward her shorts and pulled on his shirt. When the neckline drooped over one shoulder, she let it be. The hem hit her midthigh. For now, she was decently covered. But once she got wet?

Whole different story.

While he kept his back to her, she took the opportunity to study him. His sun-streaked blond hair really was too long, and now wet, the tips hung in little curls against his nape. That didn't detract from his overwhelming masculinity. Not with those wide, strong shoulders that led to a tapered waist. He had long arms, with forearms lightly covered in hair, and smooth, pronounced biceps. She visually traced the line of his spine, the deep muscles along his back, down to where his shorts hung low and a strip of lighter flesh showed.

"I feel you checking me out."

"So sue me." Drawing a necessary breath, she turned and headed to the lake. Her bare feet made rustling sounds over dried leaves and brittle grass, so he surely knew she had finished. When she reached the rocks, she said, "Well, come on then. Make sure the snakes are playing elsewhere." *And give me the chance to finally taste that sexy mouth of yours.*

Chapter Six

Mike brushed past her, a little closer than necessary and in a way that heightened her senses. Wading into the water waist deep, he splashed enough to destroy the smooth surface of the lake.

After slicking back his hair, he held those muscular arms wide. "Snakes, fish and even the turtles have vacated the area." Seriously hot, he smiled at her. "I'm waiting."

Diabolical. The way he said that ramped up her sizzling awareness even more. She didn't entirely understand the game they now played—she only knew he was winning.

Unacceptable.

"Keep your pants on," she muttered and started forward.

"Must I?"

Her toes sank into the muddy bottom of the lake. She met his gaze. "For now." Oh, good, that made his eyes widen a bit. *Take that, buddy.*

The tepid water lapped at her knees, then her thighs and finally up to her waist. "Mmmm, this feels good."

Eyes warm with approval, he murmured, "You know what you're doing to me, don't you?"

"Nothing you haven't done to me." She could attest to the fact that Mike had turned into the master of teasing.

Moving past him, she made a clean dive, submerging her head to let the water cool not only her temperature but her interest, with the added benefit of slicking back her sweat-dampened hair.

When she surfaced, he was right beside her.

Anxious for that kiss? She wanted to think so.

He moved closer. So did she.

Very lightly, he touched rough-tipped fingers to her cheek, smoothing away a wet tendril of hair. "I've been thinking about this a lot lately."

She frowned over his wording. "This...meaning me?"

"Meaning touching you. Kissing you." A fingertip trailed across her jaw, then up to trace her mouth. "And more."

"With you so far." With him. Anxious. And if he didn't get on with it soon, she'd take the initiative. She was no more shy than she was modest.

"I like my job, Ember."

What an odd thing to say. Of course she knew he did, and it surprised her. Mike Brewer was a motivated, smart, very able-bodied man. And as much as she loved... No, scratch that. Much as she *liked* having him at the farm, it was a waste of his abilities. But, whatever—he was with them, he did a great job and she wouldn't look a gift horse in the mouth.

"What does your job have to do with anything?"

He didn't hesitate to spell it out to her. "Neither of us is the type to get serious, right? I want you. Pretty sure you want me. So I think we should have fun, but it should stay just between us."

Stay between... "What does that mean?"

"No one else needs to know."

A knot of hurt formed in her stomach, but she did her utmost to hide it. "What, like a secret affair?"

He shrugged. "We'll get the chemistry out of our systems, then go back to normal."

Normal, meaning him *not* wanting her? Because that's all this was to him, an itch he wanted to scratch?

Now why didn't that sound appealing?

He took in her expression and softened his tone. "I don't want to jeopardize my job."

Okay, back 'er up. "You wanted a kiss. I don't see how—"

"And more," he reminded her, his rough fingers cupping gently around her jaw, this thumb stroking along her cheekbone. "A lot more."

More. Great. So why did uneasiness expand inside her? *Because for the first time in forever, you're interested in so much more than sex, and it appears he isn't.* Ember immediately shook her head, denying that—to herself and to him. "That would jeopardize your job...how?"

With added caution now, he weighed his words. "I don't want hurt feelings to get me fired."

And that was his biggest concern? Not her, not a relationship. His job. "Then maybe you shouldn't hurt my feelings!" *No, wait.* She didn't mean to say that. It gave away far too much. To most of the people who knew her, she denied having tender feelings. Given Mike's priorities, he was the last person she wanted to see her vulnerability.

She needed to salvage her ruse of bravado, and fast. "What I mean is, my feelings aren't involved with *you.*" They were, more than she'd realized until just this moment. Since his clearly weren't, pride put her in full denial. She was the party girl, the carefree spirit. It was time she remembered her own deception. "You can rest easy about that."

"Good."

Jerk! It took her a second to regain her insouciance, then she fashioned a silky smile. "You're a hunk, Mike. Really good to look at—"

"Ditto to you."

"Hopefully nice for a diversion. That's all."

"I promise to do my best."

His continued good humor ramped up her annoyance, and was in part to blame when she sneered, "Trust me, I'm not looking to get involved with the hired help." The second those hateful, cutting words left her mouth, heat rushed to her face. She felt like a bitch. Worse, she felt really small.

Mike, still a jerk, only smiled. "Perfect. Glad we cleared that up."

It was all she could do not to throw her hands into the air. He should have been insulted. It was a thoughtless, mean-spirited, rude and awful thing for her to say, and now she felt horribly guilty. "Look, I shouldn't have—"

"Forget about it. I'm well aware of your methods, Ember. They don't bother me."

Her spine went straight, frustration spiking all over again. "My methods?"

"With anyone who cares, you don't hesitate to bring out the claws, or to talk to other people as if they don't have feelings." His gaze searched hers. "It's a defense, I think."

Oh, no! She would not let him dissect her—

"And with me, it's fine."

Her jaw loosened. *"Fine?"* Why did that feel so disapproving?

His gaze lowered to look at her breasts in the wet T-shirt. "Because I understand you, Ember, your sarcasm doesn't detract from your appeal at all."

Of all the sexist, stupid… What made him so special, that he thought he could take her apart and study all the pieces that made her who she was? He thought he knew her motivations, that he understood what made her tick?

He had so much freaking insight that he could overlook her flaws? Screw that.

Filling her lungs with an angry breath didn't help. She had to know the truth. "Do you even like me?"

And...*he hesitated!*

Ember shoved him away, he held on, and they both stumbled, going underwater for a second. Mike came up laughing.

She came up fuming.

Until he kissed her.

As if she hadn't just insulted him, as if she wasn't royally pissed, he drew her against his rock-solid body and took her mouth. It was a tickling kiss at first, given his continued snickers, but it quickly changed, going softer, hotter. Deeper.

Hungrier.

Whew. The man knew his business. Yes, she was still piqued, but this was a kiss worth enjoying, so no way would she end it. In fact, she wrapped her arms around his neck, pressed closer and might've even given a small, encouraging moan.

His broad hand opened on her back, but didn't stay there. Little by little, seduction personified, he eased down her spine and—

A loud, jubilant "woof" broke the silence seconds before a big splash doused them both.

Breaking apart and looking up, Ember spotted Autumn standing there, a priceless expression of surprise on her face. Pavlov, the goof, dog-paddled happily toward them, thrilled to find them in the lake.

Groaning, Mike dunked himself and came up with a frown. Low, so only she would hear, he said, "Maybe next time, Ember."

Next time? But...her emotions had been up, down and sideways, then they'd come together in scorching need. She wanted him *now*.

His mouth tilted in a small, sexy smile. "By the way, yeah, I like you." And with that, he abandoned her, calling to Pavlov and swimming farther out. The dog followed him.

She was left to explain to Autumn, and since her sister now wore an ear-splitting grin, it wasn't going to be easy.

When Ember slogged out of the water in an all-but-transparent T-shirt—probably Mike's, given the size of it—Autumn had to bite her lip. She could practically see steam coming off her sister, and judging by her stomping steps, it was a combo of lust and anger.

Clearing her throat, Autumn said, "So."

"Keep watch," Ember ordered, wrestling out of the clinging wet shirt and slinging it away without caring where it went. "Make sure no one is around."

"Just us," Autumn promised, but she did look to make sure Mike was still out in the lake and that he couldn't see around the trees. As if he hadn't just been kissing her sister senseless, he played a game of fetch with Pavlov and a piece of driftwood.

"Here." She handed Ember her tank top.

After squeezing her hair to remove the excess water, Ember put it on...and slowly deflated. "Thanks." She snatched up her shorts and pulled them on, uncaring that her panties were soaked and that the shorts quickly followed suit.

After sitting on the rock to pull on her socks and shoes, she confessed, "What I just did was incredibly dumb."

There were no more rocks around that were big enough, but Autumn didn't care. She found a moss-covered spot of ground and sat there. "So what did you do?"

"I let Mike-the-ass kiss me."

Huh. That was it? "*Only* a kiss?"

"Yeah, because my sister—who has really great timing, by the way—dropped by. Thanks for that."

"The kiss wasn't good?"

"The kiss was indescribable." She twisted to look at her. "But he's worried because he works for us, Autumn."

Shrugging, Autumn said, "So?"

"Exactly my reaction, but I guess there are...laws?"

"Pfft. Not for this." How silly. Not like they were some fancy corporation.

"Good. Then we agree on that."

"We can also agree that Mike is a great guy." *Really* great. Probably one of the nicest guys Ember had ever been attracted to. "We think of him more as a partner, right? Not really an employee."

Ember didn't look at her when she nodded.

Autumn could say for certain that her mom and dad would be thrilled with this particular choice, since they already thought of Mike as part of the family. He was that kind of guy—the type who easily fit into your life. "I say go for it."

Glancing at her, Ember said, "I don't see you following that advice."

Autumn choked. "Mike isn't into *me*. You, though? I've been aware of it for a while, *and*," she continued when Ember tried to interrupt, "you're clearly into him."

Sidestepping that, Ember said, "I meant you and Tash."

"Different story." She rushed past that. "You and Mike, though? Two adults, chemistry, proximity—it seems like a no-brainer to me."

"Yeah, well, that proximity might be the biggest problem." Not giving Autumn a chance to question her, she asked, "Why are you here, anyway? I told you to sleep in."

"I did. It's after nine."

"Oh." Ember propped her elbows on her knees. "So what's up?"

Hmm. Obviously her sis didn't want to talk about that oh-so-scorching kiss she'd witnessed. Autumn decided to be patient. Not easy, but she'd manage. She knew Ember wouldn't last ten minutes.

Besides, she had sought her out for a reason, on one of the few days she'd been allowed to relinquish her duties. This was important, so she got right to it. "Not to cause you a time crunch, but when do you think you can start on the backyard equipment for Sadie?"

Now fully facing her, Ember searched her face, then shrugged. "I never hesitate to crunch your time, so I can get on it right away if that's what you want. Is there a problem?"

"This should stay between us, okay?"

Ember crossed her heart. "Goes without saying anytime we discuss a client."

True, but to her, Tash and Sadie were more than mere clients. "You know what happened last night." They'd talked about it on the drive home. "And I told you Sadie is wary about things."

Ember nodded. "It's no wonder the girl doesn't trust easily. Sounds like her mom wasn't very steady."

It was the least critical word Ember could have used. "Even more than that, she had Sadie keep secrets from Tash. I can't imagine how he must feel."

"Poor kid." Ember plucked a tall weed and rolled it between her fingers. "I'm sorry the evening went so badly off the rails for you. I really did think you'd have fun or I wouldn't have dragged you along."

"I did." Loads of fun, actually, since Tash had been there.

"But, Patricia," she said. "And finding out about that dick, Chuck. Then everything with poor Sadie…"

"First, who cares about Patricia or Chuck? I don't, so forget it." Sure, she dreaded running into Chuck, but she was a different person now, and her heart was free and clear. She could deal with him, and once she did, she'd prove to everyone that the unfortunate incident had no lasting effect on her. "As for

Sadie, I'm glad I was there. Tash handled it well, but I'm sure it angered him, and we both know Sadie doesn't need to see that."

"Both, huh? You sound like a couple of concerned parents." While Autumn sputtered over that, Ember stretched out her legs and stared at her boots. "You think work on the yard equipment will reassure Sadie that she's here for good?"

"It'll have to help, right?" Talking about her feelings for Sadie, instead of what she felt for Tash, was a lot easier. "It's what I'm hoping. She adores Tash, anyone can see that, and she wants to trust in what he promises, but the uncertainty is there in her eyes."

"Her mother did a number on her," Ember said with banked heat. "Some people aren't meant to be parents."

"Very true." Ember, however, would have been an amazing mom—and it only just now occurred to Autumn how difficult this conversation must be for her. Appalled at herself, she frowned. "God, I'm so sorry, Ember. With Sadie being older, I didn't think—"

"It's fine," Ember said, denying the pain in her eyes. "I can't fall apart every time someone mentions a kid, right? Besides, I want to help, so just tell me what to do."

Autumn knew that would be Ember's answer, and she loved her for it. "Do you think you could fit it in right away?"

"I'm almost done with the deck I'm building for Frances Richards. I could leave a few of my guys there to finish that up and I could get the groundwork going for the yard equipment right after. Is that soon enough?"

"That would be perfect!"

"I'll get all the supplies there, get some posts in the ground, let her see that it's underway. Do you think Sadie would want to help? I could give her a few small chores to do. Nothing dangerous or anything."

"I bet she'd love that, and I'll help, too."

"You? With a power tool?" Ember laughed…but quickly cut

her humor short with a wince of guilt. "I mean, yeah. I'm sure you could do anything you decided to—"

Far from insulted, Autumn grinned. "We both know I'm incompetent when it comes to that stuff, and since I like my fingers and toes, maybe I could just hammer in a few nails where you tell me to?"

Suddenly, her sister scrubbed her face. "Damn it, he has me second-guessing myself."

That had been...oh, four minutes, tops. Knowing this had to do with Mike, Autumn asked, "Who?"

"Mike. He says he likes me but I can tell he doesn't. In fact, he thinks I'm a jerk."

Autumn laughed. "Given what I saw, that can't be true."

"It is! He said so."

"Not exactly true, and you know it." Coming around the corner in a lazy stride, Mike said, "I told you I understand your defenses and I don't mind them."

Pavlov lunged forward, shook hard—spraying everyone with lake water and dog hair—then padded over to cuddle Ember.

While petting him, she said, "See?" as if vindicated. "He doesn't *mind*. Hell of an endorsement, isn't it?"

"Umm..." Autumn looked from Ember's flushed face to Mike's amusement, and decided to steer clear. "Tash and Sadie are due here soon. I think I should head back up front."

"I'll join you," Ember stated, hot on her heels. "Come on, Pavlov."

Tipping his head, Pavlov looked at her, whined and chose to lean against Mike.

"Smart dog," Mike said. "When she's in one of these moods, it's probably best to avoid her." He picked up his shirt from where she'd thrown it on the ground, saw it couldn't be salvaged, and tossed it over his shoulder.

It surprised Autumn when he belied his own statement and trailed close behind them.

Even on the wide-open farm, tension gathered, pressing heav-ily against the small group. It wasn't in Autumn's nature to stay quiet in times like these. The urge to break the ice, to attempt to smooth things over, nearly strangled her.

Mike did that, and in a big way. "Does this current mood mean you insulted your sister again?"

Hands clenched tight, Ember jerked around, now walking backward. "I *didn't*."

At the same time, Autumn said, "She didn't!"

Unfazed, Mike asked Ember, "So what were you second-guessing?"

To Autumn's surprise, Ember didn't bite off his face. Instead, she drew a slow breath…and faced forward again. She stepped over and around a tree root before mumbling, "I realize some-times my jokes are abrasive."

The moderate tone and admission surprised Mike as much as it did Autumn.

Staring at Ember's rigid back, he moved up closer to her, until their shoulders bumped. "Your jokes are fine."

Ember didn't move away. "I detest that word."

"What word?"

"*Fine.*"

Wow. Autumn couldn't stop staring. So much chemistry bounced off the two of them, she felt like a very interested voyeur.

Pavlov, unsure which way to go, trotted over to Autumn. She quietly praised him. He was such a smart dog. Beautiful, too, with his short reddish fur, and quite the character. Maybe they could both slip away… Who was she kidding? She wasn't about to budge until she saw how this war of wills played out.

They were almost back to the barn when Mike said softly, "I think we got off track a little."

Gaze straight ahead, hair drying around her face and her eyes narrowed against the morning sun, Ember stayed silent.

Undeterred, Mike persisted. "For the record, I think you're a very talented, smart, caring woman."

Without missing a step, Ember said, "Not how it sounded earlier."

On an aggrieved laugh, he dropped his head, shook it, then glanced at her again. "Horny men aren't as articulate as they could be."

Whoa. Autumn fanned her face.

Even Ember fought a grin, before she worked up a frown. "You said I bring out the claws."

Mike nodded. "Do you deny you give Autumn shit? Often?"

"Nope." She shot Autumn an apologetic glance. "But I'm going to do better."

Autumn blinked. How had she gotten dragged into this again? Though it was true, she felt compelled to defend her sister. "Ember and I are close."

"I know," Mike said. "It shows, even when your sister is defensive."

"We each have our individual personalities," Autumn explained, because he was right. Ember *was* often defensive, and more cutting because of it. Autumn knew why, so maybe Ember should tell Mike. Then he'd understand, too.

Mike slanted her a look. "She dishes it out and for some reason you take it."

Oh, Mike, Autumn thought. *Now you've stepped in it.* Definitely, her sister needed to explain a few things to him.

From her hairline to her toes, Ember stiffened. They all paused beneath the shade in front of the barn. The silence grew while Ember looked ready to detonate.

A big blowup right before Tash and Sadie arrived would be very inconvenient, so Autumn made a deliberate attempt at steering the conversation. "I'd always thought you were smooth, Mike, but you obviously insulted Ember and now you're calling me a doormat?"

"Never that." The glint in his eyes proved that he understood what she was doing, but wasn't yet ready to play along. "What I'm saying is that good times and bad, you're a natural-born peacemaker, so you temper yourself." He looked at Ember with a mix of affection and lust. "Your volatile sister here doesn't."

"See?" Ember crossed her arms. "He thinks I'm terrible."

Deadpan, Autumn said, "I think he was actually calling you hot."

Mike laughed. "That she is, and then some."

Taking her sister's hand, Autumn smiled. "You're a wonderful person." With a warning frown at Mike, she added, "As I'm sure Mike will tell you."

"Be happy to." He took a step closer to Ember. "If you have any free time right now...?"

Good. Finally, Mike wanted to get back to smooching.

Unfortunately, her stubborn sister resisted.

"Sorry—*not* sorry—but I need a shower."

He murmured suggestively, "There's a shower in my place."

Smug, Ember said, "I know, because I built it."

The whole exchange was like something out of one of her books—sort of sexy but misguided, sparks flying and emotions tumultuous. Mike wasn't a dumb guy, so there must be a method to his madness, but in her opinion, he needed to redirect.

She was anxious to hear what Mike would say next, but then Tash pulled up, and that prompted Mike to bend to Ember's ear. "FYI, your shirt is literally glued to your body."

Looking down, Ember shrugged and merely pulled it loose. "It's hot. Who cares?"

Rubbing the back of his neck, Mike said, "Guess I shouldn't admit that *I* do."

"Not if you want to live."

Yup, Autumn admitted, she and her sister were vastly different. Looking like Ember did right now, Autumn would have made a run for it until she could clean up and cover up.

Ember stood her ground, even sniped with Mike, and then turned all smiles when Sadie ran toward them.

Somehow her sister looked glorious, while Autumn would have looked like a drowned dirty rodent.

No wonder Ember's relationships with men were never anything like her own, but Autumn hadn't realized they were *that* different. Later, she wanted to know about that kiss, and she wanted a verbatim on what was said.

She eyed Tash with new interest. No one had ever called her volatile; instead she got the bland descriptions, like steadfast, calm and thoughtful. Good, solid compliments that wouldn't inspire lust in any guy that she'd ever met.

Maybe she should borrow Ember's attitude and be a little more forceful. Go after what she wanted.

Problem was, she didn't know how.

Ten minutes into the visit, Autumn wanted to strangle Mike. She didn't know what he was thinking, but clearly he was up to something. She knew him well, and their friendship had bloomed within an hour of her hiring him almost two years ago. From the start, they'd gotten along as if they'd known each other forever.

Better still, he'd become a part of the family, just naturally falling into place to help with not only farm chores and to care for the animals, but also anything she, Ember or their parents needed. He was their handyman, runner, repair guy and emergency contact. She knew him well enough to recognize that here, now, he had an agenda, and somehow it went beyond his continued interest in her sister.

Pavlov, of course, loved Sadie on sight. He lavished her with attention, keeping her occupied for a good five minutes when they first arrived. Sadie now had reddish dog hair stuck to her purple tank top and pink striped shorts.

She looked adorable furry.

They'd just finished talking about her foot, which dad and daughter both proclaimed was much better. Sadie wore soft yellow sneakers and white socks to better protect the cut, and Autumn noticed she walked without limping. It relieved her to know Sadie was feeling so much better, back to being a happy little girl.

Close to her ear, Tash confided, "She picks out her own outfits."

"Colorful," Autumn noted. "Like a rainbow. I like it." The yellow, pink and purple, added with her red hair, somehow looked very cute when pulled together.

"She's all but forgotten about her foot. The bubble bath was a hit, so thanks for the suggestion."

His warm breath sent a shiver down her back and stole her voice.

Still in that soft rumble, he said, "I'm glad you were there."

Sadie, now sitting on the ground with Pavlov soaking up attention beside her, pointed toward the distance. "Look, Dad, I can see the lake."

Aware of Mike and Ember watching her, Autumn found a smile. "Our little cove isn't as nice as the beach area, but Mike, Ember and Pavlov all went swimming there this morning."

"And someone," Mike said, looking at Ember, "threw my shirt in the dirt."

Brows drawn together in curiosity, Sadie asked, "Was it Ember?" making them all laugh.

Ember grinned at the little girl. "Mike is too big, or I'd have thrown him in the dirt, too. I had to settle for his shirt."

Tash's eyebrows shot up.

"Just a misunderstanding," Mike said. "The swim was still… refreshing. Though I think I left the lake hotter than when I went in."

That put a big smile on Tash's face. "You don't say."

Leaning toward him, Autumn murmured, "Don't ask."

"Don't think I need to."

With a child's subtlety, Sadie said, "Dad and me could swim there sometime."

Even knowing Autumn hadn't put on a swimsuit in front of others for years, Ember spoke before she could. "Consider yourselves to have an open invitation. It's also a pretty terrific spot to fish. Just so you know, my workaholic sister often doesn't get in until six in the evenings, but at seven or so we could take a nice dip to cool down." To seal the deal, Ember asked, "Would you like that, Sadie?"

"Yes! Can we, Dad?"

Tash smiled at Autumn. "When you have some free time, let us know. We'll take you up on it."

Smooth as could be, Ember hooked her arm through Autumn's and said, "I'll see that she does."

Tash looked a little confused by Autumn's silence—as if she could sneak in a word around Ember's matchmaking, anyway—but Sadie saved her from having to come up with a reply.

Jumping back to her feet, she looked out to the field and asked, "Is that Delilah and Franklin?"

"They're buddies," Autumn told her. "They always hang out together."

Just then, Matilda and Olivia came out of their pen and poked their noses against the fencing.

Sadie squealed in delight. "And it's the pigs!"

"Sadie," Tash said easily. "Remember, keep your voice down so you don't startle the animals."

Pumping her hands in front of her, Sadie whispered, "They're so *cute.*"

Her enthusiasm for the farm was catching. Autumn absolutely loved everything about it—the animals and how she helped them, the sounds they made, all of their cute furry faces, and the wide-open spaces and fresh air. It thrilled her that Sadie saw it the same way. The girl couldn't stop smiling. Like a kid at a carnival, she continually looked around, pointing out one animal after another, recalling their names and laughing softly at their antics.

Turning with an exaggerated plea, she asked, "Can I talk to Matilda and Olivia, Dad? Please?"

"I don't know," he teased. "What will you say?"

Sadie laughed. "I'll tell them how pretty they are."

"I'm sure they'd love to hear it." He lightly tugged on one of Sadie's long locks. "Go ahead, but don't get too close, okay? And remember, voice soft and calm. Promise me?"

"I promise." She hurried off in a tempered run, Pavlov sticking with her.

That's when Mike struck.

With no lead-in, without any warning at all, in front of Tash and Ember, he said, "By now, you've heard that Chuck is back."

The bald statement caught her off guard. She wasn't even sure whom he was addressing. He seemed to be telling them all.

One thought hit her before any other. "You don't even know Chuck." That whole fiasco had happened before Mike hired on at the farm. It was in the past, and she preferred to keep it there.

"Know of him," Mike explained darkly, "and the jerk is asking around about you."

Asking about her? As in, something casual like, *How has Autumn been?* It had to be that simple, so Autumn waved it away. "Small town, that's all." Chuck had dumped her, not the other way around. His interest had ended years ago.

Ember's gaze zeroed in on Mike. "I haven't told you anything about Chuck, and Autumn doesn't talk about him. Obviously you don't like him, so what did you hear?"

Before Autumn could declare the topic off-limits, Mike shrugged and explained.

"Last night Patricia gabbed to anyone who would listen. I tried to ignore her." He paused to say to Tash, "Here's a tip—

steer clear of her whenever you can. She grates like nails on a chalkboard."

"Already met her." Tash frowned. "Autumn was kind."

"Autumn is always kind."

"Seems so."

Both Autumn and Ember took in the male bonding with interest.

"I'm not her," Mike pointed out, "so I have no problem walking away from troublemakers, but then several other women talked to me about good old Chuck, too. He was a topic I couldn't avoid."

Heat crawled up Autumn's chest, into her neck, then settled in her face. "It'll die down." At least, she hoped it would. "Pay no attention to the gossip."

Folding his arms, his expression intent, Mike said, "Most of the women seemed to think Chuck was a catch."

"Ha!" Ember made it clear what she thought of that. "For desperate women without options, maybe. Trust me, Chuck might look okay on the outside, but he's rotten through and through."

"From what I heard," Mike said, "I agree."

Oh, how she loved her sister's loyalty. Yes, Mike was right that they often clashed, but when push came to shove, she knew without a doubt that Ember would back her up. Every single time.

Now, though, with Tash taking it all in, appearing more concerned by the moment, Autumn felt she had to speak up for herself. "Chuck is welcome to do whatever he wants—"

"Including visiting you?" Tash didn't look too happy with that prospect. He glanced toward Sadie and said, "Don't put your fingers on the fence, honey. That's it. Stay back at least a step," before turning to Autumn and adding, "You actually want to see that ass?"

Wishing her past wasn't the center of attention, Autumn

shrugged. "I doubt I'll ever run into him, but if I do, I'll be pleasant." It might kill her, but she'd manage. "Nothing more."

"See?" Tash said to Mike. *"Nice."*

As if disappointed in her, Mike shook his head.

Fed up with the macho posturing, Autumn propped her fists on her hips and glared at both of them. "What would you have me do? Cause a scene?"

Umbrage brought Ember closer to her. "I vote you punch him in his throat."

Tash said, "Probably not a bad idea."

"I like how you think." Putting his hand on Ember's nape, Mike offered, "But how about I talk to him for you?"

Autumn's jaw loosened. Here she'd been all distracted with the familiar way Mike touched her sister—and the way Ember allowed it after all her bluster—and Mike dropped another bombshell. "Why in the world would you do that? You don't even know him."

"I know him." Smiling with anticipation, Tash said, "I'll take care of it."

"What?" Okay, so Mike's offer made a little more sense— only a little—since he lived on the farm with them and knew them well. But Tash? Just because he'd hired her for design work didn't mean he had to get involved. "Seriously, that's nice of you, but not necessary."

Tash didn't look convinced. "If he's telling people he plans to see you—"

"He's a blowhard. Don't worry about him."

"He's obnoxious," Mike added. "And I'd relish a chance to tell him so."

When she got Mike alone... "I can handle it."

Tash wasn't ready to give it up. "It sounds like he plans to hassle you. I never liked him, so I should be the one to—"

"Okay, *whoa*. Enough already." Autumn made a *T* with her hands. "Time-out, both of you." When she had their undivided attention, she said, "First, the day hasn't come when I need a man to speak for me. Got it?"

Her sister grinned.

Tash and Mike shared a look.

"If it ever does, I'll let you both know, but until then, I'm entirely capable of handling this on my own."

Mike started to say something, but she didn't let him.

"Two, neither of you are responsible for me. I've been taking care of myself for a long time. And three, I don't want to—" Ember's elbow caught her in the ribs and she *oofed*. Holding her side, she protested. "Hey!"

Unrepentant, Ember grinned. "This is your first time having two guys argue over you. Stop resisting and just enjoy."

Horrified by that statement, because it made her sound unwanted by, and inexperienced with, men, and it was also patently untrue, Autumn considered smacking her sister. "They're *not*."

Just because both guys were trying to be…well, gallant or something, it didn't mean anything beyond that—definitely not what Ember inferred.

To make it all the more confusing, though, Mike reinforced the nonsense. "This is one of those times when you should probably listen to your sister, Autumn. Since she's often the recipient of male competition, she'd know it when she sees it, right?"

Autumn disagreed. "She's just trying to embarrass me." Seeing Ember's grin backed up that theory. Her sister could be a terrible tease.

Staging a thoughtful frown, Mike said to Ember, "I thought you were going to work on that?"

With that direct hit, Ember's face pinched…and she turned to walk away. "See ya around, Tash. Autumn, give Sadie the good news about the yard equipment for me." Ignoring Mike, she headed off for the house. Normally that'd be a five-minute walk, but her angry strides would get her there quicker.

A trail of water dripped from her wet hair, down her back and off her shorts. Autumn was surprised it didn't turn into steam.

She peeked at Tash, but he was watching her, his gaze speculative.

Mike, on the other hand, tracked Ember's every step with blatantly hungry eyes.

Because Mike seemed the easier male to tackle, she asked, "What in the world was that about? Now you've got her upset again."

Rolling one shoulder, he said, "She'll forgive me."

"*Maybe*—if you apologize?"

Drawing his gaze away from Ember's retreat, Mike shook his head. "You know your sister well, and I realize the two of you are close, but you don't understand this. Trust me, she's enjoying the game."

Just then, they all heard the door slam. Hard.

Autumn winced. If that was true, Ember hid it well.

Chapter Seven

"Sadie," Tash said, "watch where you're going, honey. Don't trip over the dog."

Loving how he divided his time between his daughter and the adult conversation, Autumn smiled. She'd love to go to Sadie and start showing her around, but sibling loyalty forced her toward Mike.

She stared up at him, sought the right words and finally asked, "That's what Ember is to you? A game?"

He half smiled at her seriousness. "I thought outside of family, games were the only type of relationships your sister wanted."

He couldn't be more wrong. Clearly Mike didn't know Ember as well as he thought.

Mike took in her gaze, then frowned. "No? Did I miss the mark on that?"

"Big-time, I'm afraid." On the surface, sure, Ember was all fun and games. But deep down? Autumn knew her sister was a very wounded soul.

"Huh. So now I have more to think about." Lower, he said

to himself, "Not that I could think about her more than I already do."

Autumn was wondering how much she should share with Mike when Tash took her hand and gave her fingers a squeeze. A silent message?

His touch, along with the look in his eyes, effectively stole all her steam. Her own life wasn't ideal enough for her to give advice to anyone else. Still, she couldn't resist, and saying, "Make Ember mad, she'll come after you. But if you hurt her feelings, she won't talk to you for a month. You might want to think about that."

His simple and sincere "Thanks for the tip, hon" cleared away the last of her annoyance.

Mike and Ember would be good together, once they got past the misconceptions.

Turning away, she watched Sadie hug Pavlov. She laughed when the dog put a wet doggy lick up the side of her face. Matilda and Olivia loved her attention. Even the skittish chickens were venturing closer, lured by her gentle manner. "She has the touch."

Using his fingertips, Tash raised her chin. "Reminds me of someone I know."

Effectively caught in his dark gaze, Autumn suffered an excess of emotion. She knew she made a difference in the lives of animals, and she didn't discount the assistance she gave her parents, or the support she supplied to Ember.

But this, with Tash, was different. At least for her.

For Tash? She didn't know. Was his gentle touch a residual effect of seeing Sadie so happy? Or was it her, specifically, that drew him?

True, she wasn't as experienced as Ember, but neither had she been a complete wallflower. She'd known plenty of men, dated some of them and understood the way things worked. Sort of.

But this? His familiarity? It kept her guessing.

That he'd attempted to defend her was one thing. Lots of good men stepped up when they thought it was necessary. Thanking her for inviting him and his daughter over? No biggie. Even smiling at her—he was so damn handsome he could frown and tempt a saint.

But holding her hand? Touching her face? Saying such sweet, heartfelt things? Mike was her friend, but he'd never done anything like that.

So what did the gesture mean?

Of course, Mike noticed. "If you two want a moment, just let me know. I'll look after Sadie."

Smiling, Tash moved his hand to the small of her back. "Actually—"

Her phone dinged with a text. "Oh, sorry."

Feeling conspicuous in the extreme and assuming it was Ember, she fished the phone from her pocket...and stalled at the sight of Chuck's name on the screen. *Oh, no.*

Pinning on a smile meant to belie her angst, Autumn said, "Sorry. Just a second."

She turned her back on them and took a few steps away for privacy before quickly reading the message.

Hey there im back in town would love to see you when are you free

The lack of punctuation forced her to read the message twice before the arrogance of his assumption—that she'd even be willing to meet with him—finally sank in.

The urge to text him back, to tell him to go to hell, had her fingers twitching, but she drew a slow breath and opted to wait. She needed time to formulate a plan. She wanted Chuck to know that she was one-hundred-percent fine without him, that she wasn't at all affected by what he'd done. An angry reply wouldn't convey that. It would show too much emotion, and she'd wasted enough emotions on him.

Despite her assurances to the guys, she wasn't ready to face him, to pretend nothing had happened. No, she didn't give a flip what Chuck did. But she did care what he thought.

She cared what everyone thought.

Damn it, she wanted the world to know that Autumn Somerset was fine and dandy on her own.

After a bracing breath, she turned back to the men...and immediately saw their suspicion.

Oh, no, no, no. That would not do.

"It was Chuck, wasn't it?" Mike growled his name like a curse. "What did he want?"

Amazed that he'd nailed it so easily, Autumn gave a short laugh. "Mind your own business, Mike."

Tash's jaw flexed. "So it *was* him. Did he want to get together with you?"

Apparently, she stood between mind readers.

Feeling like a third wheel at a testosterone party, Autumn scowled. "Boys, put on your listening ears." When they each gave her questioning looks, she announced, "I am every bit as capable as you are."

Forgoing agreement or denial, they continued to watch her.

Great. One more time, then, as firm as she could make it. "I can deal with Chuck without your help."

"He's a freaking idiot," Mike said with disgust.

She couldn't argue that point. "Yes, so?"

"Ignorant men don't respect women." Taking her hand again, Tash drifted a thumb over her knuckles in a caress that seemed even more gentle in comparison to his tone. "Obnoxious, ignorant men ignore a woman's wishes. The fact that he's been talking about you proves he's an obtuse ass. No reason you should have to deal with that."

"Correction," she said. "There's every reason for *me* to deal with it, but zero reason for either of you to step in. You have to trust me. *Both* of you," she added, when Mike started to edge away. "I won't have it looking like I need a guy to fight my battles." *Especially not to Chuck.* "Got it?" She underscored the order with stiff posture and a stern frown.

Tugging at his ear, Mike gave in, but he wasn't happy about it. "Fine."

Tash reluctantly nodded, then ruined his agreement by saying, "But if I overhear him being disrespectful, all bets are off."

Both men looked so primed for battle, she half expected them to beat their chests. She, with her big bones, could never play the little damsel in distress. Just the thought of it seemed silly, causing a laugh to bubble up out of nowhere.

"You guys, he didn't threaten my life. He didn't physically abuse me. I was jilted, that's all, and as I keep insisting, I'm well over it. Now can we let it go?"

Tash's mouth twitched, too. "Can I blame Mike? His concern was contagious."

With a pointed look at Mike, she said, "We'll definitely blame him. And you're both forgiven."

When Sadie laughed again, they all turned to see her walking along the pig enclosure, Pavlov right behind her and the pigs following from the other side of the fencing. When she turned back, they did, as well.

"She's a little Pied Piper." Autumn's mood lightened. Kids had always done that for her. Seeing their innocence and open joy in life helped to put things in perspective.

Mike held out his dirty shirt, grumbled and pulled it on. To Tash he said, "Mind if I let Sadie pet the pigs? They're gentle."

Tash deferred to Autumn. "It's okay?"

Knowing Sadie would love it, she agreed. "Mike will make sure she doesn't get hurt. But we could all—"

Tash cut her off and said to Mike, "Thanks." Tugging Autumn toward the barn, he added, "Can I have a minute?"

Now why did that make her hormones do jumping jacks? "Okay, sure." She glanced back at Mike. "We'll make it quick." His mouth curled. "Now what fun would that be?"

The suggestive question didn't help to slow her pulse.

Contrary to how movies always depicted them, barns were not romantic sanctuaries, at least theirs wasn't. Inside, a combination of scents filled her head. Earth, animals, the sweet smell of hay. A variety of tools hung from the walls, filling most of the space.

It was cooler inside, but not by much. Dust motes danced in the sunlight filtering through cracks in the aged wood. Feed barrels clustered in every corner.

She'd been in the old barn at least once a day since she and Ember had taken over the shelter, and yet now, it felt entirely different.

Closer, more private, and yes, even romantic...because Tash was here with her.

The second they cleared the doors, he led her to the side so they wouldn't be seen, prompting her heartbeat to punch into overdrive. Her hand remained in his, feeling really small and maybe...vulnerable? Dumb. Hands weren't vulnerable, but it was connected to the rest of her and suddenly all of her nerve endings tingled with a vague sense of sizzling responsiveness.

Years had passed, but how many times had she thought about being alone with Tash Ducker? Of being this close to him, having his undivided attention?

They'd both matured, but still it felt so familiar, and because he'd never been all that aware of her back then, it also felt unnerving. And sad.

That, of course, was the source of her vulnerability.

No man, definitely not Chuck, had ever made her this breathless, this alert.

Now here they were, and Tash watched her with probing intensity, yet he didn't say anything.

Mustering up her pride, she freed her hand and took two steps away to stand against a rough post. "Everything okay?"

"Yeah." His gaze dropped to her mouth…then heated. "I wanted…"

Her stomach took a free fall. "What?"

Pausing, his brows came down in a private struggle.

Refusing to be that same backward girl from school, Autumn said, "Tell me." And then she held her breath.

In a gruff whisper, he muttered, "Chuck."

Chuck? Yeah, not the topic she'd hoped for. "What about him?"

"Is he going to be a problem for you?"

Irritation erupted. Damn it, here she was, all breathless and primed, and he brought up stupid Chuck again. "I already explained a couple of times now that he's not." Did Tash really think her so weak that she didn't know her own mind? "I'm thirty-two years old. I run my own business *and* a rescue farm. I deal with my family—and trust me, that's sometimes a challenge—so it's really starting to irk that you think I can't handle one stupid annoying ex."

Her vehemence sent his brows up in surprise. Raising his hands in the universal sign of surrender, Tash shook his head. "Not what I meant, so stop killing me with that glare." He dared a step closer, a smile slipping into place. "Trust me, Autumn, I've known very few people as strong and steady as you are."

Oh, freaking great. He shared the same compliments she always got from her *mother.* Just what a girl wanted to hear. Soon he'd be telling her she was sturdy, too. "So what exactly did you mean?"

By tracing her cheekbone, the line of her jaw, he defused her anger as quickly as he'd brought it on. "I'm just saying, it took me a long time to get over my divorce from Deb. And now that she's passed away, I don't know what I think or feel other than occasional anger at the situation. Anger that she was ob-

viously unstable, anger that she didn't make Sadie a priority."
His chest expanded on a breath. "Rage that she had my daughter lie to me."

His admission had her stepping closer. "Your situation is very different from mine."

"Don't do that." He framed her face in his big, warm hands. "Don't downplay what happened to you, okay? I see your strength, Autumn. I know you can handle anything. Hell, I've seen you do it." His thumb touched to the corner of her mouth, then brushed over her bottom lip. "I also see a very caring, gentle woman and there's no way you'll convince me you weren't hurt by what that bastard did."

"It was three years ago."

"And you've put it to rest, I know. Now he's back and dredging it up again." A dimple appeared in his cheek. "I get why you wanted Mike to butt out."

"Mike means well."

"I know. It's just...with *me* you don't always have to be strong, okay? You can admit that it's going to be difficult."

With him being so persuasive, she gave in. "I'll admit I'm looking forward to it."

"Autumn," he chided.

"Right, it'll suck." Big-time suck. "But I *can* handle it." What choice did she have? In such a small town, she wouldn't be able to avoid Chuck, especially if he was determined to see her. And they'd all be watching the show, waiting to see what would happen. Blowing up on him, letting them all know she still felt humiliated, would only make things worse.

"I won't interfere," Tash promised, "but there might be a way I can help."

"You want me to talk about it?" The thought left a bad taste in her mouth. She'd grown up being the strong one. Reliable. Grounded. Calm and sensible.

But Tash said he saw her differently. With him, she *felt* different.

"Talking is a start. God knows, I've spilled my guts to you."

"That's different." Everyone talked to her. It was yet another of her assigned roles, one she appreciated because it made her feel helpful. "I want you to. Anytime."

His hands moved down from her face, along her throat, until he clasped her shoulders. "For such a small woman, you carry a really big load."

Small woman? Should she point out her big bones?

No, she wouldn't. Let him live with the illusion.

"I know I've added to it, too." When she started to object, he gave her a brief peck on the mouth that effectively silenced her. "Before you, I hadn't discussed my divorce or the way Deb cheated. Talking about it, saying it aloud, made the problems seem more manageable." Another peck, this one softer, lingering a few heartbeats. "I want you to be able to share, too." Then he said with emphasis, "With me."

Unsure what to say, she settled on honesty. "A few times, I unloaded on Ember." And though she'd always felt terrible for doing it, Ember hadn't complained. "There are times when having a sister is a really good thing."

"More often than not, I hope?"

"Definitely more often than not." Even when her sister was a pain in the ass, Autumn knew she had her best interests at heart.

"She was there for you when Chuck split?"

The gentle massage of his hands on her shoulders lulled her. "Right after Chuck ran off, I was a wreck. Did I tell you I found out from other people? He didn't even tell me himself."

"Miserable bastard."

That simple statement said it all. "For a couple of days I cried, feeling sorry for myself, humiliated and emotionally stomped, and then I'd rage about Chuck and Brenda."

"You raged to Ember?"

"God, no." Ember would have gone out looking for them both. "My sister wouldn't know what to do if I melted down on her like that. But she checked on me daily, tried to get me to go out with her." Remembering made her chest tight. "She wanted me to get even with Chuck by having a fling, but that's not me."

"So you switched to ice cream instead?"

"Ha! No, not right away. I sort of...hunkered down. Kept a low profile." It shamed her to admit it, but he'd asked, so... "I struggled with my embarrassment."

His hand smoothed her hair. "And then your pride stepped in?"

Being held by him felt so nice, she got closer and rested her cheek on his chest. His arms came around her in a welcoming hug.

"My pride—as well as my sister—told me to shake it off, be grateful for what I'd avoided, and to get out there and show the world, or at least the town of Sunset, that Chuck could never break me. Ember urged me to show them that I was happier without him than I'd ever been with him."

"A tall order." His hand moved up and down her spine. "How'd you do?"

"In public? Pretty darned good. In private?" She sighed. "It took a long time to really get back in the swing of things. I skipped life outside work for a while, using the excuse that I had things to do on the farm. Working with the animals is always soothing." She tilted back to see him. "They're pretty nonjudgmental. Feed them, give them a clean comfortable place to exist, attention and affection, and they'll love you unconditionally."

Another hug and then he set her back from him, his hands clasping her shoulders. "Chuck is a fool. I'm not."

Heat, scented by his body, filled her head. The look in his eyes, dark and compelling, thrilled her. She felt certain he wanted to kiss her for real this time.

Do it, she silently encouraged. She even tilted closer, staring at his mouth, suddenly wanting that kiss more than anything she could remember in her recent lifetime. *Do it.*

Growing sexual tension tightened his jaw. His eyes went heavy, intent, and then his mouth was on hers, gently at first, tentative. Autumn made a small sound of pleasure and he gathered her tight to his body so that her curves aligned with all his harder planes. Tilting his head for a better fit, he nudged her lips open for the glide of his warm tongue.

Yup, *this.* Tash kissing her with the same hunger she felt. Taking, giving, constantly shifting to get closer.

This was awesome. Better than any other kiss she'd known. Better than even ice cream.

Because it was Tash, her lifelong crush.

The guy she'd always wanted but thought she'd never have.

She'd had a thing for him way back in high school, and apparently it hadn't waned in all that time. One kiss from him and he'd ignited it—ignited *her*—all over again.

Need took her fingers into his hair, over his neck, his shoulders, down his chest...and Tash eased up, catching her hands in his. By small degrees he ended the kiss until they were no longer touching.

Her knees had turned to rubber and an insidious liquid warmth coiled inside her. Devastated, that's what she was. Devastated by lust.

Tash didn't look unaffected, but was he as lost as she? She saw the telltale signs of arousal on his face: glittering eyes, heightened color in his cheekbones.

His nostrils flared slightly, and he kissed her again, this time firm but quick. Then he ruined it all when he said, "I shouldn't have done that."

Those words, as effective as a dousing of ice water, snapped her out of her sensual fog. Damn it, he did not get to have regrets! Yet there he stood, looking guilty and hot and so sexy that she wanted to throw him in the empty horse stall of her nonromantic barn and...

And he'd stopped.

Embarrassment prickled, along with disbelief and denial. "Why not?"

Good. That sounded calm, as if she was merely interested instead of desperate.

"For one thing, you've sworn off men." His brows flattened with confusion and that damn regret. "I'm not an ass like Chuck, and I do pay attention to what you want. You need to know that."

I changed my mind. Or rather, *he* changed it. She opened her mouth to explain it to him, but not in time.

"And even if you hadn't," he said, frustration ripe in the set of his shoulders, "I can't be in that type of relationship, not right now when Sadie is already adjusting to so much."

Half insulted, half bemused, Autumn stared at him. "You kissed me." Under the circumstances, the reminder seemed necessary. "Pretty sure you liked it, too."

Voice husky and rough, he muttered, "You have no idea."

That was something at least.

Until he added, "That's part of the problem."

Oh, great. Kissing her was a problem.

Appearing hunted, he paced away, but surged right back like a man ready to ravish a woman. He slowly inhaled, slowly exhaled and pulled himself together. "I got ahead of myself with that kiss, and that's not fair. I'm sorry."

Hello. She'd kissed him back—or couldn't he tell? Maybe her kissing skill sucked or something. With no way to know for sure, she kept quiet. He could muddle through this without her input.

"I meant to suggest a proposition—that is, an idea that'll work for both of us."

Right now she'd give a lot to have a little of Ember's savvy and experience with men. But, no, all she had was her calm, steadfast, boring persona, so she folded her arms and asked, "Why don't you just spell it out for me?"

"I'm messing this up."

"Oh, no," she said, her tone dripping with sarcasm. "You're doing great."

Instead of being irked, amusement crinkled the corners of his eyes. "Even at the most awkward times, you're pretty damn special."

If it was awkward for him, he should try it from her side. Since they weren't really getting anywhere—beyond making her hot and bothered—she decided it was time to wrap it up. "We should get out there with Sadie."

Without looking away from her, he said, "Mike is letting her toss out chicken feed. She's having a blast."

Wondering how he knew that, Autumn leaned forward to see out the barn doors. Sure enough, that's exactly what they were doing. "Huh. A dad's eagle eye?"

"She's my daughter. Some part of my brain is always on her. Actually, that's what I'm trying to explain. Sadie adores you." His gaze dipped to her mouth. His tone dipped, as well, going a little deeper. "I like you, too. A lot."

She swallowed back her automatic "ditto," because at this point in their convoluted conversation, she wasn't sure what he wanted.

"You're easy to talk to, even easier to be around. You...fit, when I didn't think that'd be possible, not with everything we have going on. In so many ways you make it better instead of worse, and I can't overlook that."

Unsure what to make of that, she gestured for him to continue.

"Chuck coming back probably reinforces your decision about men. That's okay," he hurried to say, "because my current situation is limiting also. I have zero chance of a sexual relationship."

Her jaw loosened, then snapped shut. "I didn't ask."

That only seemed to frustrate him more. "True. Hasn't stopped me from thinking about it, though. The problem— from my end, at least—is that I do most of my work late in the evening and in the early morning."

Working around Sadie's bedtime? So when did he sleep?

"Having a seven-year-old around during the day means no privacy. I'm okay with that," he added, "especially since the plan is to help her acclimate to everything."

Finally seeing the picture, Autumn said, "But it leaves no time for—"

"Intimacy. Sex. Anything one-on-one with a woman." Full of persuasion, he edged closer. "I know, not exactly exciting, but since you swore off men, anyway, it could work, right? And to be truthful, I'm hoping you'll change your mind by the time I'm freer, maybe after school starts?" Still not giving her a chance to weigh in, he added, "For now, there'd be no pressure at all. Just friendship." He bent to see her face, his earnest eyes searching hers. "What do you think?"

What did she think? About no sex? Autumn shook her head. *Was he nuts?*

Of course she wanted sex, or at least she did with him. Until him, yeah, she could take it or leave it. She *had* left it—for quite some time.

As if to sway her, he said, "We could hang out, be together at the various town parties, like at the beach last night. You had fun, right?"

The most fun she'd had in a very long time. "Surprisingly, I did."

"You'll be working at the house and we could follow that up with dinner sometimes." Drawing her resisting body to his, he added, "There are a few movies Sadie wants to see. She'd enjoy your company. I'd love your company, too."

That sounded nice.

"Women would leave me alone—"

"Wait." Autumn straight-armed him. He'd slipped that part in there, but her brain snagged on it. "Have women...?"

"I've had a few offers," he said, like it was nothing at all. "Being with you will end that, right?"

"Being with me?" He made it sound legit, when she wasn't at all sure about that.

"Here's the bonus." Ready to convince her, he stroked a hand down her back, pressing her forward into a full-body hug. "If the town sees us as a couple, Chuck would hear about it and he'd know you'd moved on. You could avoid that whole awkward scenario."

Being up against his body, his muscles tensed and his heated scent addictive, made it hard for her to think. Otherwise she might not have said aloud, "They'll see I already have a hunk, so why would I care about Chuck."

His slow smile seduced as completely as his gravelly tone. "You think I'm a hunk?"

Pfft. "You have mirrors."

Pleased, he nuzzled against her hair. "I think you're incredibly sexy."

Yeah...she had mirrors, too. "That's why you want a pretend relationship, huh?"

"Autumn." More gently, with feeling, he pressed a kiss to her temple and eased back to see her face. "I want you. I haven't focused on a woman in a long time, not since I got news of Deb's death and I started the process of rearranging Sadie's life. Even before that, I had a casual date here and there, but most of my time was spent on advancing my career and arranging my schedule to see Sadie. With you, it's different."

Good.

"When Deb passed away four months ago, I got Sadie right away, of course. But then we had the process of me resigning from my job, selling my condo, relocating us both—everything's been up in the air. Neither of us has had a chance to regroup."

He tangled his fingers in her messy hair and gently massaged her scalp. "In the middle of the chaos, you've brought calm."

Funny, around him she felt really chaotic.

Mirroring that thought, he clarified, "Calm at least to the situation. Internally, lady, you've kicked up pure pandemonium." He looked her over, his gaze piercing...and admiring. "I can't stop thinking about you—or wanting to see you." Sadie's laughter drew his attention toward the barn doors and put a smile on his mouth. "It helps that Sadie likes you so much. I don't have to feel guilty for my divided thoughts."

"You're human, Tash. You're allowed to have feelings." And wants and desires. If she could only convince him of that, maybe they could find a way around the privacy issue.

"She's my priority."

"Well of course she is."

His smile warmed another few watts. "See, you get that. I'm not sure other women would."

Hmm...new concerns surfaced. "Are we here, doing—" she flapped her hand to indicate their close proximity "—*this*, just because Sadie likes me? You might've been with another woman, except she wouldn't empathize with your daughter?"

"That's part of it. If Sadie didn't like you, it wouldn't matter what I felt because I'm not going to put her through anything else."

"Makes sense. Keep going."

"If you didn't understand that, no matter how much I wanted you, I'd put a lid on it."

So far, he'd said nothing objectionable. But somewhere in there, he had to want *her*, for no other reason than that he liked her and found her appealing. "Got it." Hopeful, she asked, "What else?"

Framing her face in his hands, he said with forthright candor, "Sadie could claim you as her new best friend, and you could be the most understanding woman in the world. If I didn't want you so damn much, I still wouldn't be here, trying to figure out a way to make this work for both of us, and to it make worthwhile to you."

Worthwhile? Was that a joke? The man clearly didn't know his own appeal, or how much she wanted him. "So we're going to have a...relationship?" That word didn't sound quite right given his no-sex proclamation.

Giving a hint of iron determination, he said, "Let's call it an exclusive relationship."

"Exclusive," she said lightly, though it was a heady thought. Tash Ducker would be hers and hers alone. Even without sex, that sounded pretty great. "So you'll be faithful to me even though we can't—"

"I don't want anyone else," he nearly growled.

Oh, hey. The way he said that, how he sounded—and how he *looked*... Seriously, why was she still waffling?

Maybe sensing her acceptance, he pressed her back, the hunger in his eyes now mixed with optimism. "What do you think?"

A platonic relationship with the guy she'd crushed on forever? A man she respected and admired. A man she liked...and wanted. Why not? At least with Tash, she knew upfront what she was getting into.

He was right about the bonus, too. With Tash, she'd make all the ladies jealous and no one, not even Chuck, could think she was pining away.

Making the decision, she stepped back.

Out of his hold.

Shoulders back and chin up, she gave a firm nod. "All right."

Triumph glittered in his eyes. "You agree?"

That particular look made her knees wobbly, but she wouldn't turn back now. "We have a deal."

That wiped away his pleasure. "Don't make it sound like a business arrangement. It's more than that."

"Sure, okay." Knowing more of an explanation wouldn't help,

she moved toward the barn doors and he followed. To ensure a change of topic, she asked, "How is Sadie doing? I was worried after she got hurt last night."

"We talked. Really talked, I mean. I'd already made up my mind not to press her, but out of the blue, she opened up. Some of the things she said…" He took her hand. "She's sharing, and that's what matters."

His hand was large, hard and hot…like the man himself.

They paused in the doorway to watch Sadie carefully petting Franklin the sheep, who'd come to join them, only to get nudged by Delilah the goat, who wanted her own pets. Sadie laughed until she got Mike laughing, too. Having two hands, she solved the problem by petting them both. Kneeling down beside her, Mike ensured the animals couldn't get too frisky.

"We talked about Deb a little. I want her to have good memories of her mother, so I had to juggle my part a few times." He gave her a sideways glance. "She said you were nothing like Deb and that she liked you."

Maybe that's when Tash had gotten the idea for their *relationship*. "I like her, too, very much."

"I know—I told her. She wanted me to ask you over for dinner, but I thought I should preempt that with the details of my situation, just so you'd know where I stand."

Ha! She wasn't at all sure where he stood, but she'd deal with it. "Thank you for being upfront with me. I prefer honesty, always."

Lifting her hand to his mouth, he kissed her knuckles. "Me, too."

But was she being honest? Nope. She felt like a fraud, but she couldn't admit that she'd have loved to have more. More of *them*. More focus on a physical relationship.

It felt selfish when his reasons for waiting were so valid.

"Ember will start on the yard equipment Monday. I've got

the designs for Sadie's bedroom finished, too, so now we need to look at fabrics and paint and—"

Turning her to face him, Tash said, "Come to dinner tonight."

Here in the open doorway, blistering sunlight added heat to her disappointment. "I'm sorry, but I can't." Today was her day with her parents. She and Ember took turns making them a priority...much as Tash did with his daughter.

Instead of questioning her, he asked, "Tomorrow then?"

Sometimes she wished she wasn't so reliable. "Sorry, but I'm slammed until Thursday."

"Thursday it is."

Grateful that he so easily accommodated her schedule, Autumn smiled. "Perfect." Already she looked forward to it. "I'll see you Monday, too. That is, if you're around." This new relationship was loose enough that she wasn't sure what to expect. "My plan is to help Ember get things started before I head out for afternoon appointments. While I'm there, I'm hoping to set up a few other appointments with you so I can get some decisions made on the bedroom and your office."

"Sadie and I'll both be there Monday. Thursday for dinner will be even better. Okay?"

She nodded and, still determined to be different from her wallflower years in high school, went on tiptoes to put her mouth back to his.

She'd just felt the touch of his warm mouth when a shadow moved over them. They immediately broke apart and found Mike grinning.

Hand to his heart, Mike said, "Damn, I hate to interrupt, but I just got a call from your mom. She wants you to come by."

By force of will, Autumn swallowed back a groan of dread. "Did you tell her I'm showing around a client?"

"Since you two were making out here in front of God and all the animals, no, I'll admit I didn't quite put it that way."

Mortified, Autumn took a quick look around and saw no

one, not even a goat, paying attention to them. The animals kept Sadie occupied and her parents were in their small home, with no visual access to the barn.

"Mike, I swear..."

"What?" He laughed. "I witnessed it all, and that counts, right?"

Surprising her, Tash looped his arm over her shoulders and said to Mike, "You can plan to see it more often."

Already playing his part? He was good. And since he'd reminded her, Autumn leaned into him and pasted on a smile.

"It's like that, huh?" He clapped Tash on the shoulder. "Good work. She's a tough one to win over."

Autumn knew she'd actually been ridiculously easy, but whatever.

"Your mom wants to see Tash and Sadie, too. She said she remembers him from years ago." In an aside to Tash, he added, "Beware the artwork."

Oh, God, the artwork. Dread stole her voice for a second or two, but she wouldn't let Mike get away just yet. Suspicious, she asked, "How does Mom even know they're here?"

"Your sister," he replied as he headed back to Sadie. "How else?"

Chapter Eight

So far, everything was going better than Tash had dared to hope. He hadn't seen Sadie this happy in a very long time. Even before Deb had wrapped her car around that pole, his daughter had been alternately distant and then too clingy.

It pissed him off when he thought of how blind he'd been, how he'd bought in to Deb's fairy tale. So many times he'd asked about things, and Deb had lied, making up one excuse after another. She'd cheated a dozen times over, but blamed him for their marriage failing.

And her family followed her lead.

Once, when Deb had dodged out on his time with Sadie, he'd gotten hold of her mother to make sure everything was okay. She'd given him an earful that day, all of it hateful accusations. According to her folks, he'd ruined Deb's life.

He hadn't made the mistake of contacting them again after that, but he'd seen them at the funeral and it had been predictably ugly.

Sadie had grown so subdued since then, it sometimes felt like he couldn't reach her, and that scared the hell out of him. He wanted her to laugh and have fun, and he wanted her to sometimes misbehave and make mistakes, to feel secure enough to know it wouldn't matter. He loved her and he'd never stop loving her, no matter what. He needed her to believe it.

Since coming here, things had changed a little. Most especially around Autumn. Last night when Sadie had opened up, she'd given him reassurance that he was on the right track.

On the ride to the farm that morning, she couldn't stop her excited chatter. Using his phone, she'd looked up info on the various animals, what they liked and didn't like.

His seven-year-old daughter had wanted to be prepared.

God, she amazed him.

She'd also talked nonstop about Autumn.

In Sadie's mind, Autumn knew something about everything. And the kicker? She saved animals. To Sadie, that made her a superhero.

To Tash, it made her so much more. Autumn made him rethink everything he knew about women. After Deb, when physical need arose, he'd sought out slim, sexy, stylish women who disdained involvement as much as he did. Their "dates" served a purpose, but they no more cared than he did.

With Autumn, caring was an integral part of her. He doubted she knew how *not* to care. Things happened around her and she reacted in a way to make them better. Every damn time. Even with Patricia, who'd badgered her with mean assumptions, Autumn had remained considerate.

She was…a breath of fresh air. Emotionally substantial.

And incredibly sexy—maybe because of her caring nature, maybe because she didn't seem aware of her own allure.

Over and over, he studied her, trying to figure out what single feature pushed him over the edge. Her lush mouth and easy smiles drew him, but then so did the vulnerability in her soft blue eyes. Her hair, always a little unkempt, naturally drew his fingers and…hell, it was all of her. The whole package. The ripe curves of her body and her angelic face and the way she tried to nurture everyone around her, including him and his daughter.

"There," Autumn said, sliding her phone into her back pocket. "I told Mom we'd be there after I give you a tour of the farm." With a hint of hope in her eyes, she said, "Unless you have to go before that?"

No way would he budge. He wanted to know more about Autumn, and meeting her folks would help. "Sadie and I have the whole day free."

"Oh." She mustered up a smile. "Good. Okay then."

It was all Tash could do not to laugh. Seriously, how bad could a mother and father be?

For the next forty minutes or so, Autumn doted on Sadie. The chores she described boggled Tash's mind. When did the woman ever rest?

"Ember did the chores for me this morning, even though it was my turn. Mike and I will check on the animals off and on throughout the day. Especially in this heat." Eyes squinted, she looked up at the sky. "We could really use a good rain. Hopefully soon."

"How long have you had the farm?" Tash asked, watching as Pavlov rolled to his back in a barren spot of the field, only to be joined by the goat and sheep, each of them loving on him. Pavlov wallowed in their affection.

"Ember and I inherited the farm when our grandparents passed away. That was five years ago. Life was in turmoil, let me tell you. Dad had suffered a stroke, Mom had just lost her parents and we inherited a big old farm. It took us a few days to figure it out, but then we knew what we wanted to do."

"Take care of animals!" Sadie cheered, her tiny fist in the air.

"Yes." Autumn swung Sadie up and in a circle before putting her back on her feet. She bent down to look Sadie in the eyes, then explained, "But first we built a house for my folks."

"You build houses?" Sadie asked with a lot of awe.

Shading her eyes with one hand, Autumn pointed out a neat little cabin apart from the other structures. "Not exactly. Ember oversaw most of the actual building, but I designed it."

"You designed an entire house?" Tash was just as awed as his daughter.

"I wanted it to work for Dad's wheelchair, so I made everything a little lower than standard, with lots of baseboard lighting. It's superefficient, compact, but they have everything they need—including a studio off the back of the house for Mom. An intercom system makes it easy for either of them to reach the other."

Arms out, face up to the sun, Sadie turned a circle. "You all live here together."

Autumn's smile was contagious, making him smile, too. "Yes, we do." She touched Sadie's nose, then let her fingers drift through her hair, which looked an even brighter red in the afternoon sunshine.

Tash did his own perusal and thought what an amazing place it would be to raise a family. Had that been Autumn's plan before Chuck bailed?

She'd probably already imagined her own children playing outside with the animals. The devastation she had to have felt made him put his hand to his own chest, where his heart would be.

How could anyone hurt her like that? Protective instincts rose, along with a territorial inclination he'd never before experienced.

Never mind that their relationship right now was superficial at best. He'd work on that and somehow, as things worked themselves out, he'd—

"Mom and Dad aren't keen on the smells," Autumn said, interrupting his disturbing and profound thoughts. "That's why Ember didn't build their house a little closer. Plus, the animals would eat Mom's flowers and she'd have a fit. They're fenced off so critters can't get to them."

Sadie hugged Matilda. "I like how they smell."

That made both adults laugh. "You," Tash teased, "are probably the first person to say that about a pig."

Autumn winked at Sadie. Sotto voce, she confided, "I like how they smell, too."

Sadie grinned so widely, it made Tash laugh again.

"Next, we remodeled our grandparents' house to turn it into a duplex so Ember and I would each have our privacy." In an aside to Tash, she said, "I love my sister, but no way could we live together. Next door is close enough."

"So that big house is actually two places?"

"Yup. Big divider nearly down the middle. I can show it to you sometime if you want."

"Yeah, I'd like that."

As they moseyed forward, she gestured back toward the barn, where they'd already been. "We had to take down a lot of old outbuildings, repair and expand the barn, fix a few fences." A look of true contentment settled over her face. "Not long after, we got our first animal. Then another and another."

As Tash watched her, he accepted that she belonged here. The love she felt for it showed in her eyes, in the flush in her cheeks and the smile she couldn't suppress.

"It's beautiful," he said, his gaze still on her. "All of it."

A large outcropping of rock, half buried in the earth, caused her to pause. She dropped down to sit, patting a spot beside her for Sadie. "I'm lucky that I found what I'm meant to do."

Sadie leaned into her, then smiled at him.

Choosing to take that as an invitation, he settled on the other side of his daughter. His seat was a little lumpier, made up of two smaller rocks, putting him a bit lower on the ground, but he didn't mind. "It's amazing, Autumn. Everything you've done, all you've accomplished, is—"

A velvety—and slightly wet—pig snout cut him off, followed by a pig head, then feet that toppled him off the rock and into the dry dirt. Before Tash could fend her off, Olivia was on him, rooting around and cuddling, joined by Matilda, and Pavlov, and maybe a chicken. Hard to tell.

And, damn, it was nice—especially when Sadie and Autumn fell against each other laughing.

Urging the animals to the side of him instead of atop him, he'd just about freed himself when Autumn's face appeared above. Wearing a grin of barely banked hilarity, she said, "Awww, they like you. Isn't that sweet?"

"Like syrup." He swiped away a suspicious wet patch from his cheek. "Very sticky."

Cracking up, she helped to untangle him, and once he was on his feet, she took some time briskly brushing him off, clearing away the dust from the front of his shirt, out of his hair and... near his lap.

As detached as a doctor, she said, "There. You're almost good as new."

Actually, he was suddenly primed, on the verge of reacting... until his daughter said, "You look so funny, Dad."

Yeah, he could imagine. In his most fatherly voice, he said, "Not every day I'm accosted by pigs."

"And a dog," Autumn added.

"And a chicken." Sadie's eyes were bright with humor when she looked off to the side. "More were ready to join, too."

He turned to see an entire flock—or whatever a group of chickens was called—bearing down on them.

Autumn hugged into his side. "Come on. Time to meet my folks before you get any messier."

The chickens followed, but Pavlov veered off somewhere else with the pigs, no doubt in search of shade.

Using both hands, Tash tried to restore some order to his hair, but dust had mixed with sweat and he knew he wasn't at his best.

Then again, Autumn wore her own fair share of dust and dirt, as did his daughter. He tried to smooth Sadie's hair, too, but she had no patience for it and sidled away to take Autumn's hand, then snagged his, as well.

Skipping along between him and Autumn, she led them toward the home of Autumn's parents.

Autumn didn't hold back. In fact, she talked nonstop, telling them what to expect, explaining about her father's stroke and her mother's idiosyncrasies. Someone who didn't know might think she was anxious for them to meet.

He knew better. From that first day when they'd become reacquainted, he'd felt attuned to her, what she thought and what she felt. Right now, she was anxious...to get it over with.

"It'll be fine," he whispered over Sadie's head so she wouldn't hear. How bad could her parents be?

"Ha," she said just as quietly, then gave him a look of pity. "My folks are great, but a wee bit eccentric. They take a little getting used to."

"Mike likes them?"

She dismissed that as unimportant. "Mike likes most everyone and they hit it off right away. My mother thinks of him as the son she never had."

Yet Autumn thought he'd be different? Either offended by them or shocked? Determined to prove her wrong, Tash mentally girded himself for anything.

It astounded him that she'd react to this, when she'd so easily rolled with everything else. An ex who jilted her back in town? No problem. A gossipy friend spreading rumors? She responded with kindness. His suggestion for a sexless relationship?

She'd almost shrugged!

That still burned his ass a little. After his long bout of singular concentration on his daughter, he'd finally met someone who interested him—as a man, not just a dad. Hell, he wanted her so badly that around her, he stayed wired. Kissing her? Yeah, he'd be lucky if he didn't self-combust.

Yet she hadn't batted an eye at the idea of a no-sex relationship. Was it sex in general that she could take or leave, or him in particular?

Despite her assurances, did she still have feelings for Chuck? Did pride prompt her vehement denials? The idea nettled big-time.

"Mike wasn't kidding about my mom's art, okay? Just...maybe prepare yourself. I wouldn't want you to hurt her feelings."

"You think I would?"

"Not on purpose," she rushed to say, then bit her lip and gave a subtle nod at Sadie. "You might not want her to see—".

The front door flew open and a short, somewhat squat woman, dressed in a bright, boxy tunic and white capri jeans exited with open arms.

"Autumn! You brought them." She forged a path toward Tash.

Uncertain of the welcome, Tash said, "Ah—" and she threw herself against him for a big, affectionate hug.

"My goodness, you haven't changed." She pressed him back, looked him over and pawed his chest. "Still jacked, aren't you?"

Confusion wrinkled Sadie's little button nose. "What's jacked?"

Autumn said, "It means he's strong and fit in all the best ways."

Sadie grinned. "Dad has muscles everywhere."

Her mother turned her eye on Sadie. "Oh, my, and aren't you just the brightest little princess ever?" She scooped her up, squashing Sadie to her bosom. Poor Sadie, unsure what to do, held her arms and legs stiffly extended, like a dried-out starfish.

"Mom," Autumn implored, "let her breathe."

"She's just too precious," the woman said and finally loosened her hold to address Sadie. "You look like a sunset over the ocean. So very colorful."

Pained, Autumn hissed, *"Mom."*

Sadie laughed and wiggled loose.

"Oh." Suddenly twitching her nose, her mother retreated in

distaste. "You've been playing with the animals, haven't you, dear?"

Sadie gave a resounding "Yes!" Then added, "Dad rolled around on the ground with them. It was lots of fun."

"Oh, *really*?" Her mother gave him another glance, this one not so favorable.

Leaning in, Sadie whispered, "They knocked him over but he didn't get mad, even when me and Autumn laughed and laughed."

Smile indulgent, the woman patted Sadie's head. "I would have laughed, as well." Turning back to Tash, she stuck out a hand. "Since my daughter has forgotten her manners, I'll introduce myself."

Autumn sputtered. "You didn't give me a chance!"

"I'm Tracy." She pumped his hand with no end in sight. "I remember you as Tash, correct?"

"Yes, ma'am." He closed his other hand over hers, gave a gentle squeeze and freed himself, then drew Sadie to his side. "This is my daughter, Sadie."

"Your hair and those eyes." In dramatic affectation, Tracy placed the back of her hand to her forehead. "I would just die to draw you. Maybe in the sunlight, because it brings out all the red." Again she eyed Tash. "Is your wife a redhead?"

"I'm not married." His smile felt forced, but he got it out there. "Sadie's great-grandmother had red hair."

"Mom," Autumn interjected to ensure she couldn't continue her questions. "Maybe we should go inside and meet Dad, too?"

From the doorway, in a motorized wheelchair, her father said, "I'm joinin' you outside."

Tash noticed a slight slur and saw the effects of the stroke. Autumn's mother looked to be in her early sixties, but her father had to be seventy, and looked even older with his ailment. Gray hair stuck out in disarray around an expanding bald spot.

He wasn't a frail man, which surprised Tash as he watched him buzz his chair forward.

When he got close, he patted his wife on the butt, making her jump, and then reached out a shaking left hand to Tash. "Nice to see ya' 'gain, son."

"You, too, Mr. Somerset. I like your home."

"Call me Flynn." He wheeled around to look at the house. "Girls did a goo' job."

"Ember built it, you know," Tracy said with puffed-up pride. "She's so incredibly talented. She got her love of carpentry from Flynn and her free spirit from me."

Aware of Autumn standing behind her mother, miming her every word, Tash frowned, until Tracy added, "God bless her, Autumn inherited my big bones."

And with that, Autumn rolled her eyes, as if she'd heard those lines a million times in her life.

Tash saw *zero* resemblance. "Autumn's beautiful," he said, meaning it, needing her to hear it, "so I think you just complimented yourself." His smile kept it from sounding like an insult. He hoped.

"Oh." Tracy giggled with girlish delight. "She has more the look of her father...well, except for the bones." Hands on her wide hips, she posed as if to show off her attributes. "Here's what our girl will look like at sixty. Drink it in."

Tash choked.

Autumn went beet-red.

"They're both beauties, eh?" With a crooked grin, Flynn reached for his wife's behind again.

Tracy dodged him.

"The diff'rence," Flynn said, "is that my Autumn's a worker, always busy. Stays in shape."

Tracy turned her cannon on him. "You don't think I'm in shape?"

"Love yer shape." He gave a crooked, somehow leering grin. "But the most you lift is a lump of clay."

"Well..." Tracy's huff turned into a laugh. "I suppose that's true. You won't see me hefting pigs or clearing rocks or mucking out stalls."

So Autumn did all that? "I thought Mike—"

"He helps," Autumn said, then shrugged. "But there's always a million things to do and one pair of hands won't cover it all."

Dismissing all that, Tracy waved her hand at the house. "Let's go inside. I can show you my art."

Her pale throat working with a heavy swallow, Autumn closed her eyes.

"Have a little faith," he whispered to her. How bad could the art be? Then to Tracy, he added, "I'd love to see it." And he wanted to see the house Autumn had designed. "Lead the way."

"Wonderful!" Tracy swished and swayed with Flynn rolling along close behind her, blatantly admiring the view.

"She does that for his benefit," Autumn whispered. "They've always carried on, but now Mom uses his stroke as an excuse to be extra outrageous, saying it gives him something to live for."

Tash snickered. "She may be right."

Smiling up at him, Sadie slipped her hand into his. "They're funny, huh?"

"That they are." Even hot and sweaty and, yeah, maybe smelling a little like pigs, Sadie glowed with happiness. "Having fun?"

She nodded. "Oh, yeah." She snickered, then said a little too loudly, "I bet that lady smells like Matilda and Olivia now, too."

His daughter possessed a twisted sense of humor. He liked it. "Shush, or they might hear you." He glanced over and noticed Autumn grinning.

Inside, they went through an open area that included a living room, a dining room and a kitchen that astounded him. He had to pause in the kitchen to look around, and that caused everyone else to pause, too.

It was…perfect. Perfect for her father's limited reach; perfectly proportioned for two people; obviously comfortable and absolutely beautiful. In awe, he took in Autumn's anxious expression. "You designed this?"

"She drew it up," Tracy said, before Autumn could speak, "and Ember built it."

His back teeth locked but his smile never slipped. "Yes, I know." Without a missing beat, he added, "The design is incredible, Autumn. It flows so naturally."

The compliment left her flustered. "From one room to the next, I wanted it to be easy for Dad's chair."

"It is," Flynn said. "My girls are brillian'. Wife, too. I'm a lucky man."

While they moved on, Tash got closer to Autumn. "Is there anything you can't do?"

She put a small but credible fist in the air. "Hear me roar."

The teasing tone didn't negate the rosy color in her cheeks. Praise disconcerted her.

Kissing her had done the same, and right now he wanted to kiss her again. "Just so you know, I'm incredibly impressed."

Sadie said, "Me, too," though he doubted she understood. Complicated family dynamics was a tough concept for a seven-year-old.

Even at thirty-four, it amazed Tash. Autumn had created a design that showed her love and affection, her devotion to her parents knowing there'd be little appreciation.

The appreciation, at least from her mother, seemed to be exclusively for Ember.

"Thank you both." Modesty held Autumn back for a moment, but enthusiasm won out. "I helped Ember with the building once she had it under roof, though she subcontracts out a lot of stuff, too. Electrician, plumber, tile work… Even when she wasn't doing it herself, she oversaw it all, and kept it moving along without any major delays. I pitched in where I could."

Leaning closer, she breathed into his ear, "They were staying with me until we had it ready. I love them, but trust me, I was motivated to get it done, even if it meant me using power tools."

By the second, he wanted her more. How was that even possible? How could discussing her eccentric parents make him crave her?

Autumn Somerset, with her lush figure and caring nature, her inner strength and family loyalty, packed one hell of an emotional and physical punch.

"Come on," she whispered. "Just remember what I told you about Mom's art."

Curiosity took him the few steps necessary to enter the open double doors of the studio at the back of the house. Light entered on three sides, displaying wall-to-wall shelves cluttered with clay pieces and a few paintings that he couldn't begin to decipher.

"What a terrific room."

"It works for Mom's art."

"Here." Tracy thrust an ornate clay piece into his hands, then stepped back, fingers clutched under her chin, to await his reaction.

Tash looked down, and went speechless.

It looked like—

"Fruit," Autumn said cheerily, her voice a little high and shrill. "A banana, Mom? Is that right?"

Tracy scowled. "Of course it's a banana." She loomed closer to point. "Right here is a peach, and this an apple."

Well. The peach and apple appeared identical. Fruit? It looked like something altogether different. It looked... Tash twisted it this way and that. Obscene. Like an erect penis on a well-endowed guy. Was it supposed to be a peeled banana? Why were the apple and peach so small?

He didn't ask.

"I'm thinking of adding some grapes," Tracy offered, waiting for his approval.

"It's...wonderful. Very unique." Searching his brain for something more, he added, "Grapes would be good."

"Once that's done, I'll add color and a glaze." Sighing in satisfaction, Tracy said, "It'll be perfect, don't you think?"

Tash said, "Ah..."

Guessing his predicament, Flynn snickered. "She gets all her ideas from me."

Tash barely swallowed back his laugh, but with high expectations clearly showing in Tracy's gaze, and Autumn's pained embarrassment, he tried for a little more nuance. "You enjoy fruit, Flynn?"

The elder Somerset snorted.

Missing the joke, Tracy said, "That man loves his banana."

Which left Flynn sputtering.

In a stage whisper that Flynn couldn't miss, Tracy said, "My art depicts various stages of his stroke."

Yeah...not a conversation Tash wanted to have.

But like the art, the topic proved deceptive. "After he fell ill, he couldn't eat for the longest time, only something soft."

"Like bananas," Autumn explained, her face on fire.

Flynn grumbled. "I could'a ate more, but that's all she'd give me!"

"And this." Tracy produced another work with fanfare.

After one quick look, Tash shook his head. Nope. Not touching it.

Sighing, Autumn rubbed her head. "It's a rose."

"The man can see," Tracy snapped.

The petals, lying softly open, didn't look like any flower Tash had ever seen. A woman's body, however...

"My Flynn received flowers every day while he was in the hospital."

Wheeling his chair around, Flynn glared at the shelves of hapless clay, then shook his head. "She says it's all about me."

"Of course it is." She gazed at her husband adoringly. "It's very introspective, you know."

Flynn's eyes narrowed. "Come here, woman, and I'll give you something else to dwell on."

"Dad," Autumn gasped, clearly horrified. *"Child present."*

"Me?" Sadie asked, perking up in interest. Until that moment, she'd just been looking around.

Probably trying to figure out the art.

Tash considered grabbing her up and making a run for it.

"Behave, Flynn." Tracy turned away. "I want to show Tash my pineapple."

The smile cracked, and when Tash looked at Autumn, he saw her struggling, as well. He tried, but the laughter swelled inside him. Autumn's eyes started watering, her face going redder.

He could tell—she'd lose it any second.

Very carefully, Tash put the piece back on the shelf. "You have real talent, Tracy."

"Thank you. People are often overcome when they see my work."

And that did it. Autumn's chuckle started it all. Tash turned his back because watching her made it impossible for him not to laugh, too.

Around snorts and chortles, Autumn said, "I hear Mike calling me!" Shoulders shaking and eyes watering, she quickly edged her way out of the room.

Deserting him!

Knowing he wouldn't last, Tash swung Sadie up into his arms and said, "We should go, too."

Tracy rushed forward. "But I had more to show you!"

Oh, God, he couldn't take more. The phallic fruit and aroused flower were enough for one day. "Thank you, Tracy. I'll come back again soon, okay? Sadie, thank them both."

Over his shoulder, Sadie sang, "Thank you!"

Flynn waved them on, but Tracy followed, doing her best to see them graciously to the door...even though he practically ran with his bouncing, laughing daughter in his arms.

Once outside, he searched the area and found Autumn hanging over a fence post, her laughter loud and free.

And oh-so-very compelling.

Giggling, Sadie wiggled to get free.

The second her little feet touched the ground, she ran to Autumn to join in on the laugh-fest. Autumn swung her up again, then seated her on the rail of the fence. She kept her arm around Sadie's back...and Sadie hugged her neck.

Something warm and insidious wrapped around his heart, squeezing in a way that was almost painful, but more like...magic.

Until meeting Autumn, he hadn't understood how badly Deb's infidelity had affected him. After his divorce, he'd wasted so much time on the wrong pursuits. He'd thrown himself into his career. Thrown himself into meaningless relationships. And he'd worried himself sick about Sadie.

Here in Sunset, with Autumn, everything was different.

Yeah, he'd made some headway with her. Her agreement to a relationship meant a lot, because at least for now, she was his and his alone. Chuck could take a hike.

The no-sex thing...it pained him, but he'd give Autumn all the time she needed. Eventually she'd want him more than ice cream.

He hoped.

Someday she'd look at him with that same level of affection she had when gazing around her farm.

Until then, being with her wouldn't be a hardship. Autumn was always a good time, whether sitting at the beach talking, or looking at suggestive art with her parents.

At a more sedate pace, his heart thumping with new and unfamiliar emotions, Tash went to them...already a little addicted. Already a little lost.

Pondering how he'd manage a platonic relationship with a woman who made him burn with her hilarity.

It was a very special thing.

Almost, but not quite, as special as Autumn.

Chapter Nine

Apparently, a relationship took up no more time than being single—or at least that proved true for the first part of the week. She saw Tash Monday morning, and then Tuesday afternoon, too, as they worked with Ember on the outdoor equipment.

The heat wave continued with humidity as thick as butter. Though she looked a wreck within an hour, Tash didn't seem to notice. He even tucked back a damp curl, smiling at her as if he found her sweaty hair adorable. She'd have loved another kiss, but with Ember and Sadie there, it didn't happen.

By Thursday, when she joined him for their prearranged dinner, the outdoor area had really taken shape. The frame of the pirate ship was in, built around the tree rather than in it, for added stability. Six feet off the ground, it just reached the largest branches so that Autumn was able to incorporate them into the design. She'd even gotten a small skull-and-crossbones flag that they attached to one barren branch for added flair.

Sadie *loved* it. Finally, the little girl got involved, weighing on one thing after another with gleeful energy.

The beam for the swings and slide extended off to one side, braced by a climbing wall. Ember hadn't yet added the ladder because they didn't want Sadie tempted to climb it, not until the floor and sides were in.

She was a very sweet, well-behaved girl...but still a child, one who was obviously used to more responsibility and less supervision.

Autumn promised her that once the floorboards were complete, a tire swing and two-seater would hang beneath, then she'd be able to start playing.

Already the neighborhood kids took notice. Each day when Autumn stopped by, she saw that Ember had two or three extra sets of eyes with Sadie's new friends sitting on the grass and asking questions.

Given all the tension with Mike lately, as well as Ember's sometimes morose mood, Autumn worried for her. But here, working in the yard, Ember seemed in her element, teasing, laughing and patiently giving answers to the kids.

It warmed Autumn's heart to know that Sadie was already making friends, and it relieved her that Ember looked in such high spirits.

Thursday, for their dinner, Tash grilled steaks. As soon as she arrived, Sadie ran to greet her with a hug, and then Tash pulled her in for a kiss to the forehead.

It wasn't quite the welcome she wanted from him, but with Sadie watching, she understood his restraint. Because of the heat, they ate inside, but by early evening they'd settled into lawn chairs with—bless the man—ice-cream cones, while Sadie and the other children played under a sprinkler.

"She's more at ease each time I see her." Autumn noticed how two of the kids had ice cream dripping down their chins, yet Sadie was more fastidious, making only a slight mess before rinsing under the sprinkler.

"Her foot's completely healed. I'm glad now that I didn't put her through a doctor visit." Tash finished off his cone, too, his gaze on his daughter. "Last night, she told me she loves it here. We talked for a long time about the schools, her new friends, the lake, the pirate ship...and you."

"Me?" The way Tash said it, with a half smile, assured her it wasn't anything bad.

"When she gets older she wants to work for you so she can spend more time with the animals."

Touched, Autumn grinned. "Sounds to me like a goat and pig are the real draw." She finished off her ice cream and cleaned her hands on her napkin.

"She's anxious to meet Tash the turkey."

The name still made Autumn laugh. "Now that the vet has given him the all-clear, we should be getting him this weekend. He might be cantankerous for a while, but I'm sure Sadie would understand that. She's a very smart little girl."

"At least tell me he's a majestic bird."

She was amused at his chagrin and laughed some more. "A little scrawny, actually, but we'll plump him up in no time."

When her phone dinged with an incoming text, Tash's smile slipped. "Chuck?"

She knew him well enough now to know he kept his tone carefully neutral. "You're still on that?" Chuck hadn't contacted her again, so she assumed he'd given up when she didn't reply.

"He's still around, right?" And then with optimism, "Or did he take off again?"

"Don't know, don't care. Chuck doesn't concern me."

Sadie, who'd just approached, asked, "Who's Chuck?"

"Chuck is no one, sweetie." Autumn held up her phone. "And it's Ember." Her sister should have been home, showered and back out on a date by now, which was her usual routine.

Instead she'd sent a text that said: If you're around could you call?

"Something might be wrong." She flashed a worried smile at Tash and pressed in Ember's number. Some vague sense of urgency took root, making her antsy.

Ember answered before the first ring had finished. "I'm sorry. So freaking sorry because I know you're with Tash and if I could handle it on my own I would—"

Slowly, Autumn stood. "Handle what?"

She heard Ember swallow. "There's a cow… I got the call that he needed a home so I came to get him, but Autumn…"

Understanding crashed down on her. They'd been through this too many times already. "Tell me where." Headed for the house to get her purse, Autumn listened to the address, nodded and promised, "I'm on my way."

Tash and Sadie followed her.

She hated to cut the date short, but already her mind had moved on to other priorities. "Sorry, guys. I gotta run."

Before she could head back out the door, Tash caught her arms. "What's wrong?"

She briefly glanced at Sadie, but no child should have to hear of animal abuse. "A young cow that's…hurt. Ember and I will handle it." She bent to give Sadie a hug, ignoring her wet T-shirt and hair. "I'll see you soon, okay? We need to pick paint colors for your room now that the pirate ship is underway. I meant to do that today, but I thought we'd have more time—"

To her surprise, Sadie squeezed her tight and whispered, "Take care of the cow, 'kay?"

"It's what I do." She tried a smile that didn't quite make it.

Next, Tash cupped a hand around her face. "Is there any way I can help?"

She shook her head. Jerks existed, and far too often, they hurt helpless animals. "Thank you, but I've got it."

"I know you do, but if anything comes up, just let me know." With Sadie standing there watching, and her heart feeling heavy,

Tash leaned in and put a kiss to her mouth. "We'll see you to-morrow?"

"I don't know." Much would depend on rearranging her crazy schedule around this new member of the farm. Until she saw the animal, she couldn't gauge the situation.

"At least find time to give me a call, okay? When it's convenient for you."

Okay, now that felt more like a relationship, and she liked it. He was so careful, not making any demands while still showing that he cared. She was fast losing her heart, and that scared her. "I will." On impulse, she put another fast, soft peck on his mouth, then one to Sadie's cheek, before hustling out to her truck.

Which still didn't have air-conditioning.

It was an exceptional thing, at least for her, to have two people—one a hunk, the other a petite sweetheart—standing in the yard waving to her until she could no longer see them.

Trepidation grew as she drove to the abandoned farm where Ember waited. At 8:00 p.m., the summer sun still hung high in the sky, turning her truck into an oven. Windows open, her worry as hot as her hands on the wheel, she drove down the gravel drive and spotted Ember pacing outside a ramshackle shed. To her surprise, Mike stepped out of the building just as she parked.

Grateful that her sister hadn't been alone, but still sick with worry, Autumn trotted toward them.

Mike stopped her. His expression told her things that his careful words didn't. "Poor thing is scared, so go in slow, okay?"

Chewing her lip and looking haggard, Ember said, "Bastards moved away and left the cow there. Alone."

Her throat felt thick. She didn't know when the residents had left, and didn't care. Her thoughts centered on the here and now. "How bad?"

"Hungry," Mike said. "She has a few sores. Dehydrated, I'm

sure. Ember called Ivey. She knows you're on the way and is waiting."

Ivey, their veterinarian and a good friend, often donated her time for animals in need. "God bless that woman," Autumn whispered as she ducked under the sloping entry and inched her way to the back of the building. Hot, smelly and dilapidated. Unfit for a rat, much less a beautiful creature like this one.

Right behind her, Ember whispered, "A neighboring farm called. They knew she was here, but gave it a few days in case the owners came back."

Disgust reeked in her sister's tone, mirroring Autumn's when she asked, "You reported them?"

"And the monsters who left this poor baby behind." Ember wiped her eyes. "The sheriff was here and gone. He'll be in touch."

"Good."

With a shuddering breath, Ember said, "I'll get things ready outside."

Ember was far more emotional about…well, *life*, than Autumn was. Whereas Autumn would try to stay strong, Ember allowed herself to cry. She still got the job done, so Autumn didn't worry too much…except that Ember's tears prompted her own.

It had always been that way. Far too often, they fed off each other's emotions. For now, Autumn needed to pull it together so the poor cow wouldn't be more stressed.

Edging as close as she dared, she started talking to the cow. She couldn't imagine the terror the animal had felt, stuck in an indoor enclosure with no way to find food or water.

Mike had already taken care of that, having slid in feed and fresh water. The cow was listless in her eating, and only drank a little.

Worried, Autumn talked to her for a long time. Soft, gentle, nonsense words. Praise and admiration. Promises for an improved future.

Tears tracked down her face the entire time, but she didn't care, and neither did the cow.

Outside, she could hear Mike and Ember prepping the truck bed. It took longer than an hour before Autumn, with Mike's help, led the cow out and got her into the truck bed. Thankfully, the animal didn't have any major injuries.

By the time they were ready to go, the sky had darkened to gray and a few stars peeked out.

Mike stood in front of the driver's door. "So, a suggestion."

Always open to advice, especially from someone as caring as Mike, Autumn nodded.

"Even superwomen wear down. You both look beat, so even though I'm only an employee—"

Ember groaned.

Autumn had no idea what that was about, but Mike didn't give her an opportunity to ask.

"—why don't you let me get this girl to Ivey? You two should go home and get some rest, because I know you both have full schedules tomorrow."

"So do you," Autumn pointed out.

"I'm just at the farm, though, not dealing with customers. The animals don't judge me when I have bags under my eyes." His smile looked as tired as hers felt. "I know the routine, I promise. I swear I'll be as gentle as you'd be."

"Mike," she chastised, "I already know that."

"So what do you say?"

Autumn rubbed the back of her sweaty neck and winced in apology. "My air-conditioning is still on the fritz."

"I'll fix it for you tomorrow."

Not what she'd been saying. "I would never—"

"You haven't had time. As of right now, you'll have even less time next week. The forecast isn't showing a break in the temps and humidity, so I'll take care of it. Okay?"

Shoulders slumping and spine going weak, she nodded. "Okay. Thank you."

"Good. Now how about you two go home and grab some rest?"

Autumn looked at Ember, and that helped her decide. Her sis had worked in the grueling sun all day, doing a much more physical job than Autumn had. That, along with the emotional toll of finding an abandoned animal, left her utterly wilted.

"I've said it before, but you truly are a godsend. I don't know how we'd manage the farm without you."

"I'm sure you'd figure it out." He glanced at Ember. "Both of you." After the slightest hesitation, he took one big step toward Ember. When she looked up in surprise, he put a hot one right on her mouth.

Autumn took it in with interest, especially the bemused expression on Ember's face, and the fact that she allowed the kiss, even leaned into it for a bit.

After he stepped back, Mike chucked her lightly on the chin and said, "Good work today." One more peck and he left, striding around to the truck. He started the engine and slowly pulled away, mindful of the nervous cow in back.

"Wow." Autumn fanned her face, feeling a little scorched after that display. Then she fanned Ember's face until Ember came out of her daze and swatted at her. "Just trying to help." She kept her tired smile hidden as they headed for Ember's car.

Once behind the wheel, Ember kicked on the air and drew a heavy breath. "God, I need a cold shower." She realized what she'd said and turned a disgruntled scowl on Autumn. "*Not* because of that kiss."

"Uh-huh."

They drove in silence for a while, each lost in their own thoughts. As the reality of it all began to bubble up, she glanced at Ember.

"Don't," her sister warned, her voice already breaking.

"Don't what?"

"Don't...*anything.*" Ember's swallow was audible. "Don't talk about it, don't ask if I'm okay and don't you dare cry, Autumn. I mean it!" Her voice cracked. "If you cry, I'll completely lose it, so just...*don't.*"

Eyes already glassy, Autumn nodded fast and swallowed down her churning emotions. Exhaustion pulled at her, amplified by the anger and sadness of seeing an animal so neglected. "Okay." She sounded like a broken frog.

"Damn it, Autumn." Ember swiped angrily at her own cheeks, then choked out in a high-pitched wail, "Sometimes people *suck.*"

Because her sister needed her to be strong, Autumn struggled to keep her wail at bay. It took a second, but she sounded mostly contained when she whispered, "Sometimes people are amazing, too. There are very special people in this world. We have to remember that."

Grateful for the change of subject, Ember nodded and asked, "Tash?"

Just the thought of him made her squishy inside. "Yes." Tash had been through so much, but he kept forging forward, making a better life for himself and his daughter. "He is, but I meant Mike. For you."

Ember rejected that. "Another taboo topic. I can't..." Tears welled again, so she sucked in a shuddering breath. Then another and another. "I need that damn shower."

Very lightly, trying not to shatter her sister's fragile control, Autumn touched her arm. "Me, too. It's okay."

Ember gave a wobbly nod of agreement.

As they traveled, worry gnawed at Autumn's peace of mind. "You're okay to drive?" Heavy shadows filled the old country roads, and with the humidity of the hot day settling, mist made the headlights blurry.

"I am." Ember visibly focused on the road. "I promise."

Her sister was many things, but careless wasn't one of them. Autumn dug out her phone. "Do you mind if I call Tash? I promised him I would." The call would give them both a moment to regroup.

"Since I dragged you away, please do. And give him my apologies."

"You have nothing to apologize for." They both made animal rescue a priority whenever possible.

Tash answered on the second ring. "Hey," he said softly. "How'd it go?"

She nodded, knew he couldn't see her, and choked out, "Fine."

"Autumn." Even through the cell, his sympathy hugged around her, warm and comforting. "I'm sorry, babe. You okay? The cow's okay? If there's anything I can do, I swear, I'll—"

"Thank you." So, *so* amazing. As briefly as she could, Autumn explained the situation, then promised, "I'm okay, just tired. I'm sure the cow is scared, but she'll be all right, too."

"You'll make sure of it," he said evenly, full of confidence in her ability.

Wow, if only she could be that confident about herself. "Is Sadie in bed?"

"Actually...she wanted to wait up until we heard from you."

Bless her heart. Autumn had sensed that Sadie's worry for the animal would keep her on edge, and she was anxious to reassure her. "Could I say hi?"

"She'd like that. Hang on."

Sounds of shuffling reached her, and then Sadie's tentative little voice said, "Hi."

"Hey, sweetie." There went that squeezing of her heart. She wished she was close enough to cuddle Sadie, to share a few soothing hugs. "Did your dad tell you? We got the cow and she's okay."

"Are you okay, too?"

Awwww... New tears threatened, thickening her voice and

making her fight hard for composure. "Yeah." That sounded a little broken, so Autumn tried again. "I'm fine. This is what I do, right?"

"Right." With a slight hesitation, Sadie asked, "Can I see her soon?"

"You betcha." With a glance at her sister, Autumn added, "The cow is going to need a name."

A smile softened Ember's ravaged profile, and she lifted her thumb in agreement to the plan.

Sadie caught her breath. "I can name her?"

Thrilled to hear excitement replace worry, Autumn smiled, too. "Sure. Why don't you start thinking of a few choices we can go over next time I see you?"

"Okay." Two heartbeats passed. "When will I see you?"

"Oh, honey. I don't know yet. Soon, though, okay?"

"You promise?"

Being liked by Sadie was pretty special. "Cross my heart. Now you get some sleep, okay? That's what I'm going to do as soon as I get home."

"'Kay." She sounded more like her old self when she said, "Thanks, Autumn."

"Thank *you*, Sadie—for caring about animals." *And for caring about me.* "We're in this together, but we both need rest to be strong."

She heard what sounded like a kiss through the phone. "Good night."

"'Night, honey."

Seconds later, Tash came back on the line. "You're heading home for bed now?"

Obviously, he'd been listening. "Yes. Ember and I both."

"Good. We'll touch base tomorrow, okay? Same offer stands. If there's anything I can do, don't hesitate."

She couldn't see herself imposing on him, but she nodded, anyway. "Okay."

"Sadie and I insist that you two take the day off tomorrow, but give me a call when you can."

Having Tash care, too, was double the pleasure. "Will do."

After she disconnected the call, she and Ember fell silent for the rest of the drive, each respecting the other's need to stay strong. At home, they found Pavlov lounging on the porch, waiting much like a watchful grandpa might. He stood and greeted them both with a wagging tail.

"You're the best male I know, Pavlov," Ember said to him, kissing him atop his furry red head.

"You want to see Mike wagging his butt?"

Ember half smiled. "Maybe with his tongue hanging out?"

They both snickered, and then with a brief touch of hands, they parted to head inside.

Pavlov chose to follow her.

Autumn didn't know what she wanted more—a shower, a good book, or to pass out for a solid ten hours.

Watchful, Pavlov stuck close. He was a good listener, so she went to her knees and gave him her tearful explanation of the cow while he snuggled close, snuffling her neck and licking away her tears.

"She'll be okay, buddy. You'll help with that, won't you?" Pavlov always greeted new animals with loads of affection that put them at ease. "You're such a great guy." Choking a little on her tears, she said to Pavlov what she couldn't yet say to Tash and Sadie. "I love you so much."

Pavlov returned that sentiment with a wildly wagging tail.

She wouldn't mind Tash getting just as enthusiastic.

When she headed into the bathroom for her shower, Pavlov followed, sticking close even a half hour later, when she got into bed with her book.

"Now I can brag that I didn't sleep alone." She scratched under Pavlov's chin, which put a look of ecstasy on his face and made her smile. "Definitely, I wouldn't mind seeing that expression on Tash." She kissed the top of his head and settled back into the bed. After circling twice, Pavlov settled near the footboard, but with his chin touching her shins.

She was still trying to decide if she had the energy to read when a knock sounded and Pavlov went berserk.

He launched off the bed and raced down the hall, his nails scrabbling on the hardwood floor. By the time Autumn caught up, his bark had changed from warning to greeting. She knew why when she found him at the connecting door.

Worried, she swung the door open to her sister. "Are you—?"

Determined, Ember pushed in and past her. "Where's that ice cream that cures all ills? Sorry, sis, but I need some."

It was late, and still Sadie didn't sleep. Tash had finished reading to her over an hour ago, but from the desk where he caught up with work, he heard her rustling around, tossing and turning. The muted glow of the night-light in her room sent her shadow out the open door, so when he saw her sit up in bed, he saved his file and pushed back his chair.

Pausing in the doorway, he saw her arranging a pile of stuffed animals into the bed with her. Usually she picked one and slept with it. Sleeping with ten meant something was wrong.

He took a step into the room, drawing her attention. "What's up, honey? Can't sleep?"

Eyes downcast with guilt, she said, "Sorry."

"Hey." Tash moved into the room. "You don't need to apologize." Sitting on the side of the bed, he tucked in a pink elephant so worn in places, it was a wonder his stuffing didn't fall out. Tash remembered getting the prize at a local carnival when she was four.

It both saddened and pleased him that she still liked it.

When Sadie didn't say anything else, he filled the silence. "So. I was trying to work but I keep thinking about Autumn. I wouldn't be able to sleep right now, either."

"Really?"

"Really. I like Autumn, so when she's upset, it bothers me."

Sadie nodded. "Me, too."

"When you're upset, it bothers me even more. Can you tell me what's wrong?"

Clutching the elephant, she rested back in her bed but turned to face him. "She's going to make the cow okay, huh?"

"I'm sure she'll do absolutely everything she can..." Like a tsunami of sorrow, the similarities suddenly hit him, and he faltered. Yes, she'd been used by the mother who should have nurtured her, the mother who'd lied to punish him...and had hurt Sadie in the process.

Clearing his throat, Tash finished with, "She'll make the cow feel loved and appreciated."

Eyes downcast again, Sadie asked with innocent deception, "Why would anyone hurt a cow?"

Grief and anger twisted in his guts, but hopefully he hid it. "I think it's more that the cow was neglected." Because his daughter was incredibly smart, and now seemed introspective, Tash chose his words carefully. "The cow wasn't protected or cared for the way it should have been."

"I bet the cow was sad."

Tash ruined her nice display of stuffed animals by lifting her out from under her blankets and up to his lap. Hugging her protectively, he said, "The cow will talk to Autumn and that'll help."

She gave a little laugh and looked up at him. "Cows don't talk."

But little girls should. "What do you mean, they don't talk?" He put on his best face of affront.

"Cows *moo.*"

"Ah, I guess you're right. Too bad, because talking about problems always helps. But you know, just because animals don't say things the way we do, they still communicate. They relate to us through trust. They accept the love given them, and have faith that no one will ever hurt them again." *Please have that faith.*

"Because Autumn won't let them be hurt?"

He tucked a long hank of red hair behind her ear. "Just as I would never let you be hurt." He waited, but she stayed quiet, so he asked, "Will you believe me, Sadie? I will never, ever let anyone hurt you."

Hugging him, she said, "Okay."

It scared him, so damn much, but he had to know. "Did your mama ever hurt you?"

"No."

"Are you sure? Or is this one of those secrets that you're not supposed to share?"

Shaking her head, she snuggled close again. "Sometimes she would get mad."

His heart thumped hard. "At you?"

"No. She'd just…be mad." She looked up, talking fast. "She'd make a lot of noise and cry and sometimes break things."

An invisible fist squeezed his throat, making him swallow twice before he could get words out. "I'm sorry." He rubbed his hand up and down her back. "I wish I'd known—"

"She said we couldn't tell." Lifting her small shoulder in a philosophical shrug, she added, "It was just sometimes. Don't be sad."

God love her, she was an amazing child. Deliberately erasing the torment from his expression and tone, he made himself smile. "How can I be sad when you're here with me now?" He punctuated that with a kiss to her forehead. "But I am sorry. I'm your daddy and I should have known." *I should have protected you.*

"It's okay." She patted his cheek.

"What did you do when your mama was that mad?"

"I played in my room."

"With the TV on?" He imagined it would help drown out the noise. Deb had obviously suffered worse depression than he'd ever imagined.

Nodding, Sadie leaned back in his arms and assured him, "I miss her but I like living with you."

"I *love* living with you. And just so you know," he teased, quickly tickling her ribs, "I'm keeping you until you're as old as I am, and then, *maybe*, if you want to move out on your own, I'll let you." He wanted to lighten her mood, and his, as well.

He figured he'd succeeded when she giggled happily, then settled again with a sigh. "Do you think we could help Autumn?"

"With the cow?"

She nodded. "Would she let us?"

"I'll talk to her about it." Since he didn't know much about cows, he couldn't promise anything beyond that. "How would you help?"

Her auburn lashes sent shadows over her eyes. "I could maybe read to the cow, like you read to me."

Very seriously, Tash said, "You are a good reader." It helped that she loved books. "You think the cow would like that?"

Sadie nodded. "I like it so maybe she would, too."

"Then tomorrow we'll go shopping for a few new books. Maybe something to do with farms and pastures and happy cows."

Grinning, Sadie squeezed him tight, then squirreled around until she got back under her comforter. "I'm ready to sleep now, 'kay?"

Tash bent to kiss the tip of her little button nose. "On one condition. If you want to talk more, if you have trouble sleeping, just let me know. Even if I've gone to bed, okay? You can always wake me up and I promise it won't be a problem."

After a wide yawn, she said, "Okay, Dad." She pulled her elephant close, her arms around it, the elephant's head tucked under her chin. "If you want to talk, you can wake me up, too."

"Deal." He smoothed her blankets, stood to go, then whispered, "I'm so very, very proud of you, Sadie." After one last smile, Tash left the room, touched, encouraged and, as he'd said, proud of the generous caring child he'd fathered.

Chapter Ten

After greeting her, Pavlov went back to bed. Smart dog. They should probably do the same, only Ember knew she couldn't sleep, and Autumn swore by the powers of her magic ice cream...

"So." Curled up in the corner of Autumn's comfy couch, Ember dug into her chocolate-latte ice cream. Heaven. Who knew such a thing existed? But it did, and her enterprising, ice-cream-loving sister had it. "Tell me about Tash."

Autumn gave her the look, the one that said she saw through her bullshit but would indulge her...for now.

"What do you want to know?"

Anything and everything that might distract her and give her something better to think about. "Is he a hot kisser?"

"Mmm," Autumn said, her mouth full. She nodded fast and swallowed. "*Very* hot."

Waving her spoon, Ember demanded, "Elaborate."

"He kissed me in the barn the other day."

"Ooooh, do tell."

"He took me by surprise, but once he kissed me, he kept kissing me. It was pretty awesome."

"Wow. Okay, this is good. Has he kissed you since then?"

Autumn focused on her ice cream. "He has."

Curious over her reaction, Ember asked, "*Really* kissed you?"

"Pecks mostly." In a rush, Autumn explained, "It's not like we can make out with Sadie there. Neither of us wants to do anything to make her uncomfortable."

"Hmmm…" The wheels started turning. Mike made her realize how little Autumn did for herself. While Ember went out nearly every night, Autumn stayed home. Alone.

Why had she never thought about that? Her sister was loving and sweet and…okay, not great at fashion, and she definitely didn't present herself as nicely as she could, but still—

"What are you doing?" Autumn asked with a lot of worried suspicion.

Ember pulled her most innocent expression.

Brows pulled together, Autumn thunked her ice-cream bowl loudly onto the table. "You're plotting something and I don't want you to."

For her sister to forgo her ice cream, she must be pretty serious. Time to switch tactics. "How do my roots look?"

Predictably, the switch threw Autumn. "Your roots?"

"Yeah, for my highlights." She turned her head and lifted out a hank of hair. Unlike Autumn, who left her dark brown hair alone, Ember liked to play. Right now she had bold reddish highlights pieced all through her hair, and in her opinion it was a pretty kick-ass look.

"They're okay. Still look nice." Picking up her bowl again, Autumn grumbled, "Don't go plotting. I can handle my own love life."

"Do you even *have* a love life?" Cutting short the answer she knew Autumn would give, she said, "Outside of what you read in your books."

Deflating, she shook her head. Going one further, she set aside her ice cream again and dropped her face in her hands.

Whoa. What was this? Autumn never acted all dramatic and forlorn. That was more Ember's speed—coached out of her by their mother from a very young age. For as far back as she could remember, her mother had harped on Autumn being the responsible one while telling Ember she was a *free spirit*, whatever the hell that meant. Probably code for flighty, or unreliable, or something even worse.

There were times it gave her carte blanche to be bad. A free spirit had to do what a free spirit had to do, right?

She snorted to herself.

Her folks might not believe it, and obviously Mike didn't, either, but *she* could be reliable. She could be as responsible as necessary. She could—

Through her fingers, Autumn muttered, "Stop that."

Uncanny how Autumn read her even with her face hidden.

"What are you doing, Autumn?" An awful thought struck her and she asked, "Was the cow hurt? You said it wasn't, and I didn't see any injuries, but you're better at that than me, so I believed you. Now you're all morose and—"

The fingers parted for a glare. "Tash wants a relationship, but sex is iffy."

Hold the phone! Scooping the last bite of ice cream out of her bowl, Ember set hers away too. First things first. "The cow will be okay?"

"We'll make it so."

Dropping back to the couch with relief, she asked, "No sex?"

Miserable, Autumn sprawled back, too. "It's not really possible. He said he likes me, he likes being with me, and Sadie adores me." Expression softening, Autumn said, "I'm pretty nuts about her, as well."

"Yeah, she's a doll. But…no sex? Seriously?"

"Sadie is adjusting, you know? So it's not like Tash will leave her with someone just to, um..."

"Do the horizontal mambo? Light your fire? Make you scream with torrid—"

Laughing, Autumn said, "Stop."

"Autumn." Her sis might have trouble saying it, but Ember wasn't nearly that discreet. "Sex. The man won't make time to have sex. With *you*."

Autumn closed her eyes. "Yeah."

Energized, Ember sat forward again. "It wouldn't have to be a straight shot to the bedroom! You could go on an actual date, dinner, maybe a movie, then do the nasty." She bobbed her eyebrows. "God knows, you're ripe for the pickin'."

Cocking open an eye, Autumn stared. "Once more for the record—he's new to town. He doesn't have a babysitter and doesn't want to leave her yet, anyway."

"My opinion—"

"*I didn't ask.*"

"—is that he can't help her by smothering her." She picked up Autumn's bowl. "What flavor did you have?"

"Strawberry Marshmallow Crunch."

"Oh, my god, that sounds amazing." Taking a big bite, Ember let it melt on her tongue with humming satisfaction.

"Hey! I was going to eat th—"

"Delicious." Settling back again—with Autumn's share of the magic ice cream—Ember asked, "So...do you want to get him naked? Do you want him in a bed? Or against the wall, or maybe over the table?"

Autumn snickered again. "I hadn't even thought about...well, walls and tables."

"But you *have* thought about the bed, right?"

Autumn eyed her ice-cream bowl, twisted her mouth and nodded. "You've seen him. You've talked to him. What do you think?"

"I think you've been on a very—and I mean *v-e-e-r-r-ry*—long bout of denial and you've got to be primed. Like…ready to explode, right?"

"Will you stop that?"

"I mean, even before Tash, there was only *Chuck*, right?" She said his name with a sneer, then gave a delicate shudder of revulsion.

Slumping more, Autumn nodded.

"And he couldn't have been any good, because—seriously—awesome as this ice cream is, sex can blow your mind. You just need the right guy." She took another slow, savoring bite, then picked up where she'd left off. "So, yeah, Tash is yummy. A gorgeous hunk, and nice, too. I bet he's good." With any luck, he'd be a dynamo in the sack, which was just what her far-too-responsible sister needed.

Autumn heaved a sigh. "Yeah, I'm thinking he would be, too."

Hmm…given that moony-eyed expression, Autumn had been thinking about it a lot, and that made up her mind. "It's decided, then. Leave it to your little sis to take care of things, okay?"

"What? No." Alarm brought Autumn forward until she sat on the edge of the couch, looking like she might leap with the right provocation. "Don't you dare do a single thing!"

Ember waved away that order. "This really is magic ice cream. I feel better already."

Snatching away the bowl, Autumn said, "You feel better because you're zoned in on me!"

True. Solving Autumn's lack-of-nooky problem proved a very nice distraction from her own issues. She knew exactly how she'd handle things, and in no time at all—

"Let's talk about you for a bit."

Ember noted the evil delight in Autumn's tone, but she'd wanted to talk to her about stuff anyway. Autumn was always her go-to when life got a little heavy.

Her sister had a very commonsense approach to all problems. "Mike is awesome."

Surprised at her willingness to share, Autumn stared. "Yes, he is." She chewed her lip and said, "So you finally realize it?"

"I've always known. And he wants me. In the sack. Maybe in the lake, come to think of it. He would have been willing the other day if you hadn't shown up."

"I really am sorry—"

Ember sighed. Loudly. After all, it was her turn to unburden. "Thing is, he doesn't like me."

Softening in that familiar way, Autumn said, "I don't believe that."

"Yeah, well, he said he wants sex, *only* sex, and then he'll have me out of his system and we can both go off on our merry way."

Autumn's jaw dropped. "That…"

"Dick? I know. I was pretty irked, too." The more she'd thought about it, the less she wanted to tell him off, and the more she wanted to prove him wrong.

Autumn scooted closer. "Are you sure you didn't misunderstand?"

"Nope. He was real clear about it." Even with Autumn, she wasn't ready to tell her whole plan, but she could share a few of the details. "Good as this ice cream is, sex is a major cure-all for me, and Mike could be right. Maybe I'll have him once and won't even want him again."

Settling in to hear more, Autumn asked carefully, "But you do want him?"

"Oh, yeah. Big-time." And when she had him, she'd make it so damn good he'd be addicted.

It suddenly struck Ember as funny. Once she started laughing, she couldn't stop.

"Are you going hysterical?" Autumn asked with worry.

Laughing too hard to answer, Ember shook her head. She'd

eaten all the ice cream, so maybe that was part of her lifted spirits, but the facts were pretty humorous, too.

"Ember...?"

Wiping her eyes and taking a few calming breaths, she managed to get her guffaws under control but couldn't do anything about her grin. "Do you realize Tash wants you for everything without sex involved, and Mike only wants me for sex and nothing else? How's that for irony?"

"Oh." Autumn's mouth twitched. "I have a no-sex relationship, and you have a sex-only relationship."

"Except I haven't yet had the sex!" Because that started her roaring with laughter again, she slapped her knee.

Autumn started to chuckle. "Oh, man, we're a pair." Laughter being contagious, her chuckles grew until she fell against Ember, both of them snorting and choking and laughing until they cried.

"I've got it!" Ember managed to say with glee. "I'll tell Mike he can't get any until Tash gets it, and then he'll get on Tash and make him—"

"Don't you dare," Autumn said, laughing.

"It'll fix things right up. Maybe Tash can give him some pointers on actually caring while they're at it." Oops, yeah, she hadn't meant to say that.

Quickly sobering, Autumn smiled and gently asked, "Is that what you want?"

Exhaustion sent her emotions on a roller-coaster ride. "No. Screw that. Screw *him*." She snickered again. "That's the plan."

Autumn wiped her eyes and drew Ember in for a hug. A really tight you're-my-sister-and-I-love-you hug that left her completely undone. For only a moment, she clung to her. Autumn was so strong, so resilient, and she wanted to sob because comparisons sucked.

That wouldn't be fair, so she drank in a few shattered breaths and finally got herself under control.

"I'm pooped," she said, sitting back. "You?"

"Pretty much, but if you want to stay—"

Just like Autumn, always there for her, no matter what. Damn it, that almost got her crying. "We both need to get some sleep." She stood and carried the bowls to the kitchen sink, and Autumn followed. "Thanks for the laughs, the ice cream, the chitchat and the hug."

Standing quietly at the counter, Autumn asked, "Did it help?"

"Bunches." Her phone dinged and she pulled it out to read the text. "Mike says the cow is safe and sound with Ivey and her preliminary check didn't show any serious medical issues. She'll be in touch with one of us tomorrow."

Brought back to reality and the suckiness of unfeeling jerks, Autumn rubbed her tired eyes and nodded. "We'll give her lots of love. She'll flourish here. And Pavlov is going to love her."

Pavlov's nails sounded on the wooden floor and a second later he poked his head around the doorway.

"Did he hear his name?" Ember asked with amazement.

"Probably."

He'd ignored all their babble, their cry-laughing—or laugh-crying...whatever—but now he looked ready to join in the conversation.

"Pavlov, love, you are eerily intuitive."

"No kidding." Using both hands, Autumn pushed back her hair. "Get some sleep. We'll talk in the morning."

"That we will." Because she had plans to help her sis, whether Autumn wanted her help or not.

A week later, Autumn finally had a morning free. She and Sadie had already chosen all the colors for her bedroom. Painters would show up soon, so Sadie's furniture had been piled in the middle of the floor. Currently she slept in a blanket fort in the living room, with Tash on the couch.

Like so many other things, that endeared him to Autumn.

He never missed an opportunity to make Sadie feel special, and to encourage her fun.

It was because of that, as much as everything else, that she knew she was falling in love.

The days since the cow rescue, as Sadie called it, had actually been...fun. Crazy fun. When she wasn't at their house working on the renovations, they came to the farm and helped with everything. Sadie, the little darling, spent much of her time reading to the cow. Often Pavlov sat with her, his ears twitching this way and that as she spoke.

They were at the farm again this morning, invited by Ember, the rat, to take part in her day with her mom and dad. True, Tash came in handy, helping her father from his wheelchair to the old van they used when taking him to appointments or for an afternoon out. Her mother insisted that he couldn't stay home and "languish," though anyone who met her dad knew he wasn't wallowing in self-pity.

With her mom and dad both in the air-conditioned van, she and Tash went to collect Sadie.

His arm around her, Tash said, "You're great with your folks."

Meaning she did well deflecting insults and catering to requests? Probably. She knew her mother meant well, but so far that morning she'd pointed out no less than three times that Autumn had issues. Her hair needed styling. Her clothes were too loose. She should learn to wear makeup...like Ember did.

In fact, her mother wanted her to look to Ember for many, many things, including "man advice," as she'd put it, while giving Tash a telling look.

Tash had covered for her, vowing with believable sincerity, "No, ma'am. Trust me, Autumn has that completely covered just by being herself." He'd sealed the deal with a quick kiss that curled her toes and made her mother smile with pride.

Her father, ever outrageous, had tried to kiss her mom, too, but luckily, she'd dodged him.

"I love them." She glanced up at Tash, seeing him gilded by the morning sunshine, and confessed, "But sometimes they are a challenge."

His smile shared understanding, but something more. "Most parents are challenging, you know? I shudder to think what Sadie will one day say about me. I love her, but I still make mistakes and sometimes say the wrong things." Giving her a one-armed hug, he said, "You're probably too close to the situation, and I'm sure the constant judgment is a grind, but they're so proud of you. Your dad, especially, looks at you like you could handle a hurricane one-handed."

She laughed at that. "Dad is easier than Mom."

Instead of arguing that—because, no way he could—he said, "You know, I wonder how Ember feels being labeled the flighty one."

But…no. "She's not. She's the vivacious one, the pretty one—"

"You, lady, are gorgeous, so don't try to sell me that."

Wow, he sounded like he really meant that. "Um, thanks. But *they* think she's the pretty one and the lovely free spirit—"

"Meaning unreliable? Irresponsible? That's how it sounds to me, but I know Ember well enough now to see that's not true. She's different from you, yes, but she's a hard worker. She's funny, and she's kind to Sadie and all the neighborhood kids."

Holy smokes, why had she never considered that? Her mother did try to pigeonhole them both, and maybe Ember disliked her assigned role as much as Autumn did.

She leaned into Tash. "Thank you. You've given me a lot to think about."

They reached the barn and heard Sadie talking softly to the cow. The animal had proven gentle but skittish, had shied away from people, though Autumn and Ember continued to work with her, knowing she'd eventually trust them.

Now, though, with Sadie's sweet voice praising her, the cow

had moved forward and had her nose stuck through the rails of her stall. Very, very gently, Sadie stroked her nose.

Crazy, but tears burned Autumn's eyes. She sniffed, and without looking at her, Tash hugged her again.

His voice quiet, he said, "Sadie."

She looked up with a brilliant smile. "Look, Dad," she whispered. "She's letting me pet her."

"So I see."

Autumn swallowed heavily. "Have you thought of a name yet?"

Ponytail bouncing, Sadie shook her head. "I will, though."

"I know." Autumn reached out a hand. "Are you ready to go? My parents are in the van and Mike will be here soon to let the cow out to a pasture."

"Pavlov will go with her, huh?"

"Yes, Pavlov is very protective of new animals." He could do what they couldn't—get close, nuzzle and cuddle—and the cow seemed to love it. "Yesterday, I found him curled against her belly when she lay down in the field." The memory had her smiling. "I took a photo with my phone. Let's get going and I'll show you."

Going on tiptoe, Sadie kissed the cow on the nose and told her goodbye. The look on Tash's face was priceless. He appeared equal parts repulsed, amused and touched by his daughter's caring.

"She's special," Autumn whispered. "And I promise the kiss won't hurt her. I've done the same a few times myself over the years."

On the way back to the van, she handed Sadie her phone with the photo of the animals together. Sadie was in mid-"awww" when a text came in.

Handing back the phone, she said, "It's nobody."

Wondering at that, Autumn glanced at the screen and saw Chuck's name. The laugh took her by surprise. "You," she said to Sadie, "are incorrigible, but I like it."

"She means you say what you think," Tash said before Sadie could ask. He leaned toward Autumn and whispered, "But I agree with your assessment."

Are you getting my texts Get in touch Missed you

Still no punctuation, but with or without it, he spoke nonsense. She started to put her cell back in her pocket.

His step a bit more stiff, Tash asked, "Not going to reply?"

She snorted. "To him? No."

Brows coming together, he looked ahead to where the van waited, then down to his daughter. Whatever he thought, the circumstances must've convinced him to keep it to himself.

Or so she thought.

Once they reached the van, he got Sadie settled inside next to Tracy, then walked around the front. Though he'd offered to drive, Autumn had refused, yet he didn't go to the passenger side. Instead he kept her from opening the front door and said near her ear, "You need to tell him to get lost."

"He'll figure that out on his own."

"I don't think so, honey. Plus, our relationship will only work if he's told about it." With that, he opened her door for her— which meant everyone inside could hear if she tried to reply.

Dirty pool.

As she got in and buckled her seat belt, she wondered how he'd meant that. Was he reiterating the purpose of their relationship—to help get rid of Chuck? Or did he mean he felt possessive and couldn't stay in a relationship with another guy on the fringe?

Blasted men could be so confusing.

On the drive to town she tuned out her mother's complaints and let Tash deal with any questions Sadie had. Her father just enjoyed being out. Despite the heat, he'd rolled down his window a little to breathe in the fresh air.

In so many ways, he was the opposite of her mom. Always good-natured, accepting of his circumstances without letting them get him down and grateful for anything she did.

She glanced at Tash. He seemed equally lost in thought. Maybe even stewing.

What kind of husband would he be? Someday he'd remarry, right? That'd only make sense.

Into the silence, her mother asked Sadie, "Do you have any close cousins? Any other kids in the family your age?"

Tash answered for her. "I was an only child, Tracy, remember?"

"Yes, but what about her mother?"

"Deb was an only child, too."

And Sadie, innocence personified, announced, "I want a sister."

Autumn's breath strangled in her throat.

Tash twisted to see his daughter. "You do, huh?"

"Like Autumn and Ember. That'd be fun, huh?"

Autumn bit her lip, then gasped when her father murmured, "Shoul' pro'bly get married first."

Grinning, Tash leveled his devastating gaze on her. "Maybe someday."

Autumn felt his hot, speculative attention as surely as a stroke of his fingers over her skin. *Someday?* Yeah, someday sounded incredible to her, but she just kept her eyes fixed on the road and pretended a great preoccupation with her driving as they went over the railroad tracks.

"I want a sister," Sadie said again. "She should be named Ella."

In a brief show of understanding, Tash patted her thigh, then turned to look at Sadie again. "Got a name picked out and everything?"

"Yes, and she could have dark hair like Autumn and Ember."

"But your red hair is so pretty," Tash said.

"It's stunning," Autumn agreed.

"Ella." Her mother considered the name. "Ella, Ella. Hmm… Ella and Sadie. It's lovely," she pronounced, as if a sibling was a foregone conclusion. "I like it."

Oh-so-reasonably, Tash said, "You're right, Tracy. Sadie has very good taste."

Sadie went quiet in thought for a moment, then said, "Tracy is pretty, too."

"Oh." Flustered, her mom giggled. "Thank you. I've always liked it."

"I know," Sadie with a flash of excitement. "That's what we'll name the cow."

"Ella?" Tash asked.

"No." With an excess of mischievous delight, Sadie stated, "I'm going to call her *Tracy*."

Her dad burst out laughing, which made Tash crack a grin, and that made her start to snicker.

Pretty soon they were all cracking up—everyone except Tracy.

Once in town, Tracy and Flynn insisted they were fine on their own as they paused outside the restaurant.

"I need to get a few things." Tracy indicated the art-supply store a few buildings up.

Flynn said, "I'm going with her. Gotta make sure she doesn't buy out the store."

"Ha!" Tracy looked down on him with fondness. "You stick close because you think other men flirt with me."

"'Course they do," Flynn said, his affected voice a little deeper with his own affection. "No man could resist."

Ill at ease with their teasing, Autumn said, "When you're ready, Mom, just text me. We'll be at the restaurant having breakfast."

Tracy patted Sadie on the head, told them all goodbye and walked alongside Flynn's wheelchair as they headed up the walkway.

On the way into the restaurant, Sadie said, "I want waffles and fruit."

"Sounds very healthy." He kept one hand on Sadie's back, the other on Autumn's, as they started toward a back table. Almost there, Autumn tripped to a halt. He glanced at her, then to where she stared... Chuck Conning.

All around them, diners chatted, forks clinking against plates, kids slurping through straws. Tash tuned it all out, his single focus the man sitting there laughing with a friend.

As if he hadn't hurt her. Hadn't broken her heart.

Satisfaction fed into his bloodstream, burning straight to his heart to make it thump harder. Anticipation took him forward two steps. Finally he could confront the bastard.

Autumn couldn't dodge his attention any longer.

Chuck looked up, saw Tash and started to smile...until he noticed Autumn standing rigidly behind him. Chuck's smile faltered, then eased into a scowl as he pushed back his chair.

One glance, and Tash saw that he'd gone soft around the middle, his face having lost all angles in favor of rounded curves. Pudgy cheeks, the start of a double chin. His jeans fit snug beneath a thickened belly.

If he'd ever been a good-looking guy, he wasn't anymore...at least, not to Tash. Autumn must have seen something in him—*what* he didn't know.

Then he remembered Mike saying a lot of women found him attractive. Go figure.

A fake smile moved the flesh of Chuck's face. "Tash, long time no see."

Tash accepted the hand he offered. "It's been a while."

"How long have you been in town?"

"I moved back at the beginning of summer." He smiled toward Autumn. "But I've been busy."

Chuck's gaze slid to her, too. "Is that so?"

One step back, and Tash was able to put his arm around Autumn's shoulders, drawing her forward.

During his and Chuck's brief exchange, she'd recovered enough to say, "Chuck. How've you been?"

Sadie stuck close to her, nearly wrapped around her leg, her vivid blue eyes shooting daggers at Chuck.

Huh. His daughter had great instincts.

Following an uncomfortable glance at Tash, Chuck said, "I wanted to talk to you, honey. Didn't you get my texts?"

"She's ignoring you," Sadie stated, still mean-mugging him.

Taken aback, Chuck gave a short, uneasy laugh. "And who are you?"

"My daughter, Sadie." Tash wondered if there was a tactful way to peel Sadie away, but then Autumn rested her hand on Sadie's shoulder and smiled down at her.

"That's right, Sadie. And I think we'll ignore him now, too. Come on." She took two steps, realized Tash wasn't budging and frowned at him. "Let's get a table."

"I'll be right there."

Her eyes flared, then narrowed in warning. Looking between him and Chuck, she got her back up with ire. "No, I don't think so." Sadie stood in militant silence beside her.

My girls, he thought, recognizing this new sensation of unadulterated pride.

Fine. He could handle this Autumn's way. In fact, he found it preferable. No reason for false civility.

Shrugging, he turned to Chuck. "You heard the lady." Paying no attention to the few customers now interested in their exchange, Tash said, "She wants nothing to do with you, and I don't want you hassling her, so no more texts." A condescending pat on the shoulder emphasized how little Chuck meant. "I'm the possessive sort. Remember that."

Chapter Eleven

"He did *what*?" Ember asked.

"Warned Chuck off, like some, some...caveman."

"What did you do?"

"When I saw Chuck?" Hiding her face in her hands, Autumn groaned. "I froze. Like a great big coward." God, it shamed her. "All my talk of handling things, refusing to let anyone else speak up for me...and then I couldn't speak for myself."

Her voice velvety with understanding, Ember said, "You put too much on yourself, sis. What he did to you was pretty damn devastating. Of course, it'd be hard to see the dick again."

That made her choke out a laugh. "I thought for sure I'd—"

"What? Be strong and unshakable?" Ember emitted a long sigh. "Honestly, it's nice to know you're human. I mean, I'd have spared you if I could, you know that."

Her hands fell away. Ember's tone bothered her. "I know."

"It's just that I still crumble over hearing a baby cry in a store, even if I can't see him. I turn into this giant well of misery. But you talk about Chuck, you're told he's back in town, the bastard *texts* you and you just roll on like nothing happened. Like it doesn't matter."

"It matters."

She sighed again, this one more of a huff. "Right. I know. I'm still happy to punch him in the throat if you want."

"I don't think that's necessary."

"The thing is…the way you reacted makes me feel less like a weak emotional mess, because you're one of the strongest people I know."

Apparently Tash was right. Reaching out, Autumn caught her sister's hand. "I'm no better at being strong than you are."

"Ha. I'm the free spirit, remember? No one expects—"

"Don't spout Mom's nonsense to me. That's all it is, you know? Nonsense. You don't have to live up to her expectations."

"You mean live down to them?" She squeezed Autumn's fingers before releasing her. "How did I end up making this conversation about me?" Smacking a palm to her forehead, Ember said, "I'm sorry. Definitely wasn't my intent. Now, about you—did Tash at least manhandle him a little?"

"No, of course not. He just jumped in and said the things I should have said, the things that stuck in my throat."

"And? You reacted to that *how*?"

Heat crawled up her neck to pulse in her cheeks. It hadn't been her best performance. "I stewed. I did the whole stupid silent-treatment thing, at least to him. Sadie and I talked, though. Then when we got back here, Tash acted like nothing had happened. He hugged me—in front of Mom and Dad and Sadie—and he kissed me! Do you believe the nerve?" She was still confused by that and didn't know what to think. "He even stuck around to help get Dad and all of Mom's supplies into the house."

Sitting in the grass, Ember focused her gaze on Tash the turkey as he followed the hens around. "He's jealous."

Dropping down to sit beside her, Autumn said, "That's not funny."

"No, what's not funny is that you are so damn oblivious." Ember shook her head in pity. "The man wants you—in *every* way. Show some balls and ask him, and you'll see I'm right."

"I don't have balls," she argued, stalling for time to get her thoughts in order. She'd expected Ember to be as outraged by Tash's behavior as she was.

Or had been.

Something.

The more she thought about it, the more it seemed…protective instead of intrusive. He'd not only thrown her a line while she was sinking, but he'd also commandeered the ship…and steered it right into Chuck.

"So grow a pair—figuratively, at least. Go right up to him, maybe when Sadie isn't next to you listening in, because you know 'little pitchers have big ears,' and then ask him outright." Ember leaned back on her forearms. "I dare you."

Sitting yoga-style, her elbows resting on her knees, Autumn stalled. "I remember Mom saying that to Dad all the time. He'd be getting frisky and she'd say—not really in a whisper—that we were there listening and—"

They finished together, "'Little pitchers have big ears.'"

"Not like we wanted to hear him telling her how sexy she is," Ember pointed out.

With a shudder, Autumn added, "And that she had a great ass."

They both snickered, equally disturbed and amused.

"But you know," Ember said, "now that I'm older and not so geeked by the idea of my parents hankering after each other, I think I eventually want a guy like that—a guy who wants me *all* the time, whether I'm busy cooking, or sweaty from being outside, or—"

"Present," Mike said from behind them.

Ember tumbled off her own elbows, floundered around and finally got mostly upright.

Uh-oh. Autumn watched her sister's eyes narrow and her mouth compress.

"You were eavesdropping again!"

As if Ember wasn't fuming, he sat down with them. "I saw you both out here communing with nature and decided to join you, but how could I have known you'd be talking sex?"

"Speaking of sex," Autumn said before Ember could detonate. She nodded toward Tash the turkey. "He's getting a little amorous with the hens, don't you think?"

Ember looked, her eyebrows shooting up. "I think that feathered hussy is encouraging him."

Mike wisely kept his mouth shut, but he did smile. "They'll be fine. He might pursue and she might flirt, but they won't mate."

In slow motion, Ember and Autumn swiveled their heads to stare at him.

"What?" he asked, all masculine innocence. "My parents had a farm."

"I didn't know you had parents." Ember frowned over the nonsense words as soon as they were out. "I mean, I realize you must, but you've never mentioned them or anything."

Now Mike leaned back on his elbows, a man at his leisure. "Yeah, I have parents. I talk with them often, keep up on Facebook—"

"You have Facebook?"

Shrugging, he said, "Private, just for family. Overall, I dislike social media."

Autumn and Ember shared a look, because they felt the same. Once, when their mother had considered joining Facebook, they vehemently discouraged her. The last thing either of them wanted was to see her obscene art posted for the world to view.

"Do you see your parents?" Ember asked.

"In person once or twice a year."

A horrible realization hit Autumn. "Is that because you're always working here?"

He tossed a clover at her. "No, hon. It's just that they're in California and I'm here and it's a long trip. Remember I was off four days last Christmas? I flew home then."

"But…" She felt worse and worse. "You should have taken at least a week."

His gaze went to Ember. "I miss this place when I'm not here."

Whoa. That look was so scorching, Autumn wondered why her sister didn't go up in smoke. Ember looked a little shell-shocked by it, too. Her lips parted, she drew a breath…then gathered herself.

Sitting straighter, Ember made a rewind gesture. "Go back." She cleared her throat and drew another bracing breath. "You have parents, so any siblings?"

"A brother. He's in Arizona, but usually when I visit California, he does, too. I have a sister-in-law who's terrific, and two nephews who think I walk on water."

Ember gawked.

Autumn wasn't much better. Never, not ever, did Mike talk about his past. He'd showed up one day after seeing their Help Wanted sign, and the rest was history.

"By the way," he said to Autumn, "your truck now has air. Sorry it took so long. I had to order a few parts."

Ember did another rewind. "So your brother is happily married?"

"Ten years now." He stared at her with enough heat to make Autumn blush, though Ember just took it in stride. "Why is that so shocking?"

"Because you're such a—a…*bachelor.*"

"Whew." Grinning, Mike pretended great relief. "Wasn't sure what insult would come out of that pretty mouth, but that's not too bad."

Ember punched his shoulder, pulled back in surprise at what she'd done and grumbled an apology.

Mike asked, "For what?"

"Punching you."

He cocked an eyebrow. "You punched me? When?"

That got him another punch, accompanied by a shove, which made him laugh as he went off balance. He grabbed Ember to him and kissed her.

Since he was on his back, Ember sprawled over him…and didn't look like she minded.

Ummm…again, Autumn felt like a voyeur. She tried to look anywhere and everywhere that didn't include her sister and Mike, but that took her gaze to Tash the turkey, and he was turning out to be a horny little guy, his tail feathers spread, his head low as he cozied up to a hen.

Quietly, she got to her feet, ready to tiptoe away.

Hearing her, Ember freed herself from Mike. "Wait."

Misunderstanding, Mike said, "Okay."

"I meant Autumn, not you."

He rose to one elbow, the heat in eyes shifting to something else, something just as intimate and maybe anticipatory. "Yeah?"

Ember patted his firm midsection, lingered a moment, then pulled her hand away. "You just need to pause for a bit until we straighten out a few things. But before that…" Turning her face up to Autumn's, she said, "Let's get Mike's opinion."

Oh. Dear. God. Gasping on a sharply indrawn breath, Autumn exhaled with, "Don't you *dare*—"

"Tash wants Autumn," Ember blurted, "don't you think?"

There it was, thrown out for Mike and the chickens and Tash the turkey to hear. Autumn considered throttling her sister.

Until Mike said, "He's got it for her bad. Why?"

Mike took in the smug satisfaction on Ember's face, and the pink mortification on Autumn's, and wondered what he'd been drawn into.

Another of Ember's no-holds-barred, well-intentioned assaults on her sister? Apparently.

One thing was certain: Autumn didn't want to talk about it. Equally certain: Ember would, anyway.

She might assume otherwise, but he actually liked that about her—the way she did and said whatever she thought was right, damn the consequences. That facet of her personality often embarrassed Autumn, but since Tash had been around, Autumn... bloomed. A dumb word, but it worked.

Autumn had always been incredible—incredibly sweet, incredibly smart, incredibly caring...and incredibly sexy, too.

She just hadn't known it. Based on things Ember said, Autumn had always been quieter and more contained, but clearly Chuck had done a number on her, making her even more withdrawn.

Now with Tash around she'd loosened up, and good thing, because Ember so obviously loved her sister and wanted the best for her, thus this new, direct attack.

"What I don't understand," Mike said, considering both sisters before settling on Autumn, "is why you don't already know that."

"He made a deal with her, that's why. A stupid deal that—"

A thick clump of dry grass hit Ember in the chest, then small pieces of attached earth slid down into her shirt.

"*You...*" Nostrils flared, Autumn searched for words but found none. She looked both hurt and furious and it made Mike uneasy.

"Autumn—" he said, ready to reassure her, to try to smooth over the antagonism.

At almost the same time, she said, "I told *you*, Ember. *Only* you. In *confidence.*"

He watched, enthralled, as Ember frowned, then lifted the hem of her shirt, trying to shake out the dirt and blades of grass.

"I know," she mumbled, pretty much pretending he wasn't

there, a fascinated observer, as she bared her stomach and flapped the hem of her T-shirt in a way that promised—but never quite delivered—a glimpse of her breasts.

In another culture, based on how it affected him, it might've been considered a mating dance.

Decidedly *un*affected—by his attention and her sister's ire— Ember explained, "But I want you happy, Autumn, and all this ridiculous denial won't do the trick."

Yeah, a lot of the missteps Ember made were well-intentioned. He knew it, and he presumed Autumn did, as well.

Lending her a hand in the explanations, he sat up and patted Autumn's knee. "Tash has it bad—and so do you. Whatever deal you did or didn't make, I can promise you, he wants more."

After one last scowl at her sister, Autumn eyed him, gauging the accuracy of his statement. After visual resistance, she gave in to a nervous nibble of her lip. "You're sure?"

Mike took great pleasure in saying, "Thousand percent."

"How do you know?"

"I'm a guy?" When she appeared unconvinced, he nodded with more certainty. "I'm a guy."

Autumn threw up her hands. "Well, whoop-de-do. You think that makes you more observant or smarter or—?"

"I know how guys think," he said, interrupting her tangent. "I have insight, right? I know hunger when I see it." He flicked the end of her nose. "You do, too, if you'd just trust yourself."

Mouth screwing to the side, she folded her arms and grumbled, "I am not your little sister."

Meaning it, he replied, "I'd like it if you were."

Ember scowled at them both. "Hello? Third person here and she's not invisible." She nodded at Autumn. "If she's like a sis, where does that leave me?"

"*Definitely* not related." He'd decided to open up with Ember, to let her know his background, what motivated him, what he

wanted out of life, in hopes that she would soften toward him…
and maybe open up a little in return.

Night after night, thoughts of her crowded his brain until he
couldn't concentrate on anything else. The way she laughed,
how she scowled, the look of her body in his wet T-shirt while
they swam, the taste of her mouth…the hurt in her eyes that
he'd caused.

That one really ate him up.

More and more each day he sought her out. Far too often their
exchanges ended in an argument, but he knew it was his fault.

In trying to be different from the hordes of guys constantly
chasing her, he'd blundered, and now he needed a chance to
correct things.

If he didn't have her soon, he'd go nuts.

What happened here this morning, having her pull him in as
backup, felt like progress. In fact, he moved to sit closer to her,
even brushed some grass off her shoulder.

And she let him.

Yup, definitely progress.

"Don't be mad at her, Autumn." He braced his hand behind
Ember in an almost embrace. "Your sister recognizes Tash's interest, too. God knows she's had plenty of experience with guys
looking at her that way."

Ember's chin lifted. "The way *you* look at me?"

"Exactly." Using that as an opening, he brought his palm to
the small of her back, traced up her spine, and when she didn't
object, he hugged her into his side. "That would be the look."

Autumn's gaze zipped back and forth between them. "Huh."

"It's obvious, right?"

"With you two, sure." She glanced out at the yard. "It's even
clear on Tash the turkey." Her dark gaze came back to his. "But
Tash the man is different. He's motivated by other things."

"His daughter," Mike acknowledged. "That's the biggie. New
home, new job, too." He coasted his palm over Ember's back,

down to her hip, without looking away from Autumn. "Yet he made time for you. Says something, don't you think?"

Ember cleared her throat. "Well, Autumn? Tell him about the deal."

Autumn shot her another I'll-smack-you-later look, then heaved a sigh. "Tash set up this...mock relationship? See, Sadie likes me—"

"Of course she does."

"—so it's a way for her to visit with me more."

"Uh-huh," he said with a lot of blatant doubt.

"It works for me, too, because if Chuck knows I'm in a relationship, he should leave me alone, right?"

That sent a little fire up his spine. "Has he been bothering you again?"

Once more, before Autumn could say a word, Ember jumped in, rattling through the details of Chuck and the diner and Tash telling him off.

Score one for Tash.

"Yeah," Mike said, his tone dry, "that sounds like Tash faking a relationship."

Autumn's mouth opened...then closed.

Ember grinned. "Right?" She elbowed his ribs in a show of camaraderie. "You see, Autumn? The man is totally in to you."

"Totally," Mike agreed, hugging Ember closer so she couldn't gouge him again with that weapon she called an elbow.

"Then why the no-sex rule?"

The... He blinked at her. "Come again?"

"She can't," Ember said, her grin cheeky, her eyebrows bobbing. "No sex means she can't even come once, much less a second time."

Hearing words like *sex* and *come* from Ember's lips did profound things to him, made him stare at her mouth and think things he shouldn't—at least, things he shouldn't think about right now, with Autumn not just the topic, but close by.

He looked at Autumn.

She put her face in her hands.

He settled on Ember, since at least he could see her. "Seriously, there's a rule?" Damn it, he still sounded stupid, but it was a stupid rule. "You're kidding, right?"

"Tell him, Autumn."

"Why?" The question was muffled behind her hands. "You're so chatty and everything."

This time, though, when Ember was ready to speak, Autumn snapped up her head. "Tash assured me there would be no sex." Embarrassment burned her face, but she continued. "He said he doesn't have opportunity with Sadie out of school and..." Eyes widening, her words trailed off.

"And?" Mike prompted. He wanted to hear whatever other idiocy there was so he could discount it. He knew Tash. He liked him.

The guy was not stupid, so it couldn't be his stupid rule.

Autumn's eyes sank shut. "And I told him ice cream was better than sex."

"What the hell kind of ice cream are you eating?"

Ember leaned into him. "It's really good."

No. Damn. Way. "Not *that* good."

"No," Ember agreed, smiling. "Not that good." Her fingers walked up his chest and she whispered, "But it's close."

"No," he stated, catching her hand and flattening it over his thumping heart. "Give me half a chance and I'll prove to you it isn't."

This time the clump of grass hit him. Ember jumped back, startled. They both stared at Autumn.

"Could you two knock it off already? Now that Ember has blabbed my entire life to you, you might as well give me some advice."

Oh, man, Tash was going to owe him big-time. Rolling a

shoulder and hiding his grin, Mike said, "Tell him the ice cream isn't cutting it anymore."

"Ember said I had to ask him for sex."

Gasping, Ember hurled grass back at her. "I told you to ask him if he *wanted* it."

"You don't have to do either one." Getting into the moment, Mike sat forward. "Seriously. Just say 'The ice cream isn't cutting it these days.' He'll take it from there."

"I don't know." Autumn worried her bottom lip in her teeth. "I mean, there's still the issue of Sadie. No way would Tash leave her with a babysitter—"

"He totally would if he felt good about it." Ember held out her arms. "Behold, I have a solution."

Behold, Mike thought, *you have something.*

Many things, actually—all of them wicked and delicious and they tempted him more than she realized.

"Invite them over one evening," Ember instructed, animated in her sincerity. "Let me know when they can make it, and I'll finagle a girls' day at the salon with Sadie. I'll treat her to a trim, blow-dry and mani-pedi. It'll be terrific—for her and me, because she really is a little sweetheart."

Ember and a kid? Who'd have thought? But she seemed excited for the time she'd spend with Sadie.

Autumn touched her sister's knee. "Em, are you sure…?" She glanced at him, and Mike felt like something profound was happening. Clearing her throat, Autumn started again, and said, "You really think that's a good idea."

With a firm nod, Ember said, "Yes."

"But…" Another sly look at Mike.

What the hell?

"I don't want to—"

"Stress me? Make me fall apart?" With a poignant little smile, Ember shook her head. "It'll be fine, Autumn. I promise." She glanced at him, too. "I was going to tell Mike, anyway."

Tell him *what?* On alert, Mike sat a little straighter. "Everything okay?"

Ember nodded, and with Autumn's compassion-filled eyes trained on her, she said, "A little more than a year ago, I was pregnant..."

His heart nearly stopped.

"It was a little boy, and...and I loved him. So much." She swallowed heavily. "From the moment I knew, I wanted him."

Muscles from his neck to the soles of his feet tensed tight enough to cramp. "I don't..." Don't know what to say. Don't know what to do.

Don't know what to *feel.* "Ember?"

"Two months into the pregnancy, I lost him." Her lips quivered, but just for a moment, then she firmed them. "I know you won't understand, but I still miss him."

More than anything, Mike wanted to scoop her up and onto his lap. Ember's hand covered Autumn's on her knee, and they laced their fingers together.

Sisters, always there for each other, sometimes arguing, other times—like now—being so damn supportive it made his eyes burn.

He felt left out, but if it made Ember feel better—

With her other hand she reached out and drew a soft breath when he cradled it between both of his own.

Her hand was so small, so delicate, in direct contrast to her usual balls-to-the-wall attitude and her unique ability to build anything, to stand in the sun all day using heavy power tools and still look good while doing it.

Wearing a small, secret smile, Autumn pulled free and stood. Very softly, she whispered, "I'll go call Tash, maybe set up my hot date." She trailed her hand over Ember's hair, smoothing it, and then patted his shoulder.

Without making a sound, she walked away.

Mike lifted Ember's hand to his mouth and pressed a kiss to her knuckles. "I'm sorry. I had no idea."

Her smile flickered, mostly with sadness. "Because I'm the party girl, right?"

"Because you deliberately give that impression, yes."

She didn't deny it. "Mom has always said I was a party girl, the free spirit like her."

Cupping a hand to her face, Mike stroked her warm skin. "No one said you had to prove her right."

She acknowledged that with a smirk. "It became habit, you know? An easy out for me when I didn't want to follow my parents' rules. I never exactly felt bad about it, and you're right, I used it as cover after I lost my baby." She swallowed heavily, her eyes going liquid before she drew air through her nose. "Then you happened."

Unsure how to take that, Mike kept quiet.

"You pointed out how I'm sometimes unfair to Autumn."

God, he felt like an asshole. "You and your sister are closer than anyone I know. She not only loves you, she relies on you."

Ember nodded. "And I on her." She moistened her lips. "I rely on her more than you probably realize. Or maybe you do see it, and that's why you—"

"Forget anything I said. I was a dick."

That got a laugh. "A *little* dick, maybe."

"Ha! Those are two words no man wants to hear together."

This smile was more genuine. "We can discuss that later. Right now, I decided it's time I stopped hiding. I mean, I keep pushing Autumn to get out there, to go for what she wants."

His heart started that heavy tempo again, a rhythm more of hope than anything else. "Yes, you do. But you aren't wrong. Autumn shouldn't feel so uncertain with Tash."

"And I don't want to feel uncertain with you."

Yup, his heart tried to punch out of his chest. "Then don't."

"The thing is, I think we want different things. You were refreshingly upfront about sex. I want sex, don't get me wrong."

Thank God.

"But I want...more. Marriage, a family, kids—" She suddenly took in his expression—which, admittedly, was probably somewhere between shock and incredulity—and she laughed. "Relax, Mike. I'm not proposing."

Why didn't that assurance help?

"I'm just saying, I don't want a one-night stand. I don't want to have sex just so you can get me out of your system, or whatever it was you said."

Close enough, damn it.

"I want someone who likes me, who maybe wants to see where a relationship can go."

Words—they were out there somewhere, but not close enough for him to catch and form into coherent sentences. "Ummm..."

"Right." She leaned in, lightly touched her mouth to his and said, "This is my cue to mosey on and give you time to think."

Meaning...sex would not be on the immediate agenda. Disappointment was there, but something else diluted it, something like...interest? Yeah, the idea of a solid relationship with Ember sounded pretty damn sweet. Funny, because he'd soured on relationships. Or had he?

He stood with her, kept her hand enclosed in his when she would have pulled away, and smiled as he started them back toward the house. "How much time are you giving me to stew on this?"

"I said to think, not to stew. How much time do you think you need?"

Two minutes? No, she wouldn't buy that. "How about this. We start talking, really talking, so that we know each other better. No more secrets, okay?"

"I don't have any other secrets."

"Yeah, well, I have a few." Aha, that got her attention in a big way. "We'll visit until you're comfortable. You set the pace."

"So far I like your plan."

"Great, but here's the part you might not like. You spend all your free time with me." When her eyes narrowed, he explained, "No sex, until you want it. I take it you're not too shy to speak up?"

"Not shy at all."

"Terrific. Until then, no other guys."

"And no other women?"

"You're into women?" He caught her fist before she could swing it. Laughing a little, he said, "Okay, so you meant me? Sure. No other women." He hadn't wanted anyone else, not for a while now. "What do you think?"

"I think I want to know your secret."

"Secrets, plural. We'll start with one, okay?" They'd just reached the barn. She would go on to her place in the house, and he'd go around to the stairs that led to his loft. "If you want to hear another, go to dinner with me tomorrow."

Without asking for details, she said, "Fine. Lay it on me."

Oh, this was going to be too easy. Leaning in, Mike whispered near her ear, "I'm not the poor farmhand you imagine me to be."

"Mike," she began, her voice soft with guilt, "I never meant—"

He lightly bit her earlobe. "I'm fairly set financially, maybe even what you'd call well-to-do." He teased his tongue over the whorl of her ear before straightening. "Now you can think about why I've stayed, and why I like working here so much." With a final quick kiss, he headed through the barn and out the back door...aware of Ember staring at his back the entire way.

Chapter Twelve

Just shy of a week later, Autumn bustled around the kitchen, Pavlov underfoot, while she put the finishing touches on dinner. Given the relentless heat wave, she'd opted for spaghetti and salad that they'd eat indoors at her little four-seat kitchen table.

Ember, in the way almost as much as the dog, poked a fork into the spaghetti. "I like that you left your hair down."

Imagining how Ember would have reacted if she'd tied it up, Autumn told her, "I even put on some mascara." She batted her eyelashes at her to prove it.

Ember grabbed her chest as if in shock. "Tash has worked a miracle." Dropping her hand, she said, "Now tell me you're wearing pretty underwear."

Studiously avoiding eye contact, Autumn said, "Pretty enough."

"Autumn," her sister groaned.

"You sound like Tracy." She felt the need to clarify. "Tracy the cow, not our mother."

"Either way, it's an insult." Ember gave her a long look. "The underwear?"

"What? You know me. I'm into comfort. Nothing sexy or too risqué, but they *are* pretty, I promise." Cotton, but so what? She'd bet Tash's boxers were cotton, too. At least hers had a little lace around the band.

She hoped his didn't.

"I bought some really sinful stuff for when I give in to Mike. I could go grab them for you."

Stunned, Autumn halted in the middle of the floor to gawk at Ember. "First, ewww, I'm not wearing your underwear."

"Hello. I said they're new."

"Second, your underwear would not fit me." Not even close. Where Ember was svelte, Autumn was...well, not. "Now back 'er up a bit. You and Mike?"

"Yeah." Ember hugged herself, peeked over at Autumn, and admitted, "I've spent nearly every night with him."

"*What?*" Stirring the sauce one last time, Autumn turned it on low and covered it. This conversation required all her attention. "You didn't say anything!"

"I know," Ember said with apology. "It's just that I'm usually...snotty? About everyone and everything, but I don't feel that way about this. About *him*." She bit her bottom lip, but a grin pulled it free of her teeth. "Things changed after I told him about the baby."

More than anyone else, Autumn knew that had been a monumental step for Ember. God, she hoped Mike hadn't blown it. He'd had some misconceptions about Ember, based on what Ember wanted people to think.

After her sis brought up the baby, she'd left them alone to work it out. She hadn't yet mentioned it because they'd returned to the house so quickly, making her think things had gone south. When it came to that touchy subject, she tried not to pressure Ember, knowing she'd bring it up when she wanted to.

Now, seeing Ember's smile, Autumn had to reevaluate. "How'd he take it?"

"Oh, Autumn, he's been wonderful! Very understanding without pitying me. I made it clear I still want kids someday and he didn't faint. Or run. He didn't even look surprised."

"What did he do?"

"He said I'd make an amazing mother."

Oh, way to go, Mike. "Of course you will."

"He talked to me about his nephews, too—told me I'd love them as much as he does."

Wow again. "So you two?"

Ember shook her head. "I figured we should get you and Tash worked out first, right? At least, that seemed like a good excuse at first."

Putting aside her own excitement over her impending intimacies, Autumn asked softly, "Why did you need an excuse?"

"Mike is different." With a helpless shrug, Ember added, "I don't want to mess it up. Jumping in the sack makes it just about that, you know? Sex and only sex. He and I have both been there, done that. I want things with him to be different."

"I think they already are." Not that she was an expert. Far from it. But when Mike looked at her sister, he saw more than her amazing body and pretty face, more than her fluff attitude and flirting.

At least, it seemed that way to Autumn. Most of the time, he looked at her as if she was already committed to him. Not in a stalkerish, domineering way, but with…pride. Yes, that was it. He looked at Ember as if he valued her, as if she really mattered.

Ember deserved that in a relationship.

Discounting Autumn's long silence as she pondered relationships, Ember said, "The way you and Tash have handled things, with this crazy slow burn, is much better."

"You realize that hasn't been deliberate, right?" If Tash had been as obviously interested as Mike, and if the timing had worked out with Sadie, she'd have been all about it. That didn't make Ember wrong, though. It was nice, knowing Tash liked her and enjoyed her company.

Plus it was special, being liked by Sadie. She wouldn't trade that for anything.

But now she wanted more.

"I can't believe it took you so long to get this set up." Straightening a plate on the table, Ember placed it just so. "The suspense has been killing me."

"Hey, you're the one who picked the date for the salon."

"It was the only date they had available." Ember crossed her arms. "But I could have come up with something else."

Autumn waved that off. "It was only an additional week." And patience was a virtue.

Plus, full honesty, she'd been a little nervous about Tash's reaction. Without reason, as it turned out, because he'd jumped on her dinner offer. Immediately after that, Ember had asked Sadie about the salon.

So far, Tash had no idea he'd been played, but Autumn planned to tell him.

Soon as she got him alone.

It didn't seem like a good idea to trick him into sex. He'd either be onboard, or—

"Stop it." Ember gave her a light shove.

Catching herself, Autumn asked, "Stop what?"

"Wondering if he'll thank you or shy away like a virgin. Trust me, the man will go ape-shit once you make your offer."

Pretty sure she wouldn't offer, so much as explain…and then hope for the best. "Does Mike know what you're thinking?"

Shrugging, Ember went to stir the spaghetti. "We've made out some, so he has to have a good idea."

"He hasn't pushed for more?"

"No. Strangely enough, he's let me lead." She frowned over that. "Did you know he doesn't need this job? He's actually loaded, but he wanted a whole new change of pace, and I guess this was it. We're the opposite of the corporate world, shiny cars and flashy women."

Autumn laughed.

"I'm serious. When he describes his old life, that's what it sounds like.

"We embody the simple life," Autumn said expansively, "if working sunup to sundown is simple."

"I want to know why he left his old life, but so far he hasn't said." Ember scowled at the noodles. "I bet it's because of a woman."

"Did you ask him?"

"I can't. I shouldn't have to. I opened up and told him all about the baby, so he should repay me in kind."

"Ember." Sometimes her sister's mind-set seemed counterproductive to all the things she wanted most in life. More and more, Autumn thought that might include love, family and, yes, children of her own...sooner rather than later.

In many ways, Ember still seemed fragile to her. She supposed losing a child could do that to a woman. She'd only lost Chuck and it had been devastating. But a sweet little baby?

Her heart broke for Ember.

She moved closer while she considered what to say...and how to say it.

"Spit it out," Ember told her. "I can take it."

Yes, she could. Her sis was stronger than she realized. Smiling with that realization, Autumn forged on. "What you're suggesting sounds like a game, and I'm not sure that's the way to start a serious relationship. Mike deserves more than that, and so do you." Autumn was the last person who should be giving relationship advice, but then again, she was the person closest to Ember. Even better, she had Ember's own advice to fall back on. "Aren't you the one who dared me to ask Tash outright if he wanted to have sex? Well, seems to me you could ask Mike outright if he's heartbroken over another woman. The truth has to be better than whatever you're imagining."

After forking up one long spaghetti noodle, Ember nodded. "You could be right." She leaned back on the counter and snuck another noodle to Pavlov. "I'll wait until he sees me in the new underwear, though. That way, even if he does feel burned by someone else, he won't be able to think about her."

"That's genius." Struck by the idea, Autumn wished she'd gotten some nicer underwear, as well. Too late for that now, though. She wouldn't put off her "date" with Tash for any reason. "Sounds like a solid plan. I like it."

They were still laughing when a car door closed.

In Autumn's mind, it might as well have been a gong signaling the end of her celibacy. Anticipation sent her blood singing and put a riot of butterflies in her stomach.

Allowing things to happen naturally was a lot less stressful than planning a deliberate seduction.

But... *Tash*. She'd be seducing Tash and she could barely wait. She'd always wanted him, first with the shallow infatuation of youth born from admiration of his smile, his body and his popularity.

Now, his physical appeal meant less than who he really was deep down—a doting father determined to nurture his daughter, a betrayed husband who'd rallied from hurt and an overall good man with his priorities in line.

Falling in love scared her, but she'd spent too much of her life afraid. Mike was right: her ice cream didn't cut it. Not anymore.

Not since Tash Ducker had returned to town.

"Big breath," Ember suggested. "Paste on a smile and keep thinking of how things will end."

"I won't be able to eat if I do that."

Ember laced her arm through Autumn's and urged her toward the window so they could peek out through the curtain. "Just know that however much you want him, he wants you more."

She wished she had Ember's confidence. She'd gotten so used to being the big-boned rejected bride-to-be, it'd take a little adjusting to think of herself differently. She hated that she'd let Chuck affect her so much, and that his treachery managed to play off her mother's nonstop unintentional criticism.

Seeing Tash and Sadie filled her heart, when she'd refused to admit it was empty. Now that she knew them both, now that she felt so much for them, losing them would be doubly devastating.

Smiling in honest happiness, Autumn opened the kitchen door so they'd know not to go around to the front.

It was their first time inside her house and she felt a little giddy. Unfortunately, like most weeks, she'd been running non-stop with little time to prep. At least she'd gotten all the laundry done and put away, which had to be a first, and she'd had enough time to clean the dust bunnies off the floors.

Pavlov darted out to run circles around Sadie before going to Tash for a few friendly ear scratches.

"Hello, you two," she called, loving the way the sunshine reflected off Sadie's bright hair.

"Autumn!" Sadie dashed toward her, greeting her with a hug. Her arms wrapped around Autumn's knees and her face tipped up with a toothy grin. "What are we eatin'?"

"Spaghetti." She ran her hand over Sadie's crown, touched with emotion. Oh, it was a wonderful thing to be greeted so warmly, with such enthusiasm. "Hope that's okay. Your dad said you like it."

"Love it!" She skipped off to greet Ember, too.

Tash followed his daughter's example, but his hug was more complete, an open hand on the small of her back drawing her into the hard, warm planes of his tall body. Such a thrill, even here where nothing more could happen.

She, Autumn Somerset, had the town hunk holding her as if he enjoyed it as much as she did. She mentally gave herself a high five, since high-fiving Ember would only bring out questions.

"I missed you." He kissed her throat, sending a tingle of awareness straight to her womb, then breathed near her ear, "I'm dying to see your house."

"You are?" she whispered back just as quietly, feeling like they shared a secret but unsure why.

He was about to answer when Ember said, "We have ten minutes before dinner, right? Sadie's coming with me to my side of the house so I can find Pavlov's ball. She'll enjoy seeing some of his tricks."

Tash eyed the door. "You live on that side, huh?"

"Make it five," Autumn said. To Tash, she explained, "Pavlov does different tricks with different balls. He's a very smart dog."

"Back in five." Winking, Ember took Sadie's hand and they hustled through the interior door, Pavlov racing after them.

"Sadie is incredibly excited about your spa day. I just hope she doesn't come back wearing makeup or anything crazy like that."

"Don't worry." Turning back to Tash, Autumn patted his chest. "Ember knows she's not to allow anything more than a slight trim to Sadie's hair, with a blow-style, and the salon has nail colors specifically for little girls. Ember can be outrageous, but she's good with kids."

"I've already noticed that on my own." He wove his fingers through her hair, making her glad she'd left it loose. His gaze tracked over her face, then down her body. "Love this shirt." He fingered the narrow sleeve over her shoulder. "Pretty."

He couldn't know that she'd worn it specifically because it was easy to lose, but still she blushed. "Thank you."

Looking beyond her at the kitchen, he took in every detail.

Being a designer, people often expected her home to be fashion-forward and *perfect*. But she wasn't perfect, not even close. Her house was nice—at least in her opinion—but more importantly, it was functional and cozy.

The longer Tash looked around, the more she worried. "What do you think?"

"It suits you." His fingers tunneled in close, holding her head still for another quick kiss. "I've seen you at work, at the beach and out on the farm, but not here, where you live. Where you relax and shower and sleep."

"Honestly, that's about all I do here. Well, and read. I like to read a lot."

He picked up a book off the counter. "This is what you're reading now?"

"No, I already finished that one. I was going to donate it as soon as I made it to the women's shelter just outside of town. I liked it, but I didn't love it."

"You keep the ones you love?"

It'd be easier to show than explain, so she took his hand and led him to the living room and her floor-to-ceiling built-ins situated at either side of the custom television cabinet.

"Wow." Moving closer to explore the titles, he asked, "I take it these are keepers?"

Gesturing at the twenty-plus titles on the eye-level shelf, she said, "These are all from Karen Rose. She's my favorite."

"Nice covers. Suspense?"

"Romantic suspense, which makes them better." Indicating other shelves, she said, "I like romantic comedy, too, horror and urban fantasy, women's fiction, paranormal and some straight suspense."

His smile came slow and easy. "Is there anything you don't read?"

"I have a grave dislike of biographies and cookbooks."

The smile slipped into a grin. "Cookbooks?"

"Bo-o-oring." She ducked to another shelf. "But I do enjoy the occasional self-help book." She pulled out *How Not To Care.*

"This," Tash said, taking it from her, "obviously failed." He slid it back on the shelf and drew her close. "You care a lot, about a great many things and a great many people."

"You think so?" Yes, she did care—most especially about him and Sadie.

"I know so. Everywhere I go in town, people sing your praises. They love you." His lips nuzzled hers again, teasing, making her want more. "I'm surprised they haven't built a statue of you in the town proper."

She laughed. "Come on. I'll show you the rest. Just keep in mind that I put in a lot of hours, okay?"

"Since I get the scraps of your leftover time, believe me, I know."

Was that how he saw it? Did he feel she hadn't prioritized him enough? She peeked at him as she paused by the guest bedroom, used as an office for her design business. "I'm sorry if I've—"

Looking at yet more books, Tash said, "That wasn't a complaint. Sadie and I enjoy whatever time we get with you, and we both appreciate the results of all your hard work. Every kid in the neighborhood is now anxiously awaiting the grand opening of that pirate ship."

"One more week," she promised, thrilled that they were both satisfied. Once the canvas sails were installed, it'd be complete. "It really is turning out great."

"It's amazing. More than I ever hoped for."

Buoyed by his praise, she led him to the hall bath, currently in a rare state of tidiness, and then on to her bedroom. Hoping to have him back to this room soon, she explained, "Ember's place is the mirror image of this, minus all the books and with her own style of furnishings."

Drawn by a photo on her dresser, Tash went farther into the room. "This is you?"

"When I was five. My grandpa took me fishing, but said I cried every time he caught a fish, or when he hooked a worm."

"Sounds about right. You've always loved animals?"

"Much as Sadie does. I meant it when I said she has the touch.

Many kids her age would be clumsy with animals, but Sadie has this innate gentleness. She's a special little girl."

"She certainly loves the farm."

"I always did, as well." Autumn moved to another photo, one of her and Ember sitting with their grandma and a newborn sheep. "We wouldn't be able to afford the farm if our grandparents hadn't left everything to us free and clear, along with a nice savings. I think Gram knew what we wanted to do here. I also think if she saw the farm now, she'd approve."

Tash lifted the photo. "You were mighty cute as a kid."

She leaned against him. "Even way back then, my mom said I had her big bones. Look at me. I was a runt."

"An adorable runt." He pressed his mouth to her temple. "I especially like the pigtails."

Yes, her quickly accomplished pigtails…while her mother had labored over Ember's curls. She sighed.

Tash turned her to face him. "That sigh… You have to know that regardless of whatever your mother says, you are an incredibly sexy woman."

Her? Sexy? No, wait, wrong attitude.

What would Ember do? Strike a cocky pose? Give a slow smile? "I, um—"

"You're overthinking it," Tash whispered. "I'm not rushing you, just making a very male-inspired observation."

Autumn bit her lip. "You really think so?"

"Damn, how can you not know?"

She didn't want to sound like a dork, but she'd never be smooth like Ember. "I just never thought of myself that way."

"Okay, so forgive me but I'll be blunt." He tunneled his fingers into her hair and curved them around the back of her head. "For one thing, you're stacked. Seriously stacked. Screw the idea of big bones—you have killer curves that make me salivate every time I'm near you."

"Salivate?" she croaked.

"Yeah, especially since you play down your figure. It's like a present all wrapped up and waiting for a special occasion."

Hopefully today would be that occasion. The smile teased at her mouth, but wow, she liked the way he saw her.

"You being a woman, this might not make sense to you," he continued, "but you're earthy."

"Earthy?"

"You smile, Autumn. A lot. It's like a kick to my guts every time I see it. No lipstick or gloss, just your mouth…" He lightly kissed her, then put his forehead to hers. "You don't mind getting dirty…or covered in fur. And you have the kindest eyes I've ever seen. You laugh when something is funny, and don't hesitate to speak your mind."

Laughing, she pressed her fingertips to his mouth. "I—I don't know what to say." The way he described her, she sounded pretty terrific. "I'm flattered."

When his tongue touched her fingers, she pulled them away, going all breathless and excited.

"You're definitely sexy on the outside, okay? Don't ever doubt that."

No, with him, she wouldn't. Tash made her feel all that and more. She smiled at him, trying to decide how to react. "Thank you."

He nodded, his gaze full of sincerity. "It's how pretty you are on the inside that really seals the deal."

What deal? she wanted to ask, but then they heard Sadie's laughter, followed by the scrabbling of Pavlov's paws as he raced down the hall. A ball bounced in her room, careened off a dresser and got snagged in midair by Pavlov's sharp teeth.

The dog wheeled around and raced back out with his prize.

"Time for dinner," Ember called.

Autumn knew it for what it was—her sister's never-subtle way of alerting her that her time alone with Tash was over.

For now.

★ ★ ★

Things had changed. Tash felt it in the way Autumn kept stealing looks at him, the pleased smile she couldn't wipe away and the shared looks passed between her and her sister.

He never wanted to push her. Autumn did so much for so many people, she deserved to put herself first for a change—even if that meant being in a pseudo-relationship instead of having the commitment he would have liked.

He wanted her, but he needed her to feel the same.

"It's almost unfair," he said, "that you're gorgeous, funny, sweet and a good cook."

"Anything Autumn does, she does really well." Ember wrinkled her nose. "And I agree, it's unfair. If I didn't love her so much, I'd shun her out of sheer jealousy."

"I love her," Sadie announced, making everyone pause.

Ember's mouth twitched and she shouldered Sadie gently. "Me, too." Then she looked at Tash.

He wouldn't allow Ember to put him on the spot, or make Autumn uncomfortable. "Sisters like to tease each other," he explained to Sadie. "But you know they're close."

As she searched each person at the table, Sadie forked up more spaghetti. "I love Tracy the cow and Tash the turkey, too." She paused with the bite almost to her mouth. "And Matilda and Olivia and—"

Ember laughed. "We should have time for a visit when we get back, as long as it's okay with your dad."

"It doesn't get dark 'til nine. How long would your hair appointment be?"

"Long as you want me to make it." She gazed expectantly from Autumn to Tash and back again.

Definitely something was afoot…and it made his heart beat a little faster.

Autumn kicked her sister under the table and mouthed, *Behave.*

After a startled jump, Ember kicked back and a scuffle ensued until Autumn slid her chair closer to his.

Ember smiled in smug satisfaction.

To ensure he didn't spoil anything, Tash pretended none of it had happened, even though it ratcheted up his awareness to a heated level. Autumn didn't quite touch him, but he felt her all the same.

Sporting her own smile, Sadie asked, "If there's no time tonight, could I come back tomorrow to see them? Dad got me a new book for Tracy the cow."

Ever since Sadie started naming animals after people she already knew, the names had grown, as if "the" was the middle name, and the type of animal was the last.

He'd need to talk to her about that, maybe pick up a name book for her to peruse. Until then, this seemed like the perfect segue. "I've been thinking about that. Autumn, you work all the time but Sadie and I have our days free for the summer, especially since I get most of my work done in the evening. Would we be in the way if we came over to help more often?"

Sadie cheered the idea. "I could feed the chickens and spray the pigs with the hose and—"

Ember caught Sadie's glass of juice right before her elbow would have taken it out.

It pleased Tash when Ember played down the near mishap. "Oops, got it! High five for my fast reflexes." Sadie hesitated, but as Ember offered her palm, she smacked it with her own.

Abashed, Sadie said, "I got excited."

"Well, heck yeah, you did. The pigs go bonkers with that hose. I can't wait for you to get your turn. You'll love it."

Skating right past Sadie's embarrassment, Autumn said, "It would be seriously terrific if you and your dad wanted to pitch in every now and then."

Perking up again, Sadie asked, "Really?"

"The animals *adore* you. It'll be a treat for them."

"Free labor," Ember said, raising her glass toward Autumn for a toast, then tapping it to Sadie's glass, too, and lastly to Tash's. "First, though, we have to stay tidy for our salon appointment. If you like getting your nails done even half as much as you enjoy hosing down pigs, we'll be all set."

Autumn laughed. "I'm not a big salon person, as you can probably tell." When she ruffled her hand through her loose hair, leaving it extra tousled, Sadie grinned. "How about you? Do you enjoy all that spiffing up like Ember does?"

"I dunno," Sadie said, shrugging her narrow shoulders. "I've never done it."

Tash felt that now-familiar gut clench. Deb always had her nails done, and she'd kept regular salon appointments.

"Never?" Ember asked with exaggerated surprise. "You're kidding me?"

"I've been with my mom, but just to wait." Keeping her gaze on her spaghetti while she twirled it around her fork, Sadie added, "Mom said I was too young and it cost too much to waste."

Quickly covering that, Autumn said, "Ember's salon has a special rate for little girls. Isn't that right, Ember?"

Scowling, her face flushed, Ember said, "They do, yeah, but it wouldn't matter." Putting her arm around Sadie, she drew her close in a hug, catching his daughter off guard and making her almost drop her fork. "If yours cost twice as much as mine, then *I'd* just wait while you got your turn. In fact, you better like it, kiddo, because I've just decided we're going to have a regular girls' day."

"We are?" Both surprised and cautiously optimistic, Sadie asked, "What's that mean?"

"It means we'll figure out a day each month that works for us. Next time, we'll grab food out, too." Getting into that idea, she added, "Maybe we could also shop? Please tell me you like to shop?"

Sadie gave her a wide grin. "Maybe. What would we buy?"

"Anything we want! A cute top, or adorable sandals, or even stuff for your hair." She turned to Autumn and said, "Finally, you're off the hook." In an aside, she muttered to Sadie, "Autumn is not a fun shopper."

Autumn cleared her throat. "That all sounds wonderful, but do you think you should get Tash's input on it?"

Sadie jumped in. "Can we, Dad? *Please?* I think I'll like shopping with Ember."

"Guaranteed," Ember said, giving her another hug.

Amazing. Autumn and Ember had just taken an awkward, unpleasant memory of Deb's thoughtlessness and self-absorption, and turned it into a gift.

For that alone, he could easily love both sisters. In more ways than he could count, they'd accepted Sadie and made her feel part of a very special bond. Girl time. A novel concept, but his little tomboy seemed thrilled with the idea, and that left him happy from the inside out.

Thrilled by the sheer joy and ripe anticipation on Sadie's face, he said, "I think it's a terrific idea, but I can't let you pay for—"

"Of course you can," Ember insisted. "It's my treat, after all. Besides, giving me a shopping and salon buddy is a present to *me*. Or haven't you ever noticed that my sis is not a girly-girl?"

"I've noticed she's perfect."

Autumn blushed, Ember grinned and Sadie asked, "Am I a girly-girl?"

"You're the best possible mix," Autumn promised, covering her embarrassment. "Someone who enjoys reading to Tracy the cow and playing on a pirate ship swing set, but also has cuteness down to a fine art."

It was another half hour before they finished their spaghetti and salad and Ember announced it was time for her and Sadie to be on their way.

Right before they left, Ember pulled a small bag from her purse and set it on the kitchen counter. "A very small gift that you may not need," she said to Autumn, her eyebrows bobbing. "But better *safe* than sorry."

When Autumn sputtered, Tash wondered what was in the bag, but didn't ask. He took a few minutes to lift Sadie up in a big hug, telling her, "Have fun, okay?"

She cupped his face in her little hands. "You have fun, too, 'kay?"

Ember burst out laughing...and yeah, he had an inkling of the plans for the rest of the day, especially with how Autumn busied herself at the stove.

Ember gave him a long look, then slanted her gaze to her sister's back as she stood at the counter putting the leftover sauce into a bowl. When she looked back at him again, she said, "We'll be gone a couple of hours, but I'll text Autumn when we're on our way back."

To warn them? Sisters, he was finding, were handy to have around. "Thanks. Appreciate it."

Ember took Sadie's hand and as they headed out the door, she called Pavlov to her, saying, "I'll leave him with Mom and Dad."

Autumn groaned, but rushed forward to wave. "Enjoy yourselves, but don't you dare get Mom asking questions!"

Whatever Ember said in reply, he didn't hear.

However, he did hear Autumn lock the door.

The loud "click" affected him like a warm touch, making it damn hard to breath.

Just making it...hard.

To keep from pressing her, he gathered the plates from the table.

Autumn finally stepped away from the door. "You don't have to do that."

"I want to." He looked her over, making note of her nervous smile, her bright eyes and quickened breathing. "The sooner we get done, the sooner we can enjoy our time alone."

At first she was silent, then she unglued her feet and got to work. "You're right. We *are* alone, and I don't want to waste a single second."

Chapter Thirteen

Autumn knew it was ridiculous to be so nervous, but she'd never before instigated a seduction, most definitely not with her buttinsky sister laying heavy hints and innuendos to ensure the man knew he was being seduced.

Embarrassed heat continued to burn her cheeks...maybe along with a little excitement.

Or a *lot* of excitement. Whatever.

Her face was red.

Trying to pretend she hadn't just set him up, she rushed through storing the remaining food while Tash loaded everything into the dishwasher.

The silence was killer, weighing heavily on her until she thought she might burst, but she had no idea what to say. Instead, she thought about things, what she wanted to do, what she'd probably say...how he'd hopefully react.

Once they'd finished, she leaned back against the counter and tried not to look aroused. A tall order considering the chaos happening under her clothes. Like tightening nipples, tingling stomach. Warmth and sensation and...all good things.

Things she hadn't felt in far too long.

Actually, some things she'd never felt. She almost felt guilty that she'd never wanted Chuck this much. But then, Chuck hadn't deserved her, so there.

"Well. That's that." She ran her tongue over suddenly dry lips. "Thanks for helping."

With his gaze locked on hers, Tash slowly closed the distance between them...and sent her heartbeat into a flurry. "I'm happy for Sadie to have her first salon treatment, and happier still to be alone with you." He cupped her face in her hands, his concentrated expression incredibly stirring. "Not that I'll pressure you, I swear. I know how you feel about things. But I'm thinking maybe you're not quite so committed to the whole ice cream—"

"I set this up," she blurted, then winced. But seriously, she had about two seconds remaining on her patience, and then she'd be jumping his bones.

Or bone.

Whatever.

"You set up...us being alone?" He looked and sounded pleased by that confession.

She nodded, but clarified, "It was Ember's idea, and Mike seconded it, so—"

"Mike?" Confusion tweaked his brows.

She gestured to the table where they'd had dinner. "To get you alone. Mike swore you'd be onboard."

"Mike is a smart guy."

She inhaled a deep breath. "But I wanted to. It wasn't just their idea."

A fire lit in his eyes and he drew her into his body, his gaze so probing, so intense, she almost felt naked. "Tell me why."

If you're wrong Mike, I'll make you sorry. "Erm, well..." *Spit it out, Autumn.* "Ice cream isn't cutting it anymore. Not since meeting you again."

There. The rushed words were out, sort of hanging between them and—

Suddenly Tash's mouth was on hers, hungry and hot. Whoa. Mentally, she applauded Mike. That ice-cream comment had really turned the trick.

And, oh, man, was this better than any dessert, the way his firm lips moved over hers, how his tongue teased and incited, the taste and heat of him... Way, *way* better.

He kissed his way to her neck, finding places that curled her toes and flipped her stomach. Softly, against her skin, he asked, "This is your way of saying you want me?"

She nodded, then gulped out, "Yes," while running her hands over his hard shoulders. "Definitely yes." Something occurred to her and she added, "But Ember really is excited about sharing time with Sadie—"

His mouth sealed over hers again, stealing her breath and her thoughts.

"I could tell," he murmured. "But how about we don't talk of daughters or sisters?"

"Good idea," she agreed. "Except..." Stepping him back enough that she could reach the little bag Ember had left for her on the counter, she peeked inside. Cleared her throat. Peeked at him. Cleared her throat again. "I don't suppose you had these?" She flashed the bag open for him to see inside.

Three condoms.

He grinned. "I like the way Ember thinks, but yes, I had one." He kissed the tip of her nose. "Now if only we had a little more time."

"One," she repeated, considering it. With three in the bag, one didn't seem adequate, but he was right, of course. They had limited time and she wanted to get on with it.

She took his hand and, still holding the bag in the other, led him down the hall toward her bedroom.

Now that the time had come, she sort of wished she had bought new panties. Something pretty. Something exciting.

His hand moved over her rump and she caught her breath.

Okay, she told herself, *just stop it. You are who you are, sensible clothes and comfortable panties and nervousness all rolled into one. And he likes you. Don't screw it up with reservations.*

After they entered her room, she put the bag of condoms on the nightstand and pushed the door shut. With a second thought, she locked it, too. As she went to the blinds and closed them, Tash said nothing.

"I, um… I haven't done this. Here, I mean." Why hadn't she thought about her mother and father being so close? And what if Pavlov decided to come back? He'd slip right through his doggy door and then what?

"Autumn."

She locked eyes with Tash. "Hmm?"

He pulled off his shirt, tossed it aside, stepped close and whispered, "Your turn." Then he kissed her, not giving her a chance to do anything or think of a reply.

Good thing, because she was pretty sure she couldn't just whip off her top as casually as he had. But then she felt his hands sliding under her shirt, urging it upward, and he broke the kiss just long enough to tug it over her head.

Why, oh, why hadn't she at least bought a prettier bra?

Oh, but hey. He wasn't looking at her bra. Nope, he was back to kissing her again, his hands moving over her exposed skin, trailing up her spine—the back clasp of her bra opened, the cups loosened—and *then* he looked.

Seeing his face, Autumn knew he didn't give a flip about her sturdy, supportive, plain beige bra. The man was all about getting the bra off her with no thought to how it looked.

"Christ, you're beautiful."

There, see? Who needed sexy underwear? She wrestled her arms out of the straps and let it drop to the floor, thrilled with how his gaze moved over her in minute detail, followed by the touch of his hands.

And then his mouth.

A groan tore through her, especially when he licked one nipple, then drew it deep.

Locking her fingers in his hair, she wondered how she had gone so long without this.

"I want to eat you up," he whispered, and did just that, putting wet love bites over her skin, up to her shoulder, that sensitive spot where her shoulder met her neck, and then to her ear. *So good.*

Emboldened by him, she trailed her fingers over his naked shoulders, too—*love the shoulders*—and down his chest. Sparse chest hair teased her palms before she found smooth, warm skin over his abdomen, and finally her fingers found the snap to his jeans.

"Not to rush you," she whispered, barely able to talk with his mouth on her, teasing and inflaming, "but we have limited time, and four condoms, and I've been a really long time without, so—"

Again his kiss cut her off, but this time his mouth devoured hers, hungry and hot, while he made quick work of relieving her of her jeans.

It was sort of magical. Yes, she stepped out when necessary, but he did all the work and made it appear seamless. Poof. Pants gone.

Oh! Poof, panties leaving also. Huh.

"You," she accused, "have had some practice."

"You," he whispered against her breast, "are so damn sexy, I can't wait."

She tried to reciprocate by "poofing" away his pants, but it turned into a struggle so he stepped back to do it for her.

Her own private little striptease. Nice.

Naked, she stood there and avidly watched him toe off his sneakers then push down his jeans and boxers at the same time.

Oh, be still my heart. Talk about sexy.

He wasn't bulky like a body builder, but strength showed in every lean line of his body. His erection jutted out, proof that he was every bit as excited as she was.

Or at least close.

He waited, giving her time to look him over, until she said, "You look exactly as I always imagined. Maybe even better."

With a slow, provocative grin, he asked, "You imagined me naked?"

"Oh, yeah." What sane woman hadn't? "I've been mentally stripping you since way back in high school." She heaved a long, happy sigh. "Having you here is far better than thinking about it, though."

"For me, too." More kissing, this time with their naked bodies touching, until he led her to the bed.

She paused to rip away the coverlet, surprised at herself when it went halfway across the room.

Her lips twitched. "Enthusiasm?"

"I'm right there with you," he said as he took them both down to the mattress.

At first she worried for the time, but as he touched her she forgot all about it. He lingered over her breasts, not in a greedy let's-get-the-show-on-the-road way, but more like he took enjoyment from touching and kissing her.

She got lost in a haze of lust and love, and even while so affected, she knew it was special, something she'd never experienced before. "Tash?"

He pressed a finger into her, making her body bow with pleasure. "I wanted you to come first," he said low, his voice rough as gravel. "Now, I'm not sure I can wait."

"Don't," she said, almost panting, wanting—*needing*—him

inside her. "Don't wait." A tiny worry squirreled around in her brain: what if they got interrupted? What if this didn't happen?

It *had* to. She wouldn't survive an interruption at this point. She deserved this, right? Damn right, she did.

Going for a proactive attitude, she grabbed the bag, dug out a condom and handed it to him. "Showtime."

His smile was slow and sexy as he rolled to his back. "Good thing my ego is healthy or I might be intimidated with expectations."

She rolled to her side to watch as he donned the protection. Fascinating. "You've already exceeded all expectations, but let's not start slacking now. No pressure, just…keep the pace."

This time he outright laughed. "Yes, ma'am." He moved over her, kneeing her legs apart, and settled against her.

Her heartbeat pounded double-time and a rush of heat narrowed her vision to only him.

"You're beautiful, Autumn." He kissed her lightly, and sank in.

She caught her breath…and let it out in a low moan of incredible pleasure.

Watching her, he began to move, his gaze incendiary, his nostrils flaring, his jaw tight.

It felt incredibly intimate, and sent words of love to catch in her throat. That wouldn't be fair, though, especially since she understood his circumstances. This, what they did now, was because of attraction and mutual respect. She'd be an adult about it, accepting it on face value instead of making it into something it wasn't.

And really, how could she think at all right now when her entire body felt alive? Desperation, probably, because she loved him. She wanted this, and she wanted more. So much more.

For now, though, she'd take what she could get and make it enough. Tomorrow would take care of itself.

Clutching his shoulders, she met his rhythm and felt tension coiling, tighter, sweeter, with each deep thrust. Amazing how in tune they were, everything so natural, so *right*.

With a growl, Tash gathered her closer, one arm under her hips, the other braced on the mattress beside her head. She loved looking at him, seeing the color slash his cheekbones, the heaviness of his eyes, the quickening of his breath.

It amazed her how the pleasure spiraled out of control. Orgasms had never been an easy accomplishment for her, but Tash moved as she needed him to, adjusted when she did, and all of sudden a tsunami of sensation rolled over her, putting her head back, tearing a cry from deep inside her. It seemed to last forever, draining her utterly, then slowly ebbed and flowed as it began to fade.

She lazily opened her eyes to see Tash still watching her, his jaw flexing, his shoulders rock-hard, until with one final thrust that buried him deep, he groaned out his own release.

A few minutes later, with Tash resting over her, his breath on her temple, she whispered, "Wow."

She felt his smile. "Yeah."

"I'm..." Gobsmacked. Floored. "Overwhelmed." Who knew sex could be that astounding? She did...now. And she knew she'd never be the same.

He leaned up suddenly and looked toward her clock. "Not too overwhelmed, I hope. We have more than an hour left."

Yup, her jaw loosened, but he looked serious. Heck, he looked determined. And turned-on again.

She drew a shaky breath, nodded and whispered, "Yay for me."

Laughing, Tash moved to her side and tucked her in close. "Autumn Somerset, in every way imaginable, you thrill me."

She'd rung him out.

Nothing about Autumn should ever surprise him, and yet she had. Again. How was it a woman who came off so reserved could be so incredibly open and adventurous during sex? Yes, he'd most definitely planned to enjoy himself—after all, this was Autumn and he'd been drawn to her from the moment he saw her on his walkway talking to his daughter.

But he hadn't planned to be burned to cinders. She'd taken out his legs, scorched him from the inside out...and stolen a piece of his heart.

Her hair, now badly tangled, drifted over his chest when she lifted her head and peered at him. "Still with me?"

"Barely," he said, moving his hands down her back to her oh-so-perfect behind to keep her from moving away. He liked having her as a soft, sexy blanket.

Her phone made a noise and, with a groan, she stretched over him—a unique pleasure, that—and snagged it to read the screen. "Ember says they had a slight delay but should be here in thirty."

He groaned. "I'm going to need every minute."

Folding her arms on his chest, which did amazing things for her breasts, she grinned down at him. "You were pretty phenomenal."

"My line to you." He palmed that luscious behind and—unbelievably—felt himself stir again. Like most people his age, he'd always had a healthy sex drive, but what she did to him was astounding. He should have needed at least an hour to work up any enthusiasm, but Autumn's smiles were potent in the extreme.

His gaze lingered on her mouth, now slightly puffy from kissing.

Her breathing deepened and she leaned closer—

A knock sounded.

They both jumped, turning to stare at her bedroom door.

When the knock came again, Tash realized it was her front door and finally caught his breath. "Damn, I thought we were busted."

"Still might be," she whispered, as she left the bed and searched around for a shirt. "If it's my mother, I'll just die."

Given they were both in their thirties, her attitude amused him. "Want me to answer it?"

"No!" She snatched up his shirt and pulled it on. It hung to midthigh, hugged her butt and boobs and looked pretty terrific on her. "Stay put, okay?"

"Nope." Already swinging his legs over the side of the bed, Tash said, "I'll be right behind you, but out of sight. How's that?"

She scowled as the knock came again—more insistently this time—and she warned, "If it's my mother, do *not* let her see you."

"Yes, ma'am." In rapid order, Tash pulled on his boxers and then his jeans. He didn't bother to zip up as he heard Autumn hurrying down the hall.

He hustled after her and had just reached the end of the hall when he heard her mutter, "No freaking way."

The door swung open and she demanded, "Chuck. What in the world are you doing here?"

Oh, hell no.

Peering around the corner, Tash spotted Chuck, hands in his pockets, smiling at Autumn as if he had every right to drop in. He tensed, fighting the urge to step forward, mindful that Autumn wanted to handle the bastard on her own.

Then Chuck realized she only wore a shirt and moved closer, his gaze going all over her.

Autumn shot out an arm, blocking his way. "Not. Another. Step."

"You look good, Autumn. You've slimmed down, haven't you?"

Tash couldn't believe the guy was that stupid.

Autumn went rigid. She gripped the door handle and barked, "Go away!"

Before she could slam it, Chuck pressed in. "I tried to stay away, honey, but I've missed you." His voice dropped. "Let me in. We'll...talk."

"Ha!"

Oozing confidence, Chuck murmured, "You can't be over me that easily."

"Actually, getting over you was a piece of cake…or rather a bowl of ice cream." She snapped her fingers. "Just like that— me, over you."

Trying for a teasing tone, he said, "I bet you still have your wedding gown, don't you? I regret that I never got to see you in it."

With a snort, she said, "And you never will. Ember and I burned it in the yard the day after you left."

Chuck stiffened. "Bullshit. You loved that dress."

"Feel free to ask Ember, but if she punches you in the throat, that's your problem."

He looked startled for a moment, then determined. "Autumn, c'mon. You know we had something special."

"Ha!" She repeated, with even more disdain, *"Ha!"*

"Autumn…"

"You were convenient, Chuck, or so I'd thought. Having you run off with another woman was rather inconvenient. And if you think I mourned you, think again." Stepping into his space, outrage giving an edge to her voice, she snarled, "I was *glad* you left. Relieved. So much so, I rejoiced."

Chuck's mouth tightened. "I don't believe you."

Giving up on his stealth, Tash stepped out farther and leaned on the wall. Pride warmed him. Autumn in her current mood was a sight to behold and he didn't want to miss a single thing. He stayed quiet, but this way he could see as well as hear her.

Poking Chuck in the chest, she stated, "I've given thanks every day that you were such a worm because it saved me from a huge mistake. And let's be clear, that's all you were—a mistake."

Anger darkened Chuck's expression. "You loved me."

The way she laughed made Tash smile.

"I might have been gullible enough to think so at the time,

but now that I have something that *is* special, I'm doubly grateful you weren't around to complicate things."

Was he special? Nice to know. And deciding he wouldn't get a better segue than that, Tash couldn't resist saying, "She means me," with his thumbs aimed at his bare chest.

Chuck startled, staring at Tash with a slack jaw.

Autumn looked at him, too, at all of him, as if seeing him for the first time. Then she grinned. "Yes! Look at him." Rushing to Tash, she grabbed his arm and dragged him forward. "You see him, Chuck? You see that face? That *body*? You see how he looks at me? He's a hell of a sight better than you could ever be."

Scowling, Chuck went beet-red.

Tash just said, "Thank you, honey." It was a pretty remarkable thing to have Autumn gushing on about him.

"I appreciate your agreeable attitude," she told him, patting his biceps. "But I'm not done."

Tash grinned even more. "Take your time."

Jerking back around to Chuck, she said, "The thing is, there's so much more than his gorgeous face and bod. Even if he wasn't scrumptious eye candy, he'd still be ten times the man you are."

Better and better. Tash couldn't resist saying, "I don't mind if you love me for my body, but it's good to know I'm more than flesh and…bone."

Autumn caught her breath and blinked at him.

Was it the word *love* that threw her, or *bone*?

Chuck glared at them like they were both insane.

Because they now only had fifteen minutes before his daughter would show up with Ember, Tash wanted him gone.

He took a step forward. "I promised Autumn I wouldn't annihilate you, but she looks ready to do you in on her own, so I suggest you take off while you still can."

She frowned at Tash. "Damn it, I wanted to handle this myself. Wasn't I doing a great job?" Before he could answer, she said, "Heck yes, I was."

"Very true." Tash put his arm around her. "I was just watching the clock and thought you might want to wrap it up."

"Oh." She realized what he meant and said again, *"Oh."* Turning back to Chuck, she took a mean step forward.

Chuck backed up, his hands raised in surrender. "You're not the woman I remember."

"Well, hallelujah for that, because the woman you remember was dumb enough to get involved with you in the first place."

Trying to make it sound like an insult, Chuck sneered, "Have a good life."

"Plan to," Autumn snapped back, then she slammed the door on him, almost catching Chuck in the backside.

She was still fuming when Tash, standing close behind her, nuzzled the side of her neck. "Anyone ever tell you you're sexy as hell when enraged?"

Even with her breath still harsh with annoyance, she tipped her head to give him better access. "Really?"

"You were incredible." Wrapping his arms around her, Tash opened one hand on her stomach, the other on a heavy breast. "Actually, you're always incredible…especially in bed."

"Oh, if only we had time." Sounding very forlorn, she sighed but resolutely stepped away and took his hand. "Come on. We can't let Ember and Sadie catch us like this."

When they got to the room, they saw that she'd missed another text. Autumn snatched up the phone, then groaned. "They'll be here any minute!"

"Calm down and take a breath. We'll make it." It had been a hell of a long time since he'd had to dress in a rush to keep from getting "caught." It was a novelty he could do without.

After stealing his shirt back from Autumn, he couldn't stop watching her as she gathered up her own clothes—now rumpled—and dressed. This, too, he enjoyed with her, watching her bounce on the balls of her feet as she tugged up her jeans, then struggle with her bra.

Shame to put away those magnificent breasts, but hopefully he'd find a way to spend more private time with her like this. Based on all of Ember's antics, she was ready and able to assist.

Thinking of Ember made him smile. In her own inimitable way, which was very different from Autumn's calm influence, she was good with Sadie.

They'd just gotten into the kitchen when the door opened and Ember peeked in. Seeing them fully clothed and pouring iced tea, she grinned. "Well, you both look happy."

"Ember," Autumn warned.

Tash grinned. "Thank you for taking Sadie out. We made good use of the time."

Spinning around, Autumn said, *"Tash,"* in reprimand.

Laughing, Ember offered him a high five, but he caught her hand and pulled her in for a hug. "Seriously, thank you. I appreciate all the effort."

"Happy to help. Besides, Sadie is way more fun than my stick-in-the-mud sister here." She affectionately smacked Autumn on the butt. "Come on. You'll want to see this."

"Where are we going?" Autumn followed as Ember led the way back out. "And where's Sadie?"

"She's in the barn with Mike, and yes, she looks supercute. Luckily we finished early. I was taking her to get a doughnut—buying you guys a little more time—when I got a call." She waved them forward. "Come on, come on."

"A new animal?" Snagging his hand again, Autumn hurried her pace.

Tash liked how she did that—laced her fingers securely through his, treating him like a significant other when they hadn't really cemented anything at all.

Convenient relationship—check.

Burning sheets—check.

Shared affection for his daughter—check and check.

But what about them as a romantic couple? What about a relationship with real expectations and commitment?

He wanted Autumn to want to be with him, not because it was easy, because it wouldn't always be.

Not to put off Chuck, because he'd happily handle that for her, although she'd done a fine job of it on her own.

And as much as he loved Sadie, it couldn't be about keeping her happy.

Without giving it much thought, he lifted Autumn's hand to his mouth. She glanced at him with a smile but didn't slow her pace.

This time of night, the sun spilled over the horizon, painting the land in bright watercolors. The temperatures had lowered a little and the air smelled of rain. They needed it after the long heat wave.

Golden light filtered out of the open barn doors. Pavlov, even more animated than usual, ran to greet them, ran back, returned and turned again. The dog was obviously excited, but once he headed back into the barn he lowered his body and crept quietly.

"He's protective of new animals," Autumn explained as they stepped inside to see Mike and Sadie kneeling near one of the special stalls.

Sadie's hair glowed, neatly trimmed and smoother than he'd ever seen it. It wouldn't last—girls her age didn't make hairstyle a priority—but for now, he could honestly say, "Sadie, your hair is beautiful."

She flashed him a wide smile and whispered, "Thanks, Dad."

Against her body she held something small and furry, and it wasn't until they got closer that Tash realized she had a very tiny kitten.

"A whole litter," Ember said softly, "and luckily we have the mama, too."

A thin yellow tabby lounged on fresh bedding in the corner of the stall, five more kittens in various colors lined up nursing.

Slowly going to her knees, Autumn asked, "Where did she come from?"

The reverence in her voice, the gentleness, melted into Tash, amplifying the love he felt for her. In this moment, kneeling on a dusty barn floor with muted light overhead, her hair messy and clothes wrinkled from their earlier activity, she was the most beautiful woman he'd ever seen.

"Out back of the art-supply store that Mom uses," Ember explained. "Martha, the owner, called me. She was worried because the cat is so thin. She was sympathetic and wanted to help, but doesn't want seven cats, right? I told her we understood and thanked her."

"Aren't you the sweetest," Autumn said to the cat, cautiously reaching out until she lightly scratched her under her chin.

"She's supergentle," Ember promised. "After I lured her with some food and fresh water, I put her babies into a box. Soon as she finished eating, she joined them. I closed up the box because I wasn't sure how she'd react in my car, but she never made a peep."

Sadie looked up at him. Her small hands, the nails now painted bubble-gum pink, cradled the kitten with ultimate care. "I bet she knew we were saving her, huh?"

Tash's heart literally clenched. With gratitude. Affection. Pride. His daughter was clearly in her element, more peaceful and happy than he'd seen her in months. "I bet she did."

Ember ran a hand over Sadie's hair. "This one was such a help. The kittens have taken turns climbing on her."

Carefully, Tash brushed one fingertip over the kitten's tiny head. "The eyes aren't open yet."

"They're only a few days old," Autumn guessed. Pavlov had hunkered down next to her, and she kept one hand on his shoulder while looking over the mother. Large green eyes stared back. The cat seemed watchful of Pavlov, but not really concerned.

"She's a sweetheart," Mike said. "Okay for her to be here?"

"Here" was a stall enclosed in chain-link fencing, much like a dog kennel. A thick layer of fresh straw covered the floor, and over that Mike had supplied several old towels. In one corner he'd put a cat box and opposite that he had dishes of water and dry food.

"It's perfect." Autumn twisted to see Tash. "Mama cats are known to move their babies the moment you're not looking. Until we get them all checked to ensure they're okay, we don't want them to go missing."

"She'll like it here." With extreme gentleness, Sadie returned the kitten to her mother. "She won't want to leave once she gets to know us."

Us. Yes, Sadie felt part of a family, *this* family, because they'd ensured that she did. More so than her own grandparents, they had embraced her, accepted her…loved her.

"Now there's more reason than ever for you to come help out." Autumn quietly closed and secured the gate. "Seven adorable reasons."

Sadie's eyes suddenly widened. "Oh, no."

Concerned, Tash kneeled down before her. "What's wrong, honey?"

One hand in her hair, Sadie lamented, "I don't have enough names!"

With a lot of effort, they all managed to muffle their laughs.

On their way out of the barn, Autumn and Sadie went to each animal and bid him or her good-night. Autumn patiently answered Sadie's questions, sometimes their voices so low he couldn't hear.

It didn't matter. Content in new and profound ways, Tash relinquished that special time to the two of them, opting instead to help Mike and Ember tidy up.

It had been an amazing day, wrapping up with an incredible experience for his daughter. This place, and especially these two women, were pure magic…and they'd allowed him and Sadie to be a part of it.

Now if he could make it permanent, his upside-down, chaotic life would finally be perfect.

Chapter Fourteen

Mike waited until Tash and Sadie drove off, waited as Autumn bid them both a dreamy good-night, and then, finally, he focused on Ember.

Apparently divided, Ember hesitated, watching her sister leave.

"You did something with your hair."

That got her full attention on him and her smile was enough to take out his knees. Damn, but he loved her smiles.

"Instead of red highlights, I went purple." Shaking back her hair, making it shimmer under the security lights, she asked, "What do you think?"

He thought she could shave her head and he'd still want her. When she was happy like this, it made him happy, too. But even when she'd been sad talking about the baby she'd lost, he'd wanted to be with her. Hell, he pretty much wanted her at his side whenever possible, whatever her mood, whether arguing with him or smiling at him, as she did now.

Given the perfect opening, Mike stroked his fingers through

her hair, ending with his hand lightly tangled at the base of her neck. He drew her forward. "Pretty."

Ember bit her lip. "You're going to invite me up to the loft, aren't you?"

Invite? Hell, he'd beg, carry, or do just about anything else to get her there. He'd wanted her for so long now, it felt like a lifetime, but he said only, "You and I are past due."

"I have questions I want answered first," she warned.

"I have all night." With *her*. "Feel free to ask anything."

After another beautiful smile, she said, "Give me just one second," and pulled out her phone. Mouth twitched to the side, she thumbed in a text to Autumn while explaining, "She and Tash had their hot date, and I could tell by the blinding glow around them that it all went well. Normally Autumn and I would convene on her couch and go over all the juicy details."

If Ember would give him tonight, she'd have her own juicy details to share tomorrow. But, damn it, he knew how close they were, and this was definitely a big deal for Autumn, which made it a big deal for Ember.

He felt beyond stoic when he offered, "If you'd rather wait—"

"Not on your life." She finished her text, waited a few seconds and got a reply from Autumn. Grinning, she turned the screen so he could see. "She gives her blessing."

He first read Ember's message: I'm dying for details, but I'm here with Mike so...tomorrow?

And then Autumn's reply: It was blissful & I'm zonked. We'll talk tomorrow for sure. Go get him!

She cocked an eyebrow. "I think Tash has set the standard."

They were so amusing together. Mike tipped up Ember's face to put a gentle kiss to her mouth. "Blissful is a tall order, but I'll do my best."

She gave him a slow smile. "I'll help."

On the way up the stairs to his rooms, she kept glancing at

him. "I want to know all about you, Mike Brewer. Everything. All the nitty-gritty."

"All right." He'd never been hiding his past but neither had he been interested in sharing it. Now everything was different...because of Ember.

Opening the door, he gestured for her to enter. While he locked up, she looked around. Yes, she'd built the rooms per Autumn's design, but he couldn't recall Ember ever being here after he'd moved in.

He assumed Autumn and Ember both respected his private space, despite the fact he lived literally over the barn. Plenty of insulation kept out the sounds of a restless cow or sleepless goat, but wasn't soundproof enough that he ever missed an animal in distress...or the rooster they'd once had, abandoned because he liked to wake everyone extra early with his relentless crowing. Mike had heard that dude every time. Luckily, a friendly farmer had been happy to take him and the rooster now ruled his own roost.

The loft apartment was no more than a cozy sitting area that flowed into a small kitchen with a bar big enough for two stools, a bachelor-size bathroom and a comfortable bedroom.

"Wow, this is...nice." Genuine surprise kept her gaze roaming.

Because he wasn't a slob? Because his furniture matched? Mostly, anyway... "You expected something else?"

"I don't know. I mean, yeah. I guess." She took in the blinds on the windows, the end tables, the area rug on the floor. Even the shelf where he kept her mother's risqué artwork, given to him as gifts. "You're such a *guy.*"

"True," he agreed, grinning. "You need to work on those insults, hon."

"You know what I mean." She trailed her fingers along the back of his brown leather couch. "I love this."

That couch was his favorite purchase since starting over. It had the look of a catcher's mitt while being butter-soft. Fitting perfectly into the space along the wall, it faced his large-screen TV.

Glancing at him, Ember explained, "You're more rugged and…macho?" She shook her head. "You are that, but what I'm saying is you're *earthy*. At home doing the old-fashioned job. I guess…not urbane? Does that make sense?"

While opening two beers, he watched her over the divider bar, where he usually had his meals. She drifted around his small living space, soaking up every detail and looking both confused and impressed.

"You're having a hard time pegging me, and that's okay. God knows I've had a hell of a time pegging you." Getting there, though. When she looked at his coffee table, he walked over to her and, handed her the bottle, then urged her down to the couch.

Making a beeline for the bedroom would suit him, but she said they needed to talk, so he'd talk. With Ember, he wanted to do this right.

Holding the longneck in both hands, she asked, "How did you know I like beer?"

"I pay attention." He especially paid attention to her. "I used to be very urbane." Her word choice, but it suited. "I was completely citified, polished and what you'd call suave."

She snorted. "Sure, and you want to sell me a bridge next?"

Grinning at her disbelief, which he completely understood, he set aside his beer. "Shiny black Mercedes that I traded up for a new model every year. Custom-tailored suits—so many of them, they'd never have fit in my closet space here. I had a stylist who trimmed my hair every week." He held up his left hand, now rough with calluses, and examined his clipped nails. "Manicures, too."

"No way." Fascination brightened her eyes. She put her beer, only half-finished, on the handmade coffee table.

That table was one of his first efforts, a therapeutic endeavor in using his hands and body, doing for himself instead of paying others to do for him. It turned out more rustic than he'd ever intended, mostly from trial and error. But it served its purpose, so he kept it—as a functional piece of furniture, and a reminder that this was what he was meant to do, where he was meant to be, and the past no longer mattered.

"Manicures?" She, too, looked at his hands. "You?"

Moving past that with a shrug, Mike asked, "What do you think of the coffee table?"

"The table?"

He nodded at it. "You can tell that I made it."

"Really?" She looked more closely. "I just assumed you got it at one of the craft fairs or from a local furniture maker or something."

"With all the flaws?" Leaning forward, he ran his thumb over an uneven corner seam, then a dent where he'd dropped a tool on it. "I'd spent my entire adult life climbing the ladder of success. I'm good with money, know how to invest and know how to reap the rewards. It was a no-brainer for me to go into real estate."

"You sold houses?"

Settling back beside her, he smiled. "I sold high-end real estate in New York City. Deals that ran twenty million plus. Every day was a rush, from six in the morning until the last dinner party of the night. I played racquetball with clients, visited them on their yachts and constantly expanded my business contacts."

Wide-eyed, Ember stared at him.

"At the time I loved it—the energy, the high-level stakes, the flash and glamour."

She scrunched up her face. "Trying to picture you as glamorous…but no can do. And FYI, I like you like this. When I said rugged, it wasn't a complaint."

"Good to know." Especially since he liked this life a lot more than the old one. T-shirts over dress shirts? Trucks and trailers on a field over a Mercedes in bumper-to-bumper traffic? Sunshine on his back instead of club lights in his face?

Some might not see it his way, but he'd moved up in the world, and he never wanted it to change.

Ember took a swig of her beer, then studied him. "So what happened?"

"At my fiancée's request, I took on a partner. A younger, hungrier version of me."

"Whoa!" Going rigid, she scooted away from him. "Fiancée?"

"A woman I had planned to marry?" he offered helpfully. Then gently explained, "It never happened."

Silent, her jaw working, Ember searched his gaze and finally came to some inner decision. "Go on."

Since he'd expected that reaction from her, it didn't slow him down. "Having a partner freed up some of my time. I still handled the biggest deals, but he did a lot of the legwork…" He reached for Ember's hand, lacing her fingers with his and casually bringing her closer again. Her hands were small but strong, and oh-so capable. "Two years ago, right before I moved here, I got home early from a trip and found them in bed together. In *my* bed, actually."

Her jaw loosened, then her mouth dropped open. A second later she snapped it shut. "That has to be a joke. She *cheated* on you?"

Liking her incredulity, he quipped, "Hard to fathom, I know."

"It *is*." Her brows scrunched together. "What a bitch."

He almost choked on his beer, the laugh taking him by surprise. "She claimed that was the only time, but only a fool would believe her. Talk about fury… I'd have burned the damn mattress, but being on the thirty-second floor of a high-rise makes that a little tough."

"Wait a minute." Her scowl darkened even more. "You *stayed* with her?"

"No!" God no. How had she gotten that impression? "Trust

was gone, and that made the relationship pointless. Even though it was my place, I left that night knowing things were over."

"So if you left, why did you care about the bed?"

"I had to go home several times to get all my stuff." At the time it had been so incredibly personal. He'd felt stripped raw. Vulnerable. "Every time I was there, I wondered if I'd slept where another man had touched my future wife. Had I shared those same sheets? The same pillow?"

Ember made a face. "Yeah, that would suck."

"It's demoralizing. One day I'd felt on top of the world, and the next I felt like a blind fool." Breathing in her warm unique scent, Mike marveled that what had once been so horrific no longer bothered him at all. "Let's just say it was life-altering."

Softening again, Ember hugged him. "I'm sorry you went through that."

"I'm not. Not anymore." He toyed with a long purple lock of her hair. Bright, bold, unique and pretty—just like Ember Somerset. "Because of what she did, I reevaluated my life…and that brought me here. I have a very different perspective these days, thanks to the work we do." Even that, thinking in terms of "we" instead of challenging the world alone, added to his inner peace. What he did now he didn't do only for himself. It was for the greater good. It helped, and it made a difference. "I like seeing the sunrise. I love the fresh air. Here—" *with you* "—I feel more useful. What I do day to day really matters."

Her smile warmed even more. "You've been a true godsend to Autumn and me, and to all those sweet, innocent animals who wouldn't have a chance without us."

Ember was great at summing it up, but she wasn't yet letting him off the hook.

"We appreciate you so much, but why'd you leave it all? I mean, a breakup is one thing, right? Changing your whole life is altogether different."

"I didn't start out with that intent. Obviously I couldn't be partners with the guy, and I wasn't interested in making his life easy, so I cashed out. That left him scrambling…and I was glad."

"Me, too."

"She wanted to keep the condo, and I agreed. After getting my name off the lease and all the utilities, I started looking for something new to do, somewhere new to live. Things snow-balled and next thing I knew, I was changing it all. I wanted to start fresh, so I traveled south, stopping in different little towns, seeing if anything clicked."

"And you saw our ad."

"I saw your ad." He smiled, knowing that day had forever changed him. "I'd tested my wits, so I wanted to test my en-durance—and not on a treadmill at a fancy gym."

Ember looked him over. "You were always fit, but, yeah, your physique is different from all the manual labor." Leaning in, she whispered, "You're a total stud muffin now."

He kissed her for that nice compliment. "I'm stronger. I'm useful. I sleep better." *And there's you.*

"An honest day's work is good for everyone." She tipped her head. "So what happened with the cheating exes? Please don't tell me they married and are living happily ever after."

No, definitely not that. "They tried to keep the business afloat without me, but they fell flat pretty quickly. That led to them losing the condo, too."

"Ha!" She held up her palm, demanding her requisite high five for all good news.

Barely hiding his grin, Mike complied.

"Just what they deserved, right? Let them rot."

He did love her killer attitude. "Once the business failed, so did their relationship."

Her eyes narrowed in suspicion. "How do you know that since you've been living here and she's been living there?"

It didn't matter to him, so he shrugged. "She's contacted me a few times." *Saying she still loved him. Asking him to take her back.* "Just last week, in fact."

Turbulent emotion swirled in Ember's gaze. She tried to sit forward, but his arm around her kept her close.

Two inches from his nose, she demanded, "What did she want?"

"Me." His gaze dropped to her mouth. God, that mouth. He felt more than saw her deep inhalation, and brought his gaze back up to her eyes. "I told her I was involved with someone else now and wished her well."

Her eyes narrowed. "You wished her well?"

"There's no anger left, Ember. Not since you."

Something flickered over her expression. Uncertainty? Curiosity? Her chin hitched up. "Sounds to me like you want me pretty bad."

Mike tunneled his fingers into her hair, cradling her skull to keep her close enough to kiss. "At first I told myself I was on the rebound, so any pretty face would be appealing."

"Dick," she said without a lot of heat.

"Over the following year, when I couldn't stop noticing you with other men—"

She winced, then kissed him quickly and said softly, "Sorry."

"—I told myself that it was your sexy little bod, not *you* as a woman, that had me primed."

Her brows came together. "Apology rescinded."

His heart softened while other parts went rock-hard. "After that day in the lake, I think I knew one time with you wouldn't be enough. Not near enough." He drew her in for another kiss, using it as an example, leaving them both breathless. "Now I'm not sure a lifetime would be enough."

With a very satisfied, smug smile on her face, Ember whispered, "Sounds to me like you've fallen hard."

"So fucking hard."

She stilled, but then whispered, "Me, too. I wasn't looking to fall in love but—"

Love? In a flash he levered her back, his eyes searching hers, his heart off to the races. "Love?" She drew a shaky breath but before she could answer he asked, "You love me?" And again, before she could say anything, he said sternly, "Don't you dare screw around, Ember Somerset. No jokes, no sarcasm. It's a simple question and you better—"

"I love you."

His heart went into his throat, then dropped to his stomach before launching back into his chest with a furious cadence. "You love me?"

"Yes," she said with a growing threat that he saw in her eyes and heard in her tone, "and if you don't love me back you better start ducking, because I swear, I will be so pissed—"

He kissed her—a different kiss, just as hot, just as full of lust, but headier now with emotion, too.

Ember Somerset.

Love.

Happy ever after?

He felt it in his grasp, felt *her* in his grasp, and never wanted to let go.

Given how she cooperated, they ended up sprawled on the couch, him over her, her legs opening to his hips, her fingers tangled almost painfully in his hair.

He shoved up her shirt, and she helped.

He peeled off his shirt, and she groaned.

"Bed," he muttered, thinking they'd have more room there.

"Can't," she replied, trying to wedge a hand down the back of his shorts to cop a feel of his ass.

"Wait, let's slow down—"

"Nope," she said before kissing him again.

Mike almost laughed. God love the lady, he should have known she'd be just as bossy, just as take-charge in this as she was in every other aspect of her life. The difference? He wasn't Autumn and wouldn't let her steamroll him. If he had to guess, that part of his plan had been successful, at least in making him different from the pack of other men who all showed their admiration by bending over backward to lavish her with compliments.

Being easily twice her size and far bulkier, he had no problem disengaging and, before she could start complaining, scooping her up to head to the bedroom, where he'd have more room to enjoy her.

For a second she was silent, then seemed to give a mental shrug. "This is romantic."

"Yeah?" With both of them shirtless, he could think of better descriptions. Her purple-streaked hair hung over his arm, a unique tease that, when accompanied with her naked breasts, did a lot to keep his blood sizzling.

"Is it odd that Autumn and Tash got together the same day you and I will?"

"Give me one minute," he said, lowering her to his unmade bed, "and you'll forget about your sister, Tash and all other men."

"I will never forget about Autumn," she warned, unsnapping her shorts before he could and shoving them down in haste, "but I'll happily put her on the back burner for a few minutes."

"Few minutes?" Following her lead, he went about shedding his shorts, too. "You wound me, woman." He took his boxers with his shorts and then stood before her naked.

Still in her panties, balanced on one elbow, she breathed harder, faster, and seared him with her gaze. "Autumn," she whispered, making a check mark in the air, "forgotten."

His smile spread, slow and triumphant. "Yeah?"

"All other men," she added, with another make-believe check, "nonexistent." She made grasping gestures with her fingers. "Now gimme."

Mike had to laugh even as he fetched a condom from his nightstand drawer and rolled it on. With that done, he sprawled out beside her, taking her mouth, one hand going over her body to discover each soft curve, every toned hollow. For years he'd imagined exploring the length of her legs and the weight of her breasts.

Perfection—especially since she stayed busy with her own explorations. He loved her boldness, including the way she carried his hand down her body.

Such a thrill. But after waiting for two excruciating years to get to this point, he didn't mind at all. She could rush the beginning as much as she wanted.

As long as she didn't rush to the end.

A long time later, once her heartbeat slowed, Ember dragged a fingertip over Mike's broad chest, swirled it around one flat brown nipple, then opened her palm to coast over his chest hair.

How could one man be *so much* man? Never, not in a million years, could she see him in a salon doing anything, much less being manicured. And in a fancy suit?

Okay, so he'd probably look very fine.

Not as fine as he looked right now, though.

His ex—what a dummy. Ember could almost pity her—the hell she would. That lady's loss was her gain.

Mike's hand covered hers, flattening it to his heart, where she felt the heavy, steady beat.

She looked up to his eyes but found them closed. "To be fair, I think I need to warn you."

"Mmm," he mumbled, still a little dead to the world after his stellar performance.

She smiled from the inside out. "Yes, I'm multidimensional, not just the party girl that my mother has accused me of being."

"Already knew that...and I adore every dimension."

"We-e-e-ell..." She dragged that out, wondering how he would react. "I am not the patient one. That much *is* true. Unlike Autumn, I go after what I want with all I have."

"You want me." Eyes still closed, he smiled. "Done and done."

Now or never. "I also want marriage," she blurted before she could chicken out, and then, going for gold, she added, "And a family." She wanted kids *so* badly. Before now, the desire to hold a baby of her own was a vague idea, one without a specific child in mind. It was a sharp feeling, an emotional need.

Now, with Mike, she knew she wanted *their* child, one with his smile and her stubbornness.

He deserved to know what he was getting into. If he didn't want forever, if he couldn't see them as a committed couple, she needed to know now...before she fell even harder.

One of his eyes opened.

Ember swallowed, feigned nonchalance and clarified, "Sooner, rather than later."

Turning suddenly, Mike pinned her beneath him again. Man, he went from worn-out to domineering in a blink.

She liked it.

His enigmatic gaze bored into hers. "Is that a proposal?"

How could he ask that without a single hint of emotion? Such a poker face! He didn't look surprised or interested, not wary or hopeful. *Well, screw it.* She stared right back and stated, "Yes."

His gaze warmed, mellowed. With his mouth curving in a small smile, he gave a single sharp nod. "Yes."

"Yes?" she asked, more than a little confused.

His mouth twitched. "You proposed, and I said yes. I'd love to marry you."

But...it couldn't possibly be that easy. She'd gotten so used to holding men at a safe distance, that she'd expected him to do the same with her. Emotion welled up, making her voice tremble. "Because you love me?"

His gaze softened even more and his smile took on new meaning. "More than I knew was possible."

Her heart pounded in her chest. Challenging him, more by rote than anything else, she whispered, "And kids?"

Smiling now with amusement, he asked, "Can you wait until we actually tie the knot and figure out living arrangements?"

She blinked...oh, maybe ten times. Then she swallowed as a lump of emotion choked off her air. "Just like that?"

His rough thumb stroked over her cheek. "I'm many things, Ember. Too pushy, too opinionated. Old-fashioned and sometimes crude. A little too focused on sex?"

"No."

He smiled again. "But I'm not a dummy. I quickly figured out that you meant more to me than *just* sex, stupendous as the sex is."

"It really is."

"Thank you. We're good together." He stared into her eyes, maybe into her soul, showing her everything he felt...and thrilling her in the process. "I've spent enough long nights alone thinking of you to know I'd rather spend those nights with you."

Be still, my heart. "Can we start tonight?"

One brow shot up. "Making a baby?"

She nearly choked. "No, your plan for that is a good one. I meant spending the night together."

Nuzzling into her neck, he whispered, "I was hoping you'd stay. Tonight, tomorrow. From now on."

Huh. Well that plan suited her just fine.

Autumn had just gotten down the coffee can when the connecting door opened and a half-dressed Ember surged in, carrying two full cups, Pavlov at her side.

"Oh, thank God." Autumn reached for one.

Ember pulled them out of reach. "How do you know they aren't both mine?"

"Because you enjoy living?"

Grinning, Ember gave up one steaming cup and Autumn sipped. *Heaven.* "Oh, I needed that."

"Same." Appearing more asleep than awake, Ember slumped into a seat at the table.

Autumn dragged herself over to fill the dog's dish before joining her. "Pavlov spent the night with you?"

"When I was busy rocking Mike's world? No way. He stayed with Mom and Dad." Ember propped her head on a fist. "Mom caught me sneaking out of the loft this morning."

"Sneaking?" Picturing that, Autumn grinned.

"Since I wore him out, I figured Mike should sleep in a little."

More awake by the moment, Autumn grabbed a pack of cookies from the cabinet and took the seat across from her sis.

Ember grabbed two cookies. "Now Mom is full of questions—well, mostly praise for me, because I did the expected by seducing Mike."

Autumn nearly choked on her coffee. "Why do I think you're tilting the facts?"

Shrugging, Ember continued. "For *you*, she has questions galore."

Uh-oh. "Me? But why? She doesn't even know about Tash."

"Actually she does…because I told her."

The cookie fell from her hand. "Ember!"

"I needed to deflect her, all right? You weren't there, face-to-face, squirming like a teenager, so I figured you'd have time to plan a strategy."

Her strategy would be avoidance for at least twenty-four hours! If she wasn't too tired to move, she'd throw Ember out. "So…how'd Mom take it?"

Wincing, Ember said, "She's skeptical."

"Skeptical?"

"You know how Mom insists on thinking you're too responsible—"

"Aka, dull?"

"—to get laid."

Well, hell. The implied insult flattened Autumn. Was she such a hopeless cause with her big bones and responsible manner that her own mother couldn't picture her as a woman?

Enough already. More than enough.

Leaning over the table, pointing at Ember with her cookie, Autumn said, "I'll have you know I was *thoroughly* laid!" She punctuated with the cookie. "*Completely* laid." Cookie in the air. "Utterly and demonstrably *laid*."

Mike poked his head through the connecting door. "Um, I probably shouldn't have heard that." He stood there with his hair mussed, stubble on his face, shirtless, barefoot and his jeans unsnapped.

Obtuse to her distress, Ember turned with a happy smile. "Mike! You're awake."

"You snuck out on me," he replied, striding in to put a warm, firm kiss to her lips. "Your front door was unlocked, so I came looking for you, then heard voices in here."

"I wanted to let you sleep."

"Would've worked…if you'd stayed with me."

Gah! The new, recently liberated Autumn spoke up, saying, "Who needs cookies?" She tossed hers aside. "This is all so sugary sweet I'm getting a stomachache."

Pavlov gave Mike a quick greeting and then, true to his name, went through the open door into Ember's section of the house.

Mike laughed. "Sorry, Autumn. But so you know, glad to hear the thoroughly, utterly, et cetera part. You deserved it."

She hid her suddenly burning face. "Seriously guys, it's way too early for this."

"You're just jealous," Ember accused, "because my hunk is close at hand and yours isn't."

"Eh, possibly." How nice would it be to wake with Tash? Then again, she didn't wake up looking like Ember. Her sister, dressed in the same clothes she'd worn yesterday and with her hair in a high, sloppy ponytail, looked adorable.

Autumn resembled someone who'd been unearthed from the bottom of the laundry pile. After several weeks existing there.

What would Tash think of her morning face?

Yeah, maybe it was a good thing he wasn't here. She needed to fully reel him in first, make him love her enough that he'd overlook her less-than-appealing just-awakened mien and grumpy precoffee disposition.

Because it wasn't about to change. For her entire adult life, she'd been the same.

"Got any more of that?" Mike asked, nodding at Ember's almost-empty cup.

"In my kitchen." She waved a lazy hand. "Bring back the pot, will you?"

"Sure thing." Since he'd been in both sides of the house multiple times, Mike knew his way around.

Once he left, Ember leaned forward. "Quick, before he returns. It was good?"

Ah, a subject to brighten her mood. Autumn sighed. "Better than I knew was possible."

"Well, duh. I mean… Chuck? Blech." With a roll of her eyes, Ember quipped, "Tash was bound to be an improvement."

"Tash was amazing. *Beyond* amazing. It couldn't have been more perfect." Unless they'd had more time. Honestly, she didn't have the words to describe the pleasure. "How about you and Mike?"

"Same."

They shared wide grins.

Sighing, Ember sat back again. "That crack about Mike being close? It is nice, no doubt about it. But you've got something that makes me jealous, too."

Not believing that for a second, Autumn said, "Uh-huh."

"Sadie? Oh, my gawd, Autumn, that little girl is personality personified. I lost track of how many times she charmed me yesterday. She kept me smiling, tugged at my heart, and then with the kittens...?" Dramatically, Ember pressed a hand to her heart. "I love Mike, he loves me—yes, close your mouth. We cleared that up last night. Actually, leave it open, because we've agreed to start baby-making as soon as we get married, which will be soon."

Autumn had a hard time catching her breath! "You—"

"I want a baby." Ember smiled—a small smile, soft with love. "I want that so badly. And Mike, bless him, agreed."

Squealing, her exhaustion forgotten, Autumn shot from her seat and raced around the table. Grinning from ear to ear, Ember jumped up to catch her, and they hug-danced in crazy circles and excited chatter.

Mike found them like that, which put a masculine smile on his face, too. He paused in the doorway, a mug in one hand, the pot in the other. "I don't mean to intrude..."

Autumn reached out, waggling her fingers for him to join them. He quickly set the coffee pot on the stove, his mug on the counter, and then encompassed them both in his long arms.

Oh, this was perfect. Two of her favorite people, together. "I love you both," Autumn said, meaning it with all her heart. "I'm so happy for you."

Ember did a mix of laugh-crying—or cry-laughing—but went mute when a knock sounded on the kitchen door.

Chapter Fifteen

Their trio swiveled as one, arms tangled, to see Tash smiling through the glass and Sadie bouncing, anxious to join in.

Heart soaring at the sight of him, thoughts of her ragged appearance forgotten, Autumn disengaged and rushed to open the door. Pavlov had already gone out his doggy door and circled around to greet them, so he came back in, too.

The second Sadie cleared the door, she squealed and joined Ember and Mike. Mike scooped her up, and Ember, who clearly did adore Sadie, accommodated her by laughing as she spun them all in circles.

Tash's arms came around Autumn from behind and he pressed a kiss to the sensitive spot just below her ear. "Want to tell me what my daughter is celebrating?"

Oh. Right. It was hard for her to think with Tash holding her like that. Autumn turned her face toward him. "They're getting married, and apparently making a baby is a priority."

He went comically still. "Really?"

She'd never told him about Ember's miscarriage, but maybe it was time.

"Hey," Ember said, "we're heading over to my place to find better cookies." Since she held Sadie's hand, Autumn knew this was another maneuver to leave her alone with Tash.

There were times when Ember was the best sister ever.

"Once you're dressed and ready to get to work, come find us." Ember waved and headed through the door. Pavlov, of course, followed. With a sly grin, Mike closed it behind them.

And she and Tash were alone.

Autumn groaned. "I didn't expect you this early or I'd have tried to look a little more presentable."

He glanced past her to the clock. "Fifteen minutes early. Sorry."

"Oh, no, I didn't mean that." Heck, she was thrilled to see him. Turning, she smiled up at him. "It's just that I usually consume some caffeine and get a little more awake before anyone sees me."

"You look beautiful, as always." He combed his fingers through her loose hair. "How can you think otherwise? Big blue eyes, naturally dark eyebrows and lashes, and this mouth…" He bent for a kiss, but kept it brief. "You fit so perfectly against me." Saying that, he drew her closer, aligning her body with his.

With his arms around her, his heated scent enclosing her, Autumn whispered, "Thank you."

Tash gently rocked her from side to side. "For?"

How did she articulate all the ways he made her happy, how he buoyed her spirits? With Tash, she wasn't just living anymore. Now she took pure pleasure in every moment. "Thank you for making me feel better about…" She shrugged, feeling a little silly. "Actually, about everything."

"You do the same for me, you know. Probably for everyone, because that's the kind of person you are."

There he went again. The way Tash saw her was unique from

everyone else. Far more flattering. Thanks to his sincerity, she actually saw herself differently, too.

He glanced at the connecting door. "Why the celebration?"

Standing there, held in Tash's arms, Autumn explained about Ember's miscarriage and how terribly it had affected her. As usual, Tash listened intently.

"That day at the beach," he mused. "You were worried, and she worked so hard at having fun..."

"The memories sometimes hit her and it lays her low all over again."

"That's why you came out," he said, piecing it together. "I know it's not the norm for you to take part in an evening party, so I'm guessing it was your worry for Ember?"

"You," she teased, "are a very observant man." A wonderful man—who thought she was beautiful with bed-head hair and sleep-puffy eyes. A man who acknowledged that she cared and always tried her best. "Mike and Ember are now official—not only planning to wed, but ready to start a family right away."

He bypassed everything about Ember to focus only on her. "And you, Autumn? How do you feel about family?"

Odd, but no one had ever asked her that—not even Chuck, and they'd been engaged. "I love kids," Autumn said, thinking it through. "I love the idea of being a parent." She'd especially love to call Sadie her own, but that wasn't something she could say right now. "I guess I've been so busy with my interior-design business, the farm and my father's health, I've never really thought that far into the future."

After Chuck, she'd written off men—a decision that now seemed absurd. Judging all men by Chuck was as wrong as it got. She knew good men, darn it. Her dad, Mike...so many men she worked with, so many who ran the little shops in her beloved town.

Why hadn't she seen that before?

Hurt feelings, of course. It infuriated her to see just how badly Chuck's defection had leveled her.

Sliding his hands down her back to her hips, Tash said, "You would be an amazing mother."

And just like that, she shook off her bad mood. "That might be the nicest compliment of all."

"It's the truth."

"You really think so?" Did he believe she'd be a good stepmother to Sadie? The thought of it put a grip on her heart... and then didn't let go.

"Autumn." Tash rested his forehead against hers. "You're amazing at *everything* you do. You haven't realized that yet?"

Such a sweet-talker. Despite her confidence in her work, no one had ever before praised her so elaborately. In some ways, it felt like she was finally getting her due, especially since she knew Tash meant it, that to him it wasn't simple flattery.

Having her worth recognized filled up all her empty spaces. "I think you're pretty amazing, too."

Right before he kissed her, yet another knock sounded on her door, this one more strident.

Even before Autumn looked up, she knew. Still, she peeked around his shoulder.

Yup, there stood her mother. In her haste to intrude, she'd forgotten two curlers in the top of her hair. A billowing leopard-print muumuu swallowed her body and hid her feet, but did nothing to disguise the frown on her face.

Without waiting for Autumn, her mother pulled open the door and glided in. "Tash!" She giggled, arms opened wide. "I didn't know you were here."

Right, and that's why she wore her lipstick? No doubt she'd seen Tash's car and after Ember had whetted her curiosity, she'd come to get the details.

"Tracy," Tash said, accepting her embrace. "It's good to see you again."

"Would you like some coffee, Mom?" Knowing she did, Autumn moved away for another cup.

"So." Skepticism sharpened her mom's voice. "You and my Autumn?"

Eyes sinking shut, Autumn froze with a spoonful of sugar over the cup. She knew her mother would dig, but she hadn't expected her to be quite so blatant.

"I know." Tash gave a gruff laugh. "Hard to believe she'd have me, right? But I got lucky."

Autumn smiled at that wonderful reply...

Until she heard her mother say, "In more ways than one, I'm told."

Blanching, the spoon fell through Autumn's limp fingers and clattered to the countertop, spilling sugar everywhere. "Mother!"

"Mother?" Tracy repeated, snorting. To Tash she said, "She only calls me that when she's shocked, but then Autumn is so uptight, I hear it more often than I should. I knew Ember had to be deflecting when she said you two got together, but I still wondered—"

Smooth as silk, Tash interrupted, "Oh, but we did, and let me tell you, your daughter is far from uptight. In fact, I was just telling her how she excelled at everything she does."

OMG. Autumn stared at him, caught between mortification and hilarity. Her mother's face!

Mouth open. Eyes rounded. Cheeks aflame.

Hilarity won out and she had to choke down her snicker.

Clearly flummoxed, Tracy shifted her appalled gaze to Autumn.

Ha, take that, Mom. Enjoying her moment, Autumn smiled.

Clearing her throat, her mom stared. "You're saying..."

Refusing to blush, Autumn squared her shoulders and lifted her chin. "Tash and I are together."

"And I've never been happier," Tash added, moving to Autumn's side and kissing her temple. "I'll finish your mother's coffee while you go get dressed. A storm is moving in and I'm guessing there are things you'd prefer we get done before that."

"Rain?" Thrilled for a new topic, Autumn grabbed it like a lifeline. "Yes, rain can complicate things." She hurried to the window to look out. "Wow, it's really dark. Yes, I'll get dressed." Escape seemed like a very good thing. "Give me ten minutes."

"Take twenty," Tracy called after her. "Do something with your hair."

She was only halfway down the hallway when she heard Tash, as he said, "I love her hair loose like that. It's sexy, don't you think?"

The snicker escaped. Her mother had met her match. For once, Autumn was glad to let someone else speak for her.

It rained off and on the entire day. Mud became her new companion.

If caring for animals during a dry spell was hard, it was nothing compared to now.

Autumn looked down at her utilitarian knee-high rubber boots and saw that she'd still managed to get her jeans dirty. Actually, parts of her T-shirt, too. Heck, the ends of hair had somehow collected mud.

Tash wasn't in much better shape.

Only Sadie seemed to be enjoying the rain, but then as a seven-year-old, she liked to slide in the mud with the pigs. Tash, being a pro, had brought Sadie multiple outfits, two pairs of boots, a rain slicker and a hat.

Sadie needed every one of those, but Tash hadn't minded as she'd gotten mud everywhere, even down her neck. Like Autumn, he took pleasure in seeing Sadie so carefree.

This was Autumn's day to do the around-the-farm chores, but since Ember couldn't work on Sadie's play yard in the rain, anyway, she stayed and pitched in. Before long, they had the majority of it done.

Even with the added mess of mud and the ramped-up humidity from the rain, she'd enjoyed working with Tash. Both he and Mike had simply removed their shirts and allowed their jeans to get soaked.

Ember elbowed her. "Think we should use our phones to take some photos? We could make a beefcake calendar, sell them to hungry ladies and make amazing profits for the farm."

Autumn grinned. "The guys might not like that idea."

"Ha. Look at them, flexing for our benefit."

All Autumn saw was two wonderful men working hard and looking good doing it. They'd told Autumn and Ember that they'd finish up, so the sisters stood just under the barn roof, out of the still drizzling rain. Behind them, Sadie talked with Tracy the cow, who now greeted her as soon as she heard her voice.

Luckily the cow was doing well, and in between downpours she'd gotten some time in the field. Autumn had made open spaces and fresh air a priority for the sweet thing after her awful abandonment. The goat and sheep had joined her and they seemed to be pals.

The goat, being a supersocial animal, got along with all the animals. Sheep, however, didn't typically graze in the same area as cows. Unfortunately, with only one cow for now, her options were limited. She'd been talking with her vet, Ivey, about options, though so far it hadn't been a problem. The animals all got along as if they were pals.

Tracy had been resting in the grass, chewing her cud, when Sadie laughed…and just like that, Tracy had lumbered to her feet and approached the fence to greet her biggest fan. It was even Sadie who'd led the cow into the barn when the rain returned. Girl and cow had become largely inseparable.

Even the sweet little kittens, now with open eyes, fuzzy soft fur and adorable little mewls, didn't lure Sadie away from the cow for long. She loved all the animals, but had a very special bond with that cow.

"I've been thinking," Ember said.

"About beefcake calendars, I know." That earned Autumn another elbow.

"Actually—" Ember glanced back to ensure Sadie was occupied "—about babies."

Coming to attention, Autumn asked, "About your and Mike's baby?"

"For so long now, ever since the miscarriage, I've had this terrible yearning." Laying a hand to her flat abdomen, Ember said, "There were days, sometimes weeks, when I didn't think I'd ever have a baby to hold."

Autumn leaned into her, sharing love and comfort. Had Ember written off children the same way Autumn had written off men? It seemed so. "Now you'll have it all."

"That's just it, though. Since Mike agreed, I feel like…well, the urgency is gone." Sighing, she looked toward Mike, where he and Tash were repairing a fence post that had loosened on the pigs' pen. "I love him, Autumn. He loves me. I know it'll happen, but now I think I might like a year to just enjoy him." She bit her lip in an uncharacteristic show of uncertainty. "That makes me sounds really fickle, doesn't it?"

"Oh, Em." Autumn hugged her. "It makes you sound like a woman with a secure and happy future."

Ember stared at her for a few seconds, then squeezed her tight. "Do you realize you never criticize me? I realize I'm not prefect—"

"No!" Levering Ember back, Autumn feigned shock. "You're not?"

Undaunted, Ember continued. "So thank you. For always being there, supporting me no matter what. You're a very easy person to love."

Another amazing compliment? Wow, her day—regardless of the rain—was off to a stellar start. "Despite our occasional conflict, you're pretty darned easy to love, too."

They heard a snuffle and both turned.

The cow slept on her side inside her large stall. Exhausted from her earlier activities, Sadie slumped on her butt against the stall door, legs out, body lax, lightly snoring.

The cow's nose poked forward on the ground...with Sadie's small hand resting on it.

"Now that," Autumn whispered, taking her phone from her pocket, "is photo-worthy."

With rain off and on for two weeks, Tash worried about Autumn. It seemed she worked nonstop. Long after he left the farm, she had appointments to keep...and her mother to deal with.

For him, no problem. Tracy amused him more than anything else. But for Autumn, a lifetime of subtle insults and uncomplimentary expectations stole her edge. More often than not, she seemed bogged down by her mother, without her witty comebacks or even her temper.

He had a feeling mother-daughter relationships might pose unique problems that he'd never understand.

Not that Tracy was a bad person. She clearly wasn't.

Or a bad parent. She obviously loved her family.

She was simply flawed, like everyone else, and it made him hyperaware of his own interactions with Sadie.

How many times had he screwed up without meaning to? How often did he misspeak, misstep, or err with good intentions? Probably more than he cared to know.

All he could do was his best, and hope it was good enough.

For sure he would be aware of criticism, just as he'd be aware of encouragement.

Speaking of Sadie, he heard her squealing in her bedroom as Autumn put the finishing touches on everything.

Squeals of pure joy. It was a familiar sound now, and he loved it.

Autumn, most definitely, was good for Sadie...and for him, in so many ways.

He smiled without realizing it, stared toward the hall as if he could see them and impatiently waited until he was invited to view the final results.

Each day he and Sadie had helped at the farm, and many evenings Autumn had worked on some detail of Sadie's bedroom. Though he didn't get to see it, he knew what had transpired. Painted walls. A canopy over the bed. Gauzy curtains. He saw materials carried in, heard Sadie's whispers, smelled paint fumes or the sound of hammering when Ember joined in.

Most nights they shared dinner together.

Just like a family. What he'd always thought family should be, how it should feel. What it should mean.

Who knew one heart could hold so much love? Or that every single day that love would expand until he almost couldn't contain it?

Unfortunately, they'd only had two more opportunities to be alone, and he suffered nonstop need for her. Juggling everything was starting to wear on him.

He wanted his daughter secure and happy. Mission accomplished, or so it seemed.

He wanted Autumn with him always. That one was tougher, but he'd be patient for as long as it took.

What did Autumn want?

He couldn't rush her, had promised her he wouldn't. Hell, she'd only recently decided that he—*or sex in general?*—was better than ice cream.

He hoped that it was him specifically that had helped change her mind on that, but a woman as sensual, as alive and loving, as Autumn would never have sustained herself long with a frozen substitute. Eventually she'd have reached out for human contact again.

Thank God he was the one who'd been around when she did.

Now he had to do things right. Autumn deserved that. She

needed to feel cherished, loved, appreciated—for herself, not for any other reason, not even for his beautiful daughter.

Sadie poked her head out the door. "Ready?"

Tash's smile widened at the excited glimmer in her eyes. "I think so." Pretending to creep, he asked, "Will I faint from shock?"

"No, Dad!" She giggled happily. "You'll *love* it."

"I will if you do."

Too eager to suffer his slow pace, Sadie darted out and grabbed his hand in both her tiny ones, hauling him along. "Come on, hurry."

He only got one step into the room before awe leveled him. Wow. His daughter's room looked like something out of a magazine, while also feeling cozy and... Well, it felt like Sadie.

Autumn had somehow captured his daughter's bubbly personality and quirky style, her sweetness and adventurous nature, and combined it all in a picture-perfect setting.

Looking around, he took in the pale blue walls that resembled the sky on a mild day. A curtain rod high near the ceiling sent delicate, colorful panels of fabric flowing down like a rainbow to meet a unicorn bookcase filled with Sadie's favorite books.

The bed...the bed was incredible with the flexible canopy overhead. Cute, but not too fussy. He ducked to look beneath and sure enough, glow-in-the-dark stars would shine over Sadie while she slept.

A fluffy comforter and pillow sham in a print of spring flowers, a fuzzy rug under the bed, wall shelves—

"Well?" Autumn asked, her hands clasped together, her feet shifting.

"It's perfect." Organized, coordinated and fun.

"Really?" She dropped her hands, her smile flashing. "You like it?"

"Of course I do. I love it. I'm...stunned, actually."

"Did you see my dollhouse?" Sadie dragged him to the other side of the bed. "Isn't it the *best*?"

The dollhouse was huge, holding Sadie's hodgepodge collection of dolls, big enough that she could crawl into it. "Wow." The really impressive part? It looked like the barn rather than a house, which clearly thrilled Sadie.

Autumn launched into speech. "I hope it's okay. Normally for something like that I'd have gotten your permission, but then I got the barn idea and decided to make it a surprise, something from me to Sadie. As a gift, I mean, so I didn't say anything—"

Tash pressed a finger to her lips. "It's incredible."

She licked her lips—accidentally licked his finger, too—then said, "Good, because I have a few more gifts."

Sadie thrust her fists into the air and cheered.

Indulgent, Tash said, "You're full of surprises today."

Pivoting, Autumn hurried to the closet and reached to the back to pull out a bag.

Sadie bounced on the balls of her feet, her hands clasped under her chin in anticipation.

"Here you go. I hope you like them."

Taking the bag, Sadie sat down on the side of the bed and pulled out…a stuffed cow.

Her eyes rounded and her lips parted. Next she pulled out a stuffed pig and a goat, and even a turkey. After a heavy swallow, Sadie's eyes went liquid, her bottom lip trembling.

"Sadie?" Horrified, Autumn dropped to her knees in front of her. "Honey, I'm sorry. I thought you'd like—"

Launching at her, Sadie sobbed, "I *love* them." Sniffling, her arms in a stranglehold around Autumn's neck, she added, "And I love you, too."

"Ohhh." Tears filled Autumn's eyes, as well. Avoiding his gaze, she dashed at her cheeks with one hand and hugged Sadie with the other. "I love you more."

Sadie pressed back, her nose red and her cheeks already blotchy. "It's the bestest ever."

"Which part?" Tash asked gently.

"All of it." Then she hugged the cow.

Brushing a tear from Sadie's cheek, then from her own, Autumn said, "If Ember was here, we'd all be crying. She swears if she even sees a tear, it wells her up." She drew Sadie in for another hug. "I'm glad that you like it, honey. I'll finish up your dad's room soon and then we'll be all done."

That pronouncement caused Sadie to freeze. "I don't want you to be done."

Joining them on the floor, Tash drew Sadie into his lap. "Done working on projects, goose, but not done with us. We love Autumn, right?"

Autumn's eyes flared.

Yup, I slipped that in there, he silently told her, liking her reaction.

Nodding, Sadie said, "We do. And she loves us, right?"

Tash looked to Autumn for verification, so she hastily nodded...and this time the tears overflowed.

"Oh, darn," she complained, laughing shakily and wiping at her cheeks. "Ember is right. Tears are contagious." It took her a second to collect herself, and then her face was as blotchy as Sadie's. "I do love you. Very much."

Huh. Here he'd thought himself clever by sliding his proclamation into the middle of things, but Autumn just outdid him. She stated her love while looking at Sadie, which left him wondering.

Did she love him, too?

But, hey, she'd said it, and he was sitting right there, holding his daughter. Not using her as a lure, never that. But he'd happily bask in the glow of their combined happiness.

"Tissues are in order," Tash said. "Then maybe ice cream?"

Giving him an impish smile, Autumn said, "It's a poor substitute, but I'll take it." She stood and held out a hand.

Tash took it before Sadie could. With his petite daughter held close to his chest, he came to his feet. Together they went into the kitchen for a now-familiar routine.

One he never wanted to give up.

Chapter Sixteen

Tonight she'd complete the additions to Tash's office, and it left Autumn with a bittersweet sense of accomplishment.

It had taken thirteen more days to get it all done, mostly because she'd dragged her feet. Summer break would end soon and Sadie would start school. It was unfair that she hadn't wrapped up sooner, but... The time she'd spent with Tash and Sadie was the happiest of her life.

She loved their routine, all the time they spent together...and yet, they lived separate lives.

Oh, she knew it wouldn't all come crashing to an end just because summer break ended. In fact, it should afford her and Tash more time to be intimate—a definite bonus.

And yet, it would also be different. She wouldn't have a good excuse to schedule time at his house. She'd be dependent on his invitations, and with Sadie's schoolwork, how often would that work out?

She liked having dinner with them. She enjoyed helping Tash

cook and putting the dishes away with Sadie. Darn it, she missed the fun of orchestrating Sadie's bedroom changes with her.

Tash and Mike left the barn, where they'd just put down fresh straw. Both men looked good sweaty, though she'd never tire of seeing Tash like this. Here, with her.

Damn it, she more than anyone else knew he had a life in town, complete with a nicely remodeled house.

Autumn blew out a breath.

Her life was here, on the farm, and his life was there, in a close neighborhood where Sadie could make friends—and so where did that leave them?

Standing at the pigpen, Autumn idly sprayed down Olivia and Matilda while the pigs wallowed in their play. A short distance away, Sadie leaned against the fence talking to Tracy the cow, the goat and sheep. Pavlov lolled on his back in the sun beside Sadie.

Her gaze went back to Tash, and she watched him swipe a wrist over his brow. The insufferable heat wave had passed, but the highs remained in the upper eighties, and the sun was bright in the cloudless sky.

With the pigs taken care of, Autumn headed out to join Sadie. Along the way, she saw Ember pull up. Mike strode to the work truck she'd driven, opened her door and pulled her out for a long kiss.

Shaking his head and grinning, Tash started her way but got intercepted when her mother came out with a tray of canned drinks and a bottle of water.

She and Tash seemed to get along really well. He'd found a rapport with her mom that eluded Autumn.

And why did that make her weepy?

Huffing out another breath, she turned away and continued toward Sadie. For whatever reason, she felt extra uncomfortable today, like her feet were cement blocks she had to drag along. Too hot, too listless and her nose itched. Bleh.

She didn't have time to be down. Tomorrow was stacked with appointments and she'd be starting two new jobs in the next town over.

Before Autumn reached Sadie, her mother called to her. Stifling her automatic groan, she lifted a hand to shield her eyes, looked back and waited.

Picking her way along in delicate slippers inappropriate to the uneven land, her mother said, "Not another step, young lady."

What now? Autumn disobeyed and covered the five steps necessary that put her under a scraggly tree and minimal shade.

Her mother, dressed in a loose hot pink tank top and yellow capris, didn't pause until she was right in front of Autumn, then she thrust the tray at her.

"Hold this."

Left with no other option, Autumn quickly took it. Only the bottle of water and a juice box remained, obviously drinks for her and Sadie. For some reason, it felt too heavy today. "I'm sure Sadie will appreciate—"

"Hush." Her mother put the back of her hand to Autumn's head, then tsked. "Just as I thought. You're feverish."

"I'm not," Autumn denied, mostly because she couldn't be sick. She didn't have time! "It's just the sun on my face—"

"I looked out the window," her mother interrupted, "and the second I saw you, I realized you were ill. Mothers always know these things."

Ember joined them. "Know what?"

"Autumn is sick."

Ember's brows went up and she gave Autumn a thorough inspection. "You know, you do look a little putrid."

She did not need Ember encouraging their mother. With a *shut up* glare, Autumn growled, "I'm fine."

Folding her arms over her impressive bosom, her mother gave her *the look*, one she'd been giving Autumn since she was two. It was the exact expression that reprimanded, challenged and declared victory all rolled into one. "Fighting it won't make it not so. Do you want to get Sadie sick? You need to go take a cool shower, some ibuprofen, and then you need to rest."

"Mom," Autumn complained, looking past her and Ember to where Tash was heading toward them. "I have stuff I need to do."

"Mike and I will get it done," Ember said. Then she, too, felt Autumn's forehead. "Dang, you're burning up. Why the heck didn't you say something?" Before Autumn could figure out how to silence her sister, Ember turned and bellowed to the guys, "Autumn's sick!"

Short-tempered—maybe because she *did* feel like crap—Autumn shoved her. "Why the hell did you do that?"

Her mother said, "Girls, behave."

Sadie leaned into her, her arms going around Autumn's hips. "You're sick?"

Too quickly for Autumn to reply, her mother snatched Sadie back. "Keep your distance, sweetheart, or you'll catch it."

"Mom..."

As Tash closed in on them, his eyebrows together in a worried frown, her mother warned him off, too. "No closer, Tash. Who knows if she's contagious."

Oh, for the love of... "I don't have the plague!"

"Tracy," Tash said, his tone firm, "would you mind taking Sadie up to the barn to drink her juice?"

"I'll bring the cow," Ember offered, which got Sadie's immediate agreement.

Pavlov looked from one human to the other, his loyalties divided.

"Ember will handle it," Tracy said, taking back the tray. "I need to get this one off her feet."

"Allow me." Tash put his arm around Autumn and urged her forward. "Honestly, honey, you do look exhausted."

"Not putrid?" she asked with a dirty look at Ember.

"Only a little."

Well...then maybe she did. "Mom's right. You should steer clear. If I do have a fever, you might catch something. Worse, if you get it, Sadie might, too."

"We've already been around you, so the damage is done." He gave her a slight hug. "Besides, I'm not about to budge."

Autumn had no idea what to say to that.

Giving up, Pavlov trotted after Ember, Sadie and Tracy the cow, while her mother issued orders to one and all.

"Poor Pavlov wasn't sure where to go," Tash noted.

"He loves everyone, but his instinct is to stick to Sadie. He adores kids."

"And other animals."

"Yes." Pavlov was the very best welcome committee for the injured or homeless pets they brought to the farm.

"And you," Tash said. "I'm surprised he didn't insist on sticking with you, since you're not feeling well."

"He'll show up," she predicted. "Throughout the day he checks on everyone."

Tash smiled. "He really is remarkable."

Her mother caught up with them and handed Autumn the water. "You have to stay hydrated."

Odd, but for once the mothering felt nice. *Gawd, I really am sick.* "Thanks, Mom." She tipped up the bottle and drank a third, yet still felt thirsty.

With Tash half supporting her and her mother clucking out her worry, Autumn finally made it to the house, where she promptly collapsed onto the couch with no immediate desire to move a single inch.

"This won't do," her mother said. "You need medicine, a cool shower, a change into more comfortable clothes and then a nice long nap."

Tash crouched in front of her. "You have aspirin in your medicine cabinet?"

"Yes." She closed her eyes against the pounding in her head, but still said, "Thanks."

As Tash walked away, her mother plopped down beside her, making her bounce. Gently, she smoothed back Autumn's sweaty hair. "Such a warrior," she teased. "Don't fight it, honey. We all need a little help now and then."

Autumn got one eye open to peer at her. She couldn't recall ever hearing that particular tone from her mom.

"I promise," her mother continued, "you'll feel much more comfortable if you just follow my directions. I've been caring for you for a very long time, you know, and look at how you've turned out."

Autumn blinked. "Is that an insult or a compliment?"

Thinking she was joking, her mother laughed. "I don't mind saying, I've obviously done something right."

A compliment, then. "I... Thanks, Mom."

"Let me help you with your shower, then you should sleep."

Her mother helping her shower? A horrible prospect. Absolutely not.

Luckily, Tash reentered. "I'll see to her, Tracy." He handed Autumn two pills and the water. "Would you mind keeping an eye on Sadie for an hour or so? Maybe you could show her the best way to draw farm animals. She's been practicing, you know."

One brow arching, Tracy said, "I know exactly what you're up to, young man." A smile softened her expression. "And I heartily approve. Come get Sadie whenever you're ready, no rush at all. We'll be in my kitchen drawing pig snouts and goat hooves and turkey feathers." She patted Autumn on the head, embraced Tash and all but danced out.

When the door closed, Autumn turned to Tash, her eyes wide. "That was *weird*."

He grinned. "Your mother is more astute than you realize. So what do you think? Are you able to shower?"

"Of course." But, oh, it sounded like a terrible challenge. With some obvious effort, she forced herself to sit forward. "You don't need to babysit me, I promise."

Catching her arms, Tash gently brought her to her feet. "I'm where I want to be, so stop trying to throw me out."

She glanced at the door again. Closed but not locked. "You know, you're a little sweaty." And they actually had a small amount of time alone. Surely she could muster up some energy. "Did you want to shower, too?"

"With you?" Smiling, he brushed his knuckles over her cheek. "Probably not a good idea. I want you too much and I won't be able to keep my hands to myself if we're both naked."

Eh, she didn't blame him. After all, according to her sister, she didn't look her best.

"Your mother's right, you know. You need some rest. Maybe even a trip to the doctor."

"No." They headed to the bathroom. "I'll probably feel better tomorrow." Sleep, she'd discovered, was an incredible cure-all.

Unfortunately, as she showered she grew more depleted, her legs shaking and her eyes half closing. She felt foolish when Tash helped her change into a big sleep shirt and panties, then practically tucked her into her bed. Once her head hit the pillow, it was all she could do not to drift off.

He kissed her forehead. "I'm going to check on Sadie. Sleep if you can. I'll be back in a few minutes."

That was the last she heard for hours. When she awakened again, it was dark out, her house quiet, and Pavlov slept over her legs.

The second she moved, so did the dog. Elated, he reared up and barked.

Though still sluggish, Autumn managed a smile. "Hello, to you too, Pavlov." Oh, good grief, she croaked like a frog. Now that she'd heard herself, her throat felt like sandpaper.

Pavlov army-crawled up the bed until he could snuffle against her neck.

Forcing her limp arms to comply, she hugged him, doing what she could to reassure the dog that she was fine.

Footsteps sounded in her hall and a second later, Tash stepped in. He was still here? A glance at the clock told her it was after eleven.

Pushing up to sit against the headboard, she swept her gaze over him. He'd showered and changed into…sleep pants and a white T-shirt?

Was he staying the night then?

"Hey, you." Striding in, he sat on the side of the bed and put a palm to her forehead, then her cheek. "Still feverish. Think you can swallow more aspirin?"

"Um…"

He winced. "Losing your voice, huh? Throat hurt?" Taking a bottle of water from her nightstand, he unscrewed the cap and handed it to her. "Be right back."

Thoughts muddled, she watched him go, but he returned in seconds to hand her the pills.

Since she really did feel wretched, she swallowed them quickly, cleared her throat and stated the obvious. "You're still here."

"Hope that's okay. I brought over my laptop and was doing some work. I knew Pavlov would let me know when you woke." He stroked the dog. Pavlov loved it.

"Sadie?"

"She spent the night with Ember, who for once is right next door instead of in Mike's loft. Actually, Mike is right next door, too, sleeping on the couch so Sadie could share the bed with Ember."

It took her a second to process all that, and then Autumn whispered, "Wow." It seemed she'd caused a lot of trouble for everyone.

"Your mother called the family doctor, but apparently a nasty virus is going around. Fever, headache, exhaustion."

She had all three. Ugh.

"He said if you're not better in a week—"

"A *week*?"

"—or if your fever gets too high, then you should come in."

No way could she miss an entire week of work. She'd not only fall behind, but she'd also lose the new jobs and that would affect the upkeep of the farm. "I have appointments tomorrow—"

"Ember called and canceled for you."

Autumn was so appalled, no words came to her.

"She also went to the store with Sadie. They got you Popsicles, fresh crackers and ginger ale. Does any of that appeal?"

Her lungs finally filled with a necessary breath. "Ember went to the store? For me?"

"For you." He smoothed the sheet around her shoulders. "Also, your mother made you soup. She said it was your favorite." His smile sent flutters to her stomach. "I take it you don't get sick very often, because it puts everyone into a tailspin."

"I never get sick."

He cupped her cheek and gave her a level look. "You're sick now."

Of all the rotten luck…

Mistaking her frown, he said, "I hope you don't mind that I'm staying over. Your mother wanted me to carry you to her place—"

"*What?*"

"—because she didn't want you to be alone, but Flynn's wheelchair works better at their place. Ember insisted she'd stay with you instead. Mike's concerned, as well, so he manned up about it, but I thought he might end up on your couch and that seemed like more confusion than you needed." Tash spread his arms. "So you have me, and I hope you're not going to object because I figured I was the better alternative."

He was the best alternative always, in every situation. "I don't want to get you sick."

"Given we've been together all week, the doc said that's not likely. If I was going to get it, I already would have."

"Sadie..."

"She has a medical mask to wear if she comes in to say hi."

A mask. Wow. "I detest being a bother."

"I'm not bothered," he insisted, "and all I saw with your family was caring and concern."

Autumn rubbed her temples and sighed. "Thank you. You'd think I was at death's door or something."

"No, they just love you and they're not used to seeing you down." Another tender smile. "How do you feel about eating?"

He kept looking at her, his expression warm and...nurturing? She imagined he looked at Sadie like that, and it naturally made her rebel. "I'm a little hungry." She'd slept right through dinner and even illness didn't quell her appetite. "I'll just run to the john and then I can get some soup or something—"

"Autumn." He stopped her as she swung her legs over the side of the bed. "I'd really appreciate it if you let me help you."

"Help me in the john?" Mortified, she shook her head. "I can handle it on my own, thank you."

The smile cracked into a grin. "Help you *to* the john, and then I'll heat your soup." While her face burned, he continued. "You feel like eating in bed or at the table?"

"Table." She wasn't used to being a slug and felt ridiculous already. "Seriously, I can make it on my own."

When she stood, Pavlov also left the bed, standing alert at her side, watching to see what she'd do next. True, her legs were shaky and she wasn't quite up to straightening her shoulders, but neither was she an invalid.

"All right." Hand on her elbow, Tash followed her to the bathroom door. "I'll get the soup ready. Yell if you need me."

Pavlov looked between them, undecided, then sat down to await her.

Tash patted his head. "Good dog."

Sadly, by the time she'd finished, washed her hands, splashed her face and hobbled into the kitchen, she was shot. Her legs felt incapable of supporting her a second more. With Pavlov sticking close, she slumped into her chair and breathed in the scent of her mother's homemade chicken noodle soup.

Crazy how comforting that smelled, taking her back to her youth.

Seeing her settled, Pavlov went out the doggy door, no doubt for his own bathroom break. He returned a few minutes later, got a drink, then collapsed with a huff at her feet. Like her family, he wasn't used to her being sick.

Standing at the stove, Tash continually stirred a big spoon around in a pot. "Your mom said I couldn't microwave it. It has to be heated the old-fashioned way."

Her mom probably knew how insanely sexy he'd look standing there in his sleep clothes, stubble on his face, his hair disheveled. In fact, she was starting to wonder what her mom *didn't* know.

At the other end of the table, he'd left his laptop, a few folders, and some scattered papers. It hit her like a ton of bricks. "I'm interrupting your work."

"I was just about done, anyway."

Given what she saw, she doubted that. To her it looked like he'd been elbow-deep in a project. She hated to be a burden, but what could she say? He looked determined to stay, to pamper her. And honestly? She wasn't sure she'd make it back to the bed on her own.

For a brief moment, she wondered what Ember would do. Her sis was well used to men fawning on her, but she also personified independence. How to show Tash her appreciation while freeing him from obligation? Or should she even try?

In the end, she didn't say or do anything except concentrate on staying upright in her seat.

He joined her with a bowl of his own and iced tea for them both, waiting until she started to eat before spooning up a bite for himself.

His gaze met hers. "Damn, that is good."

And it felt soothing to her raw throat. "Mom's a terrific cook."

"I agree."

Her raspy voice didn't invite conversation, so they finished the meal in silence. The fact that he was eating, too, made it easier than if he'd only served her. She ate half the bowl before she lost what little energy she had. It took all her resolve not to rest her head on her folded arms and fade away.

Tash said nothing as he finished his soup and put everything away.

Amazing how comfortable he was in her kitchen, reminding her of that first day, when she'd visited his house and he'd been making tacos.

Thinking of a T-shirt she'd once seen, she said, "A man who cooks is sexy, but a man who cleans is irresistible."

He flashed a wicked smile while washing the pan. "Good to know since I plan to be here for the duration."

Her heart stuttered. "The duration?"

"Until you're well. If it's two days or ten, I'll figure it out."

He intends to stay with me the whole time. Heaven only knew how bad she'd look tomorrow...but did it matter? If he was sick, she'd want to help him, too. That rationale made the situation easier to accept.

It felt like she took a giant step when she nodded. "Okay." His first overnight. Granted, nothing sexual would happen, but still. This might be better.

This meant he really cared...didn't it?

No other man had spent the night with her. The close proximity to her parents made it impractical. When her hectic schedule had allowed, she'd occasionally stayed at Chuck's apartment, but always he'd had the expectation of sex.

What Tash did now felt far more personal.

Without appearing to work, he finished up and even wiped off the table. "I need to brush my teeth and then we can head to bed."

"Bed?" she croaked. Why did it sound like he planned to join her in *one* bed—hers?

Ears up, Pavlov shot out from under the table. Clearly going back to bed suited him.

Urging her to her feet, Tash said, "I can camp out on the couch if you want, but if it won't disturb your sleep, I'd love to hold you."

Love. Her heart tripped so fast it almost hurt. "I—" That single word sounded like gravel so she cleared her throat and tried again, going for a blasé tone. "I don't mind if you sleep with me." *Fantasy meet reality.* "If that's what you want." He'd already said he did, damn it. *Stop blathering, Autumn.* "You'll have to share with Pavlov."

His grin told her he knew she was flustered, but didn't mind. "Pavlov and I are pals, so no problem."

The dog eagerly followed them back down the hall. When they paused by the bathroom, he continued on and leaped into the bed, taking up his usual spot toward the footboard.

To Autumn, it appeared the dog had just left her in Tash's capable hands. "I should brush my teeth, too."

"All right." He let her go first. Given her fading energy, it didn't take her long. After getting her tucked into bed, Tash took three minutes for himself, then joined her.

As if it was the most natural thing in the world he closed the bedroom door, turned out the lights and crawled into bed to spoon her, carefully adjusting his feet around Pavlov's unmoving body.

"Okay?"

Mmm, better than okay. She snuggled into him, sighed and closed her eyes. "Perfect."

His kiss to her temple was the last thing she was aware of until she woke the next morning, bright sunshine bleeding through the blinds, her head pounding and her limbs wilted.

Once she got her eyes to focus, she found her father there, his eyes staring at her with laserlike focus above his medical mask. He watched her as if he expected her to expire.

Confused, she struggled up to one elbow. "Dad?"

One eyebrow shot up, he turned his head and bellowed, *"She's 'wake"* in his slurred voice.

Hurried footsteps, which definitely weren't Tash's, preceded her mother's theatrical entrance. Full of drama, she paused in the doorway, clasped her hands together and sang, "Oh, thank God." She, too, wore a mask.

Autumn tried to swallow without much success.

"It's so good to see your smiling face."

Pretty sure she wasn't smiling, Autumn asked, "Water?"

Rushing forward, her mother assisted her with a drink. "It's noon, and you've had me worried silly."

Noon?

Flattening her palm to Autumn's forehead, her mother said, "Fever doesn't feel any worse. Are you hungry?"

She didn't know what she was. Fuzzy-brained, listless, achy all over. "Tash?"

"He's helping Mike and Sadie with the chores. Ember went to a jobsite but said she'd be home in a few hours."

Ramifications swirled in her muddled mind. "The animals…"

"Mike has it covered. He knows what he's doing." Preening, her mother said, "And I've helped."

What? *No.* Autumn decided she had to be dreaming. Her mother didn't dislike animals, but she wanted as little to do with them as possible. And yet, she appeared serious.

"Don't look at me like that," her mom protested. "I can feed chickens. I can spray pigs."

In his chair behind Tracy, her dad leered. "Like a li'l country girl," he said, eyebrows bobbing as he reached out to pat her mother on the butt.

"Behave Flynn," she told him with a smile in her voice, then encouraged him by adding, "I wore this adorable scarf around my hair, my jeans with a T-shirt tied at the waist. It was a fetching outfit."

"Fetching," her dad agreed.

Somehow she got through the rest of the day—mostly by sleeping for long stretches, reading when she could stay awake and the occasional visit from Sadie, Ember and, most especially, Tash.

Tash was the only one not wearing a mask and it worried her, but he kept promising her he felt fine.

That night he held her again, and it almost made it worth being sick. *Almost.*

Tomorrow, Autumn vowed, she'd get out of bed and get on with her life, freeing Tash to do the same. She wasn't a wimp. She could—and would—get her butt in gear.

The next time Tash shared her bed, they'd get more accomplished than sleep, guaranteed.

Chapter Seventeen

For three more days, she barely got out of the bed, couldn't stay awake more than an hour and felt wretched from her toes to her pounding head. Her fever finally ended, but it left her limp as a noodle. She woke only long enough to eat very light meals, use the bathroom and wash up before crashing again.

On the fifth day, Tash came into her room and touched her shoulder. "Hey, sleepyhead. How do you feel?"

He'd done that off and on each day—checked on her and made her comfortable, seeing if there was anything she needed.

Today she was finally alert enough that it embarrassed her.

Pushing up in the bed, her back to the headboard, she stretched and glanced at the clock. Wincing, she saw it was dinnertime. "I'm so sorry."

His smile went crooked. "You did what you were supposed to do—sleep. Besides, I've enjoyed being here, helping to take care of you. The farm is amazing, but your home is nice, too. I really like it."

Her thoughts snagged on that statement, then whirled into

chaos. A hint that he wouldn't mind sticking around more, even after she was well?

No, how could he with an impressionable daughter? It was different with her sick and Sadie spending her nights with Ember, but now...

Best that she not read too much into it.

"Thank you." She pushed back the sheet, then made a face at her wrinkled sleep shirt. Shoving back her hair, she queried her body and decided she was on the mend. "I want a shower, clean clothes and real food."

Leaning over the bed, Tash touched her cheek with the backs of his fingers. "You're sleep-warm, but not feverish." He tucked a wayward hank of hair behind her ear.

She'd rather not know how bad her hair looked.

Tash didn't seem to notice. "How about I get the shower ready, then while you're in there I can put together a plate for you?"

Her stomach growled. That surely had to mean something, right? For days it had been soup and crackers, but now...? She wanted a meal. "Okay, sure." Her voice sounded normal again, too. Looking around, she asked, "Where's Pavlov?"

"Trailing your mother. She's gotten into the whole farm-girl routine, as she calls it, egged on by your dad."

"Oh, Lord."

"They're still crazy about each other. Nothing wrong with that."

If she looked at it that way... "You're right, of course." She just wished they'd show a little discretion.

"Tracy actually seems to like the animals. She's with Sadie out in the field talking to her namesake with Pavlov keeping watch." He leaned in a little and confided, "I don't think the dog trusts your mother to do things right."

Autumn's laugh sounded only a little rusty. "Pavlov is a very smart dog."

"True." Tash helped her to her feet. "Ember and Mike grilled earlier. There's a pork chop and potato left, and salad in the fridge. Does that sound okay or would you rather have soup? Sorry, but there's only canned left."

"Food that I can chew sounds like heaven." Experimentally, she took a few steps. Weak, yes, but not shaky.

In the shower, she scrubbed clean and brushed her teeth. *Twice.* That alone made her feel much better.

After towel-drying her hair and finger-combing it smooth, she slathered on lotion, then dressed into a clean T-shirt and pull-on shorts.

The mirror was not her friend, showing the dark circles under her eyes and the paleness of her skin, but recovery felt too good to complain.

Heck, just being out of the bed was a gift.

Tash sat with her at the table, drinking coffee and eating a cookie while she devoured her food. Even reheated, it was the best pork chop she'd ever tasted.

She'd just finished when a tap sounded on the kitchen door. She and Tash both looked up, only to find Patricia Schaffer standing there, all smiles and brimming curiosity.

Tash didn't look happy with the company. "I can send her away if you want."

He'd do that for her? Knowing him, he'd somehow be nice about it, too. "No, it's fine. She means well."

Visibly unconvinced, Tash went to the door and welcomed her. "Patricia. I haven't seen you since that night at the beach."

"I know, it's been *forever.*" Without taking a breath, she added, "How've you been? Playing house with Autumn, I see. Have you moved in here? What about your daughter? I've heard so many rumors."

As if she hadn't rudely grilled him, Tash nodded to the dish she held. "What do you have there?"

"Oh, *this*?" Patricia lifted a foil-covered aluminum baking pan. "It's my *very* special vegetables, ham-and-cheese quiche. Autumn favored it once, so I thought if she's feeling better, she might like it."

Wow. Even with her habit of exaggerating words, Autumn was impressed with the thoughtful gesture. "Thank you, Patricia." To Tash, she said, "Patricia brought her quiche to a community meeting and it was a big hit."

"Nice." Tash took the dish from her. "Autumn just finished eating but I'm sure she'll love it for her brunch tomorrow."

"Oh, *you'll* need to try it, too. I made plenty." Patricia gave him a look. "You'll still be here, right?"

"Take a seat," he said, again ignoring her question. "I'll get this put away."

Frowning, Patricia pulled up a chair at the table, then gave her a pitying look. "How *are* you, Autumn? Still miserable?"

Autumn almost laughed. "Actually, I'm feeling much better today."

"Oh, good. You were supposed to meet friends of mine a few days ago, but they said *Ember* called that you had an *awful* virus. I promised them you were worth the delay." Patricia beamed, waiting for Autumn's gratitude.

"Thank you," Autumn dutifully replied. "You recommended me to them?"

"Well, *of course* I did. You're the only interior designer I know, but I can tell you're good." She scooted her chair so close their knees bumped. "I wanted to visit you earlier, but after I told Chuck you were sick, he said you might be *contagious* and he didn't want *me* to risk getting sick, too."

Autumn's composure slipped. "Chuck?"

"We're seeing each other now." With a happy smile, Patricia revealed, "He promised me that he's *completely* over you—"

Tash's bark of laughter drew their attention. Even though he stood at the counter putting away the dishes from her meal, he obviously listened in.

Autumn saw him shake his head.

Patricia looked between them, her eyes narrowing. "Why is *that* funny?"

"Inside joke," Autumn lied, but sympathy forced her to say more. "If you're happy with Chuck, I'm happy for you."

"Thank you."

Ho, boy. This was harder than Autumn could have imagined. "But you know Chuck, right? You know who he is, what he is—"

"He's *changed!*"

No, he absolutely hadn't, and deep down, Patricia had to know it. Autumn didn't have it in her to press it further, though. "I hope you're right." She smiled.

After another quick glance at Tash, Patricia said, "Chuck was thinking about visiting you, too—"

No way.

"—but I told him he *probably* shouldn't just yet."

"Better not to chance it," Tash stated, his tone hard as he tossed down his hand towel. Belatedly, he turned to Autumn. "Right?"

"Exactly right," she agreed. "I'm sorry, Patricia, but Chuck isn't welcome here. Not ever."

Distressed, Patricia again looked between them. "We live in the *same* town."

"Yes, and if we run in to each other I'll be polite." Autumn took her hand. "You're a friend, and I will never deliberately embarrass you or put you on the spot. I promise."

"Thank you." Patricia squeezed her hand in return, then abruptly turned to Tash. "So you live here now?"

Autumn almost rolled her eyes. Since Patricia hadn't gotten an answer the first time, she'd asked again. Well, Autumn would nicely tell her to mind her own business, so Tash wouldn't have to.

She started to speak, and suddenly her kitchen door swung open again and her mother charged in.

"Patricia! Oh, so lovely to see you," her mother panted, obviously winded. She grabbed Patricia's arm and hauled her out of her seat. "Now you really must go."

"Go?" Patricia tried to hold back, but for a plump, short woman, her mother had strength...of all kinds. "But I just got here!"

"Yes, and you've said your hellos." Dragging her to the door, Tracy explained, "Autumn has been very sick, you know. I'm limiting her to short visits only. In fact, I'm sure Tash is taking her back to bed right now."

Titillated, Patricia asked, "You *want* him to take her to bed?"

"Don't be a prude, Patricia. Of course I do. He's taken very good care of my daughter. He's a stellar young man. Stellar." Turning her eye on Tash, she ordered, "Go on now. Autumn needs her rest."

"Yes, ma'am," Tash said around a barely banked grin.

He had Autumn on her feet, urging her down the hall, before she could take it all in. Her mother had come to her rescue? Incredible.

Over her shoulder, Autumn belatedly called, "Thank you for the quiche, Patricia!"

Whatever her friend replied back, Autumn couldn't hear... because Tash was laughing so hard.

His humor brought on her own. Snickering, Autumn nudged him. "I don't think I've ever seen my mother move that quickly."

"She's a force of nature, for sure." There, outside her bedroom, Tash smiled down at her. "How do you feel?"

"Well enough that I'm unwilling to go back to bed just to fend off Patricia."

His grin quirked. "I think I heard the kitchen door close. The coast should be clear now."

Still huffing, her mother came down the hall. "Mercy, that

was more cardio than I've done in years." She collapsed against the wall, one hand fanning her face. "Patricia is on her way."

"Mom," Autumn said, feeling ridiculously proud, "however did you know?"

"I didn't, because you, young lady, have never told me."

Autumn felt the flush climbing up from her neck. Tell her mother about Patricia snooping, carrying rumors, sharing gossip? Until this moment, she hadn't known they had that type of relationship. Lamely, she muttered, "There wasn't much to tell."

"Ha!" Her mom drank in another deep breath, then let it out slowly. "Patricia pulled up just as Sadie and I were returning to the barn. Ember saw her, but she had her hands full of tools, so she frantically *ordered* me to come run interference." She finally straightened off the wall. "'Go save Autumn,' Ember said. 'That woman is a menace and she'll upset her.' Nearly startled me out of my skin, but Ember's attitude didn't leave room for questions so I just sprinted here—*me*, sprinting!—not knowing what I'd find, but the second I saw you, I knew you were uncomfortable." Her mother peeked at her. "Did she upset you, dear?"

Affection overwhelmed Autumn, gathering in her throat, making it difficult to swallow, compelling her to do something she didn't do often. She snuggled into her mother's embrace. "No, Mom," she promised. "I'm fine."

For a second, Tracy was startled, then her arms came around Autumn, enclosing her in soft, familiar warmth. "Good, that's good." With a pat to her back, she asked, "You're feeling better now?"

"Very much so." Autumn leaned back to grin at her. "You made quite the rescue."

Her mother blushed, then blushed more when Tash leaned in to kiss her cheek.

"Very impressive, Tracy." Tash smiled. "Thank you."

"She's my daughter." Tracy lifted her nose. "No one bullies her but me."

Autumn laughed again. Maybe her mother's brand of bully-
ing wasn't so bad.

"You should be in bed resting," Tracy announced.

Luckily, Tash saved her. "I was leading her to the couch. She's
had enough of the bed for a while." To Autumn, he said, "You
could read while I help Mike and Ember finish up, then Sadie
can visit for a minute. She's missed you."

That sounded like an excellent plan. She only had one chap-
ter left in her Karen Rose book and she couldn't wait to get to
the end...because then she could start the next one.

The idea of crashing in ultimate comfort appealed, but her
mother insisted on helping. She conceded that Autumn could
rest on the couch as long as she had her feet up, a light throw
blanket handy to counter the air-conditioning and she must
consume another bottle of water.

Because her mom was currently one of her favorite people,
Autumn didn't argue. Several minutes later she was finally ready
to pick up her book when her mother took a seat beside her.

Knowing her mom had something on her mind, Autumn
asked, "Everything okay?"

"Now that you're feeling better, yes."

And...that obviously didn't cover it, because Autumn remained under her mother's close scrutiny. "What's wrong,
Mom?"

"I'm not used to seeing you down." Tracy blew out a shuddering breath as if releasing pent-up worries. "The doctor kept
stressing what an awful virus this is, and how it zaps energy
levels, so it wasn't unexpected that you'd sleep so much. But
knowing the facts didn't matter to my heart. You're always such
a stalwart example of pride, determination and responsibility all
rolled into one remarkable daughter. Seeing you sick in bed...
it shook me."

Remorse tightened Autumn's chest. "I'm so sorry, Mom."

As if she hadn't spoken, her mother continued on. "And yet

I had fun. The animals, especially when seen through Sadie's eyes, are an absolute delight." Assuming Autumn didn't already know it, she said, "They each have individual personalities!"

"Yes," Autumn agreed, her smile breaking through. "Much like children."

Her mother waved off the hint. "I've helped watch Sadie in the evenings, too. Not overnight or anything—Ember insisted she keep her—but I've been teaching her how to work with clay. She's gifted, you know. A very smart child."

"Very cute, too," Autumn concurred, enjoying her mother's newfound gusto.

That is, until her gaze snapped up to Autumn's.

Uh-oh, Autumn thought, familiar with that expression.

Her mother's chin firmed and her brows leveled. She stated with conviction, "I want Sadie for a grandchild."

The bold declaration took Autumn by surprise. "Um, Mom—"

"I want her." She grabbed Autumn's hands. "Sadie and I are good together. She makes me feel young and she makes your father laugh."

Autumn tried a smile, but it fell flat. "That's wonderful, but—"

"Do you know, Sadie can offer Flynn anything, even vegetables he abhors, and he'll eat them! Gladly. The man has never consumed more healthy food, and without a single argument from me."

Feeling her way, Autumn gave a small nod. "Sadie would be hard to refuse."

"And *Tash*," she happily gushed, pressing a hand to her heart. "Oh, Autumn, you could do worse than that one. Such a charmer he is, so very handsome, and a hard worker. He'd take on anything without complaining, and he'd do it well, too." She nodded to affirm it all as truth.

The lump forming in Autumn's throat now wasn't quite so

pleasant, and was, in fact, bordering on painful. "Yes, Mom, he's quite a catch." A catch who currently had his hands full… and she'd added to his burden.

"He's exhausted, you know," her mom added, easily reading the concern on Autumn's face. "Luckily he didn't get sick, but he's been burning the candle on both ends and in the middle, too! Caring for Sadie and you, working the farm during the day and on his computer half the night."

Guilt was a terrible thing. "I know."

Her mother gave her a light shove. "Well, then do something about it."

Good grief. Her mom went from loving on her to scolding her to sounding downright annoyed. "It's not like I planned to get sick."

"Of course you didn't! But if you two shared a household, neither one of you would have to work as hard." Her mother rushed on before Autumn could finish gasping. "Sadie loves it here and she told me she misses Tracy the cow whenever she goes home, even though she's thrilled with her new bedroom. Just think how nice it would be to tuck that little angel into bed each night."

It would be heaven…except Tash hadn't said anything about being in love with her, not directly, anyway, but he had been clear about his priorities—priorities that had apparently flown the coop when she got ill.

Remorse surfaced, making Autumn sink into the couch. "This is awful."

"But it doesn't have to be, that's what I'm saying."

The connecting door opened and Ember came in, along with their dad. They were laughing together, until they realized they'd blundered into a serious discussion.

Silence fell with heavy condemnation, then Ember demanded, "What's going on?" Circling the couch, she sat on the coffee table near Autumn's feet. "Are you okay?"

"I'm fine, yes." Physically, anyway. "Much improved, thanks."

Ember's eyes narrowed as she shifted her accusing gaze to their mother. "What did you do to upset her?"

Chin going up again, their mom said, "I only told Autumn the truth."

"What truth?" Ember asked.

Their father's wheelchair made a light buzzing noise as he propelled himself forward and around to face them. His eyebrows twitched as he took in the expression of first one daughter, then the other, and finally his wife. He nodded. "Need to marry the boy."

Autumn's mouth dropped open. *"Dad."* How in the world had he surmised the conversation so quickly?

"That," her mother insisted, "is the truth, and the only solution."

"It's not a solution at all!" Her parents had leaped far past anything that was possible and Autumn wasn't sure how to rein them back in.

And yet, after a thoughtful second, even Ember agreed. "It's not a bad idea, Autumn. You know you want him."

She couldn't believe they ganged up on her like this, as if *her* wants were the only issues at stake. "I should have stayed in the bed!"

Snorting, her mom patted her knee. "You've never shirked a day in your life. No way would you start now."

"Marry 'im," her dad demanded again. "We'll keep 'em both."

"They're not pets to be brought to the farm, Dad. Tash has his own house, newly remodeled, by the way, to perfectly suit him and his daughter."

"You're not there," her mother said, "so it does not perfectly suit them at all."

If only that was a valid point. "His house is not set up for a third, and neither is my place."

"Don't be silly. We have room." Ember looked around. "I

spend all my time with Mike, anyway, and I could easily turn this back into a single home rather than a duplex. It'd just be a matter of—"

"He hasn't asked!" If no one else would face reality, Autumn would do it for them.

With everyone now staring at her, she wanted to groan. She hadn't meant to bark that out there, but seriously, just because she wasn't passed out in the bed did not mean she was one hundred percent yet. She didn't think she'd ever be ready for this particular full-family discussion.

"This one here," her mother grumbled, pointing at Ember, "didn't sit around waiting for a proposal."

"No I didn't," Ember agreed.

"Ember," her mother stressed with pride, "went after what she wanted."

"Because she's the *free spirit*." Autumn crossed her arms, belligerence personified. "I'm the stalwart one, remember? With big bones and perspiration and—"

"Look like yer mother," her dad snapped. *"Beautiful."*

Tracy preened. "Thank you, Flynn." Then she took Autumn's hands and there wasn't a single thing Autumn could do about it.

"You are my beautiful, brave, caring daughter. You make me so proud every day."

"Us," Flynn interjected. "Make *us* proud."

Awww. That heartfelt declaration stole every ounce of Autumn's irritation. "Thank you, both."

"But if you muck this up," her mom vowed, "I will be so— so..."

Eyebrows up, Autumn waited to see what dire consequence her mother would name.

"Sorry for you. I will be so incredibly sorry for you, Autumn, because Tash is obviously the one for you."

Well. An outright insult would be easier than pity.

"*I'll* ask 'im," her father snapped as he started to furiously roll away a little faster than his usual easy pace.

Oh. Dear. God. Shot through with panic, Autumn turned a pleading do-something gaze on her sister.

Smiling, Ember stood and caught one handle on the chair. "Not how it's done, Dad, believe me. Besides, Autumn will take care of it. She's too smart not to." Keeping a firm grip on their father's chair so he couldn't get away, Ember asked, "Isn't that right, sis?"

They all looked at Autumn with varying degrees of expectation.

She slumped. "Yes, I'll handle it." Somehow. But she couldn't handle it this very minute. Hoping it would appease them all for now, she promised, "Soon."

Her dad leveled her with a long look. "Beautiful. 'Member that."

Autumn managed a smile for him. "Thanks, Dad. Love you."

"Love you, too."

"Caring," her mother added. "Smart and capable and *generous*. Sometimes too damn generous."

Since her mother rarely cursed, both sisters watched her in stunned silence.

"Tash is the first man I've met who deserves you." With a stern scowl, her mother pleaded, "Don't let him leave here without a commitment."

Nodding, Autumn whispered, "Thank you." She could barely get the words out, and sounded a little broken when she whispered, "I love you, Mom."

"And I love you." Standing, her attitude all-business, she turned to Ember and said, "Convince her."

"Yeah." Ember grinned. "I'll do my best."

Finally her mother and father left, mumbling to themselves about the many trials of parenting.

Autumn dropped her head back on the couch, and squeezed her eyes shut.

"What," Ember asked, "was *that*?"

"Love." Autumn heaved a sigh. "I think that was love and now I'll never be able to complain about her again."

"Don't go overboard." Ember dropped down beside her. "This moment will fade, I promise. It was nice, though, huh? Almost brought a tear to my eye."

Autumn snorted, then sighed again when a new worry intruded. "What if they accost Tash?"

"He's a big boy, he can handle it." Ember nudged her. "But they won't—at least not yet. Mom's counting on you to man up and do the right thing, mostly because you always do the right thing, right?"

That convoluted sentence left Autumn confused. "What?"

"The right thing." She shrugged. "You always do it."

"This wasn't right." Autumn gestured at her house. "Keeping Tash here, interrupting his life, disrupting his daughter's schedule—"

"All at his insistence."

"I should have refused.

Ember leaned back to stare at her. "Okay, so maybe where men are concerned, you've made some mistakes. God knows you're misjudging Tash now, but then I did some misjudging of my own, so I won't hold that against you. Mom and Dad, though..." She let that hang. "They're really attached to Tash and Sadie."

Autumn slanted her a look. "You scored big points with Mike. That should tide them over."

"True. In the two years Mike's been here, they've grown to care a lot for him. Sometimes they like him more than they like us." She leaned into Autumn, snuggling close with her head on her shoulder and her arm across her waist. "Think about it, sis. It only took Tash a few days to steal their hearts."

Struck by that, Autumn's brows went up. She had her mom and dad both fighting to keep Tash, something they'd never done before. "Amazing."

"You have no idea. Tash has Mom completely bowled over. Around him, she *giggles*."

No, Autumn refused to imagine it.

"Dad can't say enough good things about him. They both think he's the most amazing father they've ever met." She laughed softly, tipping her face up to see Autumn. "After all, he has to be since Sadie is so perfect."

Thinking of Sadie made it impossible not to smile. "She is pretty special."

"So." Ember sat up, turning on the couch to sit yoga-style so that she faced Autumn. "Proposing isn't so tough, I promise. I'll do it for you if you want."

That outrageous offer surprised a laugh out of her. If Tash refused, would Ember threaten him? Probably. "I'll figure it out." Somehow. Truthfully, just the thought unsettled her stomach.

"Yeah, well do it soon because odds are he'll feel the need to move back home now that you're feeling better, and we'll all miss him if he does."

Shoot. Would he try to leave tonight? Autumn looked toward the window, but this time of the year the sun lingered until late.

"Plus, we can still use his help around here. You're going to need another day of taking it easy before you dive back in. No argument," Ember said before Autumn could deny her dictate. "You know it's true."

Okay, so she did still feel washed out. She could push through. Maybe. "Ugh. You could be right."

Pulling her into a hug, Ember whispered, "Mom is right, you know. Tash definitely deserves you—and you, my crazy, too-damn-perfect sister, more than deserve him. Remember that."

Before Autumn realized it, Ember slipped away, leaving through the connecting door.

She would have felt abandoned except that Pavlov came charging in, thrilled to see her. He made an agile leap up to the couch, crowded close and covered her face with doggy kisses.

Laughing, Autumn corralled him a little to the side while crooning to him. "Did you have a good day, buddy? You kept an eye on Mom, didn't you? Such a good dog."

Tail swinging wildly, Pavlov rolled to his back, his head in her lap, and more or less demanded a belly rub.

That's how Tash and Sadie found them a few minutes later.

Autumn took one look at his face…and she knew. Tonight would be it, unless she spoke up. More than her mom or dad did, more than Ember or Mike could, *she* wanted Tash to be with her always. She wanted him to share her life. She needed him and Sadie to be close.

Because she loved them both.

Maybe it was time she told them so.

Chapter Eighteen

"**A**utumn!" Sadie ran to the couch with unending energy. It amazed Tash that the more Sadie did, the more she wanted to do. Everything from helping groom the animals to spreading straw, creating art and playing hard, she never tired.

Around his dynamo of a daughter, Tracy was a different person, not as outspoken, and more mindful of her words.

And Flynn! What a softie. The elder Somerset loved it that Sadie didn't hesitate to crowd close to his chair and gift him with hugs and cheek kisses.

"I don't have to wear a mask anymore 'cuz Dad said you're not 'tagious now." She proved that by going straight to Autumn's lap for a tight hug around her neck.

"I've missed you, Sadie," Autumn said, making room for her on the couch.

Pavlov didn't mind, but then he adored Sadie, too, and had become her near-constant shadow.

Cupping Autumn's face in her small hands, Sadie studied her. "You feel better?"

"Much, much better. Thank you."

"Dad was real worried."

"Was he?" Autumn glanced at him. "He makes an amazing nurse."

Sadie got so close, her nose nearly touched Autumn's when she whispered, "He's really good at everything."

That smile, the way Autumn's entire face lit up, her blue eyes twinkling as she held his daughter—he was pretty sure that was as close to heaven as a man could get while still breathing.

Damn, he loved them both so much.

Voice as soft as Sadie's had been, Autumn answered, "I know. We're pretty darned lucky, huh?"

Sadie twisted around to sit beside her, tucked against Autumn's side under her arm and proceeded to tell her everything she'd done over the last few days. Autumn made appropriate sounds of surprise, laughed when she should and occasionally squeezed Sadie closer.

But all the while, her gaze held his.

Tash knew he was caught. Irrevocably, happily, madly in love. Now he just needed to figure out how to handle it.

When Sadie wound down ten minutes later, Tash decided it was a good time to intervene. "You should get your bath, honey, before it gets any later."

Sadie said, "He means me."

Autumn laughed. "Thanks for clarifying."

Going glum, Sadie stared down at her feet while tapping her toes together. "We might have to go home soon." She quickly amended that complaint. "I love my room, I just wish it was here." She peeked at Autumn, hopeful.

Tash was curious what Autumn would say, too, but he didn't want to put her on the spot, so instead he gave a small reminder. "Autumn likes ice cream."

Her gaze shot to his.

He wanted to ask "Or do you really prefer me over it?" but

that wouldn't be fair. At the very least, he had to allow Autumn time to get back on her feet, so he smiled at Sadie and said, "Maybe once you're done with your bath, Autumn will share with you before you brush your teeth."

Face flushed, Autumn nodded. "I have three different kinds right now. You can choose one, or a scoop of each."

Not quite content with that answer, but anxious for the treat, Sadie slid back to her feet. "Okay. I'll get my bath at Ember's since my stuff is there." She hesitated. "You won't go back to bed, will you?"

"Not yet," Autumn promised. "For once, I want to be the one to tuck you in."

Her tone sly, his innocent little girl said, "I'd like it if you did that *every* night." Lacking even a hint of subtlety, Sadie smiled at her. "Would you like that, too?"

Autumn's entire posture wilted and she gathered Sadie close. Against her tangled red hair, Autumn said, "Oh, honey, I'd like that very much."

Sadie smiled at Tash…and said with heavy meaning, "I'll go get my bath now."

For a seven-year-old, his daughter showed incredible insight.

"Won't you need help?" Autumn asked, starting to rise.

"I'm not a baby." Sadie gave Pavlov a hug and straightened. "Besides, Ember checks on me a lot. We talk through the door."

"Oh?" Smiling, Autumn asked, "What do you talk about?"

Shrugging, Sadie said, "Fashion, hair, nails…and sometimes life."

Boggled, it took Autumn a second to find her voice. "Sometimes…life?"

"Ember is really smart." Sadie started out of the room. "I know because she said you were the best." With that cheeky comment, she opened the door and immediately Pavlov leaped down to follow her.

When it closed again, leaving him alone with Autumn, emotions and sensations bombarded Tash. He casually came to sit by her. "I've heard all about their talks before. Your sister has turned my tomboy daughter fashion-crazy. They've already bought four different shades of nail polish, and Ember even painted flowers on Sadie's toes."

"I can't wait to see." She avoided his gaze. "Ember is much better at the girly stuff than I am."

"It's fun to Sadie." He took Autumn's hand, stroking his thumb over her knuckles. "This has been such a great experience for her. Well-rounded. She loves learning about the animals from you, and enjoys doing dirty work with Mike and me. She's shown a real knack for creating art with your mother, and has a blast picking out meals for your father, and riding on his lap in his wheelchair. Ember enjoys brushing her hair and trading *girl* talk. She's outside more than she's in, gets to burn off a lot of energy in the fresh air and she's happier than I've ever seen her. She's in her element here."

With her free hand, Autumn touched his mouth. "What about you, Tash?" Her fingertips trailed to his cheekbone, tracing lightly under his eye. "You look tired."

Exhausted, really, since he'd been keeping up with his work schedule and fulfilling Autumn's share of work at the farm. But he had no reason to complain. He'd accept the same schedule every day for the rest of his life if it meant staying with Autumn. "I'm fine."

"Mom says you've worked around the clock."

"Tracy would be wrong, because I've spent at least six hours sleeping with you each night."

"Only six?" she asked with a worried frown.

It was an easy thing to lift Autumn into his lap, to hug her to his heart, much as she'd hugged Sadie. "I've enjoyed my time here as much as my daughter has."

"You're not used to farm work."

Against the crown of her head, he smiled. "Before I became

solely responsible for Sadie, I used to jog every day. It was my time to think, a way to separate from everything else, to lose tension and breathe in fresh air." He'd taken it for granted, that freedom to do whatever he pleased, whenever he pleased. "Being here, indulging in a little physical exertion, did the same as jogging."

"Relieved tension?"

"And helped give clear thought to things I wasn't certain about." Things like commitment, a future, life changes. Love.

She tipped her head back to see him. Her hair, now dry, hung in heavy tresses around her face. Color had returned to her cheeks and her beautiful eyes were bright again.

She bit her lip, released it and firmed her mouth. "I wanted to talk to you about something."

"Okay." He'd let her talk, and then he'd do some talking, too. He wouldn't pressure her, never that. But he would state his case. Would tell her how he felt. How Sadie felt. She deserved to know that they loved her…and then she could let him know how she felt about taking things to the next level. He had to be- lieve that eventually—hopefully sooner rather than later—she'd want a commitment. Marriage. A life together.

For several seconds, Autumn just searched his face.

It wasn't easy, but Tash waited.

With a rueful smile, she settled back into his arms and tucked her face close to his neck. "I love you."

His heart thumped hard and his arms automatically tightened. Had he misheard her? Given the path his thoughts had taken, it seemed possible.

She let out a small breath. "I know you haven't said how you feel—"

Squeezing her until she squeaked, Tash whispered, "Say it again."

He felt her small nod. "I love you."

"You love me?" Damn, he had trouble getting it to sink in.

Autumn pressed back. "I love Sadie, too."

She looked so earnest... "I know." Of that much, he'd been sure.

"I know it hasn't been easy being here and pitching in on everything while still keeping up with your own business—"

"I wouldn't change a single second."

"Still," she insisted, "it's a lot."

She'd just claimed to love him, and now she wanted to boot him out the door? "You've just recovered. I doubt you're ready to dive back in full speed. I'm happy to—"

"Do you love me?"

Her blurted question hung between them. Tash couldn't look away from her eyes...until she bit her lip.

"Yes." He'd been so floored with her declaration, he hadn't thought to reassure her. But, hell, how could she not know? He cupped her face, kissed her softly and nodded. "God, yes, Autumn. I love you."

And there was that beautiful smile again, tempered only by concern for their situation. "I'm sure it can't be convenient—"

"Loving you is one of the easiest things I've ever done."

That made her laugh. "Thank you, but I meant it can't be convenient being here."

Not convenient, no, but it was where he wanted to be. "A few more days, at least. Okay?"

Her smile softened. "Actually, I was thinking...maybe a lifetime?"

A lifetime? His heart nearly burst from his chest.

She rushed on before he could dredge up a single word. "You have a beautiful home, and I'm so happy with how things turned out."

"Sadie loves her room and the pirate-ship play area."

Autumn nodded fast, then offered, "I could replicate it here."

"You could?" Was she suggesting they move in?

Again she rushed on. "I'm sorry, but it doesn't make sense for me to live anywhere else."

"Agreed." On that, she'd get no arguments. The farm was a part of Autumn, and she put a piece of herself into everything she did here. Even if he tried, he couldn't imagine her living anywhere else.

"So…" She swallowed heavily. "Will you marry me?"

Dear God, if she kept zinging surprises out there, he'd keel over. "You—"

"Want to marry you. I mean, I'd be happy to just be together a little longer, to give you more time to adjust, but there's Sadie and she's only seven and I wouldn't feel right about living with you and not being married."

Finally, *finally*, she ran out of steam and gave him a chance to speak. "I love you, Autumn. So damn much."

She bit her lip again. "But?"

"Ah, babe, there are no *buts*. I *love* you. Every inch of you. Everything about you. This farm and your family and your amazing talent for making a girl's bedroom a dream come true."

"Oh." She covered her mouth, her eyes going glassy.

"You're sexy as hell, the sweetest person I've ever met…and the most caring. Stronger than you look and wiser than you should be." Tash curved a hand around her cheek. "I love you for loving Sadie, but most importantly, I love you for me. I love you for being *you*."

The tears spilled over and she threw herself against him.

Tash could feel her shaking, but he knew it was emotion, not upset. On the inside, he shook, too. "I love you, and I'd love to marry you. Sadie and I both would be thrilled to live here."

She sat back to smile at him, her lashes spiked from her tears. "Ember was right." With a little laugh, she swiped at her damp cheeks. "That was easier than I expected."

"Ah. So your sister put you up to the proposal?" That sounded like Ember, and he'd have to remember to thank her for it.

"Ember, Mom and Dad—all three. They're crazy about you,

and Mom flat-out told me she wanted to keep Sadie. Oh, but don't think I asked just for them!"

He hadn't, but he liked the way she rushed to reassure him.

"I wanted everything with you long before they started in on me. Almost from the beginning, Sadie stole my heart. And you... Oh, Tash, you are so much better than ice cream. So much better than sleeping alone or coming home to an empty house. You're...everything."

That had to be the nicest thing anyone had ever said to him. The fact that it came from Autumn also made it the most special.

He smoothed back her hair, kissed her forehead and said, "We have a lot of plans to make, but for now, I see my daughter peeking through the door."

Eyes widening, Autumn turned in time to see Sadie, trying to act like she hadn't been sneaking, slip into the room. Ember and Mike were right behind her, followed by Pavlov.

"We've all come for ice cream," Ember said, arms out and smile huge. "After all, I think we have something to celebrate?"

Sadie couldn't suppress her own grin. "You love her, Dad?"

"Of course I do."

"Me, too." She eyed Autumn. "And you love him, right?"

She replied, "Of course I do."

Sadie grinned even more. "And everyone loves me."

Together Tash and Autumn, Ember and Mike, all laughed.

"Yes," Autumn said. "Everyone loves you."

"Yay!" Sadie ran around giving hugs to everyone. When she got to Autumn, she held on extra long.

Finally, she came to Tash, her face flushed and her grin wide. "We get to stay!"

"Yes," Tash confirmed. He reached out to snag Autumn, pulling her in so that he embraced them both. "There's a lot to do, but we'll definitely stay."

"Forever," Sadie said.

Together, Tash and Autumn agreed. "Forever."

★ ★ ★

Autumn watched the kittens, now crawling about and curious about everything. Sadie had named them all, but it was difficult to tell them apart. In typical Sadie fashion, she'd thrown up her hands and said it didn't matter since they wouldn't listen, anyway.

True to Tash's promise, they hadn't moved out. He'd been with her every day since she'd been ill two weeks ago, though little by little he'd brought over their things from his house.

Mike and Tash had helped Ember make fast work of changing the house into a single home again. Mostly, anyway.

The second kitchen was closed off for now, with only an outside entrance so Ember and Mike could access when they wanted an easier way to make a bigger meal, though mostly they grilled out.

The connecting door was removed to put in a wide, open entry to the other side of the house. Ember's living room was turned into Sadie's play area, and her bathroom was decorated for a little girl instead of an eclectic woman.

Autumn moved her office and most of her books into the bedroom Ember had used, and after a fresh coat of paint on the walls, they'd transitioned Sadie's new bedroom into Autumn's house.

Eventually they'd build another house on the property for Mike and Ember—big enough for three. But, for now, Ember decided she was in no hurry to have a baby. Not when she had so much fun with Sadie. And she did truly love Mike's loft.

The only downside to the move was that Sadie's amazing pirate-ship play area stayed in Tash's yard, because it wouldn't draw neighborhood kids when the farm was so far removed from neighbors.

The upside was that a young family wanted the house right away, in part because of that play area. After all, they had four kids between the ages of four and eight. Two of the kids were girls and they loved the bedroom Autumn had created with Ember. They wanted the same only with seahorses.

They were mostly settled now, and good thing, since school would start in two weeks.

"You're hiding," Ember said, coming up to stand beside her.

Autumn shook her head. "No, just thinking."

"About why you haven't yet set a wedding date? Because that's what Mom and I are thinking about."

Hiding her wince, Autumn looked over her shoulder and found her mother bearing down on them.

Leaning close, Ember whispered, "Sorry, that's all the warning I could give."

"Autumn Somerset," her mother called. "Ember and I want to know why you haven't yet started wedding plans."

She sighed. Yeah, she and Tash had discussed it several times, but she hadn't yet set the date because she wasn't quite sure how to proceed.

Giving her mother the benefit of the doubt, and knowing Ember would play referee if it became necessary, Autumn settled on total honesty. She faced both women. They were so different, not just from each other, but especially from her. Still, she'd learned that they had incredible insight and bone-deep loyalty, so why not share her worries?

"I'm not sure what to do."

Halting, her mother gasped. "Don't you dare tell me you're changing your mind!"

"Mom," Ember soothed. "She's definitely not saying that. Right, Autumn?"

She nodded. "I love Tash. We're getting married." She had no doubts about that. "I'm just not sure...how."

"What in the world does that mean?" Her mother flapped a hand. "You've already done it once so you certainly know the process."

A look of dawning awareness passed over Ember's face. "Ah.

Yes, she has done it once…and it was a massive fail that involved the whole town."

"That wasn't Autumn's fault!"

"No, Mom, it wasn't." Ember crossed her arms. "But I'm guessing that's the issue."

Autumn blanched under their close scrutiny. She hadn't expected them both to look annoyed. "I'm thinking a simple ceremony, maybe at the courthouse, would be nice."

Her mother snorted. "You want a traditional wedding."

"With another beautiful dress, flowers, cake—the whole shebang."

Shocking how Ember aligned with their mom. Autumn opened her mouth twice before she got a word out. Yes, she'd love a traditional wedding, but she would it bring up all the old gossip again?

Trying to explain, without admitting her worries, she said, "Things are different with Tash."

"Hell yes, they are. Tash would never burn you."

Fed up with Ember's antagonism, Autumn took a hard step toward her. "Maybe Tash doesn't want a big wedding."

Again, her mother brushed that away. "He wants whatever you want. He told me so. Oh, and just picture Sadie as the flower girl. She'll be darling."

Sure she would, but that was hardly reason enough to go all out again. Rubbing at her temples, Autumn said, "I don't know if I'm up for organizing all that."

"Tell you what, sis. Let Mom and me handle it."

Autumn's head snapped up. "What? No."

"Yes," her mother enthused. "We can bring it all together in no time."

"I still have the dress I was going to wear," Ember said. "You?"

Her mom nodded enthusiastically. "Flynn and I are both ready to go. We can take Sadie shopping and get her ready in a single day. Then we only need to find a new dress for Autumn, talk to the florist and the baker—"

Autumn's heart started to gallop in mingled excitement and worry. Did she dare go all out on another wedding? First things first—she had to rein in her family. Holding up a hand, she said, *"Whoa."*

Her mother and Ember both fell silent.

Autumn stared at her sister. "I thought you'd be busy planning your own wedding."

Rolling one shoulder, Ember said, "I want you to go first."

"Why?"

"So no one is holding their breath during *my* ceremony, waiting to see what you'll do."

"Oh." Yeah, Autumn could imagine the whole town waiting with bated breath since they all knew Tash and Sadie had moved in. "I see what you mean."

"Good, then you know you have to step to it. Mike and I are going to marry near the lake, preferably in October, when the leaves are just starting to change. I already know the dress I want, but I haven't bought it yet."

Their mother came closer to Autumn, then tilted her head. "Autumn."

Oh, no, not the soft sympathy voice. Autumn forced a smile. "I'll take care of it, Mom."

"I know you could, but honestly, Ember and I would love doing it."

Ember added, "Actually, we've been sort of doing it already."

Surprise had Autumn blinking. "Sort of?"

Smile slipping into place, Ember said, "The baker wants to donate the cake. The florist wants to donate the flowers. The seamstress is ready and willing to alter anything we produce."

"Honey," her mother said, "this town loves you. What happened with Chuck made *him* look like an ass, not you. Every vendor you worked with wants to show their appreciation by being there for you now, when you're doing things right."

"She means with a really good guy like Tash, instead of that snake Chuck."

Utterly overwhelmed, Autumn laughed, but it came out a little like a sob. "You guys are both so amazing." She reached for them, this time with a laugh that was pure happiness.

When Tash and Mike walked in with Sadie, the three of them were still huddled together.

Mike grinned.

Tash looked wary. "What's going on?"

"I think they're plotting."

"I wanna plot, too," Sadie said, running forward to join the women.

Ember drew her in, then said, "We're plotting the wedding."

"Which one?" Tash asked, coming closer.

"Yours." Autumn grinned. "And mine."

"Hallelujah." He tugged Autumn away from her mother and sister and into his arms.

The place she most liked to be. "Would you mind if Mom and Ember handled things?"

"I want whatever you want."

"See?" her mother crowed. "I told you so."

"Smart man." Mike also drew Ember toward him, which meant he got Sadie, as well. He hefted her up to his chest, holding her with one arm. "Well, Sadie, what do you think about being the flower girl twice?"

"I want to!" Then she asked, "What's a flower girl do?"

"Oh, my." Her mother clasped her hands beneath her chin and sniffled. "Isn't this just the most beautiful thing ever? I need to go get Flynn. He'll love seeing all our family together as much as I do."

Sadie wiggled to get down. "I'll go with you and ride on his lap coming back." She raced out of the barn.

Then the funniest thing happened.

Her mother raced to catch up.

The two sisters watched, then stared at each other...before bursting into laughter.

"We've made Mom deliriously happy." Ember leaned against Mike, smiled at one and all, then winked at Autumn. "I don't know about you, sis, but I think this calls for ice cream."

Only three weeks later, wearing a soft, flowing white dress that was far lovelier and definitely more comfortable than the one she'd chosen before, flowers woven through her hair and her toes bare in the warm sand on the beach, Autumn became a wife.

The dress was the stuff of dreams and something she never would have chosen for herself, but it made her feel very pretty. Spaghetti straps, a low-cut lacy top and fitted waist, then a long gauzy skirt that parted as she walked.

Given how Tash had looked at her, he loved it, too.

And Tash. She sighed.

In white cotton slacks and a loose shirt, also barefoot, he was breathtaking. She watched him as he put together a plate of food for her dad and accepted yet another hug from her mother.

He'd gladly approved Autumn's theme and conceded to all her wishes. He also thanked her mother for every suggestion, and assisted them both whenever necessary.

Truly, they'd outdone themselves pulling it all together.

The beach theme was supposed to be Ember's, and her sister swore it would be—in the fall. This way, Ember claimed, she'd get to see it in action before she attempted to pull it off for herself. Being a guinea pig for her sister had never been so perfect.

Autumn had thought she'd be nervous, especially after her last catastrophic attempt at a wedding, but thanks to her mother and Ember, it was absolutely perfect.

Dancing near the water's edge, Sadie was a bright spot beneath the vivid blue sky. Yellow flowers formed a small crown on her red hair, and her big blue eyes shone with happiness. The pale yellow sundress, which matched Ember's, suited both of them perfectly.

What might have been embarrassing instead turned into a display of affection and caring that Autumn knew she'd never forget.

She looked around, still astounded at the crowd. It seemed the entire town had shown up for a wedding that, in her opinion, was a perfect mix of traditional and casual. Ember's idea of open invitations had been genius. No one felt pressured, and yet people she knew, many that she'd grown up with, had arranged picnic tables everywhere, filling them with donated food dishes meant to be shared.

Such a kind gesture. This was why she loved her home. So very, very much.

The florist had donated enough flowers for her bouquet, the women's hair and a few boutonnieres. Her mother and father had contributed the lovely arch of flowers and greenery under which they'd taken their vows.

The cake, which her mother also had chosen, was two layers of white confection, topped with cream and fruit. Not fancy, but definitely pretty and suitable to the beach.

Perfect for Autumn's style.

To satisfy all the guests, tray after tray of cupcakes were lined up on a white linen-covered table.

Near her ear, Tash whispered, "Even the weather loves you."

She'd been so involved in counting her blessings that she hadn't heard him approach.

Tipping her head back to his shoulder, Autumn smiled. "It's not ninety and the humidity is low, so, yes, I think I agree. We got lucky."

Turning her to face him, Tash looked at her with naked emotion. "I got lucky the day you showed up at my door." He tucked back a tendril of her hair. "Every minute since then has just been an additional gift."

"Tash." If she turned weepy now, she'd ruin her makeup, so instead she grinned. "I'm so glad my sister strong-armed me into proposing to you."

"She's the best sister-in-law in the world." They both heard Ember laugh and turned to see her in Mike's arms while he pretended to throw her in the lake. Ember held on to his neck, so instead, he kissed her.

Tash grinned. "Actually, this is the best family ever, on the most perfect farm, with the friendliest community...and I will love all of it, and especially you, forever."

Sadie wiggled between them. "Me, too!" Together, they hoisted her up, sharing kisses and hugs. Her flower tiara now hung crookedly, the hem of her dress was wet and she had icing on her chin.

It only made her cuter.

They wouldn't stay at the celebration too late, maybe a few more hours. After all, there was an entire farm full of animals waiting to see them again.

And they held one little girl who considered them all family.

★ ★ ★ ★ ★

Questions for Discussion

These questions may contain spoilers. It is suggested that you wait to read them until after you have finished the book.

1. Like many sisters, Autumn and Ember are two very different people who approach the world—and everyone in it— in different ways. Autumn tends to be more thoughtful and forthright, while Ember is more emotional and better able to hide her feelings. As you read the book, which sister did you relate to most and why? Did that allegiance change at all during the course of the book? If so, why do you think that was?

2. When the book opens, Tash is "the one who got away" for Autumn. Though she had a massive crush on him in high school, things between them never progressed beyond that. When the book opens, more than ten years have passed since they've seen one another. How do you think the time that has passed and the experiences they've had since they were last together have changed the way Autumn and Tash see

one another now? Or has nothing changed between them? Is there someone from your past who is "the one who got away"? Has time changed the way you see them?

3. Autumn and Ember have both had their hearts broken in very different ways. The disillusion of Autumn's engagement was incredibly public, and it has driven her to lick her wounds in the privacy of her own home, keeping people at a physical and geographical distance. Ember's miscarriage was a very private matter for her. But being around people and trying to forge new relationships seemed to help her move beyond it and try to begin again. What do you think their very different ways of coping says about them as people? How do these differences help them learn from one another?

4. Autumn, Ember and their parents share the old farmhouse on the property that their grandparents left to them, so they live in rather close proximity. How do you think that closeness has informed the relationships between them when the book opens? Do you think the close physical proximity helps change their relationship as the book progresses? Would a similar situation be ideal for you and your family? Why or why not?

5. Initially Mike and Ember seem like polar opposites. But as the story progresses, we see that Ember has feelings for Mike that she's actively trying to cover up. What do you think it is about Mike that draws Ember to him? When we learn about Mike's life before he came to the Somerset farm, did it change the way you saw him? Why or why not?

6. As much as she loves and trusts Ember, Autumn feels some frustration at the way Ember treats her and the way Ember sees her life and her choices. But Ember pushing Autumn to reconnect with Tash is what kicks off their romance. Some-

times we all need a push to try something different; who knows what might have happened if she didn't intervene? Do you think Autumn realizes that as the story progresses and gives Ember the credit she deserves? Or do you think these mutual pushes are just part and parcel of being sisters and learning from one another?

7. Tracy, Autumn and Ember's mom, is quite free with expressing her thoughts and feelings, even if they sometimes hurt her daughters' feelings. Do you think she realizes the hurt the things she says may cause in the beginning of the book? If so, why does she persist? If not, do you think Autumn and Ember should have told her how her words make them feel? How does Autumn's relationship with her mom change over the course of the novel? What do you think spurs that change on?

8. When the story opens, Tash and Sadie are trying to find their way after Sadie's mom's death. We can see that Tash feels quite a bit of guilt in not being able to see the situation sooner, but he's wholly committed to doing everything he can to help Sadie heal after the trauma she experienced with her mom, including keeping some emotional distance between him and Autumn. Autumn and Sadie get along so well, almost from the first moment they meet. Do you think Tash was partly protecting himself by trying to keep Autumn at a distance? If you were Tash, would you have handled Sadie in the same way?

9. Autumn loves ice cream and, in the beginning of the book, believes it's a perfectly fine substitute for men. Do you have a treat that you're as devoted to as Autumn is to her ice cream? What is it? What is it about that treat that makes it so delicious to you?

10. Autumn and Ember work together to maintaining the animal sanctuary they inherited from their grandparents—it's their dream. If you could do anything in the world, what would you do? Who would you share that dream with?

Read on for a sneak peek at
New York Times *bestselling author Lori Foster's*
Sisters of Summer's End,
*about two very different women who learn
that the best families are made—and not given—
and love is just around the corner.*

Chapter One

After dropping her son off at school, Joy Lee returned to Cooper's Charm, the RV resort where she worked and lived. It meant she was backtracking since she had an appointment near the school later this morning, but it wouldn't do to show up a half hour early.

Actually, nothing in the small town of Woodbine, Ohio, was too far away. In fifteen minutes she could drive to the school, the park, the grocery...or visit the new owner of the drive-in, who she'd be meeting today.

Hopefully Mr. Nakirk would continue to work with her. As the recreation director of the park, she and the past owner had put together various events with a lot of success. Halloween was coming up and she didn't want to have to completely restructure a tried-and-true camper favorite.

Coming through the grand entry of the resort, Joy couldn't help but admire the beauty of it. She'd been seeing the same gorgeous scenery for six years now, yet it never failed to soothe her.

She'd found peace here, a kind of peace she hadn't known existed. Now she couldn't imagine living anywhere else.

Large trees, currently wearing their fall colors, lined the property and served to add privacy to the costlier campsites.

A wooden walk bridge divided a pond from the large lake. Wooden cabins were scattered about, with plenty of lots for RVs and level, grassy areas for campers who preferred a tent. Even the playgrounds were well maintained, colorful and attractive.

Deciding a cup of coffee wouldn't hurt, Joy headed for Summer's End, the camp store. Maris Kennedy, a woman close to her own age, always had coffee ready. She also worked nonstop and treated everyone like a friend.

When Joy came into the camp store, Maris was busy wiping down the tops of the dining booths. She glanced up and said, "Hey."

In so many ways, Joy admired Maris. For one thing, the woman never seemed to tire. She opened early, kept it open late and rarely slowed down throughout the day. During the busiest season, Maris employed part-time help, but she handled the bulk of the responsibility herself.

Maris apparently preferred it that way.

Another admirable thing? Maris *always* managed to look fantastic with her dark blond hair in a high ponytail and a shirt at least a size too large over her jeans.

Unfair, but Maris was so incredibly nice, and she took such great care of all the employees, Joy forgave her the perfection. "Good morning."

"Is it?" Maris turned her gaze to the window. "Ah, sunshine. Better than rain and clouds, right? Coffee?"

Joy hated to pull her away from her task. "Yes, but I could—"

"I'll get it." Toting her little carrier of cleaning supplies, Maris headed to the kitchen. Joy heard her wash her hands, and then a moment later she reappeared with two cups. "I just made a fresh pot."

Of course she had. Smiling, Joy shook her head.

The café in Summer's End offered a menu of sandwiches, soups and daily specials. Positioned on the walls behind the seating area, packed shelves held basic grocery necessities and emergency items, as well as things like pool floats, sunscreen and fishing tackle. Campers didn't have to leave the park once they arrived, and if they didn't want to make use of the grills, Maris always had something to eat.

Joy took a sip of the coffee, fixed just the way she liked it, and sighed.

Instead of moving on to another chore, Maris stood there with her own coffee. "I'm wondering something."

"Oh?" She and Maris were friendly; Maris was too nice for anyone *not* to be friendly with her. But Joy wouldn't say they were close.

Sadly, it had become Joy's habit to keep some measure of distance from everyone.

"How the hell do you always look so put together?"

Surprised by the question, Joy looked down at her cotton skirt and button-up sweater. "It's a casual skirt." At least five years old, like the majority of her wardrobe. She'd updated only a few pieces since moving to the park.

"Yeah, but everything you wear looks like it came from a fashion magazine. Always, no matter what, you're styled head to toe. There are days I can barely get my hair into a ponytail, and yet you never have a wrinkle."

Feeling suddenly self-conscious, as well as amused by the irony, Joy laughed.

"Why's that funny?" Maris asked, looking genuinely curious.

It wasn't like Maris to linger, so Joy hastily explained, "I was literally just thinking how great you always look. Especially your ponytail! No matter what's going on, you...glow."

"Me?" Maris snorted. *"Glow?"*

Even more embarrassed and feeling completely out of her element, Joy continued. "You don't need makeup or anything. You always look fresh, even when you've been working all day. There's an energy about you." A wholesomeness that few other women could pull off. It was probably attitude as much as appearance that was responsible for that vibe. Maris personified friendliness, but she owned the space around her in a way Joy could never manage. "Believe me, the natural look works for you."

When Maris laughed, it made her even prettier, but before Joy could say so, she asked, "So what are you up to today?"

Hmm. Had Maris just deflected? Maybe she was as uncomfortable with compliments as Joy. "Meeting the new owner of the drive-in."

"That's right. I heard it changed hands."

"Very recently," Joy confirmed.

"Heard the new guy was a gorgeous hunk, too."

"You...what?" Joy sputtered. *A gorgeous hunk?* Definitely not what she'd hoped for, although it absolutely wouldn't matter. A man's appeal meant nothing to her—and good thing, since the guys at the park were all very handsome in varying ways. "Who told you that?"

"I'm like a bartender, you know?" Maris bobbed her eyebrows. "Everyone talks to me. You should try it sometime."

Generally the small town shared everything about everything. If a squirrel dropped a nut, someone announced it and the gossip spread like wildfire—though Joy was usually the last to hear it since she didn't cultivate those close relationships. Maybe she *should* chat with Maris more, if for no other reason than to keep up on current affairs in Woodbine. "I don't know about the hunk part since I haven't met him yet, but it's not an issue. My only interest is—"

"In recreation for the park, I know." Maris rolled her eyes in a playful way. "But there are all kinds of recreation, and I'm thinking you should try the kind that involves a man."

A nervous laugh trickled out. Since when was Maris Kennedy interested in her lack of a love life? Joy's next thought was whether or not the lack was that obvious.

Did she seem...lonely? Or, oh God, *needy*?

No, Maris more than anyone else at the park understood that a woman didn't need a man to complete her. Joy's life was already full, thank you very much.

To keep things friendly, Joy said with a smile, "Jack gets all my free time. I don't even know when I'd fit in a date." Just to clarify, she added, "Not that anyone is asking."

"Hello," Maris said. "You realize you have a big old blinking *not available* sign on you, right? Guys would—" she pinched the air "—if you'd give them just a teeny tiny bit of encouragement."

"But I don't want to encourage anyone. I mean, not for that reason."

"Why not? Jack's in school now, so don't tell me you can't eke out an hour or two."

"Hmm. Well, I guess technically I could..." Joy sat at the counter and finished with, "But I won't."

"Spoilsport." Maris joined her, taking the stool to her left.

Well, that was new. Sure, Maris conversed with Joy, but usually while she worked. She didn't sit down and join her.

She didn't focus on her.

Unsure what was going on, Joy said, "I don't mean to hold you up..."

"Already got through my routine, so I was ready for a break."

Curious, she asked, "What type of routine?"

"Coffee first—that's as much for me as it is for anyone who might drop in. Then I turn on the oven so I can make cookies from the dough I prepared the night before."

"Wow."

"I dust again, make sure all the chrome shines. Face up the shelves so they look orderly." Maris looked around her store with obvious pride. "There's always food stuff to prep, too. Soup to get in the pot, tea to make. Oh, and I have to put money back in the cash register. I like to take inventory each evening before I head home, so I know what I need to replace the next day. That means sometimes I have to restock the hot dogs or condiments."

Joy shook her head. "I have no idea how you do it all."

"Listen to who's talking, Super Mom."

"I'm not—"

"Yup, you are. I see plenty of moms here at the park, but you make it look effortless."

"Oh. Well, thank you." What else did someone say in this situation? Joy had no idea. Before moving to Woodbine, she hadn't had any friends like Maris. Her social group had been superficial, not down-to-earth. They talked about the latest high-end fashions and the next important social function. None of her so-called friends would have ever owned a wonderful little camp store like Summer's End—and none of them would have ever ended up as a single mom. Losing them hadn't been a hardship.

Other things had been hard. So very, very hard.

Like finding herself alone.

Over the years she'd adjusted, but now she shied away from getting too personal with anyone. Life felt safer that way.

"So." As if she'd been privy to her innermost thoughts, Maris gave her a direct smile—one filled with warmth and sincerity. "I'm just saying if you ever want to go out, or even if you just want some time to yourself, let me know. I'd be happy to help."

Touched by the offer, Joy laid a hand to her heart. After all her effort to keep real friendship at bay, Maris still reached out to her. It meant a lot and made Joy rethink some of her choices.

Honestly, since turning thirty, it had played on her mind, anyway. Perhaps she should begin to open up a little.

Jack certainly had. Then again, her son was one of the most personable, engaging, adorable people...and maybe she was just a tiny bit influenced by the incredible love she had for him.

Jack liked Maris a lot, and vice versa.

That didn't explain why Maris was suddenly so keen on Joy dating. "So...what's going on?"

Maris lifted her brows. "What do you mean?"

Ha! That innocent look didn't cut it. "You're up to something. We've known each other five years now and you've never asked me about dating."

"Sure I did. You just didn't answer much, so I let it go."

Ouch. That could be true.

"Gawd, don't look guilty," Maris said. "Here's the thing. You were quiet, I was swamped, so we let it go, right? But know what? I'm thirty-one now. Freaking *thirty-one*."

"Oh my God," Joy said, amazed that their thoughts seemed to be on the same track. "I'm thirty now, so I know exactly what you mean."

"Yesterday," Maris said, "this lady came in with three kids, one of them a newborn. She and her husband were frazzled and happy, and they said it was their first vacation after buying their house. Guess how old that woman was."

Joy said, "Um...thirty-ish?"

"Twenty-nine. Two years *younger* than me."

"Younger than us," Joy corrected.

"Right, but you have a kid. A *great* kid." Maris propped her head on her hand. "My point is, I can't do the whole family and home thing—but you can. Heck, you're already halfway there."

Family? Joy almost choked, since her family didn't want anything to do with her. She knew that wasn't what Maris meant, though. "You can't do it...why?"

"It's not my thing." Maris shrugged that off with haste. "You're great at being a mom. Heck, you're great at everything you do. So the least *I* can do is lend a hand, and maybe give you a push."

After all that, Maris smiled, as if she'd explained everything to her satisfaction and Joy should be jumping on board.

When Joy just blinked at her, Maris said, "Consider this your push."

It was almost laughable, but also very sweet. Joy said with feeling, "Thank you so much. Even though I don't have any hot prospects, I appreciate the offer."

"That's what friends are for, right?"

Joy had no real idea, but she nodded, anyway. "The same from me. If I can do anything for you, please just let me know."

"Great. Know what you can do? After you meet with the new owner, let me know if he's as gorgeous as everyone says he is. I'm dying of curiosity."

"Right, okay. Sure." Wondering if she'd misread this entire conversation, Joy offered, "If you want, I could mention you to him...?"

Maris blinked at her, then laughed. "We're talking about *you*, not me, but thanks." She nodded at the coffee. "Good?"

After another, more cautious sip, Joy sighed. "Mmm. Of course. You make the best coffee."

"True story." Maris suddenly sniffed the air. "Be right back."

So much for Maris's break. "Whatever that is smells delicious." Through the last five years, Joy had taught herself to cook by trial and error, but she didn't come close to Maris's skill in the kitchen. From full-blown formal dinners to the soup of the day, Maris worked magic.

Less than a minute later, Maris returned with a plateful of warm chocolate chip cookies. "Fresh from the oven. Want one?"

"I wish I could, but if I don't get going, I'll be late." Joy prided herself on her professionalism. Showing up tardy for an appointment was unthinkable.

"We stay too damn busy, don't we? We should carve out more time to visit." Maris wrapped two in a napkin. "For the road, then."

Joy's mouth already watered. "They won't last five minutes. Thank you." Smiling, she stood and slipped her purse strap over her shoulder. Hesitating, she said, "This was nice. Us talking more, I mean."

"Right?" Moving the cookies under a covered dome, Maris remarked, "We need to do it more often."

Surprised by the idea, Joy nodded. "That would be terrific."

She loved her role of recreation director at the park, and she appreciated all the wonderful people. She thought she did a good job—and yet, she'd never truly fit in. This morning, for a few minutes, Maris had been much more like a friend than an acquaintance. She didn't know if it was seeing the other couple with the three kids, or because Maris was suddenly more aware of her age.

Whatever the reason, Joy liked it. She liked it a lot.

Twenty minutes later, cold and miserable, Joy peeked in the small door window of the concession stand at the drive-in.

How had things changed so quickly?

The meager overhang barely shielded her from the pounding rain of the pop-up storm. Not that it mattered since she was already soaked to the skin.

If you could see me now, Maris…

There wasn't anything fashionable about her drowned-rat appearance. Joy couldn't remember a time when she'd been more of a wreck.

Freak rainstorms could do that to people.

Instead of knocking, she peeked inside again. People didn't usually catch her off guard like this, but for once, she felt totally flummoxed.

Royce Nakirk was everything Maris said he'd be—and more.

He stood over six feet tall, his body very…*fit*, and his dark hair reflected the blue of the concession lights.

Didn't matter. Men, attractive men in their prime, held no significance to her.

She was a mother.

A dedicated employee.

A once-burned, never-again divorcée.

My, oh my, the gossips hadn't exaggerated.

Joy wanted elderly Mr. Ostenbery back. She could deal with him. She could charm and bargain and coerce him without noticing his thighs. Or his shoulders.

Or his…butt.

All she'd ever noticed on Ostenbery was the impressive size of his nose and his genuine smile and kindness.

But this new owner was a different animal. Denim companies should pay him to wear their jeans. The way his T-shirt fit his body—snug in the shoulders, loose over a flat midsection— caused her ovaries to twitch. Until this moment, she'd forgotten she had ovaries.

Mother.

Employee.

Divorcée.

The mantra marched through her brain without much effect. She wondered what Maris would say when she told her about this.

Would she tell her?

Yes. It might be fun to share her shock. No doubt Maris would have some witty comment to contribute.

With his back to her, the owner squatted to rinse a cloth in a bucket of soapy water.

Biting her lip, Joy let her gaze track over him.

Stop it, she silently demanded, and she wasn't sure if she spoke to herself or the new, much too young and attractive owner.

When he turned, she saw his intent concentration as he scrubbed at a corner of the counter.

Joy almost envied the counter. How long had it been since she'd garnered that much concentration from anyone? Five years? Closer to six?

Scowling, he glanced at the clock, a jolting reminder that she was already fifteen minutes late.

Joy shoved wet hair away from her face and straightened her sodden clothes. No chance now for a good first impression. If the day hadn't dawned with sunshine and clear skies, she wouldn't have left her umbrella behind. The weather had held long enough for her to almost arrive at the drive-in—and *then* the black clouds had rolled in, tumbling one over the other as if racing for a finish line. A deluge split the skies, flooding a crossroad so she'd had to drive around, making her late.

The irony, of course, was that she could have walked through the woods and arrived at the drive-in within five minutes. Driving meant going around the long way, but she'd considered walking too informal. Her skirt and cute flats, which Maris had admired earlier, wouldn't have survived the woods.

Now it didn't matter, since the look was ruined, anyway.

Before she made things worse, Joy stepped to the side of the little window and gave a brisk knock.

It opened exactly two heartbeats later, making her think Mr. Nakirk must have reached it in one long stride.

Dark eyes went over her in a nanosecond and his frown deepened. He rubbed his mouth—then his gaze pinned her. "Joy Lee?"

Rain blew against her back but she barely felt it as she tried to summon professional confidence. If looking at him through a window had been disturbing, it was nothing compared to seeing him face-to-face.

He waited.

"Yes." Fashioning her frozen lips into a smile, she lifted her chin. "I'm sorry I'm late." Good. That sounded formal and sincere. She cleared her throat. "A road was closed and I had to take a detour." Pretty sure her lips were still smiling, but she turned it up a bit, anyway.

He looked at her mouth and nodded. "Come in." Belatedly,

he stepped back, making room for her. "Wait on the mat. The floor can be slippery when wet. I'll get you a towel."

"Thank you." So he wouldn't belabor her tardiness? She appreciated his restraint.

After watching him disappear into a room behind the concession stand, Joy glanced around the interior. She couldn't help noticing that the counter was spotless. The glass fronts of the candy cases sparkled, and even the black-and-white tiled floor shone. Admiring the fresh new appearance, she looked up...and found the same old stained ceiling tiles there.

"Next on the list," he said as he walked back in, startling her. He had an orange striped beach towel in one hand, a utility towel in the other. He stepped into her spreading puddle.

This close, he was taller than she'd realized. At five-nine, few men made her feel small but she had to tip her head back to meet Royce's inscrutable gaze. *And*...her thoughts fled once again. "Pardon?"

His mouth twitched. "I haven't heard that expression since my grandmother passed a decade ago."

Ohhh, he mentioned his grandmother. How sweet was that?

No, wait. Joy prided herself on her professionalism, on making a good appearance.

She did not lose her poise over a man's butt or his mention of a grandmother.

But his eyes...they were incredibly dark, framed by short, dense, ebony lashes. In a less welcoming face, she'd have labeled his eyes sinister, but the only thing deadly about this man was his bold appeal.

"Pardon," he said, as if explaining. "It's something Nana used to say. Most people aren't that polite anymore."

He called his grandmother Nana—and why would that make him more appealing?

Joy cleared her throat. "I see." Ah, yes, way to bowl him over with scintillating conversation.

He pointed up. "I meant the ceiling. I'll be replacing the tiles when I can, probably sometime over the winter so it's done before the next season." He held the beach towel out to her.

Making sure not to touch him, she accepted it, and noticed that his hands were large, his wrists thick, his forearms sprinkled with dark hair.

What is wrong *with you? So the man has hands. Most men do.* It was no reason for her temperature to spike.

She could probably blame her new distraction on Maris. If she hadn't steered the conversation toward hooking up, maybe Joy wouldn't be thinking about it now.

While she patted at her face, trying to look delicate instead of desperate, he dropped the utility towel into the puddle and moved it around with his foot.

Rain continued to drip from her hair, her clothes, even the tip of her nose. Her brain scrambled for conversation, a way to ease the awkward moment.

His nearness made that impossible.

"Well." Joy plucked at her clinging sweater. Maybe if she didn't look at him, it'd be easier for her brain to function. "I hope you've been properly welcomed to Woodbine."

"I've only met a few people."

Enough to make an impact, she thought.

"Mostly I've been stuck in here all week, trying to get it spick-and-span before movie night on Friday."

"Mr. Ostenbery was a wonderful person, but not a stickler for organization."

"Or cleanliness," he said with a smile.

For a second, Joy stared, caught in that smile, before regaining her wits. "You've done a great job. Everything shines."

The drive-in ran on Friday and Saturday nights, from March until the end of October, but Mr. Ostenbery had often hosted other events during off-hours. Joy hoped to continue that practice, and maybe even add to it.

Suddenly Royce flagged a hand toward her face. "You're washing away. Did you want to use the restroom? I can put on coffee while you do that."

She looked at the towel where she'd patted her face and saw it smudged with makeup. Oh good Lord. Cold and embarrassment nearly took out her knees. "Yes, if you don't mind."

"In fact—" He ducked back behind the counter, snagged a folded T-shirt from a stack, and offered it to her. "You look... chilled."

Apparently being faced with a sodden woman in ruined makeup didn't faze him. She accepted the navy blue shirt with the drive-in's logo on the front. "You want me to change?"

"I want you to be comfortable. Doesn't seem possible while you're shivering." He pushed aside the half door that allowed her behind the concession stand. "This way."

As they walked, Joy gave herself a pep talk. Never mind that she hadn't had sex for nearly six years. Forget that he was a specimen with a capital *S*, for *Sexy*. Disregard that she was sometimes lonely.

She would cease daydreaming about his jeans, and that fine backside in his jeans, and she wouldn't notice anything else about his body. Or his face. Or even that deep voice.

She would concentrate only on the purpose of this meeting.

"Right here," he said, pushing open yet another door to show her the most sanitary business restroom she had ever seen. The white porcelain toilet and sink shone, as did the floor and wall tiles. "There's a dryer around the corner if you need it. For your skirt, I mean."

That surprised her enough that she almost slipped on her own trail of water. "You have a dryer here?"

"I brought in a small stack unit for convenience. The mop head and cleaning towels get laundered regularly."

The positives were adding up. Joy mentally tallied them: butt. Nana. Neat freak.

Oh, and those sinfully dark eyes.

Poise, she reminded herself. *Professionalism.* "I'll only be a minute."

Accepting that, he turned away. "I'll go get the coffee started."

And... She watched him walk away, already forgetting her lecture.

When he glanced back to say, "Take your time," she knew that he knew she'd been staring.

Mortified, Joy quickly closed the door, muttering to herself about decorum. One glance in the mirror and her heart almost gave out.

Her pathetic attempts at smiling couldn't have had any impact at all, not when mascara created comical black stripes down her cheeks. Add her long, light brown hair plastered to her skull, throat and chest, and she was hideous.

The worst, though, was her sweater.

Opaque, yes, but through the soft material her chilled nipples seemed to beg for attention. *Look at me, look at me.*

She couldn't really blame them, not with a man like that standing around as if such a thing happened every day. She'd certainly never seen anyone like him before. Even in a Photoshopped magazine ad, the men weren't so...perfectly *manly.*

It was indecent.

Her nipples were indecent.

Her standing in front of a mirror carrying on a private, one-sided discussion about her nipples was indecent.

In an attempt to recover, her lungs grabbed a deep breath. *Being a good mother is your number one focus. Period. You don't care about attracting men.*

No, she didn't. So what did it matter if she looked like a murdered body washed up on the shore? It didn't.

As of right now, her hormones were going back in hibernation.

And yet, she frantically scrubbed her face and fretted over her hair.

★ ★ ★

Royce poured himself a cup of coffee and tried to quit glancing at the clock. *What was she doing in there?*

Changing her shirt and removing the tracks from her face shouldn't have taken twenty minutes. He rubbed the back of his neck and tried not to think about her tall, trim body in wet clothes, but yeah, he may as well tell himself to stop breathing. Pretty sure that image would stick with him for a while.

Funny thing, how a woman nearly drowned in rain and ruined makeup could still look so classy. She had a calm deportment that defied circumstances.

Gifting her with the shirt had been an act of self-preservation, to make it easier for him to refocus on the important stuff.

Not that breasts weren't important. They just weren't important right now.

For several reasons, this meeting had to be his priority. One, he'd just taken over the run-down drive-in and, for some ridiculous reason, he wanted to hear her opinion on his improvements. Two, he needed to first be accepted to the small, intimate town. Working with her would be a start. Three...damn, he'd forgotten three the second he'd opened that door.

He couldn't tell the true color of her hair, not with the wet hanks clinging to her face, but there was no mistaking the green of her eyes. Not just green, but a light green with shades of amber, all ringed in blue.

Pretty eyes. Startled eyes. Joy Lee had stared at him as if he'd somehow surprised her.

She'd sure as hell surprised him.

From everything Ostenbery had told him, he'd expected a polite but formal businesswoman. Maybe she was...usually.

But not today.

Not with the way she'd looked at him.

Damned if he hadn't looked back.

A foolish move since he had zip for free time. Only a month

remained of the season for the drive-in, but he planned to make the most of it, to send it off with a bang so that when he re-opened in the spring, the locals would remember. Plus he had some ideas for off-season activities, if he could get Joy Lee on board.

First, she'd have to emerge from the bathroom.

He drank more coffee, stewing over the impressions Osten-bery had given. Though the retiree hadn't mentioned Joy's age, his descriptions of her had led Royce to expect someone older. Someone not so attractive.

Someone austere and aloof.

Instead, Joy Lee had openly gazed at him while her face and throat flushed pink.

Focus, he told himself. After far too long taking care of oth-ers, this was his turn and he wouldn't get derailed by wet clothes clinging to a sweet body, or bold, mesmerizing eyes.

With that in mind, Royce strode to the door and called back, "You okay in there?"

Her head poked out, not from the bathroom but from his utility room. "Yes, sorry. You said I could use the dryer, so..." She smoothed back a long hank of still-damp hair.

Royce realized he was doing it again, allowing his brain to go down paths it shouldn't. At least this time he had good rea-son for staring.

She stood there in the logo T-shirt, knotted at the side so it'd fit her waist, with the beach towel tied like a toga skirt around her. The colors clashed, but that was the least of the fashion di-sasters.

Yet somehow, on her, the hodgepodge outfit looked like a trendy statement.

When she laced her fingers together and smiled, he felt it like a kick. Luckily, a kick was just what he needed to get back on track.

Royce cleared his throat. "I pulled some chairs up to the

counter for us." The building had a small break room, but it felt too isolated for this meeting.

He gestured for her to precede him, then wished he hadn't as she moved past, slim legs parting the overlap of the towel, giving him a glimpse of calf and thigh.

Calf and thigh? he repeated to his libido. This wasn't the 1700s. A man could see legs—gorgeous legs, not-so-gorgeous legs, young legs and old legs, plus a whole lot more—any damn time he wanted. Just because they were *her* legs didn't make them special.

Sure, the past year had been…rough. No sex, no dating. Nothing but all-consuming responsibility, focused around sickness, culminating in the inevitable end of life.

But legs?

Royce followed her, doing his utmost to keep his gaze on the back of her head and not anywhere else.

Being here in Woodbine, rebuilding the drive-in to what it could be, was *his* turn and he wouldn't let pretty green eyes and shapely legs muddle his plans.

Keeping that in mind, Royce got down to the task of building a business relationship, and absolutely, one hundred percent, nothing else.

As Royce parked at the entrance to the RV park three days later, he paused just to enjoy the view. Fall painted the landscape a breathtaking pallet of hues, from bright orange honey locusts, red maples and the purple sweetgum trees, to the softer yellow of aspen trees. The pale blue skies, interrupted by only a few fluffy clouds, met the darker surface of the rippling lake.

As a kid, every tree was a challenge to climb. Now, as an adult, he took in the colors and understood how others would see them—and why his mother had been so single-minded in her pursuit to catch the image.

Dispelling the pang of that memory, he inhaled the crisp scent in the air and glanced around at the plentiful fall flowers.

Without meaning to, he searched the various people moseying around the grounds. Most of them were likely campers, but the second he saw the slender woman, a long, patterned skirt drifting around her legs as she walked, he knew it was Joy.

He'd done his utmost not to dwell on her, but still a tension fell over him that had nothing to do with stress and everything to do with awareness. A gentle breeze teased her long, fawn-colored hair and she looked like a woman with a purpose, striding toward the back of the grounds where she disappeared into a building.

Would he run into her? Would he get close enough to see those remarkable eyes again? It seemed likely, and damned if he didn't hope he would.

Goals, Royce reminded himself, starting down the slanted drive from the extra parking area to the park itself. He was here for an appointment with Cooper Cochran, the park owner, not to indulge a juvenile infatuation.

A few campfires burned outside RVs and tents, the wood smoke scenting the air. People waved to him as he passed, friendly in the extreme. The play areas were still and empty, but Cooper had explained that with school back in session, weekdays were naturally quieter now. Weekends, though, the park would fill, especially toward the end of the month when Joy helped facilitate a site-by-site Halloween event. Guests decorated their campers, kids wore costumes, people handed out candy and the lodge hosted a "friendly" haunted house, appropriate for kids of all ages.

The evening would end at the drive-in with campers getting discounted tickets and a free bag of popcorn. According to Joy, that got the kids settled before dark, when mishaps could happen if they were still out going door-to-door for candy.

His visit to the park today was just to get to know another

businessman, since he and Cooper were neighbors of sorts, with the drive-in just through the woods that bordered the property. If it weren't for the tall trees, campers would be able to catch a free movie every weekend, minus sound.

Suddenly Joy came around the corner only a few yards away from him. She had her arms loaded down with more boxes, a large scarecrow under one arm and her sunglasses were slipping.

Royce stepped into her path. "Joy."

She stopped so abruptly the uppermost box toppled, spilling fall decorations around her feet. Glasses askew, she blinked at him. "Royce."

"Here." He reached for the remaining load she still held, setting everything aside while squatting down to collect the things she'd dropped. "Sorry if I startled you."

"You didn't," she said a little breathlessly. Pushing her glasses atop her head, she looked him over in that same intent way she had at their first meeting.

"Just throwing things at me, huh?" Trying to ignore the charge of her nearness, Royce replaced everything as neatly as he could, although he had no idea how she'd gotten it all in the boxes in the first place.

Her lips parted. Soft lips. Naked lips.

He was thinking things he shouldn't when she suddenly rushed into explanations.

"I'm running late and I'm afraid my mind was elsewhere..." She trailed off and then knelt, too, quickly rearranging things. "What are you doing here?"

She smelled nice, Royce thought, her scent subtle but sexy. Stirring. Maybe it was the October sunshine on her skin, or the warmth of her hair. He breathed her in before explaining, "I'm meeting Coop in the camp store. I'm a little early yet. Let me help you carry this stuff."

As they both reached for the same box, their hands bumped.

She jerked back to her feet. "Oh no." A nervous laugh. "That's okay. Really."

Why she was nervous Royce couldn't guess. He watched her, trying to figure her out—trying to figure himself out, too. He had no business lingering here, deliberately running into her and then prolonging his time with her.

Yet there was a pull, opposite of what he told himself he should be doing. Business, that was number one. Building a relationship in the community. Establishing himself and, therefore, the drive-in needed to be his goal.

So why was it so hard to look away from her? Seeing the flush on her face, he had to assume she felt it, too.

Like him, did she find it equally alarming and exhilarating?

Without taking his gaze off her, he slowly stood with two boxes in his hands as a natural barrier so he didn't do something really dumb. Like step up against her.

Breaking the spell, Royce asked, "Where to?"

After a deep inhalation, she forced a bright smile and snagged up the scarecrow. "This way."

Following her through the grounds, Royce continued to admire…well, the area, sure. It really was a well-laid-out, nicely tended park. But he also admired Joy. The sway of her hips. The flow of her hair. How everyone greeted her with smiles.

That is, everyone except the guy who pulled up on a golf cart, a toolbox beside him on the seat. Shoving sunglasses to the top of head, he frowned at Joy. "Hon, I told you I'd get this stuff for you. Don't you need to go?"

Royce remembered her saying she was running late. He waited, unsure who the young man might be, but assumed he worked for the park.

"I'm leaving as soon as I drop this stuff off at the lodge." She gestured back to him. "Royce is helping."

The man eyed him. "Royce, as in the new owner of the drive-in?"

"One and the same." Juggling the boxes in one arm, Royce reached out a hand. "Royce Nakirk. Nice to meet you."

"Daron Hardy, handyman extraordinaire, or so I'm told." He accepted the handshake. "You going to do a horror night for Halloween? Something really scary that'd make a sexy lady friend want to cuddle?"

Royce glanced at Joy.

She gasped, then quickly denied, "Not me!" as if that idea were the most absurd thing she'd ever heard.

Daron grinned. "Could be you, hon. You fit the bill." To Royce, he said, "Sadly, Joy gives me the cold shoulder. To hear her tell it, there's only one guy in her life."

Well, shit. Royce automatically looked at her hands, though he already knew she didn't wear a ring. Not married...but that didn't guarantee she wasn't involved in some other way.

Not liking that idea at all, he gave his attention to Daron. "We'll have a double dose of kid-friendly flicks that night, but leading up to it we're playing movies that'd probably work for you." He mentioned the latest blood-and-gore movie that'd hit the big screen.

"I'll take what I can get." Back to Joy, Daron asked, "So you'll be there Halloween weekend for the kids' flick, right? If Jack can stay awake long enough?"

Jack? Royce watched her get more flustered. "Yes, we're planning to attend that weekend, along with many of the families from the park." She adjusted her purse strap. "Speaking of Jack, maybe I'll need your help, after all, or I really might be late." She strode around to the back of the golf cart. "Drop this stuff off for me, okay?"

"Sure thing."

Royce watched the younger man, and realized he had no real interest in Joy. He was friendly in a flirting way, but he wasn't at all serious about it.

Already walking away, Joy said over her shoulder, "Royce,

thank you for your help. Just give the boxes to Daron. He'll take care of it." She practically jogged away, her skirt dancing around her calves as she headed toward a parking area.

Daron cleared his throat in an exaggerated way, drawing Royce's attention. "Seriously, dude, you're wasting your time."

"How's that?" Pretending he hadn't just been watching her, Royce unloaded the boxes onto the rear-facing seat, then secured the scarecrow there.

"Joy doesn't date. Her whole focus is on Jack."

"And Jack is…?" he asked, trying to sound casual.

Judging by Daron's wide grin, he wasn't fooled. "Her five-year-old son. Cute kid. A little shy."

Royce forgot that he wasn't interested in a relationship. He wasn't even interested in dating. He felt like he'd just taken one in the gut. "She's a mother?"

"Head to toe."

"But…single?" His brain stuck on that fact, regardless of how Royce tried to block it.

"Always has been, far as I know."

Royce looked back and saw her driving out of the park in a small yellow Ford hatchback. It took a strong woman to raise a kid alone. He knew that firsthand.

"Again, fair warning," Daron said. "Joy assigns all men to the 'casual friendship' zone. In all the time she's been here, plenty have tried to get past it with no luck."

Royce shot him a look. "You?"

Laughing, Daron tugged off his hat to run a hand through messy brown hair, then jammed it back on his head. "Not me, no. I could say I don't play where I work, but truth is, she's a mom through and through. She's also a really nice person, a hell of a hard worker and she's never given me a single hint of interest. Fact, most times she treats me like a bigger version of Jack."

Huh. From what Royce could tell, Daron was a midtwenties, fit, decent-looking *man*—but Joy saw him as a kid? Fascinating.

She sure as hell hadn't looked at *him* that way. Royce was rusty, no doubt about it, but he figured he could still pick up on sexual tension. "So she's going somewhere to get her son?"

"Kindergarten. If you're into lost causes, she'll be back in half an hour."

He wouldn't mind seeing her again, but it wasn't the reason for his visit. "Actually, I'm meeting with Coop, and now *I'm* late." But only by two minutes. "Hope I'll see you Halloween night, if not before."

Don't miss Sisters of Summer's End
by New York Times *bestselling author Lori Foster!*